Also by Imogen Robertson

Instruments of Darkness
Anatomy of Murder
Island of Bones
Circle of Shadows

The Paris Winter

A Novel

IMOGEN ROBERTSON

St. Martin's Press
New York

www.stmartins.com

Library of Congress Cataloging-in-Publication Data

Robertson, Imogen, 1973–
    The Paris winter : a novel / Imogen Robertson. — First U.S. edition.
        p. cm.
    ISBN 978-1-250-05183-7 (hardcover)
    ISBN 978-1-4668-7231-8 (e-book)
    1. Paris (France)—History—1870–1940—Fiction. 2. Psychological fiction. I. Title.
    PR6118.O2376P37 2014
    823'.92—dc23

                                                    2014026998

St. Martin's Press books may be purchased for educational, business, or promotional use. For information on bulk purchases, please contact Macmillan Corporate and Premium Sales Department at 1-800-221-7945, extension 5442, or write specialmarkets@macmillan.com.

First published in Great Britain by Headline Review, an imprint of Headline Publishing Group, an Hachette UK Company

First U.S. Edition: November 2014

10   9   8   7   6   5   4   3   2   1

Gran, Gillian and Hazel with love

Acknowledgements

The support of friends and family make the writing possible and letters, emails and so on from readers make it fun. Huge thanks to my agent Annette Green, my editor Flora Rees and all at Headline for their advice and support. Particular thanks to David Downie and Alison Harris for their expert help guiding us round Paris; to artists Caroline de Peyrecave and Claire Zakiewicz for talking to me about their training and careers; to Richard Campbell at Lucie Campbell in Bond Street for showing me diamonds; Hervé Guyot for sharing his collection of photographs of the Paris floods and to Ahren Warner and Susan Powell for their help with the research. Thank you also to my husband Ned who arranged so much of our wedding while I was in 1909. This book was originally inspired by my grandmothers and great-aunts who travelled independently in Europe in the first half of the twentieth century.

PROLOGUE

At the Académie Lafond oil on board 29.3 × 23.6 cm

This charming, loosely painted study shows a life-class in progress. The model is just visible on the left, but it is the students – bored, intent or nervous – who are the subjects of the painting. One seems to be blowing on her hands to warm them. Lafond began offering training to young artists, male and female, in 1875 and opened his first all-female atelier in 1890, seven years before women were admitted to the Académie des Beaux Arts. He managed his various studios in Paris with great success until his death in 1919. His students received a thorough training in oils and were encouraged to be both experimental and imaginative in their use of colour and in their composition.

The tonal range in this painting is narrow and the colours cold, the model almost invisible and the students placed almost haphazardly in the frame. In this way, the artist gives an impression of a snatched, unstaged moment on a chilly morning. Note the middle-class appearance of the women in the portrait. Lafond's fees for women were high, but his reputation was irreproachable.

Extract from the catalogue notes to the exhibition 'The Paris Winter: Anonymous Treasures from the de Civray Collection', Southwark Picture Gallery, London, 2010

Part One

Saturday, 20 November 1909, Paris

CHAPTER 1

HE NEWS OF THE SUICIDE OF ROSE CHAMPION reached her fellow students at the Académie Lafond on a pale wintry morning a little before ten o'clock. The heat from the black and clanking stove had not yet reached the far corners of the studio, and the women on the outer reaches of the group had to blow on their fingers to make them warm enough to work. Maud Heighton was always one of the first to arrive each day and set up her easel, which meant she could have taken her pick of places on each Monday when the model for the week was chosen, but the Englishwoman liked to sit on the far eastern side of the room. The challenge of the narrow angle she had on the model throne and whatever man, woman or child happened to occupy it seemed to please her – and she returned to the spot week after week when warmer ones, or those with an easier angle of view were available.

She was there that morning, silent and studious as ever, when the news of Rose's death came tumbling up the stairs, so she was among the first to hear it. It was unfortunate – shocking even – that the news reached the female students so raw and sudden, but even in the best-run establishments, such things do occur.

It was by chance the women painting in Passage des Panoramas heard so quickly and so brutally of the tragedy. One of Lafond's male students, a young romantic Englishman called John Edwards, lived in the room beside Rose Champion's in a shabby tenement hunkered off the Boulevard Clichy. It was an unpleasant building without gas or electricity, and with only one tap which all the inhabitants had to share. He knew his neighbour was a student in one of the all-female ateliers, but she was not pretty enough to attract his attention, not while the streets were full of French girls who made it their business to charm the male gaze; what's more, he assumed that as a woman she would have little of interest to say about art. When he took up his residence, though, he noticed that Rose kept herself and her threadbare wardrobe clean and approved of that, then thought no more about her. In the month they had been neighbours they had had one short conversation on the stairs about the teaching at Académie Lafond. It ended when he asked to see her work and Rose told him he wouldn't understand it. He had wished only to be polite and was offended by her refusal. They did not speak again.

The walls that divided their rooms were thin and he happened to be awake and waiting that morning for the matt-grey light of the Paris dawn to filter into the sky. It was the hour and the season when the city looked unsure of itself. In the full darkness, the clubs and cabarets shone like the jewels. The city then was a woman in evening dress certain of her beauty and endlessly fascinating. The air smelled of roasting chestnuts, and music spilled out of every café, humble or luxurious, into the streets. In the full light of day Paris was chic and confident. The polished shops were filled with colour and temptation and on every corner was a scene worth painting. It was modern without being vulgar, tasteful without being rigid or dull. A parade of elegant originality. Only in this hour, just before dawn on a winter's morning, did the city seem a little haggard, a little stale. The shutters were up and the cafés all closed or closing. The streets were almost empty – only the occasional man, purple in the face and stale with smoke and drink, hailing a cab in Place Pigalle, or the old women washing out the gutters with stiff-brushed brooms.

Sitting in the window with a blanket round his shoulders and his pipe clamped between his teeth, John Edwards was thinking about Matisse, his solid blocks of colour that at times seemed ugly, but with an ugliness more honest than beauty. He pictured himself making this argument to the poets and painters who gathered at *Le Lapin Agile* in Montmartre; he imagined them nodding seriously then telling their friends they had found an Englishman of talent and wisdom. They would introduce him to the most interesting art dealers in the city, the most advanced collectors and critics. He would write a manifesto . . .

He was enjoying the opening night of his first sensational solo show when he heard the sound of a chair overturning and the creak of a rope. There was no doubt where it came from. He dropped the blanket from his shoulders, ran into the corridor and started hammering at the door, calling her name, then rattling the handle. It was locked. By the time he put his shoulder to the door, the other residents of the house had emerged from their rooms and were watching, peering over the banister rails, their eyes dull with the new day. Finally the lock splintered and he tumbled into the room. She had hung a rope from one of the central beams. Her body still swung a little from side to side like a pendulum just before it stops completely. John had to scream in the face of the waiter who lived in the other room on this floor before he would help him get her down. It was too late. She was most likely dead even before he had begun shouting her name.

They laid her on the bed and one of the women went to phone the police from *Le Rat Mort* on Place Pigalle. He waited with the body until they arrived. The misery in the room pressed on him, as if Rose Champion had left a desperate ghost behind her to whisper in his ear about the hopeless vanity of his ambitions.

By the time the police arrived, John Edwards was not young or romantic any more. Once the gendarmes had been and the morgue van had taken away the body, he packed his trunk and left the building for good. He called at Académie Lafond to inform his professor what had happened and of his decision to leave Paris, but his master was not there and the rather off-hand way Mrs Lafond spoke to him irritated his already over-strung nerves. Rather than leave a note he simply told her what had happened, perhaps rather more graphically than necessary and without regard to the fact there was a servant in the room. The latter's shocked face haunted him as he prepared to return to his mother's comfortable house in Clapham and resume his career as a clerk at Howarth's Insurance Company in the City. There can be too much truth.

The servant in the room was the maid who tended to the ladies in the Passage des Panoramas atelier. She left the offices in Rue Vivienne before Mme Lafond could tell her to keep the news to herself and so it escaped, awkward and disturbing and stinking of misery.

Even though the women who studied at Académie Lafond paid twice the fees the men did, their studio accommodation was no more than adequate. The only light came from the glassed ceiling and the room was narrow and high, so that it seemed sometimes as if their models were posing at the bottom of a well. The stove was unpredictable and bad-tempered. Nevertheless it was worth paying the money to be able to study art. The rough manners of the male students meant that no middle-class woman could work in a mixed class – and sharing life models with male students caused ugliness. At the women-only studios a female could prepare for a career as an artist without sacrificing her dignity or reputation, and even if the professional artists who visited them did not spend as much time guiding their female students, at least they did come, so the modest women could make modest progress and their families could trust that although they were artists, their daughters were still reasonably sheltered. The suicide of a student put a dangerous question-mark over this respectability, and news of it would probably have been suppressed if it had been given privately. As it was, it spilled out of Lafond's office and made its way up the stairs and into the room where Maud Heighton and her fellow students were at work.

Maud, perched on a high stool with her palette hooked on her thumb, heard their teaching assistant exclaim and turned her head. Mademoiselle Claudette was making the sign of the cross over her thin chest. That done, she squeezed her almond-shaped eyes closed for a second, then helped the maid set down the kettle on the top of the stove. When it was safe, she placed a hand on the servant's shoulder.

Maud frowned, her attention snagged by that initial gasp. There was some memory attached to the sound. Then it came to her. It was just the noise her sister-in-law, Ida, had made on the morning of the fire. Her brother, James, had driven the car right up to Maud where she stood at the front of the fascinated crowd, her hair down and her face marked with soot. Ida had got out of the car without waiting for James to open the door for her, looked at the smoking ruins of the auctioneer's place of business and the house Maud and James had grown up in, and given just that same gasp.

Maud turned towards Mademoiselle Claudette the moment the older woman rested her hand on the maid's shoulder. The assistant was normally a woman of sharp, nervous movements, but this gesture was softly intimate. Maud wanted to click her fingers to stop the world, like a shutter in a camera, and fix what she saw: the neatly coiffed heads of the other young women turned away from their easels, the model ignored, all those eyes leading towards the two women standing close together by the stove. The finished painting formed in Maud's mind – a conversation piece entitled *News Arrives*. The shaft of light reaching them from above fell across Mademoiselle Claudette's back, while the maid's anxious face was in shadow. Was it possible to capture shock in paint, Maud wondered – that moment of realisation that today was not going to be as other days?

Mademoiselle Claudette ushered the maid out into the hallway then closed the door to the studio behind them. The semi-sacred atmosphere of concentration still hung over the women, keeping them silent, but no one put brush to canvas again. They paused like mermaids just below the water, waiting for one of their number to be the first to break the surface, into the uncertain air.

'Rose Champion is dead!' Francesca blurted out. It was done. A flurry of exclamations ran around the room. The high walls echoed with taps and clicks as palettes were put aside, brushes set down and the women looked at the plump Prussian girl who had spoken. Her eyes were damp and her full bottom lip shook. The high collar on her blouse made her look like a champagne bottle about to burst. 'The maid said she killed herself. She was found hanged in her room this morning. Oh Lord, have mercy on us! Poor Rose!' She looked about her. 'When did we see her last?'

'Not since summer, I think,' a blonde, narrow-hipped girl answered, one of the Americans whose French accent remained unapologetically Yankee. 'She didn't come back this year, did she?' There was general agreement. 'Did anyone see her about since then?'

'I saw her,' Maud said at last, remembering even as she spoke. She felt the eyes of the women swing towards her, she who spoke so rarely. 'She was in the Tuileries Gardens sketching Monsieur Pol with his sparrows.' The other women nodded. Pol was one of the sights of Paris, ready to be admired just outside the Louvre in his straw boater, whistling to the birds, and calling to them by name. 'It was a month ago perhaps. She was thinner, but . . . just as she always was.'

One of the students had begun to make the tea and the boiling water splashed a little. The girl cursed in her own language, then with a sigh put down the kettle and produced a coin from her pocket to pay her fine. Claudette used the money to buy the little cakes and pastries the women ate during their morning breaks. When funds were low they fined each other for inelegant phrasing. In the Paris art world, Lafond's girls were said to paint like Academicians and speak like duchesses.

'Poor Rose,' Francesca said more softly. The women sighed and shook their heads.

The room was filling with cigarette smoke and murmured conversation. '*La pauvre, la pauvre . . .*' echoed round the studio like a communal prayer.

Maud looked to see if any painting of Miss Champion's remained on the walls. Perhaps once a month during his twice-weekly visits to his students, M. Lafond would nod at one of the women's paintings and say, 'Pop it up, dear.' It was a great honour. Francesca had cried when Lafond had selected one of her pictures. He had not yet selected any work of Maud's. She had submitted successfully to the official Paris Salon early this year – the head and shoulders oil portrait of a fellow student – but even if the Academicians approved of her worked, careful style and thought it worthy of exhibition in the Grand Palais, Lafond did not think she had produced anything fresh enough for his draughty attic classroom.

Maud had written to her brother and sister-in-law about having the painting in the exhibition. Even in the north-east of England they had heard of the Paris Salon, but the reaction had not been what she had hoped for. If James had sounded proud or impressed, she might have asked him for a loan and used the money to spend the summer in Fontainebleau and recover her health out of the heat and dust of the capital. All the other women she worked with seemed to have funds to do so. Instead he had asked if a sale were likely, reminding her that she still owed him ten pounds. Her little half-brother Albert though had sent her a cartoon of a great crowd of men in hats grouped round a painting and shouting *Hurrah!* There had been no sale. Her portrait hung high on the walls, and surrounded by so many similar works, it went unnoticed.

There *was* a canvas from Rose Champion. It showed the Place Pigalle in early-morning light. The human figures were sketchy and indistinct, blurred by movement. One of the new double-decker motor-buses, identifiable only by its colours and bulk, rattled along the Boulevard Clichy. By the fountain a few rough female figures lounged – the models, mostly Italian, some French, who gathered there every morning waiting for work from the artists of Montmartre and Pigalle. They were scattered like leaves under the bare, late-autumn trees. Rose had lavished her attention on the light; the way it warmed the great pale stone buildings of Paris into honey tones; the regular power and mass of the hotels and apartment blocks, the purple and green shadows, the glint on the pitch-black metalwork around the balconies. The American was right, Rose had not returned to the studio after the summer, but the picture remained. M. Lafond must have bought it for himself. Maud felt as if someone were pressing her heart between their palms. The girl was dead and she was still jealous.

'She was ill,' the American said to Francesca. 'I called on her before I left for Brittany this summer. She said everything she had done was a failure and that there was . . .' she rubbed her fingertips together '. . . no money. I've never seen a woman so proud and so poor. Most girls are one or the other, don't you agree?'

'I saw her a week ago,' said an older woman, sitting near the model. Her shoulders were slumped forward. 'She was outside Kahnweiler's gallery. She seemed upset, but she wouldn't talk to me.'

Maud wondered if Rose had seen something in the wild angular pictures sold by Kahnweiler which she herself was trying to achieve but could not – whether that would have been enough to make her hang herself. Or was it hunger? More likely. Hunger squeezed the hope out of you. Maud held her hand out in front of her. It shook. I hate being poor, she thought. I hate being hungry. But I will survive. Another year and I shall be able to paint as I like and people will buy my work and I shall eat what I want and be warm. If I can just manage another winter.

She looked up, possessed by that strange feeling that someone was eavesdropping on her thoughts. Yvette, the model for the life-class that week, was watching her, her dressing-gown drawn carelessly up over her shoulders as she sat on the dais, tapping her cigarette ash out on the floor. She was a favourite in the studio, cheerfully complying when asked for a difficult pose, still and con-trolled while they worked but lively and happy to talk to them about other studios and artists in her breaks. Yvette was a little older than some of the girls, and occasionally Maud wondered what she thought of them all as she looked out from the dais with those wide blue eyes, what she observed while they tried to mimic the play of light across her naked shoulders, her high cheekbones. Now the model nodded slightly to Maud, then looked away. Her face, the angle of it, suggested deep and private thought.

Mademoiselle Claudette returned and soon realised that the news she had to give was already known. The facts she had to offer were simply a repeat of what Francesca had already overheard.

'Is there anyone here who knows anything of Miss Champion's people in England?'

'I believe she had an aunt in Sussex she lived with as a child,' Maud said into the silence that followed. 'But I have no idea of her address. Were there no letters?'

'We shall discover something, I hope. Very well.' The woman looked at her watch. 'It is ten to the hour. Let us return to work at ten minutes past. Monsieur Lafond asks me to tell you that in light of this unhappy event he will reserve the pleasure of seeing you until tomorrow.' There was a collective groan around the room. Mademoiselle Claudette ignored it, but frowned as she clicked the cover back onto her watch and turned to the tea-table.

'Does he fear a plague of suicides if he tells us we are miserable oafs today?' Francesca said, a little too loudly. The students began to stand, stretch, make their way to the pile of teacups and little plates of cakes.

∞∞∞

'My darlings, good day! How are you all on this dismal morning? Why is everyone looking so *terribly* grim?' Tatiana Sergeyevna Koltsova made her entrance in a cloud of furs and fragrance. Maud smiled. It was a pleasure to look at her. For all that she was Russian, it seemed to Maud that Tanya was the real spirit of Paris, the place Maud had failed to become part of: bright, beautiful, modern, light. She would chat to Yvette or tease Lafond himself and they all seemed to think her charming. Not all the other women students liked her, no one with looks, talent and money will be short of enemies, but Tanya seemed blissfully ignorant of any animosity directed towards her.

Francesca straightened up from the tea-table where she had been leaning. 'Be gentle with us today, my sweet. There's been a death in the family.'

The Russian's kid glove flew up to cover her pretty little mouth. At the same moment she let her furs drop from her shoulders and her square old maid bundled forward to gather them in her arms before they could pool onto the paint-stained floor. Maud watched as Francesca lowered her voice and explained. The Russian was blinking away tears. That was the thing about Tanya. She could be genuinely moved by the sufferings of others even as she threw off her cape for her maid to catch. She arrived late every day and one could still smell on her the comfort of silk sheets, chocolate on her breath. Then she would paint, utterly absorbed, for two hours until the clock struck and the women began to pack away. She would shake herself and look about her smiling, her canvas glowing and alive with pure colour.

Yvette tied her dressing-gown round her then clambered down from the model throne on the dais and passed the table, dropping the stub of her cigarette on the floor and grabbing up a spiced cake in the same moment. As she chewed she put her hand on the Russian's elbow and led her away into a far corner of the room. The movement seemed to wake Maud. She stood and went over to the food and helped herself, trying not to move too urgently nor take too much. She ate as slowly as she could.

The Russian materialised at her side like a spirit while she was still licking her lips. 'Miss Heighton?' Maud was startled, but managed a 'Good morning'. She had never had any conversation with Tanya, only watched her from a distance as if she were on the other side of a glass panel. 'I know it is not the most pleasant day for walking, but will you take a little stroll with me after we pack away today? I have something particular to ask you.'

Maud said she would be pleased to do so. Tanya smiled at her, showing her sharp white teeth, then turned to find her place amidst the tight-packed forest of easels. Maud steered her own way back to her place on the other side of the room and stared at the canvas in front of her, wondering what the Russian could want with her. The model was once again taking her place on the raised platform. She glanced at Maud and winked. Maud smiled a little uncertainly and picked up her brush.

An atmosphere of quiet concentration began to fill the room once more – Rose Champion already, to some degree, forgotten. The food seemed to have woken Maud's hunger rather than suppressed it. She closed her eyes for a moment, waiting for the sting of it to pass, then set to work.

CHAPTER 2

'*V*LADIMIR! WE ARE READY FOR YOU!'
Maud thought Tanya would speak to her on the pavement where the covered arcade of Passage des Panoramas gave out onto the wide, tree-lined expanse of Boulevard Montmartre, but instead she put her arm through Maud's and waved her free hand at a smart blue motor which was waiting, its engine idling, under the winter skeleton of a plane tree. It rolled smoothly towards them and stopped precisely by the ladies. Maud noticed as the chauffeur hopped out of the machine and went to open the auto-mobile's rear door for them that his livery matched the dark blue enamel of the car itself. Tanya's maid clambered into the front with the painting gear while Tanya herself ushered Maud into the back seat and said something in Russian to the driver. Maud heard the words *Parc Monceau* and the driver bowed before closing the door on them and returning to his seat.

'I hope you don't mind, Maud – by the way, may I call you Maud? Good. I need a little greenery after being shut up inside all morning. We shall run you to wherever you want to go later on.' The Russian pulled off her leather gloves and lay back with a sigh against the heavily upholstered seat. Maud made some polite reply and looked out of the window as the car pulled away into the stream of other motors, carriages and motor-buses. What did this princess want of her? Did she perhaps have a drawing pupil for her? Pupils were hard to come by in a city packed to its heaving gills with artists, but if she did, a few extra francs a month would make all the difference to Maud. She felt the curl of hope in her belly under the hunger.

Paris ate money. Paint and canvas ate money. Maud's training ate money. Paris yanked each copper from her hand and gave her back nothing but aching bones and loneliness. It was as if she had never quite arrived, as if she had stepped out of the grand frontage of the Gare du Nord, and Paris – the real Paris – had somehow retreated round the corner leaving all these open palms behind it. She was on the wrong side of the glass, pressed up against it, but trapped by her manners, her sober serious nature, behind this invisible divide. She spent her evenings alone in cheap lodgings reading and sketching in poor light. Her illness last winter – she had been feeding herself too little, been too wary of lighting the fire when the damp crawled off the river – had swallowed francs by the fistful. She must not get ill again, but she had even less money now. Sometimes she felt her stock of bravery had been all used up in getting here at all.

Even with winter closing in, the boulevard was full of activity – the shop girls in short skirts running errands with round candy-striped hatboxes dangling from their wrists, the women with their fashionable pinched-in jackets being ushered into restaurants by bowing waiters.

'Tell me,' Tanya said, 'did you know Miss Champion well? I thought, perhaps, you both being Englishwomen . . .'

Maud shook her head; her thoughts were loose and drifting and it took her a moment to recall where she was. She blinked and found herself looking into Tanya's large black eyes. She thought of

Rose, all sharp angles and anger. 'Not well at all. I found her rather . . . rather cruel, as a matter of fact.'

Tanya drew a small metal compact from her purse and examined her complexion, brushing away a little loose powder with her fingertip. Most women in Paris went into the world masked with heavy white foundation and their mouths coloured a false glistening red. Tanya's use of powder and paint was subtle by comparison, but brought up as she had been, Maud found it rather shocking and was embarrassed by her own unworldliness. She had thought herself rather wise in the ways of the world until she came to Paris. Every day that passed, she was in danger of thinking a little less of herself.

'I'm glad you say that,' Tanya said and snapped the compact shut again. 'Lord knows I am sorry anyone gets so desperate they hurt themselves, but she *was* terribly mean. I once asked her to comment on a study I was doing – it was my own fault really, I didn't want her opinion, it was simply I admired her and wanted her to praise me – and her advice was "stop painting".'

Maud laughed suddenly and covered her mouth.

Tanya grinned. 'I know! I said it was my own fault, but still – what a thing to say! She painted beautifully, I think, and in fairness she was not vain about it.'

'Yes, if one dared to say anything to her she looked as if she despised one,' Maud replied. 'She didn't think of any of us as artists at all. Perhaps she was right.'

'Nonsense,' Tanya said firmly and Maud blushed. 'There are some women at Lafond's who will do nothing more than paint nasty still lifes. There are others who are serious. You are serious, Maud. So am I. About my work at least.' The compact went back into the little embroidered bag over her arm. 'Now I shall be quiet for a minute and let you look out of the window.'

The sensation of being driven was very pleasant. Maud had been in her brother's motor a few times before, but she couldn't see why he liked it. The thing rattled your teeth and shook, and was forever making strange banging noises. This motor though was quite different; they seemed to float over the streets and the engine's regular fricatives made Maud think of contented pets. For the past few weeks, walking through the city between her classes and her lodgings had been a bleak necessity rather than a pleasure. The cold was bitter and Maud could not afford a coat thick enough to keep it from getting into her bones, and you needed money to rest in the pavement cafés, heated with braziers and defended from the winds with neat barriers of clipped box-hedge. Now though, Maud was snug behind the window seals of the motor-car, her legs covered with a rug lined in fur, and Paris unrolled in front of them like a cinema film.

The car argued its way through the traffic under the fifty-two Corinthian pillars and wide steps of the new Eglise de la Madeleine, then swung up Boulevard Malesherbes past the dome of Saint-Augustin. All movement and variety. Street-hawkers and boulevardiers, women dragging carts of vegetables or herring. The charming busy face of Paris a thousand miles away from Maud's draughty room in one of the back alleys around Place des Vosges, in a house just clinging to respectability, with its paper-thin sheets and the miserable collection of failed businessmen and poor widows who gathered around the landlady's table in the evening and tried to pretend her thin soups and stews were enough to sustain them.

Tanya grew quiet and let Maud enjoy the view until they reached Parc Monceau and the motor-car came to a gentle halt near the colonnade. Tanya sprang out before the chauffeur had time to open the door for her. 'Actual trees! Don't you feel like a butterfly pinned up in a case in Paris sometimes?'

Maud followed her onto the path. 'A little, I suppose. Though butterflies in cases are meant to be looked at, and no one looks at me.'

'I wish I could go out and about without being watched sometimes,' Tanya said casually, then turned to her maid and said something in Russian. You could try being poor, Maud thought. The conversation with the maid became a long and passionate debate that ended with Tanya stamping her foot and the maid crossing her arms over her bosom and frowning. The chauffeur had returned to the car and stared straight ahead the whole time, his face immobile.

'My maid Sasha is convinced still water is unhealthy,' Tanya said, taking Maud's arm and flouncing with her towards the little lake. 'She swears if I get typhoid she will not nurse me! You would think I had said I was going to swim the length of the Seine before lunch rather than take a little walk with you.'

Tanya's indignation had made her eyes shine and she held her chin high. She reminded Maud suddenly of little Albert, six years old and always right, and always shocked at the gross stupidity and moral turpitude of his elders. 'She had care of you when you were a child, perhaps?'

'Yes, and I was a sickly infant. Now I must spend hours every day convincing her and my aunts that I am sickly no more. You are not too cold?'

'Not at all, Miss Koltsova.'

'Oh, I am Tanya. Call me that. I love to walk here. It is the most respectable park in Paris, so my old cats can't complain, even if Sasha does.'

'Old cats?'

'My two aunts who live with me and make sure I am kept *comme il faut*. Vera Sergeyevna can tell you the order in which any company

should come in to dinner within five minutes of entering a drawing room – she is an expert in all forms of protocol – and Lila
Ivanovna, my late mother's sister, is here to agree with everything
she says. Papa would not let me come to Paris without them!
Lord, the weeping I had to do to make him let me come at all.
They are my guardian angels, apparently. Guardian gargoyles, they
seem to me.' She paused and Maud wondered if she was about
to tell her what she wanted to hear: about rich pupils who wanted
long lessons in warm houses. Instead she went on, 'The best
families in Paris send their nurses here with their little babies for
their fresh air.'

Tanya walked on with a slight swaying step as if on the verge of
breaking into a skip or a run; her long straight skirt swung and
rippled round her. Maud began to think she had been wrong about
the drawing lessons. Something like that could have been discussed
while walking through Passage des Panoramas surely, and there
was a nervous edge to Tanya's chatter. Well, she would ask eventually. In the meantime Maud had never been to this park before,
so she looked about her with pleasure and saw full, mature trees
and pathways that wandered in curves; it made the Tuileries seem
a desert.

The lake was edged with a semi-circle of Corinthian columns,
not on the monumental scale of the Madeleine, but with the same
classical decadence, narrow trunks topped with stylised foliage.
Great swathes of ivy had been allowed to clamber over them in
romantic festoons. It made Maud realise how ordered, how con-
structed Paris in general could appear. The grand boulevards
seemed like a demand for order, the tree roots ringed with gratings
as if they might escape. Here nature was controlled with a lighter
touch. A handful of smartly dressed women read novels on scattered
metal chairs, their faces hidden by the swooping brims of their

hats. Maud looked at them, the angles of their necks and hands, the physical body in the world. A formally dressed gentleman complete with silk top hat looked out over the surface of the lake and smoked his cigar, creating a personal fog-bank. A dozen *nourrices* in their high white muslin caps and long cloaks pushed prams along the gravel paths, nodding to one another like society beauties in the Bois de Boulogne.

'It is possible to see how rich the baby is by the quality of the cap and cloak of his nurse,' Tanya said, watching one young woman pass them with her little nose in the air. 'Look at those ribbons! The baby is either a prince or an American. Which here amounts to the same thing, of course. I am sure they are all shocking snobs, these girls.'

Maud wanted very much to say something light and clever in reply, but she was becoming tired and every woman here made her feel shabby and afraid. There was some trick of dress taught to every Frenchwoman in the cradle, it seemed. The *trottins* who fetched and carried for the dressmakers and milliners could be no richer than Maud, yet they seemed to know how to look neat and fresh. One of Lafond's male students told her that the French gendarmes said they always knew the nationality of a suicide pulled from the river by their clothes; the English girls were always badly dressed. Maud had not been sure what reaction the young man had been expecting, but he saw something in her face that had made him apologise and back away quickly.

'If I say something to you, will you try very hard not to take offence at it?' Tanya said.

Maud's heart sank. It did not sound like the opening of a conversation about drawing pupils, and if the Russian did say something offensive to her now she would have to leave at once, painfully hungry and further from home than she had been at the studio.

'I will try and take anything you say as it is meant,' she replied quietly.

'Very well, dear.' Tanya patted her arm. Maud glanced at her. Her face was shadowed by the brim of her hat, but one could still see the long clean line of her jaw. Her hair was beautifully black. She could not be more than twenty-two. 'I am a little worried about you, my dear Maud. You are looking too thin and too pale for a girl about to face a Paris winter. I am afraid you are spending money on colours you should be spending on food.' Maud felt herself blush and she straightened herself. Tanya was talking quickly, looking forward. 'There's no shame in it, naturally. The men behave as if poverty alone can make you a genius, but it is easier for them. So many girls come to Paris and find it rather more expensive than they had bargained for – it is Paris, after all. I am forever signing cheques to charitable foundations who are trying to get them back home before any greater harm comes to them!'

It was a sign of her hunger and the truth of what Tanya was saying that Maud's discreet good manners were not enough to stop her tongue. 'You wish to pay my fare home before I hang myself or take on a gentleman protector, Miss Koltsova?'

Tanya came to a sudden halt, and looked at Maud with wide and frightened eyes. 'Lord, is it that bad? I only thought you were beginning to look a bit unwell! You're not about to do either of those things, are you?'

'Certainly not, but—'

'I'm very glad to hear that! What a ghastly thought!' She looked so shocked that Maud suddenly laughed. One of the readers lifted her eyes briefly from her novel. Tanya gave a great sigh and hugged Maud's arm to her again. 'Oh, you mustn't tease me like that, I shall have nightmares.'

'I did not mean to tease you. I meant to tell you to mind your own business, but you rather cut me off.'

Tanya looked a little guilty. 'Yes, I suppose I did. I am sorry. Do you wish to tell me to mind my own business now?'

Maud shook her head. 'No, I find the wind has gone out of my sails rather. But I still have enough money to buy my fare home, so I need not apply to one of those charities you mention. I do not want to go home, Tanya. I find life here . . . difficult, I admit that, but I have so much more to learn and no chance of learning it back home. I'd have to live with my brother and he'd try to marry me to one of his chinless friends.'

'Urff, we have those in Russia too. When I marry, I shall choose a nice modern American. They are so beautifully clean.' She came to a halt and put her hand to her forehead. 'I have said things the wrong way about, then rattled off in the wrong direction. I had a terrible education, you know, and now I say what I think! That would never do in England, would it?'

'Certainly not,' Maud answered, thinking of her sister-in-law Ida, mistress of the pointed euphemism.

'Thank goodness I am in Paris where they see me as an eccentric and think it charming. My eldest aunt is far worse. She tells the women they all dress like prostitutes and she has become quite the social success as a result.' Tanya began walking again, pulling Maud alongside her. 'I think I might be able to help you, and I did not mean to suggest you should go home, but do you really think you have so much left to learn? I mean, the sort of things that are taught rather than found in oneself, through work. I think your painting terribly accomplished. Perhaps you just need to learn to trust yourself. Be a little more free. Don't you think that Manet and Degas have broken off our shackles? We must learn to stretch our limbs.'

Maud's head was beginning to swim rather and to concentrate on her answer took effort. 'Then I hope *that* can be taught, because I do not trust myself now. I think . . . I think if I could stay in Paris until next summer, then perhaps . . . But I cannot take charity, Miss Koltsova, however kindly meant. I would hate myself.'

It was as if Tanya had not heard her. 'Have you visited the Steins in Rue de Fleurus near the Luxembourg Gardens? Oh, I must take you there this evening then. Such paintings they have on their walls! All wildness and change and new ideas. There are no rules left, it seems. I think while those painters charge ahead like bulls, sweeping everything away before them, they make some space for us to paint as we like.'

'Tanya . . .'

The Russian paused again and blushed. 'I asked you to walk with me because I want to take you to see someone this afternoon. Her name is Miss Harris, and she has a house in Avenue de Wagram for English and American girls who find themselves destitute in Paris. Oh, don't bridle up again! She has a free registrar for work, and yes, I have contributed to her funds in the past. I am sure she might have something of use to you – English lessons or some such. You know, many ladies in Paris pay good money for a few hours' conversation a week. Now, you cannot be offended by that, can you? We shall go there at once.'

The idea of asking for help, even if it were just a recommendation from a charitable English lady, made Maud shrink away. Her pride flared up. She had got this far by her own efforts, why should she start becoming obliged to people now? What would her brother say, if he knew she was reduced to begging for a few hours' teaching English? If Tanya had asked her to teach some young relative or friend, then Maud could have felt the benefit of the extra francs and convinced herself that she, Maud, was the one granting the favour. To go and see this woman would be an open admission of failure. She felt as if all the activity in Parc Monceau had been frozen, as if everyone there, the ladies with their novels, the nurses with their pampered little charges, was staring at her to see if she would admit defeat. Whether by accident or design their conversation had carried them round the perimeter of the lake and they were once again beside Tanya's motor-car. The chauffeur had already stepped out and opened the door for them.

Maud generally ate no breakfast on studio days, trusting in the little spiced cakes to see her through to lunchtime when for a franc she might get an omelette, bread and vin ordinaire at one of the cafés near the studio. That would then sustain her till evening, or nearly sustain her. There was no way to squeeze more nourishment from her coin, that she knew by long trial. She should have eaten that meagre meal almost an hour ago and she could feel her hunger turning darker and more threatening. The idea of going anywhere, doing anything with her stomach aching and a feathery weakness beginning to spread through her limbs was impossible, yet resisting or telling Tanya the urgency of her hunger was likewise unthinkable. She let herself be guided back into the car and heard Tanya give another address then sat in the car with her eyes downcast.

CHAPTER 3

HEIR DESTINATION WAS VERY CLOSE BY. TANYA took her arm as they got out of the car and Maud felt herself sway against her. Tanya took the pressure for affection and squeezed her arm happily in return. Maud looked around her. They were in front of a good-sized building. The façade showed the familiar restrained elegance of Haussmann's Paris. Classical, stately, like all the main avenues and boulevards, it gave no hint of the poverty or fear that might be hidden in the yards and alleys behind it. English manners in stone.

Tanya pulled Maud up to the door with her, then looked up and, shielding her eyes against the grey glare of the sky, waved. Maud followed her gaze and saw leaning over the balcony of the second floor a woman of perhaps sixty, bright-eyed, bundled up warmly in a long dark-green coat and waving vigorously back.

'Miss Harris!' Tanya called up even as she pulled on the bell. 'We have come to see you. Are we welcome?'

'Always, dear!' the lady shouted back cheerfully and the white head disappeared again as the front door opened. A maid, looking particularly fearsome in tightly fitting black and solid shoes, stood in front of them. Behind her was a black and white tiled floor and a steeply climbing staircase. Everything was clean and orderly. A woman dressed in a monkish style crossed the corridor with a pile of papers in her hand and somewhere in the house, Maud heard the trill of a telephone bell.

'Miss 'Arris is not at home,' the maid said, and began to close the door again. 'If you wish to register for work, use the back-door bell. The refuge is full and the times of the free dinner and Bible study are marked 'ere.' She pointed at a little box of pamphlets attached to a railing and fluttering damply in the cold breeze.

Tanya flushed and put her hand on the wood of the door. 'Nonsense, my girl. I have just seen Miss Harris on the balcony.'

'Miss 'Arris has been working since six this morning,' the maid said darkly and not moving an inch. 'Miss 'Arris is now taking the air. Miss 'Arris is not at home.'

The lady called down from the balcony again. 'Simone, do be reasonable. I swear I have been out here twenty minutes. I have had quite enough air! Do let the girls in and come and unlock the door so I can get back to my office.'

The maid stepped out into the street and called up angrily. 'Ten! Ten minutes only!'

'Simone . . .' The lady's voice had a hint of steel in it now. The maid threw up her hands.

'Very well! We shall let these women in, we shall let you work yourself to death and then we shall all starve in the gutter or go to be registered. Much better than letting these women wait or go to the side door – oh, much better!' Simone stood aside to let Maud and Tanya in, then slammed the street door hard enough to make the vase on the hall-table rattle. She thrust open a door to the right that led into a small office with a table and chairs and several filing cabinets, and took them through into another room of about the same size, with one large desk and a number of rather sentimental watercolours on the walls. Most seemed to involve children and dogs. Simone picked up two dining chairs and thumped them down in front of the desk then stared fiercely at Tanya. 'Ten minutes!' she hissed, her finger raised and pointed. 'Starve!' Feeling her point had been made, she sighed deeply and removed a large key from the pocket of her apron, nodded over it sadly then left them.

Tanya looked a little sheepish and normally Maud would have been amused, but keeping her wits about her was as much as she could manage. She took her seat, afraid she might faint. In a very few minutes Miss Harris joined them, pink in the face and unbuttoning her coat. She hung it rather carelessly on the coat-stand by the door, closed the door behind her then smoothed her skirts and put out her hand to them both. Maud wavered a little as she stood again and had to grab onto the back of her chair. Though Miss Harris was shaking Tanya's hand with both her own, Maud thought her unsteadiness had not gone unnoticed. She shook hands with Miss Harris as Tanya introduced her and felt the quick appraising look from her small dark eyes.

'Sit down, dears! Sit down. My apologies for Simone. She always promises she will not lock me out then, hoop-la, as soon as my back is turned I find she has turned the key. She means well, of course.'

The woman settled herself behind the desk. There was a little heap of messages left in front of her and, on either side of her, paperwork was piled into towers that reached as high as her own head. She rifled through the messages with one hand, while reaching blindly behind her to pick up a speaking tube fastened to the wall. Still reading, she whistled down it and on hearing a grunt at the other end spoke. 'Beef tea and sandwiches, dear, quick as you can,' then she stoppered the tube and clipped it back into place. Her right hand now free, she picked up a pen and began to make notes in very small handwriting on the papers in front of her. For the first time since she had met Tanya, Maud noticed out of the corner of her eye that the Russian looked a little unsure of herself. Miss Harris said nothing more until the fearsome maid arrived with the tray and set it down on the desk, directly in front of Maud.

'I am very sorry to have disturbed you, Miss Harris,' Tanya said a little plaintively, 'when you wish to eat.'

'Don't be absurd, dear,' Miss Harris replied evenly. 'The food is for Miss Heighton.' She smiled at Maud, wrinkling her nose a little as she did. 'Eat up before you faint away, dear girl. Now, Tanya dear, to your left is yesterday's *Times*. I wish you would read to me the correspondence page while I finish these little notes and Miss Heighton gets her wind back.'

Tanya managed to pick up the newspaper while casting a look both shocked and a little offended at Maud. 'Maud, why did you not say you were hungry?'

'What did you expect her to say?' Miss Harris said sharply. 'I am afraid I have had more chance to see the signs of hunger in a girl than you have, Tanya. Now do read, if you can manage the English.'

'Naturally I can,' Tanya said, and while she read the various letters very carefully and in a clear voice Maud ate as slowly and steadily as she could. She could not remember the last time she had eaten good meat or bread that did not taste of chalk, and the beef tea seemed to enter her bloodstream like a drug, warming and comforting her. The room felt calm and secure as she ate everything that had been brought to her to the sound of Tanya's pretty Russian accent and the scratchings of Miss Harris's pen. When she had finished, she sat back with a sigh.

Miss Harris at once replaced the cap on her fountain pen with a businesslike click and then rang the little bell beside her. The door opened immediately and the young woman they had seen crossing the hall earlier entered. Her dress was very dark and severe in its cut. She stood very straight and unsmiling. Her hair was scraped back from her face and she wore little round eyeglasses. Tanya shuddered.

'Charlotte, dear, do take the tray away, and here . . .' Miss Harris piled her notes onto it next to Maud's crumbs, 'are the answers to the messages and notes from this morning.' She shook her head. 'I sometimes wish we had never thought to have a telephone installed. Is there anyone here for me, Charlotte?'

The severe young woman nodded. 'Two new girls and Mr Allardyce.'

Miss Harris waved her hand. 'Feed them and I will see them anon. The girls, I mean. I doubt Mr Allardyce would enjoy the beef tea.'

Charlotte did not smile. 'He is here to see if you have any unpleasant business for him this afternoon.'

'Certainly I shall. Well, you may send him in when I have finished with these ladies and look out the file on Miss Knight. I am sure he will help us there.'

Charlotte made a note in her little book then gathered up the tray and swept out of the room again while Miss Harris settled back in her chair. 'Dear Mr Allardyce! Such a useful young man. Miss Knight was forced to leave her luggage behind her in her last lodgings and her former landlord is being unreasonable about releasing it. When Charlotte went to demand it, I'm afraid she threatened him with hellfire and he laughed at her. Mr Allardyce will simply mention by name any number of officials he knows through his newspaper work and the landlord will be much more impressed.'

Miss Harris leaned forward and hunched her shoulders, speaking rather low. 'Of course, our mighty Creator is our first and final help, but Mr Allardyce's methods are certainly efficacious. He is himself an answer to a prayer. I asked God for some practical help, and the very next day Mr Allardyce appeared wishing to write something about our work for the American periodicals. I drummed him into service at once. I have no idea why anyone doubts the power of sincere prayer, I find it most reliable.' She blinked brightly as if God were a trusted tradesman. 'How is Yvette?'

'Quite well,' Tanya said without any hint of the surprise Maud felt. 'She sits for us at Passage des Panoramas this week.'

Maud's confusion must have shown on her face even if she did not manage to put it into words. Mrs Harris nodded briskly, setting a little gold cross at her neck bouncing, then gathered up another pile of papers from the tower next to her and began to go through them. 'Yvette is a soul close to God, though she would laugh at me for saying so. It was she who first encouraged Miss Koltsova to favour us with her charity.' Tanya snorted and Maud guessed that Yvette had phrased the suggestion a little more abruptly than that. 'I have no doubt it was Yvette who told Tanya to bring you to me today, Miss Heighton.' Tanya blushed a little.

'How did you come to meet her, Miss Harris?' Maud asked. It was wonderful to feel the physical effects of a good meal. She began to see the details in the room more clearly, the light glimmering on the brass bell at Miss Harris's elbow. The silver-framed photograph of Queen Alexandra hanging on the pale green wall.

'Yvette came to tell me an Italian with a nasty reputation was hiring out three young English girls as models from Place Pigalle. The oldest was twelve. Mr Allardyce and I went to see the gentleman and took the girls into our care. The Italian was most indignant. He had bought the three sisters from their parents for five pounds on Gray's Inn Road in London. They were all adopted by a most respectable family in North Wales in the end, and they still send me postcards occasionally – some of which are quite well-spelled. Now, I think you have had sufficient time to gather your wits, Miss Heighton. What do you want of me, children?'

Maud realised at last that all this chatter, the correspondence page of *The Times*, the praise of Mr Allardyce, had been undertaken solely to allow her to recover a little. She blushed and tried to answer but her tongue seemed to lock in her mouth. Tanya spoke for her.

'Miss Heighton needs a few hours' paid work a week to see her through the winter. Nothing that will interfere with her classes at Lafond's and she will still wish to study in the afternoons for part of the week at least. What do you have on your books that might be suitable? Someone requiring English lessons, perhaps?'

Miss Harris drew back a little. 'Oh my dear, I am afraid that Paris is awash with educated Englishmen and -women willing and eager to give lessons. All I have on my books at the moment are positions for governesses, shop girls and maidservants.'

Maud bit her lip. She had not wanted to come here, but having come only to find herself useless and unwanted was humiliating. She thought of an artist she sometimes saw on Boulevard Saint-Michel, his corduroy jacket buttoned up to the throat to hide his lack of a clean shirt, selling oil sketches of the Luxembourg Gardens in violent pure colours. He would be there all day, hunched by his stand, selling them for a couple of francs a time. A woman doing the same would be stared at and mocked by the crowd, and avoided by the curious tourists who were his few customers.

'There must be something,' Tanya insisted, almost affronted. 'Does no old lady need a companion in the afternoons?'

'All the old ladies in Paris have their lap-dogs and the Bois de Boulogne,' Miss Harris replied. Then she brightened suddenly like a lap-dog who has seen the shadow of a rabbit cross its vision, and began rummaging through the pile of papers to her right with more energy than care. 'Now there was something I noticed the other day – Charlotte put it to one side for some reason. Companion . . . companion . . .' Still pulling at the papers, she called out, 'Charlotte? Charlotte, dear!' The monkish female appeared behind them again and sighed at the tumble of papers. 'Yesterday or the day before? Companion?'

Maud thought the two women must have been working together for some time as this abbreviated communication seemed sufficient.

'Monsieur Christian Morel. A live-in companion for his younger sister, Miss Sylvie – a sickly young woman who wishes to spend her free hours sketching the Paris streets and must have some respectable person to accompany her. He asked for a lady with some knowledge of art.' She turned back a few pages in her little black notebook. 'Rue de Seine. Board and lodging. And a weekly stipend.'

Miss Harris beamed. 'Perfect then! Why, the dear Lord has managed everything once again.' If the Deity had been present, Miss Harris would have patted Him. 'Send Mr Morel a card, dear, to say a Miss Heighton will be calling to discuss the position on Monday afternoon.'

Maud found her tongue at last. 'But my classes . . . ?'

Miss Harris waved her hand. 'I'm sure the Lord has thought of *that*. You shall see. Give the ladies the address, Charlotte dear.' A look on Charlotte's pale round face seemed to give Miss Harris pause. 'What is it?'

'He smiled too much,' Charlotte said. She was frowning over her notebook as if she were afraid of being thought foolish. 'And he is offering too much money.'

Miss Harris folded her hands in front of her. 'Miss Heighton is a sensible young woman. She will not allow anything to occur that might reflect badly on herself or us, I am sure.'

The Dress oil on canvas 64 × 41 cm

In contrast to the painting of the life-class at the Académie Lafond, this painting contains no human subject at all. Instead, the focus falls on a luxurious pink evening gown hanging by a mirror in a white dressing room. The setting is opulent: note the gilding on the room's panelling, the chandelier just appearing at the top of frame, the amount of tissue paper and striped boxes on the floor around the mirror, and the glimmer of sequins on the dress itself. However, it is the emptiness that fascinates. Who will wear the dress that has been chosen? Any other painter might have made this scene one of feminine intimacy, yet despite the delicate colouring the image is cold and empty; the woman who should be the centre and focal-point of the scene has been removed and the image becomes one of hollow vanity and excess.

Extract from the catalogue notes to the exhibition 'The Paris Winter: Anonymous Treasures from the de Civray collection', Southwark Picture Gallery, London, 2010

CHAPTER 4

*T*HE DOOR SWUNG OPEN AND A RATHER SHORT, square woman looked up at them.

'On whose introduction are you here?'

Maud did not catch the name Tanya gave, but it seemed to satisfy their host. The woman smiled, shook their hands and their little party was ushered inside. They entered a large high room, white-washed to the ceiling, with various odds and ends of heavy-looking furniture pushed against the walls, which were filled with the most bizarre and confusing canvases Maud had ever seen.

Tanya put her arm through Maud's. 'Are you glad we have come?'

'I am.'

Maud's day had been so disorientating it seemed only right it should end here. Tanya had not wanted to release her when they left Miss Harris and invited her to spend the evening with her. Maud had agreed, was touched by Tanya's transparent delight, and within an hour was enfolded in the luxury of Tanya's house in Rue Chalgrin. Tanya ushered her up the wide curved staircase and into her bedroom. It was a massive room, exploding with white and gold, but before Maud could get her bearings she was being chivvied into the dressing room which was almost as large again.

Tanya's French maid was summoned and Maud was persuaded to try on any number of evening dresses. Tanya left her to telephone a couple of young men approved of by her aunts who would take them to the Steins' At Home and then out to supper. Maud was on the other side of the glass certainly, but if she liked it or not she was still too dizzy to say. She was wrapped in one expensive dress after another while Tanya skipped about with delight and kept offering her more food, mostly chocolate.

'The pink, Maud! There's no doubt. You must wear the pink.' Tanya was sprawled on the chaise longue in a long evening dress of gold with black beading which shimmered as she moved. Maud felt the maid's quick hands adjusting the dress that Tanya had picked out for her. Her arms felt bare and cold.

Tanya glanced at the maid then said in English, 'What did you think of that young man, Maud?'

She looked over her shoulder and the maid sighed. Tanya was unwrapping another chocolate, dropping its gold wrapper back into the box and staring up at the chandelier. 'The American? Mr Allardyce? I thought he seemed very pleasant.'

Tanya frowned. 'Just pleasant? You didn't think he was handsome?'

Maud smiled. 'Handsome too.' He *was* handsome, now she thought of it. They had met for a few moments in the hall as they were leaving the house in Avenue de Wagram, and even in the confusion of her feelings Maud had noticed how he had looked at Tanya. Could these things happen in such a way? They had never happened to her.

Tanya begin ferreting about in the chocolate box for another bon-bon, then as soon as she had found one, dropped it again. 'He has a nice voice, I think.'

The maid presented Maud with a pair of low-heeled shoes dyed to match the dress and Maud was just slipping them onto her feet when the door opened and a large woman in a wide purple dress thirty years out of fashion though crackling with newness swept into the room. She spoke to Tanya loudly and in Russian, and the tone did not sound happy. A smaller lady in a dress of a similar cut albeit in yellow silk appeared behind her. It was the second lady who noticed Maud first and murmured something to the woman in purple. The titan paused and Tanya spoke in French.

'My dear aunts, may I present Miss Maud Heighton? I have invited her this evening, and really it's very respectable – half of Paris goes to the Steins'.'

'Yes, but which half?' the woman in purple replied, her French rich and dark as Tanya's gold-wrapped chocolates.

'Maud, my aunts, Vera Sergeyevna and Lila Ivanovna.'

Maud curtsied neatly and Vera Sergeyevna lifted her lorgnette to watch her do so, then nodded slightly. 'And who might you be? I do not know you.'

She would have replied, but Tanya was too quick. 'Miss Heighton is a fellow student at the Académie.' Vera Sergeyevna's eyes widened. 'Mikhail Pavlovich Perov is taking us to the Steins' this evening,' Tanya continued in a rush. Vera's gaze shifted to her niece and her expression softened slightly, then she and Tanya had a short conversation in Russian after which the two older ladies departed rather more calmly. Vera only inclined her head to Maud as she left; the other woman smiled at her more warmly.

When they had gone Tanya collapsed back onto the sofa with a deep sigh. 'Thank goodness I spoke to Perov. They are forever badgering me to accept his invitations so they couldn't protest now.' She grinned up at Maud. 'I don't suppose you have a cousin who is a baronet, do you, darling?'

'No, I do not. Is that what you told them?'

Her dark eyes fluttered wide and innocent. 'Yes – and that you've just arrived in Paris and your luggage was lost. I had to, otherwise by tomorrow Vera would be writing to my father about my keeping low company, though it was Perov who saved us. Are you sure? I thought everyone in England had a cousin who's a baronet.'

'Not everyone, Tanya.'

'Ah well, I suppose you know best. Now what shall we do with your hair?'

The crowd in the Steins' atelier was almost as interesting as the paintings on the walls and, Maud found, far easier to look at. Tanya had told her what she knew of the place while they were dressing; a pair of Americans, a brother and sister called Leo and Gertrude Stein, amused themselves by purchasing the most extreme examples of the new art they could find in studios and from specialist dealers, then allowed anyone with an introduction to visit them and be appalled by it any Saturday evening at their home on Rue de Fleurus.

There were already a great number of people in the room when the girls and their escorts arrived, some clothed as they were in fashionable evening dress, others *à la bohème* in loose trousers and high jackets for the men, peasant skirts and blouses for the women, who hung on their arms and took the cigarettes from their mouths when they wished to smoke. Maud heard German, French, English and what she thought might be Hungarian running off the tongues around her. She tried to ignore them and looked instead at the pictures. These were the wild, animalistic paintings that had come snorting and stamping into the Salons in the last few years, the colours of nature made somehow blistering and violent, the figures simplified until they were more ideas of humans than their likenesses. There was a portrait of their host, her face flattened into planes as if she were carved. Maud stood with her arm through Tanya's, at last so lost in what she was looking at that she forgot to be self-conscious about her dress or the way in which Tanya's maid had arranged her hair for her.

The girls walked slowly round the room until without consulting one another they came to a stop in front of a painting of a pair of circus performers, a mother and father sitting with their baby, an ape squatting at their feet and looking up at them. There was something of the Nativity Scene about it, a sense of calm, the gentle warmth of the colouring. Maud felt almost as if she were intruding on them by looking at it so closely. The harlequin father of the little group wore a costume of the same pale pink as Maud's borrowed dress.

'We shall have to take it down now, I suppose,' a voice said beside her in English. Maud turned to find her host, Miss Stein, beside them, her strong plain face shining with a religious intensity. 'He is painting quite differently now. You can see the whole of the modern revolution in art between the canvas you are looking at now and that one over there.' She pointed to the image of a woman, but cut up into geometrical planes, straight-edged shapes and black curves, and lurching, animal-like towards the viewer, her face a crude mask. Tanya peered up at it, lifting her white throat so that the jewels on her neck sparkled, trying to see by the yellowish gas-light.

'When I look at that, I feel as if someone is very angry with me,' she said at last.

Miss Stein laughed, a single exclamation.

'I shall tell Pablo that, but it is the future. He and Matisse are the only painters in town.' Then she added more quietly, 'I'm afraid your men are getting bored, girls. Best take them away quickly before they say something stupid and one of the artists punches them. Happens once a month at least.' She turned to greet some new arrival and Tanya glanced over her shoulder. The two men whom she had telephoned to come with them were slouching against the desk in the centre of the room, apparently oblivious to the art. Mr Perov was examining his nails and Mr Lebedev was yawning widely. Tanya's eyes narrowed.

'Oh Lord. I suppose she is right and we must take them away before they become offensive.' She looked up again at the butchered figure on the wall. 'Is that the future, do you think? It seems very cruel.'

'I do not think it is mine, Tanya.'

The Russian girl nodded. 'Yes, I hope some people will always want pictures that resemble something in the real world. Not all Americans are like the Steins, are they? Some of them might even prefer the way I paint.'

Maud wondered if she was thinking of Mr Allardyce again. 'I am certain that is so, Tanya.' The Russian girl smiled very brightly and led Maud over to their lounging escorts.

The following morning Maud woke in her narrow room wondering if the previous day had been a dream. Not until she saw the dusky-pink evening gown with its heavy beading of ribbons and pearls could she believe it had happened at all. Rose Champion dead. Miss Harris. The strange pictures and then supper at Maxim's. The images came back to her as if refracted through glass, and the gypsy band she had heard there seemed still to be playing their insistent music inside her head. Champagne, cigar smoke and laughter. Everywhere Maud looked, men and women had been laughing, heads flung back and their throats open. They had reappeared in her dreams, braying like donkeys till they grew long furred ears to match. The two Russian gentlemen had ordered supper for them then amused themselves by abusing the paintings on display at the Steins' house.

'How do they ever expect anyone to buy such things?' Perov said, still apparently fascinated by the study of his fingernails. He had a thin sandy moustache that seemed to dribble past the corners of his mouth. 'I would rather have this glass of champagne than everything that was on those walls. And the people! At least here one sees human beings properly dressed.'

He tittered, then waved to one of the crisply attired waiters and asked for more champagne while Maud winced at the gaiety around her. There was such noise. Everyone seemed to be speaking unnaturally loudly and the women moved so much when they spoke, pushing their shoulders back even as they leaned forward and constantly lifted their hands to the level of their heads. Maud noticed that the sequins on their dresses glimmered as they did so, and the shaded electric lights caught the jewels in their hair and on their hands with shifting rainbows of colour. Perhaps that was why they were doing it. The walls were golden and the pillars marble and mirrored so that everyone was forced to see a dozen shattered images of themselves in the crowd.

The woman on the next table wore a spray of ostrich plumes in her hair, fastened at their base with a diamond the size of a sovereign.

'Fake,' Mr Lebedev said, leaning towards her. She wondered if he meant her, that he had seen through the flim-flam of Tanya and her maid to the prudish poor Englishwoman who was not related to any baronet. 'The diamonds,' he elaborated, and she realised he meant the jewel at which she had been staring. 'Most of them anyway. Half the people here are liars and frauds. All show.' He then sat back in his chair again. It was as much as he had said all evening.

She sipped her champagne slowly – it tasted acid – and watched as any number of patrons approached the tables and spoke either to Tanya or one of the two men. The noise was shocking and the smoke from her neighbour's cigar made her feel a little nauseous. There must be something else, she thought. Something between the hungry squalor in which she had been living and this. She saw great platters of expensive food and rich sauces slowly turning cold in front of the silk- and velvet-clad diners. After an hour she began to be afraid she might be ill. Only Tanya's insistence meant that their escorts agreed to take them home with anything like good grace. Her old clothes were handed to her in a bundle by the chauffeur as he walked her to the door of her lodging-house and saw her let into the building. Perhaps the Morels would offer somewhere she could be comfortable, between the sinuous insinuating richness of the café with its twisted ironwork that pressed like a fever dream and the coldness of her room; between the wild anarchy of the painters who sold to the Steins and the facile decorations of the Académies. It formed a sort of desperate hope as she lay in her bed that Sunday morning, sick with surfeit rather than with hunger but sick nonetheless, and staring at the pink dress.

After an hour she managed to get out of bed and dress and spent a little time with her sketchbook until it was time to have her lunch; she then left the boarding house to spend the rest of her Sunday in the Louvre. Monsieur Pol was there in the gardens as always with his birds, and she thought of Rose Champion as she stopped to watch him whistling his songs. The birds settled on his outstretched arms and shoulders and they chirruped insistently back to him. Sparrows pretending to be canaries. She closed her eyes and hoped for deliverance.

On the Monday morning Maud took rather longer than usual making herself ready before she left for Lafond's. She tried to make her dress as neat as possible and brushed and bound up her hair three times before she was content with what the ragged glass could show her. It did no good when she tried to tell herself to be calm; her imagination had begun to rage. What if M. Morel and his sickly sister did not like her? Might she seem too young? Perhaps a more matronly woman would be more suitable to be a companion for the sister. She thought of the elderly relatives – the 'cats' – who guarded Tanya. Perhaps she could say she was twenty-four rather than twenty-three. She smiled into the mirror. 'Delighted to meet you,' she said to herself then turned from the glass with a groan. She felt like a child about to be interviewed by a strict headmaster. And what if the Morels themselves were not quite right? What if they were vulgar or unpleasant? Rude or off-hand? She tried to decide what level of respectability or otherwise would be acceptable for her comfort, what would the shy small-town miss in her think? Perhaps he would smell of drink. Perhaps *she* would. The thoughts argued and twitched at her all the way to the Académie then through the first hour.

At the first break in their work she stayed at her easel, too nervous to eat and too distracted to exchange pleasantries with her fellow students. Tanya had yet to arrive. She studied the portrait in front of her and thought of those strange cut-up bodies at Miss

Stein's. It seemed to her they were about the painter not the subject, a painter trying to see everything at once and consume it, rather than know one thing and communicate that. She dipped her brush in linseed oil and then in the purple madder on the palette and with it began to thicken the shadows so that Yvette's pale skin would seem more fragile by contrast. When Yvette spoke to her she started.

'Miss Heighton? I was hoping you'd look a bit more cheery this morning. I passed by Miss Harris's yesterday afternoon and heard they might have something to suit.'

'Oh, good morning, Yvette.' Maud blinked and turned away from the painting, becoming aware of the continuing bustle and chatter around her. The model held her tatty silk dressing-gown around her, her weight all on one jutting hip and a cigarette in her hand. There was something childlike about her thin face, a quickness, those large eyes that seemed to draw everything in, shivering with an animal glee. More fox than cat. 'Yes, I am to go along and see a Monsieur Morel this afternoon with Miss Koltsova. Perhaps they won't like me.'

'They will. You know English is all the rage. Half the girls I know who normally make their money looking after kiddies can't get work at the moment, because every mother wants their little ones to learn "proper cockney". Any Frenchman would love to get his sister a real English miss as a companion.'

Yvette leaned forward to study the picture of her on Maud's easel and blew a long lungful of smoke over the depiction of her own naked skin. 'You're coming on, Miss Heighton.' She suddenly straightened and set her feet more widely apart, clasping her hands behind her back. The collar of her dressing-gown opened and Maud could see the bluish tint to her skin. 'Your tone sense improves, but watch your lines around the model's elbow, Miss

Heighton. Anatomy! Anatomy! Is Yvette a human or a horse? For
that is the joint of a horse, not of a beautiful Frenchwoman.'

Maud laughed. It really was a very good impression of Lafond.
She put out her hand. 'Call me Maud.' Yvette shook it and gave a
little bow, still in the character of Lafond. 'I understand it was
you who suggested Tanya take me to see Miss Harris. Thank you.
If this Mr Morel and his sister like me, you'll have made my life a
lot easier.'

Yvette wrinkled her nose. 'He'll like you, and Tanya will be able
to tell you if it's a proper establishment for a lady like yourself. Her
aunts have drilled that into her well enough, I think. It's being
poor she doesn't understand. She sees in straight lines sometimes,
and only looks for the pretty and charming. Not a bad way to be,
but she assumes because she's well fed, everyone who speaks nicely
is well fed too. She never thought what a difference a bit of
respectable work might make to someone like you. And never
noticed you were too proud and lonesome to go and look for it
yourself.'

Maud looked down at her palette, the grain of the wood as
familiar as her own hands. 'You seem to know us very well, Yvette.'

The model stretched her shoulders. 'I spend half my mornings
up there watching you all, and I know how hard Paris can be.'

Maud frowned suddenly, realising. 'Yvette, did you try to help
Rose?'

The model winced as if Maud had hurt her and twisted her
body away slightly, looking tangled and upset. 'I told her about
Miss Harris, but I mucked it all up and she just swore at me.'

'That's why you asked Tanya to speak to me? You didn't think
I would swear at you, did you?'

'No, but . . .' She scratched her neck. 'I could see you admire
Tanya and I thought to myself, if she spoke to you, it might do

some good. Would you really have taken advice on how to live from someone like me?'

Maud tried to imagine what she would have done if Yvette had spoken to her. She would have been offended, certainly. 'I almost told Tanya to go to hell, so no, probably not,' she admitted. 'But I'll try not to be so stupid in future.'

Yvette gave her a small, tight smile. On the other side of the room Mademoiselle Claudette clapped her bony hands and the students began to return to their places. Yvette dropped her cigarette and wound her way back to the dais. Maud watched her go. She was still a young woman – not more than twenty-five, Maud guessed – but thin as a boy around the hips and shoulders, and there was a wary edge to her that Maud normally associated with much older women. A certain guardedness even when she was teasing. Perhaps not always. When, a little later, Lafond arrived and during his progress round the room told Maud to watch the structure of the upper arm, she glanced at Yvette. The model was biting on the material of the collar of her dressing-gown to hold back her giggles. Maud only managed to keep her own composure by looking down and fixing her attention on her teacher's shining black shoes.

CHAPTER 5

CHRISTIAN MOREL WAS A HANDSOME MAN OF SOME years past forty, judging by the lines around his eyes; clean-shaven, though his dark hair reached to his shining white collar. From the moment he opened the door to Tanya and Maud he gave the impression it was he and his home that were on trial, that he was campaigning for the privilege to have Maud with them. Her nerves leaked away under his quick smile, his concern for their comfort and air of sincere supplicant.

He began by apologising for the very beautiful apartment. He had meant to stay at his club, but his cousin, with whom his sister was supposed to lodge while he was away had become ill, so they had little time to find somewhere suitable for them both in town. Tanya sympathised, but to Maud the accommodation looked palatial. The drawing room was narrow but long, with high windows draped in lace that let in the winter light, and a fireplace at each end of the room. Starburst mirrors hung above both. The south end of the room was occupied by a chaise longue, a piano, and a few armchairs upholstered in yellow; the other end was dominated by a round, lace-covered dining-table and dresser. All the light-coloured wood in the room was worked into long supple lines; electric lamps were dotted around on the occasional tables.

Maud thought of the heavy dark furniture in her father's house; every piece of it had seemed hulking and angry. Here everything was cheerful but not overwhelming, comfortable without being oppressively rich. She was delighted.

'There is a maid's room,' Morel was saying, 'but we'd rather not have a servant live in. The house girl comes in every morning and prepares our lunch. In the evening we order up from the café on the corner.' He looked at Maud, gently questioning. 'They have a good chef. It's not the Café Anglais, but who can eat like that every night? We live simply and dine early. I hope that is acceptable, Miss Heighton?'

'Oh, quite,' Maud said politely. As Morel led them out into the main corridor, Tanya pinched Maud's arm. Maud turned and made her eyes wide. Tanya stifled a giggle. Morel had reached a door, the first in the corridor from the entrance to the apartment. He pushed it open gently with his fingertips.

'If Miss Heighton were willing to stay with us over the winter, this would be her room.' With a bow he invited her to walk in ahead of him; as she did so she was shocked by the pricking of tears in her eyes. Stupid to be so sentimental, but it was just as she had imagined her room in Paris *might* be when she had climbed onto the train in Alnwick two years ago. It was a large room. The bed was brass, wide and covered in white linen, the washstand was ash, the floor carpeted with thick rugs in red and brown. Soft shadows rested comfortably in the corners and draped themselves over the bed. Mr Morel was watching her anxiously.

'But I am so foolish, you cannot see a thing.' He crossed the room and opened the shutters. Light and air tumbled into the room and seemed to wake it; Maud felt it greet her as a friend. She went to the window and looked out. It gave onto a courtyard at the rear of the building where white-washed walls gathered the afternoon sun and flung it into the room. There was a lean-to by the entrance to the communal cellars and a girl was sitting on a rough stool outside it. She was plucking a chicken for the pot, her red apron a sudden splash of colour over the earth floor. Maud looked down on her, resting her hand on the windowsill.

'Naturally, this room is a little shaded in the mornings, but I understand you ladies work elsewhere in those hours.' He looked at his feet. 'Miss Harris explained to me you have lessons every morning, Miss Heighton. I wish you to know that would be no difficulty, no difficulty at all if you are content to live here. My sister keeps to her bed in the mornings.'

Maud realised they were waiting for a response from her. 'It is a lovely room,' she said. 'Absolutely lovely.'

Morel looked relieved, then started as he heard a clatter of cups from the drawing room. 'Ah, our tea. Let us go and refresh ourselves.'

∞∞

Over tea, served in the English fashion, Tanya set about questioning Morel. Maud watched her surreptitiously. Yvette had been right about her willingness to sniff out any threat to Maud or her reputation. She was polite but thorough, smiling as she asked questions about the background of the Morel family and nodding as they were answered. Her aunt would have been proud of her.

Morel was born in 1867 in Luxeuil-les-Bains, the only son of a prosperous merchant in the town and his first wife. This lady had died in 1871 but Morel's father had eventually remarried and was blessed with a daughter in 1889, Sylvie. Morel spoke with the dignity and restraint of an Englishman when telling them of the carriage accident that killed their father and Sylvie's mother in

51

the year 1904. Sylvie had been with her parents at the time and the injuries she had suffered had made her health delicate. She was easily tired even now. Morel had taken on her care and support. Then, having given the two young women the facts of the case, he moved the topic on and spoke of how impressed he had been by Miss Harris and her good works. He hoped Maud and Sylvie would speak English together. He wished to go to America in the spring, he informed them, to pursue some promising business opportunities, and wanted to take Sylvie with him. To have her English fluent and practised would make her life there much easier.

This gave Tanya the chance to enquire as to what his business was. He smiled and waved his hand. 'Moving money! Trains and planes and automobiles, the telegraph and now telephones. Money has to learn how to keep up in this modern age. But it is dull business in comparison with yours. Let us talk about you young artists instead.' He turned towards Maud. 'You are an artist, Miss Heighton? Tell me what your family think of you living so independently and so far away from them. Do your parents approve of your coming here?'

Maud put down her cup. 'My father was an auctioneer in the north of England, Mr Morel. He died three years ago. My mother died when I was twelve.'

'An orphan like my poor sister and me? But not alone in the world, I hope.'

'My elder brother James is a solicitor in Darlington. I have a younger brother too, only six years old, from my father's second marriage. He lives with James and his wife now.'

'Perfect woman!' he said, lifting his hands and looking upwards as if thanking heaven. 'You understand then the bond between Sylvie and myself.'

She thought of Albert, his round face always dirty and his wide blue eyes.

'I do.'

'And there is no better man to do business with in my opinion than an English solicitor,' Morel continued. He seemed more at ease now than when the girls had first arrived. He picked up his teacup again and arched one eyebrow. 'One always knows exactly what they are going to say. I think I can quite easily imagine what they are likely to say about a young woman living in Paris alone.' He frowned slightly. 'Or am I being unfair?'

Maud shook her head, trying not to smile. 'No, you are quite right. James thinks Paris a very dangerous place, and his wife thinks any city a mortal danger, and art only ladylike if taken in moderation. Perhaps they are right. However, they have little to say on the matter. My father's property was insured and the money divided equally between the three of us. It is not enough to provide an income, but enough to support me during my training until I can earn money of my own.'

She felt his eyes examine her threadbare cuffs, but he made no comment and when he found he was being watched, smiled at her warmly.

'Ah! You are one of the new women. Independent in thought and deed. Excellent.'

'Christian? We have visitors?' A woman's voice. They stood and turned towards it and Maud saw Sylvie Morel for the first time.

She was much lighter in colouring than her brother, with white-gold hair loosely tied up and pale skin. She leaned against the doorframe looking as if she had just stepped out of a Burne-Jones painting. Her afternoon dress of ivory silk suited her slim figure and had some suggestion of classical drapery about it. It was as if Canova's marble sculpture of *Psyche* in the Louvre had woken and dressed herself. Maud looked away, suddenly shy.

'My dear, we have woken you,' Morel said. 'I'm so sorry. Please, come and join us.' She approached slowly, not quite looking at either of them. 'This is Miss Koltsova. Miss Koltsova, my sister.'

'Delighted,' Tanya said, putting out her hand. Miss Morel took it with a smile and repeated the word, drawing it out as if she were enjoying the taste of it.

'And this is Miss Heighton,' Morel continued. 'I hope, if you think you might like each other, that Miss Heighton will spend this winter here as our guest.'

Mademoiselle Morel turned towards Maud and after a moment smiled with more warmth. Maud put out her hand and for a moment held Mademoiselle Morel's fingers between her own. They were dry and cool. 'I think I should like that,' Sylvie said. 'Will you come? It might be very dull for you, but we will do our best to make you welcome.'

'Then I shall come,' Maud said, and released her hand.

'Very good, come tomorrow if you can. I get so bored with Christian away all hours. Forgive me, I must go back to my room. This is not one of my good days.' She turned to go at once, then looked back over her shoulder. I wonder if she will model for me, Maud thought. One would have to thin the paint so as to create only a suggestion of colour. 'May I ask your first name?'

'Maud.'

'A proper English name, I am glad. *Queen rose of the rosebud garden of girls . . .*' she quoted in English, her accent giving a heavy new fragrance to the line.

'My mother was a great admirer of Lord Tennyson.'

'It suits you. My name is Sylvie.' She left them, her slippers whispering across the hardwood floor.

'Then it is settled!' Morel said, looking triumphant and relieved.

He hesitated as if to say something more, then looked uncertainly between his guests. Tanya at once put out her hand to him.

'There is a darling little bookshop on the corner I noticed as we came in. Would you think me terribly rude if I take the chance to have a look at what they have? I can see myself out. Maud, I'll be waiting for you when you are ready.'

Morel bowed over her hand and did not speak again until the door had clicked behind her. 'What a charming woman! Are you very good friends?'

Maud smiled. 'I hope so.'

He cleared his throat. 'I should like to offer you a consideration of five louis a week, Miss Heighton, as well as your board. Would that be acceptable?'

'You are too generous,' Maud replied sincerely. She lived on that amount a month.

'Do not be too quick to say so,' he said. 'Please, sit with me a moment more.'

Maud took her place in front of the cold teacups again. Morel reached into his pocket and produced a cigarette-case, blue enamel and decorated with a tiny circle of brilliants. He asked her permission with a raised eyebrow and she nodded her consent. She found she was holding onto her little purse quite tightly on her lap. The fear that something would deny her that room, this company elegantly balanced between champagne or gruel, reared up again. It was so comfortable here.

Morel lit his cigarette and then exhaled; the smoke curled upwards in the light. 'My sister . . . Sylvie . . .' He crossed and uncrossed his legs. 'This is a matter of some delicacy. My sister has a weakness that I know is tolerated in some parts of Paris, but I cannot condone it. I was not perhaps the guardian I should have been to her during these last few years, and she was introduced to bad influences in my absence. I hoped bringing Sylvie to Paris might break these connections with certain corrupting influences, but I find she cannot now manage yet without . . .' His voice trailed away and he scratched suddenly and hard at the underside of his chin.

Maud shook her head. 'I am so sorry, sir. I do not understand you.'

'Of course not. You know that laudanum can be of great help to those in pain?'

'Yes, I have heard it can do a great deal of good.'

'So it can, so it can, and properly administered under the care of a professional medical man it did help my sister a great deal. Then she was introduced by a "friend" into taking the drug in a vaporised form – that is, smoking it in the fashion they do in the East.'

Maud was startled. 'Opium?' she said faintly. All she knew of opium came from the cheap novels her step-mother had left lying around the house. The illustrations showed hovels in the bowels of London full of emaciated, corpse-like figures and sinister Chinamen rubbing their hands. It all seemed rather at odds with this elegant apartment and the beautiful girl. Though she was rather ghostly, a little lost in her own dreams.

'You are shocked, naturally. Perhaps I can reassure you. I purchase the poison for my sister and she has sworn to use it only in this apartment. She knows no one in Paris. You will not be dragged into any low or dangerous places, Miss Heighton, I assure you. No one visits us, no low company will offend you here. Though, I admit her use of the drug does make Sylvie very reluctant to leave the apartment in the evenings. I would be happy for you to go out from time to time if I were at home, but I am afraid you will find this a dull place. No parties, no visits to the theatres or cabarets. If the consideration I offered you perhaps seems a little high, let us say it is by way of compensation for robbing you of the delights of Paris to a great degree over the winter.'

Miss Charlotte's fears were explained away. Maud felt a sudden relief. Not only could she live here through the winter, she could be useful to the lovely girl and her concerned brother. She would distract Sylvie with sketching and English conversation and keep a watchful eye on her.

'Please, Mr Morel, I came to Paris to study art, not for the cabarets. I also know very few people in the city. You would be robbing me of nothing.' He looked greatly relieved. They made their arrangements for her belongings to be removed to Rue de Seine the next day.

Later in the afternoon Tanya and Maud walked arm-in-arm past the secondhand book stalls that lined the embankment opposite the solid square towers of Notre Dame. The sky had cleared slightly, and they were both a little giddy with their success. They drank in the cold air as if it were fresh water in the desert. It was strange for Maud. She had never made friends easily, having been isolated as a child and reserved throughout her youth. She wished that some of her old school fellows who had thought her such a strange girl, always sketching and never joining in with their gossip and whisperings, could see her now, in step with this glamorous Russian girl, strolling the Paris pavements as if they owned them. She felt as if her old tired skin was being shed and she, fascinating and original as Paris itself, had suddenly emerged at some moment between Miss Harris's beef tea and the handshake with Morel.

'My eyes, what a beauty! I declare I hate her,' Tanya said. And when Maud laughed at her: 'I do! We brunettes are expected to be fiery and clever and passionate all the time. It's exhausting. With her colouring, all Mademoiselle Sylvie has to do is recline on a day-bed and the world will drop to its knees in admiration. It is very, very unfair.'

'I shan't pity either of you for being rich and beautiful,' Maud said.

'Well, that's very cold-hearted of you.' Tanya dropped Maud's arm to pick up a volume of Baudelaire from the closest *bouquiniste*, but after reading a couple of lines, she made a face and replaced it. 'Oof, I am glad I am a painter. Poets are never cheerful – but not all writers are like that, are they? Mr Allardyce is a journalist.' Maud smiled at Tanya and she blushed. 'So your father, Mr Heighton, he was an auctioneer?'

'He was a drunk,' Maud said, surprising herself.

'Ah.'

'And his name was not Heighton, but Creely. Heighton was my mother's name before she married.'

'My dear Maud, you are full of surprises. Why did you change it?'

On the pavement behind Tanya an elderly man with long, well-groomed whiskers and a long black cloak was arguing over the price of a book with the stall-holder. Each bent forward from the waist and argued their point nose to nose. Behind him on the pavement and apparently waiting for him was a handsome young woman very fashionably dressed and leading a tiny dog. Her lips were painted a deep crimson and her figure drew glances from the cabmen driving by.

Maud looked too, as boldly as a born Parisian, and sketched them in her mind as she replied, 'It would not surprise you if you had met my father, or seen the shop. The name Creely reminds me of him and of that horrid place. I was delighted when it burned down. I was cheering on the flames. Everyone in the crowd thought I was distraught. Poor Miss Creely losing her father, and now this! But it was all I could do not to burst out laughing. It was a wonderful fire. They couldn't save a thing.'

The man in the long cloak concluded his negotiations and huffing into his moustache handed over a number of coins. The young lady took his arm and they set off again along the pavement. Her skirt hung so straight and narrow from her hips she could take only tiny rapid steps. Her stride seemed to match that of the toy dog that trotted beside her. The man with the book, she with her skirt and dog. Money was paid and collections formed, passions indulged. Maud felt wise and amused by the pageant, then there was an unexpected pang inside her – a distant warning of a storm coming. It was all too sudden, too perfect.

'Tanya, what do you think of them, truly?' she asked. 'Is this wise of me? Is there not something a little . . . strange about them?' She had said nothing to Tanya about the opium, and Morel seemed a gentleman indeed, a concerned brother and Sylvie so young. Drink was a worse addiction, surely? She thought of her father's sudden rages and repentance.

'They seem respectable enough to me. I would say it does not look as if you will have much fun, but judging by our night in Maxim's you will not mind that.'

Did Tanya sound a little hurt? The Russian girl had taken her in and dressed her and shown her a side of Paris she would not otherwise have seen. Maud felt ashamed. 'I do not mean to be ungrateful, Tanya.'

'Well, I certainly don't want you to be *grateful* either!' She bit her lip. 'Do you think, Maud, I can be a good painter but still enjoy my clothes and my evenings out?'

'I see no reason why not,' Maud said, surprised by her sudden vulnerability. 'I think you are a fine painter, Tanya. You cannot doubt it.'

'No,' but she did seem doubtful. 'It is hard to find the time to work when one must go to dressmakers every other day and change one's clothes three times in the course of an afternoon. My aunts feel it is a disgrace to my family to do less. When I have a family as well, how shall I find the time to paint? I do want a family.'

Maud did not know how to answer her. Tanya seemed to shimmer and dance through her life so, Maud could not see her as a woman with worries of her own.

Tanya shook herself a little and said firmly, 'Morel seems to have the proper respect for an Englishwoman's virtue. If he tries to force himself on you, come running to me. I shall send Vladimir after him.' She put her hand on Maud's sleeve. 'Wouldn't the comfort there do you a little good, Maud? If someone gives you a free horse, do not check the bridle.' Maud thought of that bright little room again and what Miss Harris had said about prayers being answered – but Maud had not asked God for anything for a very long time.

'Charlotte was right, he does smile a lot and he is offering a great deal of money.' Tanya had become brisk again. 'You can leave if you are unhappy. I shall be in Paris all winter and will not desert you. Always have the means to a graceful exit to hand – don't you think that is one of the best lessons we learn? I always have a gold sovereign sewn into my travelling dress. Actually half a dozen, so the line isn't spoiled.'

Maud considered. Mr Morel had offered her board, her own room and a weekly consideration that he called a trifle and that Maud called a fortune. She could simply wait and see how matters unfolded. The wind had been fierce yesterday evening, rattling her windows while she sketched her memories of the day, giving birth to new cold draughts, harbinger of the freezing depths of winter.

'Thank you, Tanya. Even if I only stayed there a week it would do me good. It has been difficult these last months.'

Tanya squeezed her arm again then looked up. 'Oh Lord, the rain is coming again, and I am expected back at the cathouse.' She turned and lifted her hand, and the dark blue motor materialised beside them. Vladimir and Sasha were staring out of the windscreen like dolls in a shop window. 'Can I give you a lift somewhere? No? Do you have an umbrella? Vladimir, do give Miss Heighton an umbrella, please, there's a dear. And that package.'

Tanya thrust a bundle tied in brown paper and string into her arms. 'It is only an old walking dress of mine, so don't say no. You cannot wear your working dress every afternoon while you shepherd that beauty round the streets.' Before she could thank Tanya or refuse it, the umbrella had been placed in her other hand and Tanya had scrambled up into the back seat. She leaned out of the window and took Maud by the hand.

'The angels have given you a gift, my dear. Embrace it! Now say you shall. I shan't let go of your hand until you do.'

She looked quite determined and Maud said, 'Very well, I shall!' Then as Tanya released her grip, Maud held on. 'Tanya, why have we not been friends before now?' The car was beginning to cause an obstruction in the road. A carter shouted and Vladimir yelled back something in Russian.

'Sweet, you always seemed so sober and serious, so contained, I've been quite terrified of you. Somehow I knew you weren't the type for Maxim's. Even if you did look charming in that dress.'

Maud let go of her hand and Tanya blew her a kiss as the car pulled away. Maud watched it retreat into the stream of taxicabs, omnibuses, carts and motor-cars heading along the quayside. It was a few moments before she remembered the umbrella and opened it to protect her and her package from the increasing pace of the rain. It had a tortoiseshell handle and bore the name of a shop in Rue de la Paix. Maud knew the place. She had walked past it shivering in the cold every day for a month when she lived off Rue de Lille, and each morning had wondered who could possibly be rich enough to spend such a vast number of francs on an umbrella. Now she held one over her head – an elegant, oiled-silk shield of money. She leaned her back against the wall, the wave of relief spreading over her so quick and full she would have fallen otherwise under its force.

CHAPTER 6

23 November 1909

*S*OMETIMES WE DO NOT REALISE HOW MUCH WE HAVE been suffering until that suffering is removed. On her first night in Rue de Seine, as Maud undressed she realised that her hands were shaking. She was a wrecked sailor crawling onto a sandbank and only then acknowledging the pain in her muscles. She wondered what would have happened to her if Yvette, Tanya, Miss Harris and the Morels had not intervened. The thought frightened her so much it hurt her.

Morel had been there when she arrived, to see her trunk stowed into her new room and to host her first lunch in the apartment. It was a pleasure he could not promise himself every day, he sighed. He asked if Maud was happy with the arrangements he had made for her comfort. The daily maid would leave luncheon for them. The ladies were then at liberty to do whatever they wished. Supper would be fetched for them, if they required it, at seven. He would join them when he could; but he expected to dine often at his club.

Sylvie was quiet but pleasant at that first lunch. She seemed content in a self-contained way. Her brother made all the conversation. He asked Maud a hundred questions about herself and gave every impression of finding the answers fascinating. There was nothing offensive about the questions or the way he asked them, but Maud found herself drawing away from him slightly as she gave her usual responses. Not lies, but truths that concealed some of the misery of her youth.

The food was excellent, though he had apologised for it as simple fare just as he had apologised for his palatial apartment. Maud had been subsisting on ten-sou omelettes in the worst of the respectable cafés, so to see game pie and *hâchis portugais* set out, with cheese on the sideboard for later and white wine dripping with chill . . . She had to be careful not to eat too quickly. She wondered if, under his flow of talk, Morel had noticed her hunger and was teasing her with his questions when she wanted to eat. She glanced at him. His expression was open and friendly.

'When did you discover you were an artist, Miss Heighton?' he asked, filling up her wine glass and piling more potatoes onto her plate.

'I am not an artist yet, I think. I am just trying to be a painter.'

He laughed. 'I shall remember that! But you are too modest. To come here as you have, leave home and family, suffer hardships to study here. That suggests a greater calling.'

She shook her head. 'My mother drew and painted. I think I began by copying her, and I never stopped. Drawing was simply what I did. She was my first teacher and when she could, she would take me to the galleries nearby, and find me books of reproductions.' The child's voice in her head whispered in awe, *some in colour*. She remembered the hours she had spent with those books curled up under her mother's dressing-table. She had had one with coloured plates from the Louvre and would study each one for an hour before she allowed herself to turn to the next. When she had first seen the originals in the museum the day she arrived in Paris, it had been like seeing much-loved, long-missed friends, but so much brighter and more alive. Her father had sold all of the art books to a London gentleman three months after her mother died. He had been disgusted by her distress when she found them gone. He had got five pounds for them, which was four pounds more than he had thought they were worth. She had been too busy crying to see the blow come that time.

She took a careful sip of her wine; it was fruit and acid on her tongue. 'All the best moments of my life have been bound up with painting. *That* is perhaps why I have come here, rather than some great calling, or particular talent.'

Morel nodded to himself, as if this confirmed some idea of his own, and then, by chatting to his silent sister about a letter he had received from home, let her eat in peace.

When Morel left them Maud felt suddenly embarrassed by this enforced intimacy with Sylvie. The maid cleared the table and Sylvie sat down at the pianoforte and picked out a few stray notes. Maud waited until the maid had said her farewells. They had spoken in French while her brother was present, but Maud was thinking of her duties now and switched to English.

'Perhaps you would like to show me your drawings, Sylvie? So I can see what instruction I might offer.'

Sylvie twisted round from the piano and sucked in her cheeks. 'I am afraid that you will think I am a great fool. I am not good, not at all. It is my brother's plan to keep me occupied. He will buy me opium when I show him sketchbooks filled with pictures of fruit. Is that not a strange,' she searched for the word, 'trade?'

Maud was shocked to hear her speak about the opium so plainly and wondered if there was some element of challenge in the confession. She said calmly, 'If you must do them, you might as well do them to the best of your ability, Sylvie.'

The young woman sighed, but with a nod left the piano and returned a few minutes later with a sketchbook covered in green; she sat down beside Maud on the sofa, holding it on her knees for a moment before handing it over. Maud opened the pages with an encouraging smile and looked at the drawings. They had been done in haste, certainly, but they proved that Sylvie could see what was in front of her and had some idea of how to hold a pencil.

'They are bad, is that not so?'

'Not at all. You just need a little guidance.' Maud pointed at the opened page, a drawing of the table in front of them with a lamp-stand on the centre of it. 'You see, you are drawing what you know is there, rather than what you see.' Sylvie touched the weave of the paper, apparently concentrating hard. 'You must avoid drawing outlines if you are to make progress, Sylvie. We see edges to things because of changes in light and tone, not because they have a line around them.' Sylvie nodded slowly, then slid the book back onto her own lap. Maud was afraid she had discouraged her. 'The best thing we could do is to go somewhere and try to draw something together.' She looked up and out of the window opposite, just as the wind threw a scatter of rain against the window like a handful of sand.

Sylvie laughed. 'The gods say no, Maud!' Then at once the light faded from her eyes and she yawned. 'I always rest for a little while after lunch. Perhaps in an hour you could knock at my door and we will go out then.'

'As you wish.' Maud was unsure. She had not thought in any depth about her relationship with Sylvie and what it might entail. Her considerations had centred solely on whether the position was respectable, followed by a happy vision of food, warmth and comfort; now she realised she was to some degree Sylvie's creature, though a polite fiction might be maintained.

'If you want to go out for a walk before then, Maud, you must do so. This is not a prison. Do as you would at your own house,' the girl went on. Maud felt she had been dismissed, but on balance was grateful for a little time on her own. She could think more about how to instruct Sylvie – look for interesting places where they might sit and draw when the weather was good.

Sylvie stood and with the sketchbook held loosely at her side, made to leave the room. On the threshold she paused and looked back.

'There is no need to come into my room, Maud. You may knock at the door and I shall join you here a little while later.'

Maud retreated to her room. There was an envelope on the bed with her name on it. She picked it up and her fingers brushed the cotton of the bedspread on their way to the thick paper. Comfort. The envelope held two fifty-franc notes and a message from M. Morel asking her to make use of the money for any little items she might need to make herself at home with them. He added that this was, of course, in addition to her weekly stipend. Maud sat suddenly on the bed and stared at the pink and blue notes, the paper smothered with engravings of anchors and cherubs. No Empress has ever felt their wealth as wide and inexhaustible as Maud did in that moment. She lifted her head: there was a faint sweet smell in the air, heavy and pungent, reaching into the room. She tucked the money away in the lid of her box of painting materials and left the apartment.

Funeral oil on canvas 64.8 × 76.3 cm

The narrow range of colours gives the suggestion of physical and spiritual chill to this picture, and the framing forces the viewer to be part of the scene rather than the observer. The grave is at our feet; the figures jostling the frame are at our shoulder. In the distance and on the right, a break in the cloud allows a glimmer of sunlight and warmth of colour into the scene, though whether this is hope, or a false dawn, we cannot say. None of the figures surrounding us at the graveside have noticed it; it is a beam of light offered only to the artist and now the viewer.

Extract from the catalogue notes to the exhibition 'The Paris Winter: Anonymous Treasures from the de Civray Collection', Southwark Picture Gallery, London, 2010

CHAPTER 7

*T*HE DAYS QUICKLY DEVELOPED A PATTERN. MAUD left the apartment every morning before M. Morel or his sister had woken; had her breakfast at a zinc by the entrance to Passage des Panoramas, and was ready to begin her day's work with an unfamiliar lightness and ease. The studio had become a more welcoming place now. Tanya had made a pet of her, and having decided that their figures were practically identical, had given her two more of her old dresses: a working dress of soft grey, and another walking dress that meant she needn't be ashamed of wandering the boulevards with Sylvie in the afternoons. The other women began to warm to her too. They teased her about her luck and when she laughed along and agreed with them, they liked her for it. The following week, when the dais was filled with another of their regular models, Maud realised she had no idea of the life Yvette lived when she was not in the studio with them. She asked Tanya about it as they drank tea.

'Oh, Yvette is a child of Montmartre, you know,' she said, waving her hand and almost knocking Francesca's cup from her hands. 'When she's not here she'll be with the other models at Place Pigalle. Old Degas has used her a fair amount in the past. And she normally has some boyfriend or other to keep her amused.

I envy her freedom, don't you?' Maud shook her head. 'Truly you don't?' Tanya seemed a little disconcerted. 'Am I being stupid? I know it must be hard to be poor, but it is hard to be as harried and pursued as I am. My aunts are giving a dinner next week and that means I must go to Rue Taitbout again this afternoon for a dress fitting when I would rather be working.' When Francesca almost choked on her tea, Tanya looked genuinely distressed. 'Oh, do not laugh at me.'

Maud offered her a pastry. 'Tanya, I promise I do not envy you either.'

The Russian appeared to be slightly mollified. 'You are very kind, Maud. Would you like to come to the dinner? I could lend you the dress again?'

'No, thank you. I do not think I can use the Morels' flat as if it were some sort of hotel. Sylvie does not go out, so neither can I. In the spring when they have left Paris I shall come and visit you whenever you wish.' At that moment, Maud realised that Mademoiselle Claudette was at their elbow waiting for an opportunity to speak.

'Ladies, I wished to tell you that the funeral of Rose Champion will be held tomorrow morning. Her aunt has arrived in Paris to see it done. I shall attend. If any of you wish it, we may leave from here together.'

'Monsieur Lafond . . . ?' Francesca asked and Claudette shook her head. They understood. Their master's income relied on his good reputation and his attendance at the burial might draw attention to the squalid nature of Miss Champion's death. Tanya spoke for them.

'We shall come.'

∽∾

M. Lafond might not wish to attend the funeral himself, but he did provide Claudette with the fare for a taxi to take them there. It was a cold but clear day and the women found themselves drawing in great lungfuls of clean air, enjoying the contrast to the centre of the city until they remembered their business and became quiet.

Miss Champion's aunt and the priest were already waiting by the grave. There were no other mourners. The aunt introduced herself as Mrs Fuller and seemed distracted and exhausted as well as distressed by the death of her niece. Her hat, dark purple and heavy with black blooms, was rather crushed and her woollen skirt and jacket showed signs of travel. She peered at them short-sightedly and her hand, when Maud shook it, was damp and limp. The priest recited his lines mechanically, the grave-diggers began their work. As Maud made the proper remarks the damp grip tightened slightly.

'You are English? And an artist?' Mrs Fuller sounded hopeful.

'I am.'

'Oh, please tell me what is to be done with the paintings Rose left. There are only four of them. I have them in the taxicab, but I know my husband and my son will not like them. They are not cheerful. I prefer the paintings Rose did when she was little, though not many of them were cheerful either . . .' Her words trailed away and she came to a halt in the middle of her memories. 'She was always such a difficult child. I had always wanted a little girl, but she never liked me. Still, I cannot throw away her paintings. Oh, I hate to travel this time of year. Still a pretty day, but so many cars.' She pulled a handkerchief from her bag and blew her nose.

Maud was at a loss. Perhaps some dealer would take the paintings, though Rose's poverty suggested that she had not managed to sell very much work. Even if she could find someone who would take them, the idea of dragging the canvases from one shop to another then arranging for the money to be sent to England seemed a thankless task, and in any case she was engaged to spend her time with Sylvie.

'I shall buy them,' Tanya said. Mrs Fuller looked up at her in surprise then let her eyes travel over Tanya's fur-trimmed coat, her wide picture hat and the pearls in her ears.

'But you haven't even seen them,' she said suspiciously, her rumpled face lined like damp linen being wrung out.

'No matter. I know Miss Champion's work and thought highly of it. I shall take all four and pay you fifty francs for each of them.' Claudette rolled her eyes and even Francesca looked a little shocked. Mrs Fuller looked up at Maud, her tongue darting out of her mouth a little to moisten her lips.

'Is that a proper figure, Miss Heighton? After all, I hear that some paintings my husband says are the most terrible scribbles are sold for thousands, and poor Rose will paint no more now. Does that not make them worth rather more?'

Maud could see the attendants of the cemetery continuing to fill in Rose's grave behind them. She tried to speak evenly. 'Rose was a talented artist, Mrs Fuller, but entirely unknown here or in London. It is unlikely you would ever sell those canvases at all to anyone else, let alone for eight pounds each. Miss Koltsova's offer is extremely generous.'

'Is it now?' Mrs Fuller narrowed her eyes and looked sidelong at Tanya again, and even though it must be clear to her that she was understood, she said, 'Is the young lady Jewish?'

'I am not,' Tanya said. 'Though I fail to see what the significance is of that.'

Mrs Fuller smiled thinly. 'I am sure you are very clever with money at any rate. Still, I suppose I must believe it is a fair price.

Poor dear Rose, such a terrible loss to us all. Do you have the money with you? I have the cab waiting at the gates.'

Sylvie agreed to go with Maud to the Jardin du Luxembourg that afternoon as the day continued fine. They took their sketchbooks with them and found a seat near the grand octagonal pond at the front of the palace, where the children pushed their rented sailboats across the rippling waters. Maud suggested that Sylvie try to draw one of the ornamental urns, thinking the curve of its body and the mass of its high pediment might give her hand some useful practice, particularly as the long afternoon shadows fell across it and turned it into strong patterns of light and shade. Maud watched the children for a while, smiling at the fierce concentration of the sailors, the pressure of the wind on the hand-kerchief sails, and she listened to the scud of running footsteps on the gravel paths, the shrieks of laughter. Opposite them, tiny in front of the walls of the pale palace, a girl no more than six years old was playing with her diabolo, running the cylinder along the string, throwing and catching it again while her mother sat nearby, occasionally looking up from her sewing to applaud her daughter's efforts. Still, nothing caught her eye and Maud started to sketch what she had seen that morning, the clear day and the tiny band of mourners shivering around the grave. She began to tell Sylvie about the mean little funeral, and the greed of Miss Champion's aunt.

'But Maud, simply because you knew that her niece's pictures were worth very little, it does not mean that she did. And consider, are you English not taught from the date of your birth that every foreigner you meet is trying to take away your money? She was doing that which she was taught to do, and you cannot reproach people for that.' Sylvie swore softly under her breath. 'I shall never manage this. It looks like a plant pot.'

Maud leaned over and examined her work. 'Do not press so hard, or try to make such long strokes.' Sylvie tried again. 'Yes, that is better. I think you are too kind to Mrs Fuller. She was standing in front of her niece's grave and thinking of what profit it might bring her. How can that ever be proper?'

'Proper? Bah! So might anyone if they were not very attached to the person who died. And I think it would be a very easy mistake to make. Who knows what makes one painter rich and another poor?' She tapped her drawing with her pencil. 'What if I hold this up high and say it is the new art. Very rare and valuable. Give me two hundred francs for it.'

Maud looked at the rather misshapen drawing with its heavy lines. 'No one would believe you.'

Sylvie looked triumphant. 'But that is nothing to do with my poor picture. It is only because I haven't published a manifesto first. Everything that is worth money in the world is so because someone says very loudly, "This is beautiful and rare". Every piece of art is rare because a person has only so many hours to live, so many bits of art they can make. Now all you have to do is convince them the art is beautiful . . . or clever at least. I shall write an article for the newspaper proclaiming myself a genius then we can sell this,' she flicked the page with a smooth fingernail, 'for a hundred francs. The rare work of a genius.' She bent down and picked up a piece of gravel between her finger and thumb; it was a pale lilac. 'Now if there existed in the world only a very little of this, and a million tons of diamonds, this is what queens would wear in their crowns and we would put diamonds down on the walkways. Beautiful and rare. Beautiful because it is rare, or beautiful because we have been trained to think it rare. Then we can make it into money.'

Maud felt strangely sad at the idea. 'You make it sound like a trick.'

Sylvie shrugged. Whether it was because she was unhappy with her drawing or because she had not rested after lunch, her mood had become suddenly brittle.

'Come. Perhaps it is just I know too little of art. You must educate me. This place is full of art shops, books on art. Let us go at once.'

Maud began to put away her materials, sensing Sylvie's impatience, then allowed herself to be dragged down Rue de Tournon. The bookshop Sylvie happened upon was in Rue Saint-Sulpice, but though the impulse and the plan were hers, as soon as the two women entered the shop, it was clear she wished to be gone. The bookseller, a young man with a ready smile, obviously wanted only to help, but Sylvie made her purchases distractedly. Maud found a translation of Ruskin, and though she thought him a little old-fashioned, she offered it as a useful place for Sylvie to begin her reading.

'Very well, Maud. Whatever you wish,' Sylvie said briskly. She picked up two or three more of the volumes the bookseller had put in front of her on his polished counter, then handed them to him without more than a glance. 'And these.' Maud thought of her lost, loved books and wondered where they had ended up.

As he bound up the package, Sylvie tapped her foot and when she handed him her money, her fingers shook. Maud stayed silent and let herself be whisked out of the shop and back to Rue de Seine without comment. As soon as they were back in the apartment, Sylvie put the package into her hands. 'Open them if you wish.' She went into her room without another word.

Maud took the books into the living room and untied the paper wrapping. Her education in the history of art had been all at second hand until she came to Paris. It had been a wonder to see in life the images she had learned to know in hazy reproduction, as if the sun had suddenly appeared to drive off the mist on the dale and reveal the landscape below it. She removed her hat and gloves and sat at the table, but did not open the books. She thought instead of the strange ugly pictures that Tanya had bought from Mrs Fuller and what Sylvie had said about art. They had returned to Passage des Panoramas before examining Rose's pictures, and had done so in a sort of sorry silence. The palette of each was limited and muddy, purple lake and brown madder with sickly touches of citron to suggest sources of light weak and out of the frame. They were loosely painted, sketchy in places and oddly placed, flattened, the perspective lost and lurching. Where the eye expected to see most within the frame was a dingy absence of form; only at the edges of the whole did figures lurk, pressed down in the composition as if irrelevant, yet the only interest the artist offered. The gutters of Paris. A long table surrounded by gaunt and stooping figures, their grey fingers curled around wooden bowls. A woman leaning against one of the elegant lamp-posts, but crushed by the darkness around her. No street was as dark in the city of light as Rose had painted this one. When you looked long enough, that darkness seemed to seethe with half-realised faces, painted as a layer of darkness on a deeper dark.

Mademoiselle Claudette had touched the half-seen figure of the woman, feeling the thickness of the paint. 'I do not understand,' she said, and Maud realised she had tears in her eyes.

The American girl looked over her shoulder and shuddered. 'You've wasted your money.'

Tanya looked up sharply. 'I do not think I have. She was trying to do something . . .'

Francesca had hooked her palette over her thumb again and

taken her seat by the stove. 'I can respect the attempt, but I have not learned to paint to make the world miserable. I paint the world to celebrate it.' There was a murmur of agreement around the room.

Tanya bit her lip and set the painting down. Maud was not sure if she did so with respect or fear. 'What do you think, Maud? I think Rose might have been almost a genius. But some of this seems clumsy and Francesca is right – even if it is clever, it is still very ugly.'

Maud said nothing, only sighing and continuing to prepare her palette for the remaining hour of the morning. Rose's pictures crawled behind her eyes, insisting on overlaying themselves on her vision. *What can paint catch?* they said. *What can it make visible that is hidden? Are these pictures more true than your pretty women posed on a model throne with their lips a little reddened?*

At Rue de Seine, Maud smelled the heavy sweet scent in the hallway and went straight to her room, taking Ruskin with her for company. For a moment it seemed that she had carried Rose Champion's ghosts with her into the room. The deepening shadows seemed to be full of her whispering demons carrying darkness on their backs. Their breath smelled heavy and sweet. She turned on the electric light and opened the window, sat by it and let the cold air stream in until the demons were gone and the room was hers again. The fierceness of the light rather overwhelmed her, and only when she had wrapped a thin scarf round the shade could she read in comfort. Ruskin had no doubts or demons, it seemed. His heavy baroque sentences made her think of the rose window in Notre Dame, their thick colours hanging off his phrases like coronation robes.

Maud ate her supper alone in the drawing room that evening and was asleep in her room long before M. Morel returned home.

CHAPTER 8

*A*S THE DAYS PASSED THEIR WALKS GREW LONGER, then when they came home Sylvie began to look into the art books and ask Maud about what she found. Maud sketched her for the first time a week after she arrived. Heavy rain had kept them indoors, but Sylvie had not retreated to her own room and oblivion. Rather she stretched out on the chaise longue under a Lavery landscape and turned the pages of one of her books. Maud began her sketch and quickly became lost in it, not thinking of anything but the line on the paper until Sylvie asked in a strange, whining voice, 'Are you nearly finished, Maud?'

Maud looked at her, changing her way of seeing from the model to the girl.

'Almost. One moment more.'

Sylvie was staring at the clock behind Maud's shoulder. It might have been a little more than a moment, but the second that Maud put down her pencil, Sylvie scampered from the room leaving Maud wondering. She emerged for supper with her though, her manner vacant and gentle, her half-smile drifting over her lips – and though she ate very little, she did eat.

Maud's health improved. The rest from worry, the good food, the calm of life in Rue de Seine was making her a better artist. Her hand was steadier, her lines more confident; at the Académie her use of colour grew bolder and more her own. She could almost feel the shackles that Tanya had mentioned coming loose, their weight falling from her wrists, and when she walked through Paris between her classes and Rue de Seine she did so with her head up and watching. The shouts of the street-sellers accompanied her; the old woman with her cart of glistening blue and silver fish arranged in fans on a bed of green grass, the girl her own age with milk-white skin and cap, her cart piled with potatoes with thin gold skins and deep mounds of cabbage, all arranged and turned to face any passing customer with their folds of malachite green frothing round them like crumpled lace. Each seller sang their calls to the housewives of the *quartier* like birds, each with their own particular rhythm, rise and fall: '*les haricots verts, les pommes de terre*', '*J'ai les poissons pour quinze sous*'. While the models were resting from their poses, Maud joined the women in conversation, no longer obsessed with the provisions laid out for them. She and Tanya looked through the old illustrated catalogues of exhibitions, comparing the lines of composition, the gauzy fantasies of the Symbolists or the strange bare spaces of André Sureda with his Turneresque pursuits of light through mist.

⚭

Some afternoons, Sylvie rebelled against sketching and demanded that they take a turn through the Jardin des Tuileries then along Rue Saint-Honoré so she could peer in at the windows. The displays were becoming more splendid by the hour as Christmas approached: sweet shops filled with great banked displays of pastel-coloured macaroons or truffles like scrunched scraps of silk peppered with flakes of gold; stationers, their windows heaving with reams of butter-coloured writing paper and glistening silver fountain pens; haberdashers plumed in an explosion of lace.

On one such expedition Sylvie claimed she was still not tired as they reached Place de la Madeleine, and despite the threatening weather insisted on turning down Rue Royale. It was a confusion of dark umbrellas as on the crowded pavements the shoppers of Paris protected themselves and their purchases from the sudden squalls of rain. The clanging of metal wheels against the stone cobbles seemed louder than usual, and Maud felt the strangeness of being on the wide streets of Paris with such a fragmented view. When she looked behind her, the towering colonnaded frontage of the church of the Madeleine appeared occasionally through the stormy sea of oiled silk like a fevered dream of Ancient Greek temples.

'Here.' Sylvie took her arm to lead her into the relative calm of a jeweller's shop halfway down the street. The interior was a different sort of dream, mirrors and wood painted white, gold and pale green, and carved in places to imitate drapery. The light from above was stained turquoise and pale yellow. The clerk stood behind a small circular station in the centre of the room, and at his back a mosaic peacock spread its wings over the wall.

Sylvie went at once to a case held up on narrow curving wooden legs that contained a single necklace of opaque glass. It looked as if it had been fashioned out of snow. There were three other women in the shop, all moving with the slow graciousness of wealth. They were as magnificent and polished as the shop itself. The clerk stepped out from behind the desk and approached Maud. His polite smile did not reach his eyes. 'Miss, is there anything I can show you?' Maud felt the expensive gaze of the other women settling on her, her black merino dress and the loose arrangement of her hair. She straightened her back and answered with a not-quite smile of her own: 'I doubt that, Monsieur. Your goods are a little too gaudy for my taste.'

The smile was fixed and he remained in a half-bow as if carved by the same snaking hand that had created his surroundings. 'And all so terribly expensive!' he said very quietly. 'A number of English ladies remark on it every day. I wonder why they come in at all.' He let his eyes travel over her poor dress and her unpowdered skin, pink from the cold. 'They do not seem to understand Paris fashions.'

Maud would have dearly liked to slap his face but she could not help seeing herself over his shoulder in one of the many mirrors. She looked like a country wife at court.

Sylvie left her contemplation of the frosted-glass necklace on display and glided across the mosaic floor towards them. 'I am sorry to keep you waiting, Maud dear,' she said, and then turned to the clerk. He took in the sable collar of her winter coat and bowed a little more deeply. 'Brooches, please, Monsieur. I need a little something to cheer me up now the weather has grown so dull. Will you oblige me with a selection?'

Maud waited by the door watching the people pass outside while Sylvie examined whatever Monsieur offered. The other women circulated, more came in or out and Maud observed them admiring themselves and examining each other until Sylvie was ready to leave. She and the clerk both had a vague air of disappointment clinging to them. It seemed they had concluded there was nothing quite right for her among the blue and gold and enamel. They shook hands with mutual expressions of esteem and regret then Sylvie took Maud's arm and led her back onto Rue Royale then down towards Place de la Concorde with her shoulders slightly drooping.

Maud was expecting her to suggest they returned home until they rounded the corner and found themselves outside the new

Hôtel de Crillon. At that point, Sylvie suddenly put her head back and laughed – a deep, throaty laugh Maud had never heard from her before and liked. She pulled Maud under the shelter of the colonnade. The afternoon shadows were lit by crystal chandeliers blazing inside the hotel dining room. She opened her palm and Maud saw sitting on her white glove a brooch the size of a hen's egg. It was an oval of turquoise enamel, edged in gold with lotus shapes in a darker blue fanned around it and a milk-white opal pendant on a single stripe of gold.

'Ha!' she said, grinning so her small white teeth showed. 'That will deal with the nasty little invert. How could he be so rude to my friend? He will have to work a month to pay them back for losing this.' She spoke in French and there was a vicious edge to her voice.

Maud looked around her, terrified. 'Sylvie, you did not *steal* this?'

The other girl slipped it into the deep pocket of her coat. 'Yes, I did, and I was very brilliant too. He won't know a thing about it for hours, the disgusting wretch.' She returned to English, sounding like herself again. 'Now, will we take some tea at Smith and Sons? You may read *The Times* while we drink Earl Grey and I shall imagine myself in London.'

She made to move, obviously delighted with herself. Maud put a hand out to detain her. 'Sylvie, you cannot steal. You must take it back at once.'

'I don't want to! Maud, I did it for you, after all. Now do come and have tea.'

'I shall have to tell your brother, Sylvie.'

'I do not care what you do as long as you come along now. I shall freeze to death if you keep me talking here a moment longer.'

She left Morel a polite note before she went to bed, and found him waiting for her the following morning in the living room. He wore a long dressing-gown of patterned silk and the remnants of evening dress. His face was a little grey in the lamplight and Maud realised he had not yet been to bed. She explained what had happened while standing in front of him in her working dress, ready to leave for the studio. She thought that if painted, the pair of them would appear as some sort of allegory of Dawn – she all upright industry and he jaded decadence.

Christian sighed deeply when he had heard her out. Then, to Maud's surprise, he shrugged. 'Rue Royale, you say? Very well, I shall call there today, explain the mistake and pay for the thing.' He looked up at her, a cautious smile on his face. 'I think you are shocked, Miss Heighton?'

'I'm afraid I am, sir.' She had her hands clasped in front of her. She felt like a governess.

'Then please accept my apology on Sylvie's behalf. I feared that as she started using less of the drug she might take these odd fits. You are doing her good.'

'The drug, sir?'

He looked up at her with his eyebrows raised. 'She has been spending more hours of the day with you than resting, I think. The hour when she starts to smoke is gradually being pushed back, and so a little more of Sylvie returns.'

'That may be so, but you cannot condone theft, Monsieur Morel!'

He looked amused, as if she had done something charming. 'Naturally I do not, but I do welcome her recovery. After all these years of her being only half-alive, caught in her dream and hardly seeing the world outside . . . Whatever the inconvenience, I delight in seeing her take interest in life again.'

With that Maud had to be satisfied and she left him to make her way to the Académie in distracted mood. Her work did not go well in the first hour, and she was still brooding about Sylvie's larceny when Tanya arrived. Perhaps that was why she did not notice the Russian's dangerous mood until the next rest period in their work. As they gathered round the stove complaining of the damp, Francesca said something to Tanya. She replied in a high cracked voice though Maud did not catch the words, and then fled out of the room, already in tears. Her maid Sasha sighed and began to pack up her knitting but seemed to be in no great hurry about it. Maud put down her cup.

'Francesca! What on earth did you say to her?'

The Czech was a little red in the face, but looked angry more than ashamed. 'Nothing! Only she's been sighing for the last hour about how hard her life is in Paris and how long her fitting took yesterday and I said perhaps she'd paint better if she spent more time working and less shopping. I know she's your friend, Maud, and there's no malice in her, but I couldn't think for her complaining.'

Mademoiselle Claudette was looking at her questioningly. 'I shall go,' Maud said. As she left the room and lifted her skirts a little to climb down the narrow stairs, she noticed that Tanya's maid had taken out her knitting again.

She found Tanya sheltering in the lobby of the Hôtel Chopin. She was collapsed in one of their deep leather armchairs and crying her eyes out. The man behind the desk looked relieved when Maud went across and sat down beside her.

'Tanya? My dear, what is the matter?'

Tanya sniffed and struggled with her handkerchief. 'Oh, nothing! How could anything be the matter?' She turned away from Maud so that all she could see was the quivering lace across her shoulders.

'Now Tanya, don't be foolish. Something has upset you, so do stop crying for a moment and tell me what it is or I shall fetch your maid. Have your aunts been unkind? Come now – I promise not to be angry with you for being rich and beautiful for at least half an hour.'

The crying slowed down a little. Maud lifted her hand and the nervous young man behind the desk hurried over and bent low to hear whatever she commanded. 'A little brandy and water for my friend.' He reversed away from them before standing up with a quick shimmering step to rush away and do her bidding. Maud wished Tanya had seen it. By the time he had returned with the brandy in a balloon glass the size of her head, on a silver tray perched on his fingertips, and made his obeisance, Tanya's crying had given way to the occasional damp sniff. She drank a little of the brandy, which made her sneeze like a cat.

'Now can you speak?' Maud asked. 'Is it your aunts?'

'Everyone says I am to marry Mikhail Pavlovich Perov,' Tanya said very quietly, and tucked her handkerchief back into her sleeve. 'He has written to my father to ask permission and my aunts are taking it as a settled thing. We were at supper at the house of one of their ghastly cronies last night and they were dropping hints to everyone there.'

Maud remembered. 'Oh, not that young man with the horrible laugh?'

'Yes,' she whispered. 'His father is very rich too – grain import like my father, so it would be a merger more than a marriage. Mikhail Pavlovich told my aunts it would suit him to continue living in Paris while he learns the business. Then in five years we will return to St Petersburg where I can show off my Parisian polish. He actually said that to them. They thought it was charming, though he laughs at them behind their backs, the dirty hypocrite.'

Maud remembered him staring at the dancers at Maxim's but not even pretending to look at the paintings at Miss Stein's house.

'You can't possibly marry him,' she said.

Tanya turned towards her with her eyes black and wide. 'No one has thought to ask *me*, Maud. What can *I* have to say? He is rich and I am rich and he will let me *shop* all I want. After all, that is all I am good for, is it not? Shopping and a way . . .' she waved her hand in the air, 'a way for men to give money to each other. I am not a woman at all. I am a saddlebag filled with gold.'

Maud laughed. Tanya looked down at her hands and the corners of her mouth twitched. 'I must marry someone though, Maud. And there are not many suitable men. My family are all so pleased.'

'Surely that cannot be enough?' Maud asked. 'There must be some liking, some affection?'

'I don't know. I must be taken care of. I have never had to look after myself, and perhaps it would not be so bad. There would be children, I suppose, and I think he would let me carry on with painting.'

'Tanya, don't say such a thing. Perhaps you should learn to look after yourself. But would your father cut you off for refusing to marry a man you didn't like?'

Tanya took the great balloon glass of brandy in her hands again. 'Perhaps not. Though I think he would if I decided to marry a man without money. He fears adventurers, of course – that is why my aunts are so often with me – but he thinks if I enjoy the wealth of the family I have a duty to add to it, rather than take it away.' She lifted the glass to her lips and took a smaller sip. 'How many happy marriages have you seen, Maud?'

Maud's mother had married a man in no way worthy of her and had suffered for it. Maud's step-mother had married thinking she was taking a step up in the world and found herself saddled with a self-pitying drunk. Though the times she had visited her son Albert, now in James and Ida's care, she had come with the drover she had married shortly after her first husband's funeral. The couple seemed affectionate and happy together, although of course, it was early days.

'See? You have nothing to say,' Tanya said, 'so if I cannot have a happy marriage perhaps it would be better to be rich than fall in love with someone who may seem rather wonderful but who would have to work every day, and expect me to work adding things up in notebooks and finding out where to buy cheap clothes. It would be boring and I would be bad at it, and even a very nice man might get impatient with me then.'

Maud watched her drink the rest of the brandy and wondered about the slightly wistful tone in her voice. Some remark of hers from another day crossed her mind. 'Tanya, have you seen much of Paul Allardyce?'

She blushed. 'My aunts were driving us in the Bois. They think the atmosphere in the studio is damaging my bloom. He came and spoke to us for a while and asked after you. I told you that.' Maud nodded. Tanya's attempt to be casual about seeing the handsome American again had been charming really, but Maud, too busy with learning about the Morels and settling into her life in Rue de Seine, had not pressed her about it. 'Then he happened to be at the Circus when we went the next night. And I have seen him once or twice at the theatre. He is a writer so he will never have any real money.'

'That is not what is important, Tanya.'

The other girl put her brandy glass down on the table and straightened her back. Her eyes were still a little red but she was in control of herself again. 'Would you have said that a few weeks ago, when you were still hungry, Maud?' She didn't wait for an answer. 'I think I might do one brave thing in my life, but to live without plenty of money, that would be doing a brave thing every day. Only a fool would think otherwise.' She stood up and smoothed the long folds of her dress then spoke to the clerk at the desk, her head tilted to one side and smiling. 'Thank you so much. I will send my maid down to pay the bill.' He whispered his delight in being of use and as she swept out of the door with her head high, Maud followed like a bruised shadow in her wake.

CHAPTER 9

The Drunk oil on prepared board 45.7 × 40.7 cm

The background is roughly sketched; in places the prepared board is left unpainted and the brushwork is light and loose as if the brush can hardly bear to create the face. Note the lowered brow and the blotched pink and white of the skin, the mouth slightly open and the eyes wide. Its raw power disturbs even now.

Extract from the catalogue notes to the exhibition 'The Paris Winter: Anonymous Treasures from the de Civray Collection', Southwark Picture Gallery, London, 2010

15 December 1909

The late-afternoon calm of the apartment in Rue de Seine was shaken by a hard and rapid knocking at the door. Maud closed her book and left her room, then hesitated in the corridor. They never had visitors and the waiter who brought their supper in the evening was not due to arrive for another hour at least. And he never struck the door so violently, rather announced himself with a tap and delivered their food with the gentleness of a ghost. Sylvie's door remained closed.

The thought that M. Morel might have had some accident decided her. Maud opened the door but instead of the concierge with an urgent message she found herself faced by an elderly woman. She held herself very straight but with her head jutted forward, her lips pursed tight, and she was frowning so hard her eyes seemed to have disappeared into their sockets. Her coat was threadbare, old-fashioned; her hair was coming loose from its pins and her hat was a little battered. Around her neck she wore a ragged fox fur, the thin head still attached and its black bead eyes glinting. The woman's expression was one of violent disgust, though in the twitch of her thin lips there was something of triumph.

'Where are they?' she demanded at once, peering round Maud into the apartment. 'Where are the devils? I have found them! I have run them to ground at last, the dirty monsters! Oh, the pretty little devils! How can they sleep so comfortable, knowing they have stolen every penny from a poor widow! Not that I was poor then. Oh no, I was rich when I met them – and hardly a bone to gnaw on now! All charity!'

The creature was obviously insane. 'Who are you and what do you want?' Maud said.

'I want nothing from *you*, you silly tart. I want Christian Gravot and his bitch childwife!'

Maud started to close the door. 'There is no one here by that name. Good day.'

The old woman was too quick for her, and put her hand round the doorframe. Maud could only close it now by slamming it on her fingers, and she did not have the courage to do that.

'Morel, then! That's what they call themselves.' She was very close now, but if Maud stepped back she was afraid the woman would push her way into the flat. She felt her heart thudding in her chest.

'They are not at home. Perhaps if you left your card.'

'Ha!' The woman reached into her bag, continuing to block the door with her shoulder, and pulled out a piece of card which she flung straight at Maud's face. Maud flinched away, covering her eyes, and it fell at her feet. The woman pushed the door fully open and loomed hideous as a witch towards her. Maud felt panic tightening on her throat. 'There. Do you think he'll call? Do you think he will visit me at my hotel? After all the letters and telegrams from me and nothing, nothing from him in six months?' She took a step forward again and stared about the apartment, at the flowers on the hall-table, the gleaming floors, the calm polished comfort of it all. 'Where is he? Where is he now? Tell me, or I shall smash up your pretty home – and don't think you can stop me. I will have what is owed.'

'Monsieur Morel is at his club – The Travellers in the Champs Elysées. If you have any business with him, go there.' Maud's voice was high, protesting. The woman smiled, seeing Maud afraid, and her own voice became soft and wheedling. She looked up at the girl through her thin pale lashes with lizard eyes.

'What of the bitch who used to hold my hand and call me Granny? Where's she? Where has she hidden my diamonds? Did she eat them? Did *he*? I will have what I am owed.' Maud could not help herself; she glanced towards Sylvie's door and the old woman saw it. She began to glide towards the door with her wrinkled hand outstretched. Maud tried to make herself step forward, but failed.

There was a shout on the stairs and the concierge appeared with her husband lumbering up behind her. The old woman left the door to Sylvie's room to face them.

'There's the old monster!' the concierge said, her thin chest heaving with indignation and red spots showing on her cheeks. 'Sorry, miss, but she got by me. Now will you leave the ladies in peace, or will Georges here have to pick you up and carry you?' She put a hand on the old woman's shoulder and was shaken off.

'Paid in advance, has he, dear? Paid with a bit extra for you to keep an eye out? Count your silver before he leaves. That's all.'

The concierge's husband hunched his shoulders. 'What are you thinking of, Granny, coming round and disturbing people? What sort of house do you think this is? Come on, out of here, you old baggage.'

The woman looked back at the door to Sylvie's room. Maud wondered if she was thinking of making a dash for it, forcing the door open and attacking the girl. Maud could see it in front of her: the horror of the struggle, the vase smashed, Sylvie's screams and the howls of the madwoman.

Georges took a small step forward and the old woman looked back at him and growled. 'All the same to me!' she said, sniffing and pulling her coat around her. 'I'll be off to the club then, now I know where to ferret him out. And I'll sing my songs there.' She turned on Maud then, her eyes small and angry. 'And you, you silly tart, if you've got a shred of decency left, you should put your coat on and clear off out of it right now.'

Maud said nothing, unable to speak or act in her own defence or to save Sylvie.

'Enough of that! Time to go,' Georges said, his voice rising, and the woman let herself be jostled away. Maud found she could move again and followed them on to the landing to see them go. The old woman kept turning to look at her as they went down the stairs, muttering to herself. In the hallway below, she burst out again: 'I shall have you, Christian Gravot! I shall have you in this world or the next, you monster!'

Maud turned back into the flat. The door to Sylvie's room was still closed; for a moment she considered knocking, but to what purpose? The card that the woman had thrown at her was still lying on the floor. Maud bent down to pick it up. It was a visiting card. *Madame Prideux, 4, Place Saint-Pierre, Luxeuil-les-Bains.* She carried it back into her room and stared at it while her heart slowed to its usual beat. The old lady had not seemed the type to have a visiting card. Perhaps she had found it on the street.

Maud sat in her usual seat by the window and took out her sketchbook, tucking the card between the back pages. She thought about what she had said to Tanya about being brave, about taking care of herself, and felt ashamed. She then pulled the pencil free of the book's spine. She had thought she was going to draw that hard angry face with the threadbare fox fur and its dead glass eyes staring up from under the woman's pointed chin, but instead she found herself drawing her father.

When Maud's mother was alive her father had been a ghost in her life, a brooding presence slouched in an armchair with the whisky bottle at his side, staring into the fire while her mother sewed or read to them. Maud thought her mother had been beautiful, though she had never been photographed and Maud's memories of her face were hazy and ill-defined. When she died, quietly and quickly when her illness could no longer be concealed, Maud and her father were strangers. She realised then how much of the work of Creely & Sons, the auctioneers business her father had inherited, her mother had been doing. As long as Maud could remember, when she came down for breakfast her mother was already at the table working at long columns of figures in black account books or writing letters with neat scratches of her fountain pen. Later in the mornings Maud would accompany her mother as she made her calls around the town, playing with the black and white cat at the grocer's while her mother placed her order for the boy to bring round in the afternoon, or sitting on a sofa quietly while her mother talked to her friends in their dark living rooms full of heavy furniture and loudly ticking clocks. She was told that she was a good child and given paper to draw on, then her mother's friends would tell her how clever she was. She revelled in being a good child, a quiet child, an obedient child, rewarded with praise and her mother's love. It never occurred to her she could be anything else.

She had no hope of taking her mother's place. She was far too young and had not been trained to it. A month after her mother's funeral she began to see the home she knew becoming neglected. Two maids left in quick succession and her father spent days now as well as his evenings in his armchair with the bottle at his elbow. She went for a fortnight without a bath and only realised it when she overheard the butcher's wife saying she needed to be washed. She became deeply ashamed and hid away from the town as much as she could. She was no longer a good child to be admired so she stayed at home, only occasionally going to the back of the grocer's to meet her old friend the cat. The grocer's wife would bring out biscuits and milk and look at her with troubled eyes.

Maud's father started coming home less, and when he did he stank of tobacco and beer. The latest maid never looked at her and fed her on bread and butter and the occasional herring. Maud wanted very much to sit in those rooms with the ticking clocks again with her hair brushed and be told she was a good girl. One night she put on the cleanest pinafore she owned and waited for her father to come home. He looked surprised when he saw her sitting on the stair. She stood up and went to stand in front of him and asked if they might have their old maid back because she needed to be bathed and did not want any more bread for her supper. He bent towards her, his breath wheezing in and out of his lungs as if he'd been running, and his face red. His nose was covered with little broken veins but the skin around his eyes was oddly white. He watched her for what seemed an age, then he pulled back his arm and slapped her hard across the face. It knocked her to the ground. She heard him go into the parlour and slam the door behind him. A week later she was struck because she cried over the sold art books. Another time because he heard her complaining to the maid about her food again.

Someone must have seen the bruises. The grocer's wife probably. Maud's elder brother James arrived two days after the last bruising. He had qualified as a solicitor the year before and was freshly established as a junior partner in a firm in Darlington. She saw him walking up the road from the station in his high white collar and brown waistcoat and did not recognise him until he turned up their garden path. He was nine years her senior and as much a stranger as her father. Doors opened and closed downstairs, and before long Maud could hear her father's voice buckled with rage. A few minutes later, James came into her room and told her to pack her things. She was to go to school in Darlington.

She still had to come home during the holidays. Before her first full year had passed, her father had married the barmaid from the local pub. She at least dealt better with his drunken rages than Maud had done, happy to strike back when he raised his hand. She had a child and made her husband work, rationing his drink and screaming at him to support his children. Maud remained in her own room sketching and reading. Her step-mother tried to be kind to her, but Maud shrank from her loud laugh and her teasing. Her step-mother thereafter confined her efforts to her husband

and child, though Maud was not struck again and was grateful.

For all her step-mother's efforts there was very little of the business left when her father died. He fell one day in the shop when Maud was at home for the Christmas holidays, and the first she knew of it was the jangle of the bell on the ambulance. He died three days later in hospital, and though her step-mother asked if she wished to go, Maud did not visit. She did not go back to school in Darlington but remained in Alnwick under her step-mother's care. After years of having little to do with each other, they developed a wary sort of mutual affection. Her father's will split his estate equally between his wife and surviving children, though other than the building itself, that amounted to only a few pounds. It was a shabby place, and her step-mother could find no one interested in taking it on.

Three months after the funeral, her step-mother left, saying only that she had met a drover from Newcastle she liked the look of and would be on her way. It seemed to Maud that she was miserable to leave her son, Albert, but James and Ida were married by that time and offered to bring him up as their own. Maud watched the woman decide, and having decided she acted. She took three pounds out of the savings account in her and Maud's name and said they were welcome to keep whatever the building fetched, she'd rather be shot of it. James invited Maud to join them in Darlington. She refused and for a month lived alone in the family home. Then came the fire, her share of the insurance money and Paris. She left many things in Alnwick, but more than anything she wanted to leave her father dead among the ashes. Now he appeared on the page in front of her in profile with his chin lifted.

The time unrolled and Maud was surprised when a far lighter knock came at the front door: it was the waiter from the corner café bringing them their supper. M. Morel arrived as he was bowing his way back out of the apartment.

CHAPTER 10

*I*T WAS NOT UNTIL AFTER THEY HAD FINISHED EATING
that Maud mentioned the strange old woman who had
visited, and apologised for giving the address of the club.

'I'm afraid she rather frightened me. I hope she didn't give any
trouble.'

'Oh, it was you who sent her, was it? That was kind, I must say.'
Morel pushed his plate away from him. Maud started to apologise,
but he stopped her and said more seriously. 'Poor lady, no, you did
quite right to give her the address. Though I am afraid I was not
there when she called and she caused quite a row. The porters saw
her off the premises and threatened her with the police. By the
time I got back there, she was gone. I came here this evening to
warn the concierge to keep an eye out for her. I hope she has
decided to go home. Perhaps I should send a telegraph to her son
and say she has been up to mischief before she does any worse.'

'Who was it, Christian? Maud, you didn't say anyone had
called.' Sylvie had as usual eaten very little, just picking at her food.

'You were resting, Sylvie.' How deep must her dreams be, Maud
thought, not to have heard that.

'It was poor Madame Prideux,' Morel said. His voice was
solemn, like a clerk of the court reading a charge. He scraped at the

lace tablecloth with his fingernail. Maud noticed how neatly trimmed and polished they were.

'Madame Prideux? Here in Paris?' Sylvie half-sat up, then dropped again into her chair and turned her head away. 'What an awful bore. I hate her. You must take the proper precautions, Christian. I have only just begun to explore, and now I fear I will see that foul crone round every corner. It could ruin everything. Did it cause a problem at the club? Did she tell the porters where she was staying?'

Morel looked across the table at her, his nails still making a little scratching noise on the lines of the cloth. 'They understood the lady was a little mad. Yes, she told them where she was staying, and you are right. I shall deal with it in the morning.'

Sylvie shook her head, all at once more animated and more present than she was normally at this time in the evening. Maud had not realised her dream-like state could be set aside so easily. 'No, I shan't be able to sleep. You had better go now.'

He sighed. 'If it will make you happy, Sylvie.'

'It is what should be done,' Sylvie replied simply. 'But first perhaps you should explain to Maud who she is.'

Morel folded his hands in front of him on the tablecloth. 'You spoke to her, Miss Heighton. What did she say to you?'

Maud felt deeply embarrassed. She could think of nothing but her own cowardice when the woman was reaching for Sylvie's door. The amount of money that Morel was paying her above her bed and board would entitle him to expect her to make some effort to protect his sister, but she had done nothing of use. She had let the old woman into the apartment, given up Morel's club at once when a lie would have served just as well, and then stood there without speech or action until the concierge arrived. 'She said many things. But you have no need to explain yourself to me. None at all.'

'She said we stole from her, I imagine. I can assure you she is a confused old woman and we did no such thing,' he said.

'Naturally, I did not for one moment believe it. The lady was obviously quite mad.'

'We are grateful for your confidence, Miss Heighton. You see, Sylvie, ladies of sense like Miss Heighton are aware that she is nothing more than a mad old woman to be pitied. We need say no more about it.'

Sylvie shook her head again. 'I think you had better tell her the whole story, Christian. The siege and the diamonds. Then she can understand why Madame Prideux is as mad as she is and not think me a coward for wishing to avoid her.'

Sylvie got up from the table and fetched her cigarette-case from the side-table. 'Let him tell you, Maud. Or I shall worry you will think him a fiend. I am sure she told you we are man and wife.' She settled back down, lit a cigarette and dropped the case on the table. Maud still found the sight of women smoking rather shocking and flinched. 'See, Christian? Maud is blushing. She did say so.' The enamel stripes on the case were of subtly different blues. French ultramarine, brilliant ultramarine, new blue.

'Perhaps you can tell her the story as you see fit, Sylvie, after I have left.' Morel's voice was a little clipped.

'Oh no, Christian. You tell it so much better than I do.' She tapped the ash off her cigarette and sat back in her chair watching him.

Maud put her hands together on her lap. 'If you do not wish to tell the story, sir, I am sure I do not wish to hear it.'

'Unfortunately, Miss Heighton, Sylvie wishes the story told and wants you to hear – and we must in all things be ruled by her.' He took a cigarette himself and leaned forward so Sylvie could light it, cupping her hand to protect the flame from an imaginary breeze.

Maud said nothing. Morel filled his glass. The apartment was particularly silent this evening. The slight creak in the chair, the rub of cloth on cloth as Morel settled himself was quite audible. 'Miss Heighton, do you know anything of the Siege of Paris? And the terrible week that followed the break-up of the Paris Commune?'

'A little.' The electric lamps around the room shed a dull orange glow about them; the smooth curves of the furniture seemed to shift a little in the light, like the vines of a forest floor caught in the act of growth. She recalled a hot summer's afternoon and her teacher reading from *Lessons of History*. In 1870 the Prussian army had defeated the French and for a year laid siege to the capital. The poor suffered the worst of it, but in the end even the rich who had not escaped in time were eating rats. Napoleon III fled and the new government made terms, but the militias formed for the defence of the city wanted something more for their sacrifices than the new government were offering. Suddenly France was at war with herself. For a little while the Paris Commune made its laws and decrees before the new French government sent in troops from Versailles and slaughtered them.

'Madame Prideux was born and has lived most of her life in our home town,' Morel said, 'but she was in Paris in 1871 with her husband and her young child – a boy of about four years of age. Her husband was a diamond polisher who worked on Rue de la Paix. It was possible if he was skilled and lucky that they could have had a respectable, even a comfortable life – but seeing those diamonds every day made him greedy. It became harder and harder for him to work with such priceless rarities and then take home only a few francs for his wife and child. The chaos in Paris seemed too good an opportunity to miss, and with the help of his friend who worked in the same establishment, he managed to steal half-a-dozen good-quality stones. He needed only to pay off his accomplice and meet his family before returning to his native soil with the means to buy a good-sized farm. His accomplice was a man named Christian Gravot.'

Morel drank slowly from his glass and Maud noticed him seeking out Sylvie's gaze. She smiled brightly at him and blew out a long thin stream of smoke from between her pale lips.

'This was just the time when the troops were beginning to pour through the streets. They were searching for the ring-leaders of the rebellion, but in truth anyone not obviously bourgeois who had remained in the city was regarded as guilty. A patrol approached him when he was in sight of the place where he had agreed to meet Gravot, and in a desperate attempt to conceal his crime and protect his plunder, he swallowed the stones. The patrol was not put off. Perhaps they had taken fire from that building. No doubt Prideux looked guilty and afraid, perhaps his hands were dirty and they took him for an arsonist. For whatever reason they shot him where he stood. Many others met the same fate. Often the bodies were buried in the roadways where they fell. There was no trial, no arrest and examination in those days.'

Maud remembered her history lessons. The bodies stacked in piles like wood ready for the fire. The stories of the burning of Paris when the Tuileries Palace was reduced to rubble and Notre Dame itself was threatened by the mob. She tried to imagine Paris in chaos: the fresh-washed streets she walked along every morning pooled with blood, the sound of soldiers marching, of men and women trying to build barricades across the wide streets, and gunfire, a man hauled off to be shot with a group of strangers against the shop windows where now rich women bought their silk gloves. The bodies rotting to nothingness under their satin slippers.

'How horrible,' she said.

'Oh, just wait,' Sylvie said, blowing out another smooth flow of smoke. 'It gets a great deal worse.'

'Oh!'

'What is it, Miss Heighton?'

'Only the old lady, Madame Prideux, said she wanted her diamonds. She asked if you'd swallowed them.'

Sylvie made a noise of disgust in her throat, and Morel's skin became a little grey. Maud tried to imagine that angry old woman, young and caught among the gunfire and flames.

'So the diamonds were lost?' she asked.

'I wish they had been. This is where, as Sylvie says, it gets worse. Madame Prideux was waiting for her husband nearby. He did not come at the appointed time and she could hear shots being fired so she went to find him at the place where he was supposed to meet his accomplice, Gravot. His plan too must have been to leave Paris at once as he had his pretty wife and their bundles with him. Madame Prideux saw them bent over a body in the street and ran towards them. She was just in time to see her husband's corpse being gutted for the diamonds he had swallowed. She threw herself on them, but Gravot's wife held her back. All she could do was watch.' Horror made Maud's skin crawl. 'It is terrible what people will do for a little wealth, Miss Heighton, terrible.'

Maud felt a touch on her arm. Sylvie had put out her cigarette and now drawn her chair close. She lowered her head onto Maud's shoulder. Without thinking, Maud put out her hand and Sylvie took it. Their hands lay loosely entwined on Maud's lap. Morel stubbed his cigarette out fiercely on the edge of his plate.

'Tell her what happened next,' Sylvie said.

'She went home, borrowed enough money from her family to open a grocery shop. Ran it for more than thirty years and told that story to her child every night for his bedtime story. I fear he did not turn out well.'

'Did she want revenge?'

His mouth twitched – a sad quick smile. 'No, Miss Heighton, she wanted the diamonds that they had cheated her of. She believed her husband's sacrifice should have made her a rich woman. Instead she spent her life scrimping for the basic necessities of existence while watching richer women come and go in her shop, and sacrificing any ounce of comfort to pay back the money she had borrowed. She was always a bitter woman with a sharp tongue. She would flatter her customers and spit acid when their backs were turned. Her son was no better. He was sent to the prison camps in Guiana in the end after he was caught stealing.'

'A harsh punishment,' Maud said quietly.

'He was caught stealing diamonds. A lot of them. I suspect he meant to give them to her.'

Maud squeezed her eyes shut for a moment, trying to think. 'But why does she believe *you* are Gravot, sir?'

'She is mad,' Sylvie said without lifting her head. 'It came on her slowly. I remember she was found once or twice on the street apparently unaware of where she was. Christian was away on business at that time, but when he returned, her mania fixed on him. There was some resemblance perhaps. I am not sure she understood that it all happened forty years ago. She began to call at our house. I tried to be kind, but it was a terrible strain.'

Maud looked down at her profile; the young woman's skin was golden in the lamplight. 'Is that why you came to Paris?'

Sylvie shook her head. 'No. Her son came home, claiming to be a reformed character. He took over the shop and kept her off the streets. She must have escaped him.'

Maud was silent for a while. Her father used to rant about

Quakers, claiming that the fact he was losing business to an auctioneer in Darlington who was of that faith was proof of a conspiracy against a good Methodist like himself. The conviction would grow on him as he talked, and when Maud and her step-mother could take no more and left the table to go to their separate pursuits, he could be heard continuing his monologue with only the walls for audience. Outside, a drunk was singing to his lady-friend, his slurred swooping songs punctuated by her laughter. 'What a terrible story.'

'I am sorry to tell it, sorry that Madame Rémy did not do a better job of protecting your peace, but perhaps Sylvie was right and it is best you know, having seen her.'

Sylvie moved and stretched; the fabric of her gown slipped down her arms, showing them smooth and glowing.

'You will take the proper steps, Christian?'

He stood, tucked his chair under the table and brushed down the sleeves of his coat. 'I will, at once. I shall telegraph. Her son must come and retrieve her. She shall not spoil Paris for us, Sylvie. I promise.' She kissed her fingertips to him. He came round the table to kiss his sister on her white forehead. Maud noticed there was more blue in his skin than usual. She looked up at him.

'I know it is a difficult story to tell,' she said, 'but you tell it beautifully. It almost reminds me to be sorry for her and her son again.'

'Then I suppose it is worthwhile. And now, dear ladies, I must leave you. I may be late back.'

CHAPTER 11

MAUD DID NOT ENJOY HER WALK TO THE ACADÉMIE as much as usual the following morning. The story haunted her and she found herself examining the smooth classical façades of the buildings for bullet-holes, or waiting for the dead to reach up through the pavement and grab her ankles. The sounds of the street seemed a little jangled and out of tune and she felt watched, persecuted. She was afraid of meeting Madame Prideux on the street, afraid of her withered hands and the acrid bite of her breath.

Sylvie showed no sign of nerves when they met at lunch. She chattered about how much her sketching and her English was improving under Maud's care and made a great show of serving Maud with the best pieces of meat from the stewpot and piling her plate with thick greens. Then, as soon as Maud had put down her fork, she was itching to be away, drumming her long fingers on the cover of her sketchbook while she waited for Maud to change. She did not lead Maud in the direction of one of their usual sketching spots in the Jardin du Luxembourg, however, but instead turned in the opposite direction towards the river. She wanted to walk along the Quai de la Tournelle and then cross the Seine at the Pont Sully. It was no hardship to Maud. Sylvie's mood, the sun and the clear cold breeze drove all the demons away. Paris became a romance again and the life of the riverside always pleased her eye, such was its variety. Barges loaded and unloaded gravel onto the lower embankment where young boys climbed the piles like conquerers then slid down their flanks in giggling heaps. The little steam-boats carrying the curious travellers for a penny an hour chugged between the piers, each papered in advertisements with letters two feet high and backed with burnt sienna orange or Prussian blue, while the floating white buildings of the public swimming baths looked down on them like duchesses watching a lively toddler at play.

Sylvie chattered while they walked, pointing out the men washing and trimming the poodles of the rich by the water and exclaiming on the brightness of the day. Three times Maud suggested finding a place where they might stop and sketch the broad views in front of them, the river heavy and placid rolling through all the noise and activity of the city, the houses on the Île St-Louis seeming to hang over and watch it as it passed, but Sylvie would not stop as yet.

'Have you visited Père Lachaise, Maud?' she said over her shoulder as they crossed the river a second time on to the right bank. Then when Maud shook her head, Sylvie took her arm and pulled her close to her side. 'Then we must go at once. Christian took me there before you came and I think you shall like it.'

'I have heard of it, of course,' Maud said. 'But are you sure you would like to go there now? Are you not tired?' She did not know the precise time, but she was sure that Sylvie would wish to return to her room in a little while.

Sylvie waved her hand. 'Not at all. I do not wish to go home at all. Shall we take the omnibus? It is only right to go there when the weather is good. Who knows when it might be so pretty again, and

there are many nice places to sit and we can rest and draw there.'
She was wearing a long winter coat that Maud had not seen before.
It was fawn in colour but there was something darker mixed into
the weave so it looked to Maud like the pelt of a lioness. Its collar
was of some glossy black fur.

'If you are sure, Sylvie.'

'Oh, quite sure,' she said, all but dragging Maud up Boulevard
Henri IV past the sudden stalls on the pavement selling children's
toys and bundles of mistletoe.

When they reached Père Lachaise Sylvie chose to rest on a bench
on Chemin Denon opposite the tomb of Chopin. She did not, she
said, feel any great sympathy for the man's music, but she
remembered liking the kneeling angel that guarded the tomb.
Maud wondered if she realised it looked quite like her. She had
lost the strange vivacity with which she had begun the trip but
made no complaint when Maud handed her her sketchbook and
suggested she try and copy the musician's profile, stamped on his
tomb. Maud herself, however, did not begin to draw at once. Her
eyes were still too full of the place, its peculiar gothic beauty.
The cemetery where they had buried Rose had been a flat and
dreary sort of a place. Rows of square low tombs without greenery
or flowers to cheer it. Père Lachaise was quite different. The hill
on which the cemetery was built was covered with a city of its own,
complete with avenues and squares, poor quarters and rich. There
were rows upon rows of tiny mausoleums about the height of a
man and with pitched roofs like sentry boxes, but their designs
were not uniform. Every one was marked out by some individual
feature – iron grilles, gothic touches at the roof-edge, a medallion

or carved quotation, and dotted among them were weeping angels, busts of generals, carved drapery.

On the Avenue des Acacias were a number of larger establishments, mausoleums built like Grecian temples with broad staircases leading from their porticoes to the damp cobbles of the avenue. The jumbled edges of the crowded monuments tricked the eye. The contrast of the stone with the trees that grew between them, the dank mossy shadows, the distances of the city below offered a puzzle for Maud to work out in her sketches. There was too much to take in; she had to select the details to find the peculiar mood of the place without making the viewer drunk. People walked along the paths in twos or threes with their guide books in their hands, visiting the tombs of the illustrious dead. They peered at the names, giving a sharp nod if they recognised it, as if the sight confirmed something they had always thought, then moving on to the next.

A young woman had followed them up the path, and as they sat down she stood in front of the composer's tomb with her head lowered as if she were waiting to perform. She had a white rose in her hand. Maud began to sketch her, then stopped. It was a storybook picture being offered to her: the beautiful girl with a rose in front of a tomb would be a classic Victorian *memento mori*. She might as well paint a faithful hound. She could imagine her father sneering at it at some house sale – the sentimentality of it. Instead she shifted her position on the bench so she could look past the tomb and down the path. Sylvie's silhouette, her chin tucked into her collar, became the edge of the picture, the path that reached away from them; that way, the eye could understand the confusion of statuary around them.

'What will you do when you have finished in Paris?' Sylvie said quietly, looking between the tomb and her page. 'Will you go and paint portraits of your town dignitaries and give drawing lessons?'

Maud smiled slightly but the idea seemed a good one. She pictured herself in rooms of her own where there was good light to work by. She had been seeing it through a haze of desperation in the past year. Now it reappeared in her mind's eye quite clearly. There were not many artists trained in Paris living in Darlington, but there was money there. James's business was flourishing and his occasional stiff letters were full of the names of influential people whom he had met. It would appeal to the vanity of the local officials to have someone trained on the continent to immortalise them, and the surrounding countryside was beautiful. She would then be able to spend time working for her own pleasure as well as theirs.

'Something of that sort,' she said.

'That does not sound like a good life. Stuck in some provincial backwater where there is nothing to see and nothing to do,' Sylvie said. Maud said nothing, only thought how Sylvie's English was improving. It was quite possible that tomorrow Sylvie would demand to know all about her home town, the landscape, the people, and sigh at how much she wanted to visit. There was a pause, and Maud noticed her companion had stopped in her work, and was simply staring at the angel and the girl with the rose.

'Madame Prideux is dead,' Sylvie said suddenly.

At first Maud did not quite understand her. 'Did you say dead, Sylvie?'

'I did. A traffic accident on the Champs Elysées last night. I suppose she was too distracted to see where she was going. My brother had not managed to send his telegram to her son before he heard. The porters were discussing it at the club. He told me to tell you. I am sorry she is dead, though I cannot think her life did anyone much good.'

Sylvie did not seem to feel that any more needed to be said and turned back to her sketch. Maud did not know what to feel; she should be sorry, shocked. Perhaps she *was* shocked at the suddenness of the news, but she was not sure she was sorry. Perhaps it was better to die quickly like that, rather than be confined in an asylum, or rotting away behind the walls of your home – and to her, Madame Prideux had seemed unimaginably old. However, even surrounded by tombs, the idea that a person could be in the world one moment, then disappear from it the next felt extraordinary. The glass eyes of Madame Prideux's fox fur seemed to glimmer at her for a moment from the shadows in the path. Again she wondered what she should have done the previous day, whether she could have found words to calm the old woman.

'Her family will be informed?'

'I imagine so. Christian will write to them perhaps. Are you sorry for her, Maud? She was a wicked old woman.' Sylvie was looking at her over her thick fur collar.

'I am sorry for anyone who is so lost. Her life seems tragic to me.'

Sylvie smiled. 'If it was tragic, perhaps it is better her life is now over.'

Maud could not think how to reply so returned thoughtfully to her work. The ghost of the old woman retreated and the world became once more a series of visual problems to be solved. She made her notes, ideas for the tints she might use to recreate this scene on canvas, the variegated greys and greens. At last she felt the familiar ache between her shoulderblades and sighed, placing her pencil on the pad and spreading her fingers wide. Sylvie was still sitting very quietly beside her, but there was some tension in her shoulders. Her right hand still held her pencil but it did not move. Her breathing was a little shallow.

'Sylvie? What is it? Have you been getting cold? You need only tell me.'

The girl started as if she had been sleeping, but didn't look at her. Instead she took out her cigarette-case, shook one free then lit it. Maud watched her, frowning. Her fingers were shaking.

'Maud, I think I've done something stupid.' Maud waited. 'I threw away my *chandu* last night. The opium.' Maud closed her sketchbook and slipped the pencil she had been using into the hollow of the spine. 'I was thinking of America. How nice it would be to be free of France, how much better it would be to go there with clear eyes. I thought . . . I felt I did not need it at the time. Now, I am afraid.'

Tears appeared in her eyes and she tried to blink them back, tilting her head so she looked into the empty grey sky above them.

Maud felt her heart go out to her, poor strange Sylvie who had tried to break free of her chains. Yesterday she had failed the Morels, today she would not. Maud began to think in small, practical steps. 'Are you in pain?' A quick nod. 'We must go home.'

Maud put away her book, helped Sylvie to her feet and threaded her arm through hers. Sylvie leaned on her as they walked quickly down the slope to the main gate, her head lowered. Her grip on Maud's arm spasmed. As they walked down the Avenue Principale, a gentleman with a face like a bulldog turned to stare at them, ignoring his companion who was trying to point out Rossini's empty tomb. Maud thought of how she might look with Sylvie's thin pale form hanging on her arm. As if she was stealing one of the ghosts away from the place, no doubt.

If the cab driver they found at the stand by the gates noticed that Sylvie was unwell, he said nothing. Sylvie lowered the blind and leaned into the corner of the carriage as they drove. Her breathing was quick and harsh and she pressed her hand to her stomach. It had come on her very quickly. Maud's first thought had been to telegram to Morel in his club as soon as they were safely back in Rue de Seine, but he might not be there – and even if he were, what could she say in such a message? She could hardly mention opium openly, and if she said Sylvie was ill he would certainly hurry back to Rue de Seine, but then he would have to go out again to buy whatever Sylvie needed. She was suffering so greatly now, Maud was very afraid of what her condition would be in a few hours. She felt she had not the authority to summon in a doctor, since that too would surely bring scandal, would be a betrayal of trust. A panicked English miss might call a doctor, but an experienced woman who could take care of herself in the world would be more circumspect.

'Sylvie, do I understand rightly? You do not wish to continue with this attempt to abandon the drug?'

'I cannot. It is too sudden. I was stupid.'

'And your brother has no supply in the apartment? I will happily force a lock on his bureau and explain later what has happened.'

Sylvie shook her head and sank further into the corner of the cab, closing her eyes. Maud thought of her father. When he was taken into hospital, the nurses had stopped him drinking. Maud's step-mother stood by Maud at the grave staring fiercely at the earth as it covered the coffin, Albert's little hand held tightly in her red fist. 'It was the cutting off the drink that killed him. Seen it before when a drinker gets taken in by these religious types. So keen to do you good, they'll kill you in a minute.'

Maud put her hand on Sylvie's knee and said quietly, 'Can I fetch it for you? Do you know where I should go?'

The girl did not look round or open her eyes, but Maud felt her shudder with relief. 'Oh Maud, will you? Thank you. I am sorry to be so much trouble.'

'I am happy to help you in any way, my dear.'

Sylvie half-laughed, half-gasped and brought her hand to her face. 'There is a little place in the Rue Croix des Petits Champs – it sells prints and ornaments from China. Ask the girl for "a box" – she'll know what you mean. Just wait till you are the only customer there.'

Maud didn't ask her any more, letting her rest in the shadows while the cab danced and dodged along the streets. Once back inside the building, Sylvie straightened up as they passed the concierge's door, but the effort came at a cost. Maud wondered if she would be able to get her to her room, but somehow they managed. In the safety of Sylvie's bedroom, she helped her undress, and when Sylvie was in her shift, Maud pulled back the covers so the sick girl could crawl into her bed. Maud fetched water then opened her purse. Sylvie saw her.

'Maud, no. Don't use your own money.' Sylvie rummaged in the single drawer of the bedside-table. 'Here, take this. Please – I insist.'

Rather than a coin or a note, Maud found she was holding a small brooch, a bar set with diamonds with a sapphire in the centre. 'I've no paper money to hand. Pawn it, please. Rue des Blancs Manteaux. I never wear it.'

Maud would have argued, but Sylvie had already turned away with a low groan. She decided she would do as she had been asked, pawn the jewel and buy the opium. The decision made her shiver with complicity. She was no longer the same as other women of her class and country. She dropped the brooch into her clasp bag and snapped it shut, then let herself out of the flat feeling like a woman of the world for the first time since she had come to Paris. The skies were growing dark and fat with rain.

Shop Interior oil on canvas 152.4 × 182.9 cm

A bravura riot of pure colour, but notice the presence of the shopkeeper in her dark tunic. She ignores the viewer, is a point of calm and control in the centre of this profusion of oriental luxury and excess. Chinese and Japanese art and artefacts were extremely fashionable throughout the Belle Époque and were a profound influence on artists from Manet to Pierre Bonnard.

Extract from the catalogue notes to the exhibition 'The Paris Winter: Anonymous Treasures from the de Civray Collection', Southwark Picture Gallery, London, 2010

CHAPTER 12

THE SENSE THAT SHE WAS DOING SOMETHING difficult and dangerous for someone she cared about made Maud brave. She went to the government pawnbroker's shop prepared to meet any sort of insult or insolence but found in fact a clean and efficient office, and the people waiting with her did not seem desperate or ashamed. There were ladies in fashionable walking dress talking to each other with the same ease as if they had run into each other in the glove department in Printemps. Some men in worker's overalls sat with bundles of clothing between their knees, but several of them were comfortable enough in their surroundings to lean back on the benches with their flat caps over their eyes and sleep until it was their turn to magically transform their property into a few coins.

When Maud's number was called, the man behind the desk greeted her with a polite smile. He examined the brooch through a jeweller's loupe that left a crease in the skin below his eye when he removed it. He wrote for a few moments in a notebook and handed her one of the carbon copies, stamped and sealed, explaining that she should take it to the cashier. Then he put the brooch into a little labelled bag and shut it inside one of the drawers below his desk, wishing her a good day as he did so.

The shop on the corner of Rue Croix des Petits Champs was very different. The air was perfumed with sandalwood and every available inch of space was crammed with fancy goods decorated in strong colours. The ceiling was hung with opened parasols, all painted with birds of paradise and trailing greenery, and the shelves were packed with bowls, some painted with blue dragons chasing their tails, others in vivid red and green cloisonné work. There were dozens of little figurines, dragons and lions in blue enamel seated on plinths and showing their teeth, half-open ivory fans and black lacquer boxes inlaid with mother-of-pearl. A Chinese woman stood behind the counter at the back of the shop, her dark hair pulled back from her face and wearing a high-collared dark tunic. She was wrapping a scarlet bowl patterned with chrysanthemums for a gentleman with thick white whiskers. She used a great quantity of newspaper and chatted to him in fluent French while she worked. When the package was tied the gentleman left, touching the brim of his hat to Maud as he let himself out of the door, leaving the bell jangling behind him. The woman cleared away her paper and string and folded her hands, waiting till Maud approached.

'I was told to ask for a box,' Maud said, trying not to blush. The woman's expression did not alter. She lifted her hand and with her palm flat indicated the shelves surrounding them. 'There are many here, miss. Would you like one of these?'

Maud shook her head but said nothing.

'Very well.' The woman slid from her stool and went into the back of the shop, returning a little later with a box the size of Maud's clenched fist. It was decorated with a picture of a phoenix lifting its heavy body away from the dark brown of the wood. The woman named a price, about half what the pawn shop had given her for the brooch and Maud counted out the money. The phoenix disappeared into wrappings of newspaper and string, and though the woman did not chatter as she had done to the man with the white whiskers, she was perfectly calm and the pleasant smile never left her lips. Maud realised she had expected something sordid; that the shop would be dirty and half-empty – an obvious front for vice; that whoever served her would be skeletal and creeping. She looked back over her shoulder as she left. The shopkeeper had picked up some sewing from the basket beside her and did not look up. Maud hurried back towards the river and Rue de Seine through the courtyard of the Louvre feeling oddly diminished, the colours she had seen in the shop beating behind her eyes.

Sylvie's bedroom was large and rectangular with a polished brass bedstead draped in white linen, the twin of Maud's own. The bedside-table was piled with cheap editions of English novels, the only books Maud had seen in the apartment other than the ones she had brought into it herself. The shutters were closed but letting in the last light of the afternoon through the slats. Two small armchairs upholstered in malachite green, embroidered with pale yellow and pink silk, sat in front of the fire. Sylvie must have heard the door to the apartment open, for she was sitting up on the edge of the bed with her dressing-gown on when Maud tapped and opened the door.

'Did you get it?'

Maud nodded and reached into her bag for the phoenix box, but Sylvie had already stood up and padded round to the other side of the bed, her bare feet making no more noise than a cat's. She dropped to her knees and pulled a tray from under the pleated valance. The tray was narrow, perhaps eighteen inches long and richly enamelled in scarlet and a dark but powerful green; its geometric patterns were studded with white circles, each containing a Chinese character in black. Cloisonné work. On it was a lamp with a glass chimney, the base decorated to match the tray, and to one side of it lay a pipe – a tube about the length of a conductor's baton, but thicker, with a bowl in blue and white porcelain attached to its side which looked strangely like a door knob. The mouthpiece at the other end was ivory. On either side of the lamp were a number of small tools and boxes, all decorated with the same enamelwork. Maud was reminded of the luxurious dressing-cases for rich travellers that had occasionally passed through her father's sale room. Every convenience at hand.

'Fetch me a cushion,' Sylvie said. She was trying to light the lamp, but one match after another failed.

Maud placed the cushion beside her, put the phoenix box containing the drug on the tray and took the matches from Sylvie's hand. She bent over the little lamp to light it and fitted the glass cover over it again while Sylvie twisted the lid off the wooden box, lifted it to her face and inhaled deeply. Something in Maud told her she had crossed a line in her life, that the act of lighting the lamp for Sylvie was one of great significance, but what that significance was, she could not say. She felt worldly and wise again after the challenges of her shopping excursion.

Sylvie was lying down on the floor with the tray beside her. Maud curled her legs underneath her and watched while Sylvie pulled a twist of waxed paper from the box and teased it open. It held a dark brown, slightly oval ball which glistened in the lamplight. Maud watched fascinated as the girl prepared her pipe. A tiny morsel was separated from the greater mass of the ball then needled to the edge of the bowl and heated on the lamp. Sylvie then put her lips around the mouthpiece and inhaled; there was a slight fizz and crackle as the drug vaporised. Her body seemed to relax at once. She did not fall into a stupor, nor behave as if she had become instantly drunk; nor did she seem to see visions – all of which Maud had suspected might happen. There was just this loosening in her muscles and a slow cat-like smile.

Almost immediately, she lifted herself onto her elbow once more to prepare another pipe and inhaled it in the same way. Maud could hear the faintest bubbling sound as she drew in the smoke. She then set the pipe down and looked at Maud. The tray in front of her, iridescent in the lamplight, was a burst of prime colour. In the outer glow of the flame Sylvie had become a spirit of greys and pale purple shadows: the lilac silk of her dressing-gown with its cream trimming of antique lace, the girl herself, her blond hair falling around her face and large grey eyes. Maud had left her sketchbook here when she had first put Sylvie to bed. She reached for it and drew the pencil out of the spine.

'May I?'

'If you wish, Maud.'

She began to draw. It seemed no time at all before the knock at the door heralded the waiter and their evening meal.

Sylvie oil on paper, mounted on canvas 69.2 × 64.7 cm

A woman reclines in half-light with the paraphernalia of opium smoking laid out in front of her. This is a sensitive, intimate painting of what was seen at the time as a dangerous vice. The drapery around the room, the subject's dressing-gown and even her skin seem to be painted in shades of smoke.

Extract from the catalogue notes to the exhibition 'The Paris Winter: Anonymous Treasures from the de Civray Collection', Southwark Picture Gallery, London, 2010

The weather was becoming more and more unpredictable, and inclined to turn viciously cold without warning. Sylvie said it was too chilly to sketch outdoors so instead took Maud driving through the Bois de Bologne in a hired car or on shopping trips in the grand department stores. Maud saw Sylvie smoking on one more occasion, when she asked if she could paint rather than sketch her. There had been some discussion at the Académie about the advantages of producing a work in a single sitting, and Maud was keen to experiment.

They established themselves on the floor of Sylvie's room, Maud pinning her oil sketching paper to a deal board to support it then choosing her tints, squeezing each onto the palette in abstemious amounts, attaching the little tin cup with its reservoir of linseed oil to its edge, setting out her hog-hair and sable brushes. As she did so, Sylvie prepared her tray with a similar satisfaction, and Maud was aware that the ritual was important to them both. Then each settled to their addiction.

Time ceased to consist of one moment following another. Maud's hand travelled with a will of its own; she felt as if she were hardly present. Her body was obeying its training to observe and record without intervention. Each tint she required she could mix at once, and the sensuality of the process took over her senses. Moving the brush along the paper was like brushing soft skin with her fingertips. The long lines of the picture appeared beneath the gentle pressure of her brush, the shape of the dusky shadows behind Sylvie, the pattern of light through the shutters . . . She painted for two hours then slowly put down her brush; it rattled with the others in the jar and it sounded like applause. Sylvie seemed to have fallen into a half-doze and Maud left her, to clean her palette and brushes before the evening meal arrived.

Maud managed to persuade Sylvie to visit the Louvre once – but almost immediately, they ran into Francesca. Maud was very happy to see her out of the studio, and the two women began to talk about the painting in front of them for a few minutes until they realised that Sylvie had, rather pointedly, wandered away. It was clear she did not wish to be introduced. Maud did not know how to apologise for her.

'She is not used to company,' she said, rather awkwardly.

Francesca rolled her eyes. 'Tanya did say she was a bit of an odd fish. Beautiful, though.'

'I should go after her.'

'Of course, treasure. But you should also take my advice and get married. It's so much easier to be dependent on a man for one's bed and board. As long as my husband is fed and I tell him he's a handsome devil once a week, he's as good as a lamb. Now hurry along.'

Every time Maud suggested going to one of the museums after that, Sylvie accused her of wanting to see her artist friends and of being bored with her company. During one of his brief appearances in the flat, Maud mentioned this to Morel. He nodded and chewed his lip. 'I understand, Miss Heighton. Sylvie has never been fond of company or crowds. I can only say that your friendship and patience has improved her greatly. You would have to have seen the stupor in which she lived in the past to truly appreciate this. I only fear that our home will become tiresome to you. A healthy young woman like yourself should not be so confined.'

Maud protested. 'Please, Monsieur Morel! I am more than happy.'

He did not seem to believe her. 'I know what happened a few days ago, Miss Heighton. Sylvie would never have attempted to give up the drug without your example; even if that attempt failed, it gives me hope. But I must arrange some thank you fitting to your help for us. Let me think on it – a Christmas gift!'

Maud slept badly that night. It was the first time she had not enjoyed a full night's rest since she had arrived at Rue de Seine. She lay, uncomfortably awake, staring at the shadows on the ceiling, trying to account for it. She thought of the picture of Sylvie. She had stored it with her other sketches in oil in the lid of her painting box and she could feel it glowing there. The picture, and her ability to paint it, to bring it so close to what she saw in her own mind, excited her. It was a bold piece in the narrowness of its range of hues, shocking perhaps in its subject, but not vulgar the way she found some of Manet's nudes vulgar. There was none of the flat, blatant invitation of Olympia, or the contrived nudity of the Académie's bound Andromedas, fastened to a rock for the sea-beast or for the critics to examine the quality of her skin. Still, it was certainly true that the painting of Sylvie was sensual; frankly so.

Maud turned over in her bed, echoing the pose of the painting, wondering what her brother and sister-in-law would say if they saw the picture. She had nothing to be ashamed of, she told herself. Nothing – so why this creeping sense of shame as if she had lost something? She had absorbed in her youth an idea of herself that could not, it seemed, include pawn shops and opium lamps. They put her outside her class in a way that having a drunk as a father had not. He had never left the house without a collar and tie, and people would exchange a 'Good day' with him in the street though they crossed the road to avoid her step-mother.

Maud wondered why it had been so important to her to stay in lodgings that could be thought respectable even when she was starving, why she paid the fees at Lafond's to paint the nude with no men in the room. She felt as if she were on a tower of Notre

Dame looking down like one of the gargoyles at herself – herself as she had been, spinning in little circles in her sensible black working dress, as confined in her movements as a child's toy, when all around her, experiences and lives which she could not think of, could not admit to knowing, existed just out of sight.

Feeling suddenly vertiginous, she opened her eyes, sat up to pour a glass of water and went with it to the window. The gaslights shone ghostly in the thick dark and although she could not see the river, she could sense it, the mass of water between the embankments, pushing itself towards the eventual relief of the open waters of the English Channel.

Catching sight of herself in the glass, she toasted her reflection then set the glass down; as it clicked down she heard another click – of a latch in the hall. She stepped noiselessly across the floor in her bare feet and knelt down, peering through the keyhole like a butler in a peepshow film. Sylvie's door opposite was ajar and the light fell across the corridor for a moment before it was blocked by the shadow of a man emerging from the room; he turned to say something in a low voice and Maud saw it was Morel. His shirt was untucked, his braces hanging down from his waist. He was laughing a little, showing his white teeth. Sylvie appeared beside him, her body hidden by the angle of the door. She put a hand to his face and reached up to kiss him, her lips pressing his face just by his mouth. The warmth of their affection gave Maud a pang of jealousy. She thought of her mother, and wondered if she would ever be loved like that again. They said something more, too softly for Maud to hear, then Morel turned towards his own room and Sylvie quietly shut the door behind him.

CHAPTER 13

*W*HEN MAUD RETURNED TO THE APARTMENT THE following day and was shaking her umbrella off in the passageway, she heard the voice of M. Morel greeting her. He was beside her at once, helping her off with her damp coat.

'Mademoiselle Heighton! I am delighted to see you. Do come in. I hope you'll forgive my rudeness but we are already at table. I only had a moment to dash back from the club.'

Caught up in her coat and bag, Maud had no time to do more than assure him no apologies were needed before she was ushered through to the drawing room like a favoured guest rather than a girl who ate there every day. Sylvie was at the table looking far brighter than usual and dressed to go out.

'Maud, darling! Are you famished? It's boiled chicken for lunch again, I'm afraid, but they know we like it and their imagination seems to be running out. Christian has arranged his treat for us though.'

Morel pushed in her chair behind her and while Sylvie piled stew on her plate and fussed with cutting more bread, he leaned over Maud, his eyes wide.

'Now Miss Heighton, have you heard tell of the splendid, the refulgent Madame de Civray?'

'Naturally.' Everyone had. She was a French Countess though American by birth, and very rich. Rumour said she bought a great deal of art and said a great deal of stupid things about it which the painters all repeated to each other with great glee while they spent her money in the Montmartre cafés. Or so it was said at the Académie. Maud had never been near enough to a café in Montmartre to know what was said. Yvette was their only connection to the artists on the hill and all they knew of what was discussed there, they heard from her. She had told them her own story of the Countess too. She had been modelling for M. Degas one afternoon when the Countess arrived at his studio with her footman and her little yapping dogs.

'Well, Master was not best pleased to see her, but even he cannot drive a woman like her out once she has her foot in the door. "Am I disturbing you, *maestro*?" she says. "Yes, you are, Madame," he says, and looks as angry as all hell. "Well, honey, I'm only here to pick up a couple of little things for the smoking room," she says, and I promise you she picks up the first two canvases she can put her hands on and passes them to the footman. Then she draws out a wedge of notes the size of my fist and pops them on the table. All this time, old Degas is too angry to speak. Then she backs out of the room with, I promise you, her finger on her lips! As soon as the door closed he threw his palette so hard against it, it cracked. Then she was heard the next day in Galérie Georges saying she couldn't understand why people were so rude about him, because he was such a sweet old stick!'

Morel dropped down into the seat next to Sylvie, his arm still slung around the back of her chair. 'The Countess and I have friends in common. I begged a favour. You and Sylvie are invited to her home this afternoon – early, mind you – to see her paintings. She leaves for her husband's country estate for Christmas today.'

Maud didn't know what to say. Morel lowered his voice. 'You know, Miss Heighton, that Sylvie finds public places rather a strain on her nerves, but there you will be free to feast your eyes on pictures in privacy. Sylvie is more and more ready to brave the outside world, in this limited way. It isn't even a formal visit. Come, haven't I done well?'

Sylvie put out her hand and covered Maud's. 'It is all good, isn't it? I hate for you to be shut up here all the time. Christian tells me I have been selfish, and I agree.'

Maud looked at her and said, 'Not at all. You know I take such pleasure in your company.'

'No, I can be strange and cross and I know it. But we are hoping this might make up for your patience, and to thank you for your help.' She jumped to her feet. 'See? I am already dressed. Now say you'll come, Maud, do. Tell us how clever we have been, then eat quickly.'

Maud looked at her with pleasure. 'I'll be delighted, but you must let me change.'

'No need!' Sylvie said. 'She knows it is a poor friendless painter Christian wishes to see her collection. Spend the moments we have eating, Maud. Christian shall go and fetch a cab.'

Maud looked back at her plate. Sylvie was as brutal as a child sometimes.

CO CO

Sylvie was unusually animated on the way to the Countess's house, and in spite of the crowds thronging the pavements, she made the cab stop twice in order to dart into one or other of the shops on Rue de Rivoli. Each time she made Maud wait in the cab and emerged with a number of parcels and boxes. 'Presents,' she mouthed as she returned. She stared out of the window at the passing streets with renewed excitement. 'How happy everyone looks! Perhaps this time next year I shall be well again. We will be in America by then. They understand business there. And now I speak English very well. You will come with us to Midnight Mass tomorrow, will you not? Did you go last year?'

Maud was becoming used to her whirring changes of subject. 'I was unwell. But there was a little party in the boarding house where I was staying, and the landlady brought me up some of the food.'

'How horrible it is to be unwell, particularly at Christmas when everyone else is so happy. This year you shall enjoy it more.'

'I'm sure I shall, Sylvie.' Maud had prepared her gifts. To her brothers and Ida she had sent French confectionery and picture books. For Yvette and Tanya she had made cards with portraits of them both. Morel was to have a tie from Charvet, and for Sylvie she had found a pretty fan in ivory, painted with peacock colours. They were all of them modest gifts, but she felt a certain pleasure in giving them.

'Oh, we are here!' Sylvie counted out coins from her purse for the cabman while Maud stepped out onto the pavement and looked up, amazed. The Countess's house on Place Saint-Georges was astonishing, a can-can dancer among a row of stately matrons. Four storeys high, each window surrounded by stone Graces and Muses, garlands, flourishing black ironwork – all exuberance. It was a frivolous, pretty building that seemed to be laughing sideways at the flat, self-important front of the Thiers Library opposite.

Sylvie appeared beside her. 'I hope the lady is not too like her house,' she said, 'or I may find her exhausting.'

The manservant took Sylvie's card and within moments his mistress was approaching with quick steps, her hands stretched out in front of her and a pair of yapping dogs dancing around her heels.

'Oh Miss Morel! Delighted! And this must be Miss Heighton, I think? I'm so pleased you could drop by and see me at such short notice.'

Maud had always liked the American accent. It sounded friendly to her, its easy musical swing so unlike the clipped English of glass and china she had learned at her mother's knee. The Countess was wearing a day gown of green silk rippling with pearls set into its lace bodice and sleeves. Maud waited for the familiar long contemptuous look her own clothes tended to draw in Paris, but none came. Instead the Countess shook hands very heartily and gave her an open smile. 'Now, I want to hear your opinion on something straight away. Then I shall be very rude and leave you to wander about as you see fit. I have to get the evening train for the Loire and there's not a thing packed. This way! You too, Miss Morel!'

'Are you going to be away long, Madame?' Sylvie asked as she trailed behind them, staring up at the high ceilings, the baroque mouldings and gilt and red velvet furnishings. It was like being in a private Versailles.

'Only a week, thank God. We are paying our winter visit to my husband's family. A whole château full of titles and unmarried aunts and not a chin between them.'

Maud smiled and the Countess winked at her. She thrust open a pair of doors off the hall then turned to face them as they waited in the corridor, her arms still wide and holding the doors apart, a firm but glorious guardian of the space beyond. 'Now, Miss Heighton, it seems to me in this day there are three sorts of painters. Those who paint what they *want* to see, those who paint what they *feel* they see, and those who paint what they *think* about what they see. Which are you?'

Sylvie spoke while Maud was still considering. 'That is very clever, Madame. Did you read it somewhere?'

'Seems unlikely!' she said cheerfully. 'Unless it was in a Sherlock Holmes novel.'

'I hope I paint what it *feels like* to see,' Maud said at last with some hesitation.

'There! Just when Miss Morel has said I sounded clever, you have invented another category. I cannot allow it. I shall put you in category two, as that seems closest. It is my favourite. The first lot are too pretty, and the last lot think such ugly thoughts. Now what do you make of this?'

She took hold of Maud's arm, walked her into the middle of the drawing room then pointed to a still-life that hung above the fireplace. It was difficult at first to see the painting properly in these surroundings, for it was small for this room – perhaps twenty inches in length and almost square. It showed a rough wooden table with two bowls on it, one containing cherries and the other peaches, on a ruched-up tablecloth. But the perspective was all wrong. The cherries were facing towards the viewer, the peaches turned upwards. Every angle was impossible and clumsy; the brushwork strange, hurried, with variegated hatchings; the colours, other than that of the fruit, oddly muddy; the light source hard to trace. Still it had a mass, a weight that was tangible.

'Cézanne,' Maud said.

'Uh-huh,' the Countess replied, standing by her side and staring with her. 'But what do you think?'

'It seems crude, but I would never stop looking at it if it were mine.'

The Countess clapped her hands. 'Exactly! That's exactly what

I felt! How can something be revolting and so beautiful at the same time?' She stared at it. 'I own a lot of beautiful things, Miss Heighton. I'm as rich as Croesus and I like to spend my money, but if this place was on fire and the people were safe, this funny little painting is what I'd come back for. Isn't that odd? My husband had a huge portrait of his mother here until I bought this. It felt like an act of Yankee rebellion replacing it, but when you really look at it, all this other stuff . . .' she waved her hand at her private palace '. . . just seems to melt away. I think the Count was a little angry with me for a while, but you know what? I now believe it is what he would save too.'

'I'll never paint like that,' Maud said.

'Would you want to, honey?' the Countess asked. Maud thought, and then shook her head.

'Me neither. The world only needs one Cézanne and we've had him. You have to find your own way. Now, I have to run around like a fool getting ready for the train. The servants all know you're here, so you wander about just as you like. The Degas paintings are all in the smoking room. The Count and his male friends think they are connoisseurs, but when it comes down to it, they just like looking at the ballet dancers' legs while they have their cigars. You know I had to chain them to the walls? The first painting of his I bought, he came and took back, saying he wanted to alter something – and I cannot get him to return it! Always, "tomorrow and tomorrow, Madame"!' Maud began to think a little differently about Yvette's story of her raid on the master's studio. 'There's a Fantin-Latour in my dressing room too you shouldn't miss if you want a more classical fruit basket. So do have a good poke around. We can have a proper visit when I come back from the Château of the Dead in a week or so. Nice to meet you, Miss Morel!'

And she was gone.

Maud was intensely happy during the two hours she spent in the Countess's home. There was such a profusion of canvases, and each one offering some fresh revelation. Here were pictures that belonged neither to the violent crudities on display at the Steins' house, nor the polite pastorals of the Salon. And she was alone with the pictures. No matter how early she arrived at the Louvre or how late she stayed, the rooms were always full. The same people she saw in Père Lachaise were there too with their Baedekers and Ward Lock guides, glaring studiously at the paintings, comparing them with the fuzzy reproductions in their guides and reading off, loudly, the appropriate paragraph, before striding onto the next. She tried to ignore it, tried to tell herself it was right that these people too had the chance to look at these great paintings, but they irritated her nevertheless. She wanted to snatch their guidebooks away and stamp on them. 'Just *look*!' she'd complain in her head. 'That's all you need to do. Just stop for a minute *and look*!'

The private galleries kept all their best pictures locked away to titillate their customers with goods unsullied by the inferior eyes of the poor, and the Salons? Packed society occasions that befuddled the eyes. At Madame de Civray's, Maud feasted in solitude. It was indeed an eclectic collection. Impressionists jostled up against Symbolist works, the soft edges of Renoir alongside. There were names she did not know: Rousseau, Utrillo, who painted blank walls and somehow made them live. Some Maud liked, some perplexed her, but each one demanded attention. If the Countess did choose them at random, then her luck was the devil's. Maud wished Tanya was with her. She'd change her mind about the catty gossip surrounding Madame de Civray just as quickly as Maud had.

Sylvie sauntered around with her for a while, but was more interested in the Countess's dressing table than her art. She began picking up the jars of ointment and reading the labels of each one slowly as if committing it to memory. Maud went on and found herself in an upstairs library face to face with a painting of Pissarro's of a meadow in sunlight. A woman, the suggestion of a woman, stood under a group of trees, looking out of the frame. In the distance were the roofs of a small town. It was all so perfectly light and alive; the air moved, the woman would walk away at any moment. Maud closed her eyes and opened them again, trying to fix the image in her mind, trying to see the individual colours and brush-strokes. And all this in peace. No one dragging on her arm. No loud voice behind her, pronouncing. She could reach out and touch it . . .

The door opened and she flinched. It was the Countess.

'Sorry, honey. I won't disturb you but I wanted you to have this.' She handed over a flat black cardboard folder tied with ribbon. Maud took it. 'Open it up.'

She did. It held a slippery mass of photographs of the paintings she had been admiring. 'Oh my goodness!'

'I know, I'm just too kind – don't even say it! Happy Christmas! It was just I thought, Hell, I'm giving that poor girl a couple of hours to take it all in, then throwing her out again. It seemed cruel. We had them done for the insurance in the summer, and I had them make up a few extra sets.'

'Are you quite certain, Madame? I can return them.'

'I'm always sure, honey. It's one of my many virtues – and keep them, for crying out loud. You don't treat me like an idiot and that makes you one of my special friends in Paris. Now, where is that floaty friend of yours?'

Maud laughed. 'I'm afraid she's not as fascinated by these as I am.'

'More fool her. Now I have to go for a fitting, it seems, so stay as long as you like and scoop her up on your way out. Wish me luck in the ghastly Château.'

Maud held the portfolio to her chest. Her heart was lifting and rising; the pictures had made her giddy. 'Good luck, and thank you – thank you so much!'

The Countess sketched a wave as she left the room. 'Pleasure, honey!'

CHAPTER 14

HE VARIOUS STUDIOS OF THE ACADÉMIE LAFOND gave themselves over to pleasure on the morning of Christmas Eve. Lafond himself went from studio to studio drinking a glass of punch at each and giving his blessing to his students. He always came early to the women's ateliers, since a man as careful of his reputation as he was would not visit his young ladies after drinking the punch mixed by his male students. Even at ten in the morning, though, he was jovial and pleasant with them all, released from judging them as they too were released from being judged. He beamed at them all over his fantastic white moustache as he told them it was at this time of year he most enjoyed counting his blessings, to revel in his old age, crowned with friends and prosperity. All his students felt caught up in his pleasure: it was as if Père Noël himself, having swapped his tunic for a tailored suit and high collar, had graced them with his presence.

Maud rather shyly gave her cards to Tanya and Yvette, and was delighted when they both laughed heartily at them.

'You see too much, Maud!' Tanya said. Maud had drawn her in an evening gown and clutching a canvas under her arm, fleeing a Russian Bear who wore a top hat and monocle. 'Oh, I shall keep it forever.'

Yvette's card showed her seated on the edge of the fountain at Place Pigalle with a queue of hopeful artists in front of her. 'I wish it were so!' Yvette groaned when she saw it. 'Still, all the girls with rich friends will be off and holidaying for the next few days so I might have the fountain to myself.'

Mademoiselle Claudette became a little sentimental and handed each of them a little printed card from the studio itself as they left. Classes would begin again on 3 January 1910.

It was all very different from the previous year for Maud. She went to Midnight Mass with the Morels and for the first time since childhood felt moved to prayers of gratitude. After they returned to the apartment, brother and sister fussed over their gifts from her. Morel played cabaret songs on the piano, bashing them out with more enthusiasm than accuracy and making Sylvie and Maud dance around the drawing room behind him. Maud had Morel's gift – a scarf from Worth – tied loosely around her neck and her gift from Sylvie – a brooch in the shape of a butterfly – pinned to her blouse. Sylvie played the coquette with her fan, and Morel wore his new tie over his old one. Maud went to bed at three leaving Morel playing slower songs and Sylvie curled up on the chaise longue watching him. Her bedside-table was a little forest of cards including ones from her brother's family, wishing her luck and success. She felt, falling asleep, she had nothing left to ask for.

After the giddiness of Christmas, the days that followed felt peaceful. Sylvie encouraged her to go out still in the mornings and Maud spent them wandering round the museums, but she left her sketchbook at home and let the works she saw flood over her. She studied individual works, feeling her fingers twitch with the urge to experiment, but avoided her easel. It was a holiday, after all, and should be treated as such. She strolled by the Seine, watching the smoke rise from the barges. It felt as though an early spring had come even as the weather continued cold and damp.

On 30 December Maud spent the morning at the Musée Carnavalet among the histories of Paris and admiring the caricatures of Jean-Pierie Dantan. After lunch she and Sylvie walked together in the gardens watching the students and their models eating pancakes which steamed in the cold air. Sylvie was affectionate, but seemed more subdued than usual. Maud wondered if she was preparing for another attempt to give up the pipe. Later she read contentedly in the flat and was surprised but pleased to hear Morel's voice in the hallway just before the usual hour for supper. She heard the brother and sister speaking but remained in her room until the waiter brought their food. She joined them with the expectation of pleasant conversation, but Morel was quiet and withdrawn. Sylvie was silent too. Maud wondered if they had received bad news from home, or worse, that Morel's business in Paris had suffered some reverse and they would have to leave at once. She was ashamed that her reaction to the idea of their leaving was purely selfish. She would have to find miserable lodgings again while the weather was still bitter, and although the money they had given her already would keep her going through the spring, it would not permit any comfort. She needed another month's wages for that. The way they both piled her plate high and filled her glass made her feel even more sure it was all going to be taken away. She ate and drank hungrily, like a peasant who has sneaked into a feast. When she could eat no more she felt a sudden wave of disgust at herself, the animal which fear of poverty had made her. She was too hot; the rich food had made her sleepy.

'Might we open the window for a moment, Sylvie?' she said at last.

'Not just now, dear,' she said without looking at her.

Morel wiped his mouth and stood up from the table. With a clarity that felt unnatural Maud noticed that his lips were still a little greasy with the sauce. He went to the side dresser and opened it with a key from his waistcoat pocket. Maud watched fascinated as he removed a small striped box and handed it to her.

'Could you tell us about this box, Miss Heighton?'

He looked so grave that she laughed. 'You know I cannot. I have never seen it before.'

He looked away from her, out into the street. 'Open it, please.'

She did so, though it took a slight effort to pull herself up from the table. She set it down, then took off the cardboard lid. 'I don't understand. What is this? Oh, Lord.'

The box contained a blaze of white light. Maud blinked to clear her vision and saw a tiara, made only it seemed of diamonds and air.

'Take it out, please.'

She did. It was far lighter than she had expected. There was one large central stone the size of a pigeon's egg, surrounded by curling fronds of smaller stones. 'I don't understand,' she said again, and reached forward to touch that central stone. It shone like the crystal glasses Morel kept for his whisky. 'Is it yours, Sylvie? Oh, my dear! Please tell me you didn't steal it!'

Sylvie gave a sharp bark of laughter and lit a cigarette. Morel continued to stare out of the window as he spoke.

'My sister found it in your room this morning, Miss Heighton. It belongs to Madame de Civray.'

'How could you, Maud?' Sylvie said.

Maud was confused; the room was so warm she could feel sweat trickling under her hair on the back of her neck. 'How could I what, Sylvie? Stop being so silly. I've never seen it before in my life, and it was most certainly *not* in my room this morning. This is some sort of joke. And it isn't funny.'

Sylvie was watching her with a sad smile. Morel remained at the window with his back turned. 'Some moment of madness, much regretted now I am sure,' he said.

Maud was too surprised to be frightened yet. 'Are you suggesting I stole it? You can't be. I would never do such a thing. Sylvie, you had all those packages with you. You must have picked it up by mistake.'

Sylvie turned to Morel. 'The Countess just leaves her treasures lying around – the temptation must have been too much. Have you not noticed how unhappy Maud has been this week, Christian? How distracted and upset? She has been walking the streets of Paris by herself.'

'The museums, dear,' Maud explained. 'You don't like them.'

Sylvie carried on as if she hadn't spoken. 'Without even taking her sketchbook. I think it began just before Christmas. And you know, Christian, I think she almost wanted me to find it. It was sitting on top of her bed, plain as anything.'

Morel smiled sadly at his sister. 'Perhaps the effects of opium have, as some have suggested, destroyed her moral sense. This cannot be forgiven, Sylvie.'

Maud tried to smile, her eyes going back and forth. 'Sylvie, Mr Morel, do stop. It's not kind. You know I've been happier these last weeks than I think I ever have been before. Do stop.' Her head swam and she put her hand on the table. Her limbs felt alien and unwieldy. She felt she had somehow forgotten the trick of moving them.

Sylvie sighed. 'The papers are full of such things. Poor women, trying to be respectable then falling into temptation. So sad. How long have you been a victim of opium, Maud?'

Maud tried to speak firmly, but her mouth had become dry and her voice came out thicker and lower than usual. 'I have never touched that drug, as you well know.'

'Please don't deny it, Maud. I thought I smelled some strange scent in the air but I had no idea, not until I looked under your bed after finding the tiara.'

'There is nothing there. You are talking nonsense.'

'Oh, but there is!'

Maud would wake up in a moment. Didn't this feel like a dream? Her body so reluctant to obey, her vision blurred. She stood up. There was nothing under the bed. She would show them and that would be an end to it. She had to keep one hand on the wall of the corridor to stop from falling as she went. They followed her and she thought she could hear Sylvie's sympathetic sigh as she stumbled. She shoved open the door to her room and fell to her knees by the bed, then stretched out her arm under it until she touched something. A tray. Her fingers feeling fat and unhelpful, she pulled it towards her. Sylvie must have put it there as a joke. Part of her stupid joke. She was a child at times. She realised she was speaking out loud, but the words were emerging ugly and slurred. She managed to pull the tray out from under the bed. It was not the cloisonné treasure of Sylvie's but a dented metal serving platter like those used in the most down-at-heel restaurants. On it was a cheap-looking brass spirit lamp, a bamboo pipe, a porcelain bowl the shape and size of a door knob. She picked it up, confused and lost in a deep fog that made her arms impossible to lift. The world began to feel very far away. 'That's not mine.'

Sylvie and Christian had come into the room after her and were standing just in front of her window looking serious and sad, and watching Maud as if she were some exotic, but faintly repulsive reptile. An elegant couple visiting the freak show. Maud could see the volume of Ruskin she had been reading lying open on the windowseat.

'Did you see if she was carrying anything when you left Madame de Civray's home, Sylvie?'

Sylvie tilted her weight to one side. 'She *was* carrying a few things, and she seemed very excited.'

'You had boxes – that box. I was carrying some for you but all I took from that house was the portfolio! The photographs!' The words stumbled through her lips and she was no longer sure if she spoke French or English. It seemed suddenly very important that they saw the photographs. If they did, they would understand. They would stop this. She half-crawled towards them, towards the side-table to the left of the door where the portfolio lay, but her hands wouldn't work. She fell towards them, knocking the photographs onto the ground as she went. Neither Sylvie nor Christian made any move to help her.

'Poor Maud!' she heard Sylvie say.

The last thing Maud was aware of was Sylvie stepping over her body to leave the room.

She was wearing her long coat and a hat with a wide brim. Her legs still wouldn't work, but someone was holding her up. The air was freezing cold and she could smell tobacco and brandy. It was a man – a man was holding her. She tried to push at him but her hand hardly moved. She saw it. Why aren't you moving, hand? she thought. It must be part of the same dream. She felt the grip the man had around her body tighten and for a second she was lifted onto her toes, then suddenly set down again. There was the sound of footsteps approaching. They echoed as if they approached down a long stone corridor.

'Everything all right?' said a male voice she did not recognise.

'Yes, all fine. The wife's had a bit too much to drink. Her sister's birthday.' That was Morel's voice, only he was speaking strangely, like a worker rather than a gentleman. Why was she here with Morel? There was another sound too. Water; water moving. No matter, it was just a dream – just a funny dream.

'Well, we'll all be like that tomorrow night with any luck! You need some help getting her home?'

'No, we'll have a little rest here, then it's only round the corner. Marriage, hey?'

'Too right!' the man said and laughed. 'Happy New Year!' Maud heard his footsteps fade.

'OK, my little rabbit? My sweet little cabbage? Oh, you're waking up. Not for long.' Morel was holding her face up towards him, his other arm tight around her waist. His face was so close she could see his eyelashes, delicate as the hair on a sable brush. The light came from above and from far away. She felt a high stone wall at her back and over his head she saw the blank silhouette of the Louvre. The lights on the far embankment were bright as starlight, their aura almost blue. He held her hard against him for what seemed like an age. No man had ever held her so close before. Then he looked to right and left. Such silence. She had no idea Paris could be so quiet and so full of shadows. She could hear someone whistling as they crossed the Pont des Arts above her head. Ah, so that was where she was, on the quayside under that long beautiful bridge, untroubled by horse or motor traffic. She could see the lace patterns of the ironwork. The song faded and the quiet returned; now there was just the lap of the water and the shifting of the boats tied up at the quay. None showed any light.

'Time to go, Miss Heighton.' Morel half-lifted her, half-dragged her a few feet. Her shoes scraped against the cobbles. She could feel the heat from his body. And then her right foot slipped over the edge of the quay and touched nothing. Something in her understood and she felt herself seized with panic. She started to struggle against him but she could feel the weakness flowing through her. He released her suddenly and she felt a sudden blow to her stomach, something between a push and a punch, sending her back into space. Too fast. This couldn't be. Only as she fell did she realise completely that she was awake, that this was in truth happening to her. She struck the water as if falling through glass; the water raged up around her white and freezing, leaping into the air in a shout of spray – then there was nothing but coldness and darkness as the river closed over her.

Part Two

CHAPTER 1

31 December 1909

*H*AVING CONSULTED AT LENGTH AND FOUND OUT who was likely to be where in Paris on New Year's Eve, Tanya's aunts informed her that they had accepted the invitation of the Swedish Ambassador to join his table at the Bal Tabarin in Montmartre. Tanya was surprised until her aunts told her that Perov was a great friend of the Ambassador and instructed her to make herself as pretty as possible. She had a rather sick presentiment that Perov was planning on asking her to marry him tonight. In a slight panic she sent Sasha to the telegram office and snapped at her French maid when she was trying to arrange various items from Lalique's latest collection in her hair.

The streets were full of the signs of festival as they drove through Paris. Music and light pouring out of the cafés, the buildings lit up and the crowds surging back and forth. They stepped out of their car on the stroke of ten. Tanya was nervous of being too early, but there was a steady procession of ladies and gentlemen entering under the canopy and they found the grand ballroom already full and loud with the galloping music of the can-can. The walls, balcony and ceiling were hung with great ropes of flowers, the musicians were sweating over their instruments and the whole hall was brilliant with coloured electric lights. As they made their way over to the long table where the Ambassador was entertaining his party, a group of women in huge picture hats were occupying the centre of the floor, dancing, kicking their legs up in the air to show the snow white petticoats beneath their hooped skirts. Aunt Vera lifted her lorgnette just as one gentleman got a little too close and found his hat knocked into the mocking crowd by one of the dancer's high-heeled shoes. Tanya paused, waiting to see if Vera would be too shocked to stay, but instead she laughed and watched the man struggle to retrieve his hat from beneath the feet of the crowd with apparent pleasure.

Tanya's heart sank a little. She was sure Perov meant to propose now and had told her aunts as much. Ribbons curled down from the balcony in a continuous stream of emerald and scarlet. 'I must ask for time to think,' Tanya said to herself. Above their heads hung large hoops filled with New Year's souvenirs. She could see paper flowers and model aeroplanes, cardboard cigarette-cases and matchbooks marked *1910*. She tried to look further into the crowd, but there was no one she recognised. So taken was she by looking at the faces in the distance, Tanya hardly noticed where she was being seated, but found herself next to a man her own age with an oddly pointed chin. The seat to her left was unoccupied, and for a moment she was afraid Perov would drop into it at any moment – but then she saw him at the far end of the table sitting between her two aunts and looking smug.

The man on her right was thin to the point of emaciation and told her he was a writer. He had a monocle squeezed into his right eye which seemed to require frequent polishing. He peered up the table towards Vera and Lila. They had insisted as always on wearing the styles of their youth in bright silks, and had bullied the weeping fashion gurus of Rue Royale into supplying them with puffed sleeves and pinched waists. Or rather Vera did the bullying. Lila laughed at her for it, then cheerfully wore whatever she was told to. It should have made them ridiculous, but the two women were swiftly surrounded now as ever by a number of young men in tight-fitting dinner jackets who fought for the honour of fetching them champagne and strawberry mousse. Tanya knew they would be trying to make her aunts say something shocking enough to amuse them, and had no doubt they would succeed.

'They are quite the success of the season, these Russian old maids!' remarked the writer. 'It shows how jaded we are become in Paris when our novelties are so . . . *novel* . . .'

Tanya took the flûte of champagne offered by a waiter bending low over her shoulder and looked at him coldly. 'You are speaking of my aunts, sir. Vera Sergeyevna is a widow, not an old maid.'

He seemed quite unabashed. 'Ah, you are the artist we have to thank for bringing them among us! Is it true you labour all morning in an attic and refuse any invitation that might take you away from your work?'

'There are many reasons I might refuse an invitation. I attend the classes of Monsieur Lafond, but that was my whole reason for coming to Paris – so how else should I spend my mornings?'

His expression showed a slight disgust. 'Oh, you will destroy yourself! Leave art and science to the men. It is in our nature to innovate, to adventure into new worlds, while it is woman's duty to support and inspire us. Do not make yourself a half-creature, learning to paint. You are in Paris – it is the place where you should learn to become a woman! To charm and infuriate, to drive us to new heights. *You* are the work of art, my dear. Stop your lessons now before your beauty fades and your charm dulls.'

'And what great heights has my sex inspired *you* to, sir?'

'I have had my successes, though one shouldn't expect the acclamation of the vulgar crowd for works of high art.' The monocle was polished ferociously for a few seconds and replaced.

'You must admire the genius of George Sand,' Tanya said.

'Naturally, but indeed, she proves my point.' He jabbed his long finger towards Tanya with such vigour that his monocle sprang free from his eye and swung on the end of its ribbon; such was his pleasure in the argument he ignored it. 'She was not a woman at all but a half-breed. Her genius *proves* she was not a woman but an hermaphrodite. And look at her! An unfortunate freak. Such intellectual activity crushes feminine charm like your own, the female mind becomes overheated and loses its bloom, its frivolous ability to please.' He smiled kindly. 'Come, Miss Koltsova, I am sure you must agree.'

'I do not. But as you think I am half-witted at best, I am sure that cannot be of the least concern to you.' She was aware as she spoke of a man sliding into the chair on her left.

'Gustave,' he said with an American twang to his French, 'I swear you will turn every woman you speak to into a suffragette. Hell, I listen to you for ten seconds and I want to bop a policeman over the head just to show fellow feeling.'

Tanya turned in his direction, aware that the room had grown suddenly brighter and warmer. 'Mr Allardyce! I did not know you were to be of the Ambassador's party.'

'Neither did I, nor the Ambassador until an hour ago, Miss Koltsova. Then I had a sudden and urgent need to change my plans for the evening. Now, have you had a turn around the room yet? There are lots of shiny lights and rich people in pretty frocks to look at. That should appeal to your feminine fancy, shouldn't it?'

She grinned into her champagne. 'It should.'

'Excellent. Then do stand up with me at once, but be careful not to look back in the direction of your aunts. I am fairly sure they will make it clear they wish you to stay in your seat if you do.'

Tanya got to her feet very gracefully and didn't look round. He led her to the edge of the dance floor to a stop where they could pretend to watch the dancers. 'Well, I am here. What's the emergency?' He spoke in English, his voice dry and tired.

Tanya fixed her eyes on the conductor of the band. He squatted and leaped as he led his musicians, exhorting them to greater efforts with extravagant grimaces. 'There is no emergency. I did not mean you to think such a thing.'

He raised an eyebrow. 'You certainly did. I'm sorry, Miss Koltsova – I've been working hard and that makes me more plain-spoken than usual. What can you want of me? I've chased you round town for a month trying to make myself amusing and dodging your aunts. You know, I don't think in that time I've seen you in the same dress twice?'

'Paul . . .' she whispered. He controlled himself and looked out onto the dance floor again. It was the first time he'd heard her say his first name, but there was such fear in her voice, such sadness. He looked around at all the show and spectacle and felt a black bitterness run through him.

'So it's true, then. Perov is going to ask you to marry him. I've heard the rumour. Have you got me here to make you an alternative offer?' Tanya's eyes felt hot. 'Sorry kid, but I can't make you one – though it's sweet of you to offer me a chance to counter-bid. I've nothing but what I earn, so if you were hoping I've got some railway stocks laid by, you're out of luck.'

The band leader sprang in the air and spun about, aping the movements of the can-can dancers. He looked to Tanya at that moment like a devil.

'You horrible, cruel . . .' She still looked straight ahead, a polite smile on her lips as if she were enjoying some pleasant conversation with an acquaintance. 'If that is what you think of me, why are you here? Even if I were stupid enough to agree to marry you, you would not want me, would you, without all . . . this!' She touched her evening gloves to the diamonds in her ears, the pearls and diamonds at her throat. 'You're just as money-minded as any millionaire in the room. If I didn't change my dress every day you wouldn't chase after me for long.'

'I'd take you in rags,' his teeth were gritted, 'but how could I ever live with myself afterwards, knowing the life you could have had? You'd make me a failure just when I am beginning to get my start in the world. I could never dream of keeping you in the style—'

'Keep me!' She faced him, hissing. 'Am I a horse, a dog? Offer me your arm and smile, you idiot, then take me back to your friend Gustave. At least he is honest about his contempt for women.'

He took her arm and drew her back towards the table, blistered with rage and feeling that though he was greatly injured, he was somehow also in the wrong.

He could not leave, though, but rather sat in heavy misery listening to Tanya sharpening her feminine charms on Gustave for the next hour and sinking every glass of champagne he could get his hands on. Then he noticed that the heavy hoops of souvenirs were being lowered just to within reach of the gentlemen's canes, so some of the souvenirs might be knocked down and claimed. Pushing back his chair with a violent scrape, he set out into the scrum, returning some minutes later rather red in the face and with his blond hair dishevelled.

Tanya looked up at him in surprise. He bowed very formally and presented her with his prize. It was a cheap cardboard cigarette-case printed with one of the advertisements of Bal Tabarin and a border of glass beads, glued not quite straight. She took it from him a little dubiously then laughed; her black eyes lit up and she pressed it to her heart. 'Mr Allardyce, I will treasure it.'

He sat down, feeling a glow of satisfaction that spread painfully from his stomach to his fingertips. She leaned towards him and said softly, 'I will ask for time.' The warm glow became ashy and cold.

'The horse could learn to talk,' he muttered.

'What?' He was about to explain when Tanya straightened and looked across the room like a pointer bitch who had spotted game. 'Oh, is that not Madame de Civray? Are you acquainted with her? A friend has told me about her and I would love to meet her.' She looked so enthused, her fingers were already drumming out a tattoo on the white linen.

'I do know her,' Paul said. 'I write for her father's papers about Paris affairs from time to time, so she invites me to her At Homes. Not that they're very exclusive. Shall I introduce you now?'

'Oh do!' and once again Paul offered his arm. He noticed before she stood up that Tanya slipped his cardboard cigarette-case into her shimmering evening bag and whatever else he felt, he was briefly as happy as he knew how to be. He ushered her through the crowd and subtly made space for them in the circle of the Countess's court, then when she had greeted him with a slight nod of recognition, he bowed and introduced Tanya.

'I am so delighted to meet you,' Tanya said, with a curtsy. 'My friend Maud Heighton told me of your kindness in showing her your collection. She is absolutely thrilled with the photographs and has promised to bring them to the studio in the New Year.'

The effect of this little speech was not what either Paul or Tanya had expected. The Countess's polite smile disappeared and her face became pale. 'You have not heard then,' she said, then looked around the faces of her friends. 'You must excuse me, dears. I have to speak to this young lady.' She took Tanya by the elbow and guided her across the ballroom floor to an alcove behind the band. 'Let us sit down for a moment, honey.'

Paul felt rather aggrieved. He half-followed the women, being discreet but keeping them in sight, watching them through the crowds of dancers. Midnight was coming up fast and the dancing seemed to be getting wilder. There were shrieks of laughter coming from all sides of the room. He could just see them through the bobbing and braying heads of the revellers. Tanya was facing him, and he saw her polite smile vanish, to be replaced by an expression of sudden shock. She had one hand over her mouth and was shaking her head. The Countess de Civray was holding onto her other hand and appeared to be speaking to her urgently. Miss Koltsova wrenched her hand away and bent forward, covering her face. The Countess looked round and caught his eye. Paul forced his way through the crowd towards them. He looked down helplessly on Miss Koltsova's shaking shoulders.

'Allardyce, thank goodness! Could you fetch Miss Koltsova's aunts and explain to them that their niece is unwell? Then speak to Monsieur Guyot at the front desk. Have their car sent to the back entrance at once. Hurry along now, there's a good fellow.'

He went off to do as he was told, leading the aunts to the alcove and arranging for the car. Then he remembered Tanya's evening bag and ran across the room to fetch it. When he returned, Tanya was already getting into the car. She took the bag, and as she thanked him distractedly, he tried to squeeze her fingers with his own. Her eyes were red but before he could ask anything or even tell if the pressure of his fingers was being returned, the more fearsome of the aunts reached across and pulled the car door closed;

he had to move quickly to avoid losing an arm. He slipped back into the ballroom before Guyot closed the door on him too and hurried up to the Countess.

'Madame, what . . . ?' She shook her head and pointed upwards. The apelike band leader was standing on the upper balcony with a pistol in each hand and both arms raised in the air. That instant, the lights went out and in the utter darkness twelve shots exploded, the muzzle flashes singeing the eye. The crowd counted in a great shouted chorus after each shot ' . . . *dix, onze, douze!*' The cry of twelve became a general cheer and the electric lights glowed and burst forth again. Strings of them in mauve and yellow were lowered from between the festoons of flowers that canopied the roof. The band let fly with a fanfare on the trumpets and the room erupted into more rolling cheers. As another cascade of ribbons came curling down from the balcony, the back doors opened and a succession of beautiful women, carried on platforms resting on the shoulders of men dressed as Roman slaves, began to parade round the room. Above her head each woman waved a flag sewn with large scarlet letters proclaiming *Love, Beauty, Peace* – and finally and most splendid in her bower, a girl under a stiff arch covered in paper roses and emblazoned *1910*.

Confetti fell over Paul's shoulders. The Countess had disappeared back into the crowd and the dancing had begun again, even less inhibited than before. Paul leaned back against the pillar behind him, exhilarated and confused. A red ribbon fell over his shoulder, and without thinking what he was doing, he curled it and tucked it into his breast-pocket.

CHAPTER 2

1 January 1910

*T*ANYA WOKE SLOWLY, BECOMING AWARE OF LIGHT and movement within the room. Her old maid Sasha was already there, bustling about Tanya's discarded clothes and books. As always, her first thought was, I am in Paris – and for one moment she was happy. Then her memories of the previous evening returned. She saw the Countess's face and heard her saying gently but firmly that Maud was a thief, and dead. Tanya squeezed her eyes shut. Her blood felt suddenly hot and painful in her throat as if she were choking on it. She had managed it all so beautifully; introducing Maud to Miss Harris and seeing her safely established at the Morels' for the winter, and more than that she been sure, *sure* that Maud liked her and that they were friends. She thought of the card Maud had made for her, and the sketch in oil she had done of Maud at work, her suddenly frank and open laugh when she had seen it.

Tanya could never tell if the Frenchwomen she met liked her or not. They treated her like a child, laughed at her for working at Lafond's when she could be sleeping and shopping, writing catty little notes to each other as they did and despaired over her every time she turned down some invitation in order to attend the evening lectures on anatomy. Whenever her aunts dragged her round the fashionable At Homes in the afternoons, their hostesses made sly jokes saying they hoped she would not get paint on their upholstery though she was better dressed than any of them. The aunts would not let her visit her friends from the studios where they lived, nor invite them formally to the house. Even Francesca, though her husband was at the German Embassy, was forbidden to dine with them. Apparently the Ambassador himself, a huge man who looked permanently bored, was a third cousin of theirs, and to invite the wife of one of his juniors to the house when he himself had only dined here twice would be a gross and grievous insult. There were rules about these things. There had been trouble enough when she had only hosted Maud for an afternoon, but as it had not been a formal visit and Maud had seemed perfectly genteel, they had let it slide in the end. Had she been too distracted by her interest in Paul Allardyce, the threatened proposal from Perov, to notice that Maud was still in real danger, in real need? She had seemed so calm and happy. She had not been terribly understanding about the pressure on Tanya to marry wealth. Tanya had thought perhaps that was just the famous English commonsense, something she could learn from that might in time make her stronger. Or perhaps it had only been jealousy, after all.

Tanya loved Paris, but she felt she was kept in a small, rigorously policed corner of it, and had been plotting a means to move the velvet ropes out a little way. She hoped in some part of her soul that if she spent more time among those people who worked for their living – practical men and women who did not devote themselves to fashion and leisure – she might be able to imagine a life among them. She saw Maud as an example. She was so moral, so correct and hardworking, no one could think she was not a suitable companion, but she intended to earn her own living when her training was done. Tanya had been carefully mentioning Maud to her aunts since she began to live in Rue de Seine, repeating the lie about her being the relation of a baronet, only making the relationship a little more vague. Weren't the Morels wise to have a young, respectable companion for Sylvie? Weren't they lucky to be able to practise their English? Wouldn't it be hard for Miss Heighton to go back to an ordinary, albeit respectable boarding house, when the Morels left Paris, having been so comfortable?

Tanya bunched the silk sheets in angry fists. Now Maud had ruined it. She had lost herself in opium. Could she have fallen so far without Tanya even noticing it? She had seen Maud's hunger and her hope that day in Parc Monceau, her longing for the comfort of the apartment in Rue de Seine. She must have been tormented by the idea of losing it again, and then, just at the season of Christmas when all the wealth and light of Paris is on display, so available if you have francs in your pocket, that stupid, stupid American woman had left her diamonds lying about. If Tanya had just told Maud her clever plan, that she should come here when the Morels left Paris, that she would save her from the cats, help her plan an independent life and laugh at the *mesdames* with her; if she had just said to her, 'This is my plan, Maud. Help me,' then the Countess could have left wallets of fresh banknotes around and Maud would never have thought of taking any. But she hadn't said anything, not wanting to disappoint, and now Maud was gone and everything was broken. It was her fault. She drew her knees into her chest and groaned.

'Oh, so you are awake, cabbage? Sit up and drink your tea like a good girl. I've held them off as long as I could but your aunts are pawing at the door. Fainting away in the car might have worked last night, but it ain't going to work this morning.'

Sasha arranged the pillows behind her, then handed the girl her tea. The cup started rattling in the saucer at once. Tanya's shoulders started to shake again and she sobbed. Sasha sat down beside her and lifted her chin in her hand. 'There, there, my little darling! No more crying! Are you sick?' Tanya shook her head. 'No one has been cruel to you?' Another shake. 'Bad news then? I wondered, but who do you know in Paris to cry over so? Not any of those fools who take you dancing when you'd rather be home, I'd lay my savings on it, and I have a few. Did Perov propose? Did he frighten you?'

'No, no . . . not that.'

There was a tapping at the door. 'Is she awake, Sasha?'

'Here we go! Now mind what you say! No scandal, no illness and no nerves! Vera Sergeyevna would have written to your father already this morning, demanding that you be taken home at once – if I hadn't hidden the ink.'

Tanya nodded and prepared herself as well as she could for the onslaught.

'Are you ill?' Vera Sergeyevna said before she even came to a halt by the bed, then without waiting for an answer, she turned to Lila and snapped, 'I knew this was a mistake and I told Sergei so! I did! "She is fragile, my dear brother," I said. "Do not send her to Paris! Her nerves will not take it." And see? I was right!'

Lila Ivanovna placed the back of her hand briefly on Tanya's forehead. 'She has no fever. Some private sadness? Has someone hurt you, Tanya?'

Lila's voice was always softer. She had been the first person to encourage Tanya to hold a pencil. If she had been with Tanya alone she might have soaked all her secrets from her, though what she might have done with those secrets was anyone's guess. Tanya shook her head.

'Poor Mikhail Pavlovich was *so* disappointed when we left,' Vera continued. 'And who could blame him if he decided he did not want a sickly wife, always pulling him away from his pleasure with her fits and fancies.' Tanya gritted her teeth. 'Your father will be extremely disappointed also. Perhaps we should get you back to Saint Petersburg at once. If you drive off the only suitable men in Paris with your fits, then we shall have to find you a husband there.' Tanya kept her head lowered, staring at the folds of her disordered sheets. There was a pause, then Vera said with the air of a visionary pronouncing, 'The Rhum Saint James.'

Tanya was startled enough to look up at her. Vera was standing with her fists on her wide hips. 'I'm sorry, Aunty Vera?'

'You haven't been taking it, have you?' Tanya dropped her eyes. 'You foolish, foolish girl! It was recommended to me by Monsieur Claretie himself. I am only surprised that you are not fainting away every day. I dare say my cousin and I would hardly be standing without its support.'

'I do not doubt it, Vera,' Lila said, and for a second Tanya thought she caught the ghost of a smile on Lila's lips.

Vera tapped her slipper on the floor, frowning, and her eyes fixed on the moulding in the corner of the room. 'Perhaps if Mr Perov is made to understand it was a rare lapse from your usual health . . . The richness of the Christmas diet without taking proper precautions. Men like women with delicate tastes as long as they don't cause too much trouble. Makes them chivalrous.' She sniffed hard. 'You must stay in bed today so I suppose we shall have to do the *whole* round of New Year's Day calls by ourselves. And no doubt every maid will want her tip. You are very thoughtless.'

'I am sorry to have been so foolish,' Tanya whispered. 'And to have ruined your enjoyment of the ball last night.'

'Oh, it is not for *myself*, dear, that I complain.' Vera swept her arm wide with the palm upright. She might have been performing Racine. 'Balls and champagne mean *nothing* to me. But your poor Aunt Lila was not brought up with the same luxury as I was. Your selfishness cost her a *unique* pleasure.' Tanya said nothing but kept her eyes lowered submissively, while Vera Sergeyevna sniffed again. 'I suppose we must go. It will show we are not seriously concerned for your health and we can convey to Perov your apologies for not wishing him a good night and a Happy New Year. If only you had not been talking so much to that American.' Tanya felt her heart clench angrily. 'Allardyce. He has sent you roses this morning. Foolish extravagance! No doubt the servants will talk.'

If Paul had sent her roses yesterday, Vera would have been able to tell what they meant to her, but today in the horror of Maud's death and disgrace, Tanya showed no signs of caring.

Her aunt was reassured. 'Well then. Go to sleep again. And take your tonic. What a *blessing* I never had daughters.' She leaned forward over the bed so that Tanya could kiss her powdery cheek. 'Well. Good girl.' She strode off while Aunt Lila bent for her kiss too.

'I am sorry I spoiled it for you, Aunt Lila.'

'I do not think you can help it. And I do not like the taste of champagne.' She straightened up. 'That young man Allardyce is clever. He wrote a note with his flowers, addressed to us. He was afraid that we would not have had a chance to collect a souvenir because of your falling ill and sent a little box of them; it was prettily done. But Tanya, your father will not support you if you marry him, and you can have no idea of the misery it is to be poor. I escaped it because my sister was beautiful enough to make your father love her and allow her to help her family. I thank her in my prayers every day.'

Tanya had no idea that Lila had seen so much or guessed so

well, but the mention of the misery of poverty made her think of Maud, not Paul, and she felt the useless tears gather in her eyes again. 'Poor treasure,' her aunt said again softly then Lila left the room in the purple wake of her sister.

When they had gone Tanya tried to sleep again but could not. Tried to write in her diary but could not. Sasha brought in Paul's roses and she barely looked at them. She was nothing but miserable. An hour after her aunts had left the house to begin making their calls, Sasha let herself in. She began to tidy up a little, straighten out the silver and pearl hairbrushes on the dressing-table, but all the while she was shooting sidelong glances at Tanya until the girl could ignore them no longer. 'What do you want, Sasha?'

'A little farm, two pigs and some chickens. You?'

Tanya gave a half-laugh, picked up a clean handkerchief from the bedside-table and blew her nose. The first of her angry grief had settled into dull misery, and she gave her answers automatically. 'Paint, canvas and a forest.'

'You can sit on the porch of my farm, if you like.'

'As long as I help feed the pigs.'

'That's right.' It was a ritual exchange and it comforted her. Sasha sat beside her and put her arm around Tanya's shoulders. The young woman leaned into her.

'Maud Heighton is dead, Sasha.'

The servant crossed herself. 'Lord have mercy on her! That nice English girl?'

'Yes.' They sat together in silence for a while and Tanya breathed in the scent of her old nurse's blouse. Sasha received a small bottle of eau de cologne from Tanya's father every year at Christmas and wore it, carefully rationed, every day. It made Tanya think of home. Eventually Sasha shifted.

'Lord, you're getting big. Thanks be to God. There's a letter for you.' She pulled it out of her blouse and handed it to her. It was slightly crumpled. Tanya wiped her eyes and opened it, but as soon as she saw it was addressed from Rue de Seine, she guessed it would be another account of Maud's death and she pushed it back into the envelope. 'And there's a person waiting for you in the kitchen.'

Tanya looked up. 'Who? Why didn't you tell me? Did she bring the letter?'

'A Frenchie. And no, she didn't bring the letter. Says her name is Yvette. Has the manners of a street cat. She can hold on while we have a cuddle, can't she? Anyway, I had to wait until Vera and Lila were well out of the way. Lord, they haven't changed. Those two were just the same twenty years ago.'

Tanya scrambled out of the bed and reached for her dressing-gown. 'Yvette from the studio? The model? Didn't you recognise her?'

Sasha crossed her arms and sank her chin into her chest. 'Models? How should I recognise her? I don't like to look.' But Tanya had already run out of the room.

Yvette was sitting in front of the fire with her feet up when Tanya came dashing into the kitchen. The cook was filling Yvette's coffee bowl for her and the model held a half-devoured meat pie in her other hand. As Tanya came in, she swung her legs to the ground and stood up, swallowing her food and wiping the crumbs from her mouth with the back of her hand.

'At last!' She gulped coffee from the bowl and gave a swift approving nod. 'Have you got any money?'

'What are you doing here? Why?'

'I'm here to get money, because I need it.'

'I'm not going to give you money for no reason!'

'It's not for no reason. I told you, I need it.'

'Why do you need it, Yvette?'

'Because I went on a spree over Christmas and I haven't got any at the moment.' Tanya stamped her foot and the cook found she had pressing business in the far corner of the room. 'All right! Don't fly at me! I can't tell you because if I do, you'll keep me here an hour, and I need to leave right now. But I swear, if you knew why, you'd be glad to give it to me.' She crossed her arms over her chest and looked Tanya straight in the eye.

Tanya drew a deep breath. 'How much do you need?'

'Oh sweetheart, I could kiss you. Twenty francs should do it for now. You got it in silver?'

'In my desk.'

'Then go and fetch it, will you? Come on, get a move on!'

Tanya obeyed in a sort of daze and when she returned she found Yvette pacing in front of the fire. The purse was snatched from her hand.

'Yvette, about Maud – have you heard?'

Yvette looked wary. 'Heard what?'

'That she stole a diamond tiara from Madame de Civray, then when the Morels found it she . . . threw herself into the river.' Tanya's voice broke over the last words.

Yvette looked stunned for a second, then thrust the purse into her pocket and swallowed more of the coffee. She was looking at the broad back of the cook.

'That's bad. Look, can you get away today? I'd like to talk to you.'

Tanya looked towards the cook as well. 'I have to stay at home,' she said clearly, while staring at Yvette with her wide, tear-reddened eyes.

'Shame. If you *could* get away you might look in at the bar next to my office and ask for Daniel. He might give you an address nearby.' Tanya nodded. 'Take heart, princess.' And then she was gone.

$\infty\infty$

Two hours later, Tanya found herself standing on the doorstep of a rather shabby house on Impasse Guelma.

'You brought your maid with you?' Yvette was standing in front of her looking angry and dirty with a dusty apron tied over her dress.

When Tanya looked up from under the brim of her wide hat, Yvette noticed that her eyes and nose were still red. 'I can't go wandering around Paris without Sasha.'

'But you sneaked out of the house!'

'Still, Yvette, there are rules.'

Yvette looked as if she was about to give her opinion of the rules then stopped herself and tapped her foot. 'Can she be trusted?'

'Of course she can. Yvette, what is all this about? I don't like going and asking for waiters by name in bars. If anyone had seen me – particularly when I'm supposed to be sick in bed . . . Is this your house?'

Yvette raised her eyebrows. 'No, it is not my house – and if you don't want to be noticed, have you thought of not wandering about in white satin with a maid, a chauffeur and a hat you could serve a roast boar on?'

Tanya touched the brim; it was loaded with wax cherries and feathers dyed green.

'Oh,' she said, and looked so surprised at the idea that Yvette laughed.

'You are priceless sometimes, princess. Still, I'm glad you are here, maid and all. Get your driver to go and wait in Place Pigalle though before anyone notices, then come on in. But mind your skirts. I've been cleaning for hours and the place is still as filthy as all hell.'

Tanya gave Vladimir his instructions, then Yvette ushered her and Sasha into the hallway and pushed open a door to the right of the uneven staircase. It led to a good-sized room, dim with shadows and dust. Broken bits of furniture were stacked against the walls, old packing cases and general detritus. In the corner, under the single window and next to a cane armchair was a single low bedstead. There was a girl lying on it under thin grey blankets. A wolfhound was stretched alongside her, one forepaw over the sleeping girl's shoulder. Tanya took a step forward and the dog looked up.

'It's all right, Tanya. The dog is friendly. Go and see who it is,' Yvette said softly.

Tanya felt a sudden lurch of hope and ran forward.

'Maud! Oh, *Maud*!'

The sick room oil on canvas 64.8 × 76.3 cm

This beautiful and unusual picture was once thought to be the work of Maurice Utrillo. It shows part of the walls and ceiling of a room as seen, we assume, by a sick person lying in bed. A small window is just in view at the top right of frame, though the sky seen through it is uniform cream white, and at the bottom left, note what appears to be a handful of holly stuck into the top of a bottle. Note also, however, the multitude of colours used to make up the grey of the walls. A picture that seems so empty is, on close examination, shimmering with colour interest.

Extract from the catalogue notes to the exhibition 'The Paris Winter: Anonymous Treasures from the de Civray Collection', Southwark Picture Gallery, London, 2010

CHAPTER 3

ANYA COLLAPSED INTO THE CHAIR BY THE BED AND burst into tears. Every few seconds she would wipe her eyes so she could again convince herself that the girl in the bed was her lost friend, then start to cry again. Yvette put a hand on her shoulder and squeezed, then moved away, biting the side of her thumb.

Sasha had followed them into the room. She closed the door and crossed herself on recognising Maud, then started examining the stove in the centre of the room. After a minute or two she opened it and began to work on the fire. Tanya managed to stop crying. Maud's eyes had not opened and her breathing sounded uncomfortable, viscous. Her skin was bluish-white and her hair was plastered to her forehead with sweat. Tanya touched her brow with the back of her hand and felt the heat of a high fever.

'Oh, Yvette! I think she's very ill.'

'Yup.'

Yvette had settled into a beaten-up armchair at the other end of the bed, her legs hooked over one of the arms and swinging. Her mouth was a thin line and Tanya noticed for the first time how tired she looked. Sasha appeared to have finished work on the stove. It did seem to be giving off a more even heat now. She approached the sickbed as Yvette and the wolfhound both watched her suspiciously, and took Maud's hand. The girl was sleeping very deeply, somewhere beyond sleep. Sasha said something to Tanya without looking at her.

'She wants to know if a doctor's seen her, and if so what he said.'

Yvette shifted in the chair, pulling her legs beneath her. 'That's where half your money went. He gave her a draught of something – laudanum, I think. Though, bless her, she didn't like it much. Ended up with half of it down his shirtfront. He said to keep her warm, and try and get her to eat. Keep her quiet and wait it out. She'll live or she won't.'

Tanya blinked rapidly then spoke briefly in Russian. This provoked an angry-sounding stream of words from the maid. Yvette watched, amused in spite of herself as Tanya tried to interrupt, but she never got further than a syllable. Eventually the maid ran out of breath and put her hand out. Tanya meekly extracted some coins from her purse and handed them over. The maid tied her shawl over her grey hair and stalked out of the room.

'You know, I think I like her,' Yvette said at last. Tanya bent over Maud and brushed a strand of hair from her face.

'Sasha doesn't like doctors a great deal, but she knows how to look after the sick. She'll cook up something foul-smelling on the stove and it'll help. I hope. What happened, Yvette? The Countess told me she'd stolen the tiara . . . How did you find her?'

Yvette watched as Tanya carefully removed her hat and set it, after a microscopic hesitation, on the floor beside her chair. 'I have no idea what happened. One of the river rats turned up at the party last night at the Bâteau-Lavoir looking for me. His father pulled Maud out of the river two nights ago and would have sent for the gendarmes straight away but she bribed them not to. Asked them to let her stay until she recovered.'

'But why did she send for you?'

'Because she didn't recover, you ninny. She gave them the rest of her money to come and fetch me. At least, I suppose she did. I couldn't find another penny on her. Anyway, the kid found me. I guess his people don't like the cops much after all, so that might be another reason they bothered coming to me. So I went and found her.'

'Was she awake?'

Yvette swung forward in her chair and put her head in her hands. 'Not really. She recognised me and said some things, but the only bit I could understand was I must not take her back to Rue de Seine so I thought of this place. I spent all my coin on the cab to get us here. Miserable bastard, that cabbie was. Oh, I hate them, snooty self-satisfied lot.' She stared angrily at the floor. 'If I'd spent a bit less at New Year I could have got a doctor sooner.'

Tanya pulled up the blankets over Maud's shoulder; the dog stirred and then settled again. 'Sasha will help. God would not give her back to us then snatch her away again.' Yvette looked unconvinced. She stood up and began to pace. 'Do you think she did it? Stole that tiara, then threw herself in the river?' Tanya asked. 'The Countess said it was very valuable.'

'I don't know. I'd have laughed in your face if you suggested such a thing last week. I've been thinking about it every second since you told me. She's frightened of something. So maybe she did take it, but . . .'

'But what, Yvette?'

She put her arms out. 'I don't think she's *stupid*, Tanya! If she wanted to steal from the Countess, there must have been a dozen little things lying around. Why take a bloody great tiara? Something impossible to sell, that would be missed? It's the sort of thing a child would take if it wanted to dress up.'

Tanya nodded slowly. Her right hand went up to her earlobe, twisting the pearl she wore there. 'But the temptation . . . being poor is difficult.'

Yvette shifted her weight to one hip and lifted her eyebrows. 'Is it? It's hard, is it?'

'I mean for a girl like Maud . . . Oh, don't look like that at me, Yvette. The Countess said she was a dope fiend.'

'Rubbish. She's been reading too many detective novels.'

'No, she said Morel told her so! He said that Maud was addicted to opium and had been stealing his sister's jewellery and selling it.'

Yvette paused, then shook her head. 'Then I don't believe a word of it. This stinks, Tanya.' She turned on the Russian girl, suddenly triumphant. 'She had money enough on her to bribe the bargemen. The kid said she had coins sewn into her skirt hem. That's not what a dope fiend does. As soon as they have a franc, they spend it on what they need. They don't spend hours at classes, or sketching when there's some spare cash. Anyway, I'd have known if she smoked in any of the Paris dens.' Her voice was bitter and tired.

'How?'

There was a long pause while Yvette pulled at a loose thread on her cuff. 'Because I would have seen her there. There aren't many places to smoke in Paris, but I know them all.'

'Oh, Yvette!' Tanya said.

'Don't "oh Yvette" me. I'm not a fiend. Just sometimes . . . When you have a pipe in your hand you don't have to worry about anything else, about growing old or having no money or a way out. You are just happy. And I don't do it often. And Maud would never . . . I mean, look at her. She's English!'

'You're right,' Tanya said after a pause. 'It does stink.' Then her voice rose a little. 'I just don't understand what's happened.'

'Oh, give me strength! Will you stop saying that, princess? Who does?'

There was a long silence. Tanya blushed and Yvette felt awkward and cruel.

'Where are we?' Tanya said quietly at last. The stove was crackling away now and, looking around, Tanya could see the work Yvette had been trying to do. The floor had been swept, though it was only bare boards and there were still piles of dust in the corners of the room. There were other stools and chairs against the walls. A table, its broken leg tied together with string, stood between the bed and the wall. There was a clean glass and water jug on it and behind them a vase improvised out of an empty wine bottle with sprigs of holly in it.

Yvette pushed the hair off her face. 'A friend's place. Suzanne Valadon has rented it as a bolt-hole now she's left her fancy banker boyfriend for her new lover. I knew she'd never last long as a bourgeoise. She has the studio upstairs, but she'd no use for this room and wanted to sub-let it. That's where the rest of your money has gone. Rent.'

'We are safe here?'

Yvette nodded. Then: 'There's no way to know what happened to her until she wakes up. *If* she wakes up, the poor chicken.'

'You like her, don't you?' Tanya said after a pause.

'I do.' Yvette sat back down again and sighed. 'Most women in Paris seem only to think about being looked at. It makes me sick sometimes. *She* watches.' Yvette stared up at the cracked grey plaster of the ceiling. 'You think she's just all bound up in herself, then she'll say something and you realise she's been listening.'

'It's your job to be looked at, Yvette.'

She yawned. 'It pays. As you so cleverly observed, being poor is difficult. Though when my looks have gone I'll end up scrubbing those rooms I've modelled in for forty centimes an hour. If I'm lucky.' She shrugged and bit her knuckle.

'I told Maud I always sew money into my clothes in case of emergency.'

'She listens, she learns.' Both women were silent for a while, listening to Maud's painful, dragging breaths.

'Oh, Lord,' Tanya said, and began rummaging in her purse.

'What?'

'Blast, I know I have it. Sylvie Morel wrote to me. It arrived this morning. I couldn't bear it, so I just . . .'

Yvette was on her feet at once and almost grabbed the bag out of her hand. 'How the hell could you have forgotten until now!'

Tanya looked up. 'I thought Maud was dead. I brought it to show you, didn't I? Oh, get your hands off, you're not helping.'

Yvette lifted her palms and backed away. At last Tanya pulled out a blue and slightly crumpled envelope. 'Oh, look. She uses the same stationer's as I do.'

'Tanya!'

'All right. You may as well come and read over my shoulder.' Yvette scurried round behind her and leaned on the back of her chair.

'Move your head, will you, and hold it steady.'

Tanya straightened the pages with a vicious snap. 'Better?'

'Much.' For a few minutes they were silent. Tanya turned the page and read on. Four sheets in all. They reached the end and Yvette whistled. Tanya's neck had turned an angry red. 'It is just the same story the Countess told me. But I don't believe it. They are lying.'

'What's their game?' Yvette said. 'Why make her out to be a thief?'

'I don't know. They gave back the tiara, so what could they possibly . . .' Tanya read part of the letter out loud. ' "*My brother and I visited the Countess the same afternoon she returned to Paris, yesterday*" – New Year's Eve, in other words, "*and returned the tiara. She most generously agreed never to repeat the story of the theft publicly in order to safeguard Miss Heighton's reputation. We feel though that you, as a friend of poor, lost Maud, deserve the fullest explanation.*" Well, that's nice of her. Oh, Yvette, what are we going to do? Can't we go to the police?'

Yvette hunched her shoulders. 'And say what? *Someone* took the tiara and the Morels gave it back. Maud's poor. She'd be in prison before she even wakes up. Let's stay out of the way for now until she can tell us what happened. You just look sad and say nothing.'

'What about our host?'

'Valadon? She won't say anything. Too bound up with her lover boy and enjoying her freedom. She's been giving dinner-parties in the suburbs for the last year, so she needs it. Says she can't stop painting.'

Tanya nodded. The door was pushed open and Sasha reappeared with a basket over her arm, uttering a stream of complaints in Russian about the shopkeepers of Paris. Then she began to unpack her cures.

CHAPTER 4

2 January 1910

*T*HE FIRST TIME MAUD WOKE AND WAS SURE IT WAS not a dream, she found herself staring into the eyes of a woman; a square-faced stranger with chestnut curls of fringe hanging over her fierce black eyes. She blew a lungful of smoke out of her nose like a dragon.

'The mermaid wakes!' Her voice was dark and low. 'Got all your senses this morning?' The face did not wait for an answer but retreated, leaving Maud looking up at a low ceiling supported by heavy blackened beams. She could not see properly. Her lips were dry and her throat ached; her head was thick with pain that struck her skull from within with every beat of her pulse. She tried to think. The tiara, the river. Then she had been on a boat with a smoking stove in the corner; there had been scolding and question-ing, another ugly and suspicious-looking woman with a baby tied onto her back watching them, then she had been taken somewhere else in noise and darkness. Lights seemed to blister and break in her eyes.

Maud tried to lift herself onto her elbows. The iron springs of the bed groaned and fought against her. She saw a room, the woman standing against the wall with a cigarette. She seemed very far away now. There was a bunch of holly in a bottle near to her. Something warm moved next to her and she started, only to see some huge tawny dog was sharing the bed with her. He stirred as Maud moved and wagged his feathery tail a couple of times before settling against her again. She reached out to touch his warm flanks.

The woman was dressed like a respectable bourgeoise. She wore an apron over her blouse and skirt, and her over-sleeves showed traces of paint. There was a twist to her mouth.

'I think Hugo was a monk in his past life,' she said, indicating the dog. Her voice sounded to Maud as if it were coming from the bottom of a well. 'One of those who used to patch up the knights when they were off crusading. He finds whoever is sick in the house and stays with them while they are in danger.' Maud lay back down again, her belly cramped with nausea. 'There's water there. Can you hold your glass?' Maud turned and saw it and reached over the dog's head to take the glass and drink. It took all her strength. The light fell in through a single smeared window. It was a grey, comfortless sort of room but it was not Rue de Seine and it was not a prison cell and it did not move under her.

'Who are you?' she said. The effort of speaking set off a fresh cascade of pain.

The woman came closer and Maud saw that her long fingers were stained with nicotine.

'I am Suzanne Valadon, Artist. And you are Maud Heighton and either a dull little student of the Académie, a victim of terrible injustice, or a rather pathetic thief. Which is it?'

'I didn't steal anything,' Maud managed to say.

Valadon dropped her cigarette and ground it out on the floor. 'Your friends don't seem to think you're a thief.' She folded her arms in front of her and studied Maud's face. 'The Russian princess, the French model and the English miss. Sounds like the start of a bad joke or a good brothel.' Maud said nothing and Valadon laughed. 'They think your friends in Rue de Seine set you up. Yvette tells me they've been saying you're an opium fiend. Perhaps I am harbouring a dangerous criminal.'

Maud reached for the water glass again and finished what was in it. Criminal. Opium. Thief. 'It doesn't seem to worry you.'

Valadon gave a one-shouldered shrug. 'Why should it? I have nothing to steal.' She walked round the bed and took the glass from her hand before Maud dropped it, then filled it up again from the jug. She was older than Maud had thought at first. There were lines around her eyes.

'Where am I?'

'My house. You're my first lodger. We're in Impasse de Guelma on the Butte.' She gave Maud the glass and this time she drank greedily but the burning pain in her head and throat continued.

'Montmartre?'

'With the drunks, *apaches* and the only artists worth a damn. Thrilling, isn't it?'

Maud felt sick. Her stomach ached and her mouth tasted of riverwater; pain pressed into the side of her head. She handed the glass back to Valadon. 'I didn't steal anything,' she said again.

Valadon replaced the glass on the side-table. 'No. I think if you stole something, you'd hang onto it, wouldn't you? Till they broke your fingers to get it away.' She put her head on one side, watching her. 'I think that they made a mistake, your friends in Rue de Seine.'

Maud lay back on her pillow and turned her face towards the wall. 'You seem to know a lot about it.'

That low gravelly laugh again. 'Oh, I do. It's my job now to watch you while your nursemaids are out pretending to mourn you. It is the second of January, by the way. You missed New Year. Welcome to 1910.' She sat down on the cane chair. 'Did you throw yourself in the river?'

'No. I was thrown in.'

'How calmly you say it. Interesting girl. They didn't know who they were trying to kill, did they? I've seen you sleeping with your jaw clenched so tight the muscles on your neck stand out and your fists pulling the sheets apart. There's a little fighter in there under the English manners. A little demon. Your friends in the Rue de Seine would never have risked throwing you in the water if they'd seen you sleep.'

Maud stared at the plaster on the wall by her head. It was unpainted, but in the pale grey were a hundred points of colour. Mud browns, ochre, yellow, moments of titanium white . . . they shifted and blurred and she closed her eyes.

'What is it like to drown?' Valadon asked.

'I don't remember.'

'Liar.' She stood again and went to the stove. 'The Russian's maid left this soup. I'm to spoon it down your throat whenever you are awake or Yvette will scream at me. Sit up a bit, will you?'

In the early evening Tanya arrived and exclaimed to see Maud open her eyes. Maud managed to squeeze her hand and the Russian burst into tears. She found herself being fed again, this time by the Russian maid. For the next three days her periods of consciousness were still short and painful. She was aware of Yvette from time to time curled at the bottom of the bed, reading. The dog continued to share her bed, leaving only occasionally, and when she woke she was grateful for its animal warmth. Valadon flitted in and out, taking her turn at feeding her when the others were away, and other footsteps hammered up and down the stairs outside her door. There always seemed to be people laughing or arguing in Valadon's studio from late afternoon until dawn. The daylight hours passed in moments, a series of shaking snapshots. The nights were long and suffocating. Then at last the hours began to mean something. The dog returned to Valadon, and Maud realised that this, as much as anything else, meant she would live.

That afternoon, when Yvette and Tanya arrived, she began to ask questions and Yvette told her the story of her rescue, the doctor. Tanya told her about her meeting with the Countess on New Year's Eve.

'Do they not miss me at Lafond's?'

Tanya hesitated and for the first time the name Morel was spoken in the room. He had been to see Lafond with the same story. At first her teacher was sceptical, but he had visited the pawnbroker's office and the shop in Petits Champs, and the Countess herself. After that, he was just amazed. Tanya had suggested they say Maud had been called home over Christmas and Lafond had agreed.

For the first time, Maud told them what she could remember of that last evening in Rue de Seine; the accusation, the strange heaviness in her limbs and her collapse.

'Laudanum, probably,' Yvette said quietly and continued to bite her nails. About those last moments by the river Maud could say nothing, and her friends, watching her carefully, did not press her.

At first Tanya would not read her the letter from Sylvie that described Maud's crime and suicide, but Maud insisted, and Tanya, seeing the fierceness in her eyes, felt afraid and relented. Valadon had drifted in, escaping the chaos of her studio to listen. Her son

Maurice and some of his friends had been drinking since the previous evening and she had grown bored with them and come to look at the women instead. She lounged against the doorframe smoking, her wolfhound at her feet while Tanya read the letter with her rolling Russian accent. Sylvie wrote that a number of small items of jewellery had gone missing in the weeks since Maud had arrived. Her brother had successfully traced them to a pawn shop near Rue Croix des Petits Champs, and the man remembered Maud. She mentioned the sweet, sick smell of opium that they had tasted in the air coming from Maud's room. They said they had tried to speak to her, but she had denied everything. Only when they found the tiara had she become wild, and fled the house in spite of their efforts to restrain her. Christian had gone out in pursuit, only to see her throw herself from the quayside. He had raised the alarm, but the river had already swallowed her. Sylvie concluded by saying that the tiara had been returned and the Countess was deeply sorry that poor Maud had been tempted.

Tanya put her hand on Maud's shoulder. Her body was stiff, rigid.

'Maud? Sweet-one? *Did* you go to the pawn shop?'

She closed her eyes. 'Yes. Sylvie was the opium addict. Morel told me the first day. I went for her, to the pawn shop, to get money to buy the drug.'

'Of course she went there,' said Yvette. She was sitting on the floor with her back to the bed and her knees drawn up. 'They wouldn't write it if they couldn't prove it. "Oh Maudie dear, could you just pop in with this" and little Maud does it because she's so grateful to the nice rich people for feeding her.'

'Sylvie needed it,' Maud said. 'She'd thrown away her supply and was suffering for it. I was trying to help.' She felt her heart clench tight like an angry fist. 'How was I to know?'

'Needed it, did she? Was she throwing up? Doubled over in pain? Cramps in all her bones? Covered in snot and shaking so hard you could hear her teeth rattle?'

'No,' Maud sighed. 'It was not like that.'

The French girl shrugged. 'Then she was faking a nice polite version of needing it for you, Maud, to set you up. If you'd seen what needing it really looks like, you would have run away.'

Tanya gave a little gasp. 'Yvette, you've . . .'

'No, I've never been that way. But I've seen it and it's enough to stop me from visiting those places most days.' She scratched the back of her neck. 'People die.'

'But *why* did they do all that?' Tanya said, still holding the letter in her hand. 'What was the reason? They gave the tiara back. Why go to all this trouble and expense to make Maud look guilty of a crime then give it back?'

Valadon straightened and the dog immediately scrabbled up and yawned. 'Stop asking questions and send that girl home,' she said. 'They wanted her dead. She's alive. She was strong enough to live through the fever and the police aren't looking for her. That means she's winning, as far as I see it. And whatever scheme the Morels had – who cares?'

'But . . . ?' Tanya protested.

'Who cares?' Valadon said again. 'We live, we die. You've got deep pockets, Tanya. Pawn a bracelet yourself and put her on a train tonight. She's got family. Send her back to them and let the rest lie where it lies.'

'They told the Countess I was a thief,' Maud said thickly.

'What? The nice Yankee Countess? Yeah, I know her and I can just imagine.' Valadon bunched her fists and rubbed her eyes. ' "Oh no, that nice English girl was a thief! I am so sad! Now what shall I wear tonight?" And the Académie? The girls are wasting good colour and fat old Lafond is grateful the scandal's not going in the papers to scare away his shit-eating sycophants.' Tanya blushed.

Valadon swept her eyes over them. 'Go home, Maud. You'll never be artists, either of you. Princess, you want everything to be pretty and Maud, you want everyone to think well of you so neither of you will ever tell any truth worth a damn.'

'Leave me alone, Suzanne,' said Maud. 'Madame de Civray was kind to me.'

'Oh, you moth,' Valadon answered, her voice cool. 'Now I shall leave you babies and go back to my work.' She looked at Tanya. 'God, women are stupid sometimes.'

CHAPTER 5

10 January 1910

*I*F IT HAD BEEN A FINE DAY TANYA WOULD HAVE HAD
some warning, but the rain had been falling steadily, thin
and unbroken all morning, so Passage des Panoramas was unusually
full when she left Lafond's at midday. There was a slightly low
feeling in the air. The shop windows were offering discounts on
Christmas goods and everything seemed a little shabbier, more
grey than was usual in Paris, but still the Parisians came out in
flocks to shop and crowd into the covered passageways to hunt for
pretty bargains out of the rain. At times like these, when the gold
and black shop-fronts and the polished mosaic floors were hidden
by crowds of silk-lined coats, and the thick low bodies of the men
seemed to press near to her, Tanya felt smothered.

Now she was free of the distractions of her work, the image of
Perov in evening dress making his proposal returned to her.
Thinking of it was like pressing on a bruise. He had come to dinner
with her and her aunts as a close family friend, as if the thing were
settled already. He had enjoyed his port and cigar, then as soon as
he came into the drawing room to join her and her aunts at the
tea-table, Vera and Lila had remembered urgent errands in other

parts of the house and left them alone. Perov took a seat next to her, made himself comfortable and began to speak as if their marriage were already agreed. He spoke of where in Paris they might live and the size of house he thought suitable; it was some minutes before Tanya could interrupt him.

The memory was strongly tainted by the smell of cigar smoke, the stale sweetness of wine on his breath. Eventually she managed to break in and ask for more time before committing herself to be his wife. He was offended, pursing his lips and blinking rapidly. Only when she forced herself to smile shyly and ask submissively for his patience and understanding did he seem mollified. At no time did he express any sort of feeling for her. He was telling her the result of his negotiations with her family, not asking for her love. Tanya thought of her father and her aunts, the comforts and security of her life. The idea of being without them made her afraid. She had never met a problem before that could not be solved with money. How could she make problems go away without it?

Paul Allardyce she had seen only once since New Year, once again while walking in the Bois and with her aunts on either side of her. She could only thank him for the roses and look at him with a sort of desperate appeal, but he looked at her as if she was something he had already lost. At this thought, she turned her eyes upwards to the glass and ironwork roof of the passage, the light grey and the glass rain-spattered, trying to convince herself there was air here, there was space, but she felt caught in some low deep current.

Some of the men tried to get out of her way, others did not seem to notice her in their hurry to peer in at the shop windows, and her world was crowded with high shoulders in dark cloth. She was starting to pant. It had been useful to her many times in her dealings with her father, her ability to make herself faint when the drama of the moment required it, but it meant she was now liable to faint when she really didn't want to at all. She was just about to break free into the rainswept freedom of Boulevard Montmartre when she felt a touch on her arm and turned to find herself face-to-face with Christian Morel. She stared at him, horrified. His smile became uncertain.

'Dear Miss Koltsova, I am so sorry if I frightened you. I have been waiting here hoping for a moment of your time.'

Her concerns for herself disappeared like smoke in the wind and at once her nervousness in the crowd became simple rage. She wanted to strike him. She wanted to beat him to the ground and shout *murderer*. She had a vision of this pressing crowd closing over him, kicking his worthless body on the slippery stone floor till he was rags and nothingness. He gestured to the little table thrust into the crowd where he had been sitting. There was the half-drunk coffee of the murderer, the folded copy of *Le Matin* the thief had been reading. She wished for a knife, for a gun, for the strength to pick up the table and smash his head in with it while the crowd cheered. 'Might I ask you to join me? Just for one moment?'

She managed to nod and he pulled out the other chair for her. His fingers brushed the back of her coat as he pushed it back in for her and it was all she could do not to turn round and spit in his face. The waiter hovered: no, Miss Koltsova required no refreshment but M. Morel would take another *petit noir*. He watched her while he waited for it to arrive. Tanya looked at the shoes of the men and women passing by. She could not kill him. She must be clever. He thought Maud dead, and he must not suspect otherwise. So Tanya should show not rage, but what? She thought hard of what she should be feeling as the low-laced boots of some idle Parisienne pivoted into the shop opposite. Grief and shame for her friend? With a sickening turn she realised she should be apologising to him, for helping to introduce a drug addict and thief into his home. She was already trembling – well, that would do for grief and shame. So much the better. His coffee arrived and he crossed his legs and sat back while he drank it. She glanced at him. So handsome and so respectable. She pulled a handkerchief from her pocket and touched it to her eyes, preparing her performance.

'I cannot believe this has happened, Monsieur Morel. Poor Maud. I should have answered your sister's letter.' He could take it how he pleased; she could not manage more at first. He set down his coffee cup and nodded. He must be here to see if I believe them, she thought. Why? Because I am the one person who might ask questions, who might have known Maud well enough to see he is a murderous lying thief. *Oh, why haven't you gone away? Why aren't you in hell?* She lowered her face, then lifted it again and looked straight into his deep brown eyes. 'I had no idea her case was so desperate. The mention of opium in your sister's letter was a terrible shock. I am so sorry. I did not know her as well as I thought.' She blinked rapidly.

It was a tiny change in him, a slight relaxation in his shoulders, in the muscles of his face. The smallest disturbance on the surface of a pool fading and leaving it darkly smooth again.

'I hope you do not blame yourself,' he said. Tanya concentrated on her own hands. 'Remember, we lived with Miss Heighton for some weeks and were thoroughly deceived.'

'You are generous,' she breathed, her mouth ashy.

His voice was comfortable now. 'I have sought you out for two reasons. The first is, I know Miss Heighton had relatives in England. She mentioned a brother? I can find no trace of their address in her belongings and Lafond does not have it; his correspondence to her was always addressed to the post office. Hiding her ambitions from the respectable lawyer brother, I suppose. I hoped you might know it. We must write to them, but perhaps it would be kinder to say she met with some accident, rather than reveal the full ugly story.'

'Her family have a right to know the truth,' Tanya replied quickly, then groaned inwardly – too fierce. 'Don't you think, sir?'

'Even in such circumstances as these?' He shook his head slowly, his smile indulgent. 'No, Miss Koltsova, you have the proper convictions of your youth. But I think that at times it is kinder to lie. Why poison whatever memories they have of her?' He sighed and was serious, stroking his black eyebrow with the tip of his index finger. 'Paris, Paris. So beautiful, so full of traps. Even the most virtuous can find themselves . . . lost. Do you have the address?'

'I do not.' She tried to concentrate on the newspaper between them. The wife of a former Governor of the Bank of France had been found dead. MYSTERY OF A TRAGIC DEATH the headline read, then just below it: *Was she assassinated?* Tanya looked away quickly.

'How unfortunate. I have left my address at the Académie, but I think my sister and I will be leaving Paris at the end of January for America. If no one comes in search of her before then . . .'

The thought of Morel pawing his way through Maud's possessions was repulsive. The headline kept pulling her back. *Yes, she wanted to scream, yes, she was assassinated!* She moistened her lower lip.

'I have no plans to leave Paris until the summer,' she said slowly. 'If her brother comes, I would be willing to see him, and pass onto him anything you care to leave with me.'

She could feel the gentle smile in his voice as he replied, 'You are too kind.'

'It is the least I could do in the circumstances.' *I want to tear you apart with my teeth. I shall buy a dog the size of a wolf, like Valadon's, only with a warrior soul, and he will hunt you over the city, run after you until you are sweaty and desperate and screaming.*

'There are her painting materials, of course. And her sketchbooks. Her clothes we thought it best to give to the poor.'

'Perhaps you will have the rest sent to me.'

He smiled. 'As it happens . . .' he gestured to the floor under the marble table, and for the first time Tanya noticed a small suitcase sitting there. 'I had hoped you might have the address and I could write my letter here and now. It has been difficult for my sister this last week or so, knowing these things were still there in her room.'

A huge dog, with great powerful jaws to rip your lying throat from your body.

'Naturally that would be uncomfortable for your sister, Monsieur Morel. I shall take them with me at once.' Tanya stood and he did the same before picking up the case and handing it to her. She hesitated. 'Madame de Civray? What did you say to persuade her to keep this affair quiet?'

Morel gave a half-smile. 'Oh, the dear Countess – she is as sentimental as every other American I have met. They are like children.' He stroked his eyebrow again. 'She was distressed indeed to hear of Miss Heighton's fate. I am convinced the tiara means very little to her. She hardly looked at it, and the suggestion that the theft be suppressed was all her own.'

'She is a good woman,' Tanya said fiercely, then afraid she had been too emphatic, managed to smile. 'I shall take proper care of these things, Monsieur Morel. Thank you for letting me take them.'

He bowed and she walked out into the street and out of his sight before stopping on the pavement and lifting her face so the light rain could freshen her skin. Sasha lifted the umbrella over her head and waved to Vladimir.

'Was that the man, pudding? Oh, I knew it! Oh, he looks like my cousin's eldest – and a devil that boy is. Half the bastards in the village are his.'

'What shall I say to Maud, Sasha? He wanted to write to her family, but he hasn't the address.'

'Tell her that then. And be grateful you haven't worse news to share. Now are we going to that old tart's place or not? I've more soup for Miss Maud.'

Maud heard Tanya's voice in the hallway, shouting up a greeting to whoever happened to be in the studio above. One of Valadon's regular visitors was a crazed Italian. He came almost every day and Maud could often hear him, slightly muffled by the floorboards, declaiming Dante as he sat at Valadon's feet while Maud lay drifting in and out of an uneasy sleep below them. The door was pushed open, and there was Tanya as bright as morning with her peasant maid trotting behind her and a fat bundle in her arms.

'Dear! How are you this afternoon?'

The maid began clucking round the stove at once as Tanya trotted up to the bed.

'Better.'

Tanya felt her forehead with the back of her hand and tutted. 'But still not well. Not to worry, Sasha has driven half the French staff out of the house roasting bones and making all sorts of jellies. They taste horrid, but they've cured me every time I've been ill.'

Maud managed to smile, but Tanya became serious. 'Now, my love, I am not sure how to say this to you, so I am just going to talk very fast.' She did, watching Maud's face. Maud made no sound, so Tanya watched the colour in her cheeks, the white of her throat.

Eventually she ran out of words and set the suitcase down on the floor. She could hear Maud's breathing.

'Perhaps I should have kept quiet. Should I put this out of sight?' Maud nodded and Tanya crouched by the bed to slide the case underneath. There was nowhere else to hide it, after all. She remained crouching and put her hand on Maud's arm, trying to read her expression.

'I can't bear that they should go on in the world, Tanya. I know what Valadon said, but I bet if they had done this to her . . . Why? Why should I run away?'

Tanya nodded. 'The whole time I was talking to him I was longing to shoot him through his black heart – if I could find it.' She moved till she was sitting on the floor by the bed, her chin on her arm next to Maud's face. 'Perhaps if you shot him and we explained what happened, they would forgive you.'

'I would like that.' The two women were silent for a while. Sasha turned from the stove and sighed when she saw Tanya curled up on the floor. She decanted her soup and shuffled over with it. Tanya smiled when she saw the bowl. It was one of a grand dining set Vera Sergeyevna had brought from St Petersburg, stuffed in straw and only produced on the most splendid of occasions. Sasha had obviously taken a liking to Maud. Tanya wrinkled her nose when she smelled the soup, but Maud showed no sign of distaste and took the bowl carefully. Thinking about shooting Morel had calmed her a little.

'How do you say thank you in Russian, Tanya?'

'*Spaceeba*.'

'*Spaceeba*, Sasha.' The old maid blushed and she patted Maud on the shoulder before returning to a stool by the stove and rummaging around in her workbag for something to mend.

Maud was just finishing her meal when Yvette came charging

in, her hair and coat damp with rain. She kissed Sasha before dropping the coat over a chair and throwing herself down on the bed. 'Urff, what a day. Rain and rain. And nowhere warm in this whole damn city. Let me share your blanket, Maud, there's a dear. I've spent the morning freezing my tits off for Adler, then when he's done for the day it's all, "Sorry – I'm a bit short at the mo! Come back for the rest on Tuesday when I've sold my canvases!" Arsehole. No one's going to buy his stuff for more than firewood. The canvas was worth more before he started daubing all over it.'

Tanya tutted. 'Why do you have to be so crude, Yvette?'

The French girl shifted round to look at her. 'Why do *you* have to be so prissy? You know I've got tits. Painted them often enough, yourself.'

'It's not ladylike!'

'*Ladylike?* Oh, save it for the ballroom, princess! I thought all you ladies loved my dirty comments. It's as close as you virgins can get to roughing it in Paris, isn't it?'

'I wish you'd stop calling me a princess. I'm not! And even if I were, it's not my fault.'

Maud put the soup bowl carefully aside and lay back down. 'Oh stop it, both of you. Yvette, Tanya saw Morel today.'

Yvette's eyes widened and she gathered the blanket round her and burrowed across the bed so she was closer to Tanya. 'No! Tell at once! That bastard. How did you keep from throttling him?'

Tanya launched into her story at once while Yvette cooed and whistled. 'Thank God he didn't have your address, Maud. You think he was checking whether you believed them, Tanya?'

'I think so.'

Yvette reached forward to stroke Tanya's cheek with her knuckles. 'Clever girl. Oh, by the way, has Perov proposed?'

Tanya picked up the pearls that hung around her neck and

began running them through her fingers like a rosary. 'Yes. On Saturday.' Morel had driven the thoughts of Perov out of her mind. Now they came back, she could almost smell cigar smoke again.

'And?' Yvette said, her eyes wide.

'I asked him to let me finish the spring classes at Lafond's before I gave him an answer.' The pearls were twisted so tightly around her fingers their tips turned pale and bloodless. In the quiet they could hear the rain beating in sudden squalls against the high window. 'My father has written to me. He talks at great length about the advantages of the match.'

'And Paul Allardyce?' Maud said, shifting on her bed so she could see Tanya's face.

'He doesn't ask me to choose. He just stands by and watches. I wish he'd just take me away. I'd go with him if he did, and I think he knows that – but he does nothing.'

Yvette got more comfortable in the bed, making the springs groan. 'How can he? Oh Tanya, we all know you love the poor man and don't like the rich one much. How is waiting until Lafond's spring classes are done supposed to change that?'

Tanya scowled. 'I don't know. But something might happen.'

'The horse might learn to talk . . .'

She looked round at Yvette. 'What does that mean? Paul said it, and I don't know what it means.'

Above them there was a muffled exchange of shouts and the sound of something being thrown across the room. They all looked upwards and waited for the drumroll of footsteps down the stairs and the front door to slam. Another of Valadon's family dramas.

Yvette put her arms over her head, stretching out her shoulders. 'It's a story. A man is about to be executed but he says to the King, "Don't kill me. If you delay chopping my head off for a year, I'll teach your horse to talk." The King says, "Fine, go ahead," and the man's friend says, "What are you doing? What's the point in that?" The man says, "A lot can happen in a year. I might die, the King might die. And who knows – the horse might learn to talk."'

Tanya frowned over this for some moments then said quietly, 'Am I the horse?'

Yvette laughed under her breath, then clambered off the bed and kissed Maud's cheek. 'Come on, Tanya, let's leave Milady here to rest.' Tanya got to her feet, still looking thoughtful, and they left their friend to the sound of the rain and what good sleep could do.

CHAPTER 6

M AUD WAS WOKEN BY A PEAL OF LAUGHTER FROM above. It was deep dark outside, and she lay still for a moment, wondering if she could get back to sleep again. Upstairs, someone had begun playing the flute. It was a strange, open song. Almost too subtle, too gentle, flowing on as if the rules of music meant nothing to it. The voices grew quiet. Maud swung her legs out of bed and lit her candle; match after match failed until she managed it. She remembered Sylvie's shaking hands over the opium lamp, the feel of her skin as she took the matches from her. She tried to stand, bent over and still half-leaning on the bed. Her muscles were weak and complaining, as if they had forgotten the way to keep her upright. She waited, then stood straight in the shadows. It was a small victory but it felt like her first in a long time. The wooden floor was cool, almost soft under her bare feet.

She knelt down carefully, leaning on the bed again as she did so, then reached beneath it till she touched the varnished wicker of the suitcase. She pulled it slowly towards her, unbuckled the leather strap and opened it. Her materials were all in their usual places; her sketchbooks just as she had left them. She looked at her hands, spread out the fingers then relaxed them again. It was almost two weeks since she had drawn anything, and her fingers felt stiff and old. It was the longest time she had gone without drawing since she was an infant.

She undid the ribbon that held her palette to the inside of the upper lid; it tilted into her waiting hand and she saw tucked beneath it her oil sketches, one of Tanya and some from the atelier, and the painting of Sylvie, all where she had left them, pressed flat against the lining of the case. She laid them down to one side without looking at them, then pulled at the slippery upper lining of the case with her fingernail until it came loose. There was her collection of fifty-franc notes, her savings from her time with the Morels. She stared at the notes in her hands as she had done on that first night, but rather than feeling rich, looking at them now she felt a tearing darkness in the middle of her chest. This was what she had cost.

She put the money back in its hiding-place and was about to replace the oil sketches, but the portrait of Sylvie stared up at her and she could not put it away with the rest. All the while the flute continued to play, meandering, exploring the air. She placed the painting on the floor while she tucked away the others, then twisted round, her legs folded under her, to look at it properly. The candlelight gave it movement, as if the smoke of the pipe was still moving in the air. She reached forward and touched the line of Sylvie's shoulder, feeling under her fingertips the texture of the paint. How had these things come back to her, found her among the dead?

She closed her eyes and she could see Morel in her room, in black and white like a film, his movements jerky, bundling her few clothes up to send to the poor, burning the cards she'd left by her bed in the fireplace, leafing through the sketchbooks and wondering if they could be turned to his advantage, an opportunity to check that the story had taken.

Maud opened her eyes and let her fingers brush Sylvie's hair, half-pinned up. The interview with Sylvie and Morel on that last evening came back to her in all its details, the injustice of it, the cruelty. She tried to believe she had seen in Sylvie some softening or regret, but she could only think of her casual ease as she stepped over Maud's body after she collapsed. For a moment Maud felt too sick to live. She was nothing, she had meant nothing, and she had not belonged in those comfortable rooms. She belonged nowhere. She bowed her head and listened to the slow flow of the flute then she clenched her fists. A sigh went shuddering through her, then she stood, staggered a little, set her jaw and found her balance. The wall of her cell was covered in drawing pins. Holding her painting by one corner she shuffled across the floor then pinned up the portrait where she could see it from the bed. As she turned away, the strange song of the flute ceased and there was a burst of applause, cheers and whistles. A man was calling for more wine, someone began to scrape at a violin.

Maud stumbled back into her bed and pulled the blankets round her. Her eyes closed, and with terrible familiarity she found herself returning to the scene of her drowning. The waters and darkness surrounded her as soon as she slipped into sleep. The shock of the cold never lessened. Her confusion was as complete as it had been in that first moment. Horrified, betrayed, stupid and trapped in her useless body. 'It will be over soon,' the dark water said to her. 'Breathe me in and you will never be lost again. Let go, and be with me.' For a moment in her distress she did let go: warmth, peace soaked through her and pulled her down. Then her self called out to her. Images and sounds. She saw her mother dead, her father drunk. She held her little brother Albert in her arms and whispered him promises, she threw dirt into her father's grave and watched her step-mother ride out of town, blowing kisses and waving like a spring bride. She tried to move in the water, close her mouth to it. The lonely warehouse full of rotting cast-offs. She cheered the flames chewing up the walls, roaring and ripping apart the humiliation of the place with their red and yellow teeth. *Not like this.* She would not die like this.

She pushed against the black waters, broke the surface and sucked in air and water – one breath, two – before the drug and the cold pulled too hard on her and took her down. Once more she fought, once more for the hours spent sketching in the Louvre, for every moment she had been hungry, for the loneliness and the fear; once more for the betrayal, the cruelty, the easy violence. Rage lifted her, the phoenix on the opium box. Another breath, and she was spent and fell again. If she heard the shout from the boatman, the flurry of activity from her rescuers, she did not know it. She drowned; she slept.

When she woke, Valadon was standing by the painting of Sylvie. Maud shifted in her bed and Suzanne looked over her shoulder.

'This yours?' Maud nodded and stretched her fingers. They were sore and stiff every time she woke. 'You're not as shit as I thought you would be.' Valadon whistled and her wolfhound trotted in from the corridor. She crouched to greet him, taking fistfuls of his fur in her hands and shaking him while she shoved her face into his neck. The dog panted and wagged its tail. She looked back at Maud. 'I'm going out. There's coffee there and more of your soup. God, I love that old maid. What a face!' She stood back up and lifted her arms above her head. 'No rain this morning. I shall run up the hill and down again before I pick up a brush today.'

'Suzanne? Thank you.'

The older woman lowered her arms and smiled crookedly. 'Don't think of it. We are at home to every waif and stray here. You're just the latest. When I die I shall go to Saint Peter and he will say, "Suzanne, you've been a very bad woman, but I have to let you into heaven anyway because you are kind to outcasts".'

Maud smiled. Her head felt clearer today. 'And because you are a great artist.'

Valadon lit a cigarette and walked towards the door. 'That should count for something, shouldn't it?'

'Suzanne, I need to write a letter.'

'Can you make it down to *Le Rat Mort* on Place Pigalle? They'll have all you need there.'

Rain oil on board 35 × 25 cm

It would seem from the fountain, just glimpsed in the background, that the painting is seen from the perspective of the interior of *Le Rat Mort* café on Place Pigalle, Montmartre. The café was a favourite for the artists and models of the area during the Belle Époque. Note the strong sense of movement from right to left across the secondary frame of the café window; figures dash past the viewer, sheltering under umbrellas or with their coats pulled over their heads. Note as well the heavy yellow light in the atmosphere and how the rain shows itself in the disturbances in reflections, the thinned and distorted edges of the gutters and figures seen through glass. *Rain* is a tour de force that makes us feel we too have just escaped a cataclysmic storm.

Extract from the catalogue notes to the exhibition 'The

Paris Winter: Anonymous Treasures from the de Civray Collection', Southwark Picture Gallery, London, 2010

Maud should not have left her bed, let alone the house in Impasse de Guelma. She paused from time to time as she dressed to sit a moment and wait for the faintness to pass. She had only the clothes she'd been drowned in. They had been laundered and pressed, but she seemed to put the waters on with them and shivered. There was a broken mirror propped up behind the washstand. She wiped it on a corner of the bedsheet and looked at herself. Strange, she looked much as she remembered, only thinner in the face and with dark circles under her eyes. The good effects on her health of her stay in Rue de Seine had been wiped out when her hosts tried to kill her. She almost smiled at the thought then began to pin up her hair. The movements were familiar and mechanical and she wondered at them. How could anything be the same? Yet her fingers twisted her dark hair into the usual neat pile on top of her head and the pins held.

She pulled out the suitcase from under the bed, took out the sketchbook and turned to the last empty pages. It was still there, Madame Prideux's *carte de visite*. She tucked it into her pocket, along with one of the fifty-franc notes.

On the Boulevard Clichy a man sat on an upturned tea-chest playing a violin. On his knee perched a little monkey in a red jacket with its own tiny instrument and bow. A long chain ran from its neck to the man's waistcoat pocket. It watched him, copying his movements, checking and chattering. The trams rang their bells all the way along the road in front of them. The sky was an orange-grey and Maud was not sure if it was the weather or her own illness, but the air seemed to press on her. She looked up.

'Find cover, miss,' the violin player said. 'There's a storm not a minute away.' He started to pack up his instrument as he spoke. He stood and the monkey clambered swiftly up from his lap to his shoulder and crouched under the rim of his broad-brimmed hat. The man touched his forefinger to it in salute and sauntered up the road.

Maud crossed the clanging and blaring boulevard in the crowd, protected from the motor-cars by the mass of people around her, and found a place in the interior of *Le Rat Mort* just as the first fat raindrops began to fall. She sat in the warmth and comfort of the interior, listening to the civilised murmuring of the morning customers behind her, the snap of newspapers being opened and the chink of spoons on china cups as the readers stirred sugar into their bitter black coffees. All the surfaces were freshly polished and glowed with reflected electric light. Before the writing materials and her coffee had arrived the street outside was washed with rain, the gutters choked and plashed. The atmosphere outside was strangled with a thick yellow glow and the people fled past as if the thunder had let demons loose on the streets. She looked at the paper in front of her, let her head clear and began to write.

Maud was worse that afternoon, and when Sasha was told her patient had been out wandering the streets in the morning and got caught in a shower on her way home, she let forth a stream of Russian that Tanya refused to translate. Yvette grinned up from the floor. 'I think we get the idea.'

Maud pulled herself up in the bed and drew the blankets around her.

'Tell her I'm sorry, but I had my reasons,' she said. For the first time she told them about the strange visit of Mme Prideux to Rue de Seine, Morel's bloody story of the Commune and Sylvie's casual announcement that the lady had died in a traffic accident.

'Why didn't you tell me then, Maud?' Tanya said. She looked upset. Maud shook her head, not knowing how to answer.

'They had you all tied up, didn't they, sweetie?' Yvette said sadly. ' "Sylvie smokes opium – but don't tell. Here are more of our secrets about the crazy lady because we trust you." You weren't going to gossip once they had you all grateful and helpful. I'd lay money that was why she pretended she'd chucked her supply that day – same day that she told you Prideux was dead. Nothing like making people feel part of your secrets and troubles to keep them quiet and loyal.'

Maud hugged her knees. 'You're probably right. Anyway, I wrote to Prideux's son at the address on the card this morning. I told him I had met Mme Prideux and gave a hint at what Morel said of her. Then I wrote that I was thinking of investing money with Morel, but what she had said before her accident gave me pause. I mentioned that she called him Gravot too.' Tanya had been softly translating for Sasha and the old lady looked startled and afraid, tutting and crossing herself as she listened and worked the stove.

'Could that be done? To kill someone in traffic? Do you think Morel killed her?' Tanya asked.

'Yes,' Maud said, wondering what it felt like to be well, to be free of this creeping sickness in her stomach, the pain in her head. 'Tanya, I wrote the letter in your name. I'm sorry. That means the answer will come to you.'

'Nothing easier than killing someone in traffic,' Yvette put in. 'Friend of mine died like that last year. I always thought her lover pushed her out into the road. He was so jealous and she liked to tease him.'

'You were right to do that, Maud. And I'll bring any reply as soon as it comes. My aunts will think I'm getting love letters, but as long as it's not post-marked Paris, it should be fine.'

'Where do they think you are now, your cats?' Yvette asked.

'At the Louvre. It is one advantage of Perov proposing – they don't want to parade me around so much and it makes my request to stay on at Lafond's seem more sincere if I spend all my free hours in the galleries. I have more time to think now.'

CHAPTER 7

14 January 1910

*Y*VETTE WOKE COLD AND UNCOMFORTABLE, HER head a little thick from the night before. *Tant pis.* She had needed a bit of a spree after spending so much of her time in a sick room, but she had not gone to one of the smoking dens and lost a day. That was good. She could be pleased at that, even if her head was pounding. The damp had got into the blankets and it was like trying to warm yourself with fog. She pulled what she could grab around her and shut her eyes, trying to will herself back to sleep. There was a groan next to her.

'Yvette, you demon! I shall freeze.' An arm snaked round her waist and pulled her back towards the middle of the bed. She could feel the strong lines of his thighs pressing against her own. One hand stroked up from her belly and cupped her breast. She could feel his stubble on her neck. 'You'd better warm me up again.'

She was tempted. Then his other hand pressed on her bladder and she wriggled away from him and out of the bed. The floor was icy under her bare feet.

'Oh, warm yourself up! I'm off.' It was light already. She trotted behind the screen and squatted over the pot while he laughed.

'Why can't you be like little Marie? Stay here and sit by my side and darn my shirts. Play the housewife. I bet Marie keeps her friends warm in the mornings.'

Yvette emerged and started looking for her stockings. 'Why should I care what she does?' Damn, another hole. Still, it wouldn't show. 'Harley? Can I ask you something?' She sat down on the bed beside him as she put on the stockings and pulled the ribbons tight.

'Anything!' He propped himself up then looked more serious. 'My allowance from home doesn't come for another week, but I do have a few francs still. I'll share, even if you don't darn my shirts.'

She grinned and kissed his forehead. 'Save your money for paper and ink, there's a good boy. No one keeps me but me. But I wanted to ask you: why would you steal something, then give it back?'

He yawned. 'Depends what it was.'

Yvette studied him. He was two years younger than her, and at times like these, all tousled and sleep-warm, he looked like a child in a false moustache. He had come to Paris from London to write, but as far as Yvette could tell, whenever he was awake he was in one of the bars that clustered round Place du Tertre, talking and arguing with other young men. When she asked to see what he wrote, he said he was still gathering material. She was always happy to see him and liked talking to him about books. He blushed when he looked at her, which she found more touching than any practised flatteries. When he had money, he was generous and when he was poor, he did not ask her for her cash so sometimes she went home with him even though she knew his room would be cold and there would be nothing to eat.

'Say, like a diamond necklace, something like that,' she went on.

'You planning to rob someone?'

She leaned over him to pick up her skirt and stepped into it.

'Fine, if you can't think of anything. I just thought, you're supposed to be a writer, have some imagination or something . . .'

'No – wait.' He sat upright and rubbed the back of his neck. 'What, give it back straight away?'

She sat back down and leaned against him, facing the other side of the room. 'No, maybe a week later. Say you blame somebody else for it. Say you found it and are now returning it.'

'Like the honest girl you are.'

'Exactly. But you're not honest. You're not very honest at all.'

He put his arm round her waist again; his forearm lay across her narrow belly and she stroked the hairs on it as if he were a pet.

'Maybe you're not giving it back. Maybe you're giving back something that just looks like it.'

Yvette snorted. 'I don't care who she is, a woman will recognise her diamonds.'

'Are you sure?' He sounded enthused, as if the idea had caught him. 'I mean, what if you lever out a few of the stones and replace them with good glass imitations or something? Then the woman gets her necklace back, it looks the same, feels the same. Most of it *is* the same and you get to keep a few diamonds.'

Yvette stopped stroking his arm. 'You could get a lot of money like that, couldn't you?' she said.

He stretched back out in bed again. 'I suppose you could, if you knew what you were doing – thousands and thousands.' He sighed. 'I wouldn't know a diamond if I found one in my glass.'

Yvette sprang up and struggled into her blouse. 'If one turned up in your glass, you'd swallow it before you even saw it. I need my shoes.'

'Over by the door. Are you really rushing off? I hate to see you go. Perhaps I've fallen in love with you.'

'Men fall in love with the woman who is leaving or the one who has just arrived.' She stepped into her shoes and picked up her jacket from the back of the chair. He was looking miserable.

'Do you like me at all?'

'When you say clever things, I do.' She bent over the bed and offered her cheek to be kissed. '*Au revoir*, Harley.'

He took his kiss then rolled on to his side to watch her go. 'What clever thing did I say? I'll say it again.'

⌒⌒⌒

Tanya brought the letter to Valadon's that afternoon.

Dear Miss Koltsova,

My thanks for your condolences. As to your questions, I can only say it causes me great pain to reply in detail, but I feel it is my duty both to correct any errors and give you fair warning if possible. I have never heard of anyone named Morel, but the name of Gravot is only too familiar to me. If my mother told you this man you know as Morel is in fact called Christian Gravot, then that is who he is – and a worse scoundrel has never walked the earth. He is a thief and a confidence trickster.

Forgive the vigour of my expressions, but from your letter I must conclude you have been told a number of slanderous lies about my family, and it grieves me excessively. I am therefore willing to lay before you the true facts regarding our dealings with Christian Gravot and his wife Sylvie, which led to my mother's sad derangement.

My father was not a rich man, but he was honest. He worked as a clerk in our town hall from the age of fourteen until his retirement. He was awarded a medal for his distinguished service in 1893 and died in the autumn of 1905. My mother was housekeeper to the Widow Rochoux in our town from her marriage until 1907. She was a loyal servant, and on the death of her mistress she was generously remembered in that lady's will. That same lady also provided for my education and that of my brother: her generosity has allowed us to become professional men. I am now senior partner in our town's law firm. My brother holds a similar position in his wife's native city. As these simple facts must make clear we are a family devoted to respectable service.

It is not the story of my mother and myself you have heard, but that of Madame Claudine Gravot and her son Christian, the snake you know as Morel. He was the child who saw his father's body defiled, not I. You ask yourself perhaps how can I assert this with such confidence? I shall tell you. He and I are of an age and were school fellows in our youth. He told me the story himself, though I knew his mother beat him for doing so. Gravot wished always to be admired, courted and respected, but as he had neither the station, learning nor character likely to inspire such feeling, he instead told and re-told his lurid stories to gain the attention of the weak-minded and lead his more impressionable fellows on tours of petty and spiteful vandalism in our town. I was glad to leave his company. When he heard news of my improved prospects, he made an enemy of me. He was not unintelligent, and I think resented the opportunities offered to me and my brother. I shall not distress you with the details of his campaign against us; let me just say it confirmed him in my mind as a twisted and malicious child.

In 1883 at the age of eighteen he stole a diamond necklace

belonging to one of the rich ladies who come and take the spa waters in our town from time to time. He was transported to Guiana for the crime. His mother owned a grocery store in one of the less pleasant quarters in town and died, bitter and spiteful before the new century began. I sold the business on his behalf and sent him the money when he returned to France at the end of his sentence. What happened to him between that time and his reappearance in our town in early 1908, I cannot say. He returned here with a wife and some appearance of wealth shortly after the death of my mother's patron. He made great show of being a reformed character, and as such was welcomed into our community. His wife, Sylvie, was charming and beautiful though very young, and he himself seemed to have acquired a great deal of polish in his years away.

I am deeply grieved to say I did not realise how intimate this young couple had become with my widowed mother until it was far too late. My only excuse is that I had recently become a father myself for the third time, and had also taken on new responsibilities in my work. I deeply regret I was not more aware, but I was, in truth, as taken in by Gravot's reformation as my mother was. I was simply glad she was not lonely.

The couple left our town in the middle of last year. Shortly afterwards, my mother came to me in some distress. It was only then I learned that she had 'invested' with Gravot all that she had inherited from my father's modest estate as well as from her benefactor. She had also been persuaded to raise money against the value of her small house for the same cause. She believed she had invested in a diamond mine in Angola of all places, but the papers she had from them were worthless. That it was a gross criminal act is without doubt, but Gravot and his wife had so phrased the documents as to make the money appear a gift. My mother was not practised at reading legally phrased documents and had trusted the young couple too much to do more than sign them.

The house my parents had shared through forty years of marriage was sold and my mother joined my own establishment. Her last months with us were not happy. She felt both humiliated and angry, and nothing my wife or I could do would make her accept what had happened or see the impossibility of seeking redress. She would take no ready money from my hand, and sold what trifles she still possessed to fund her trip to Paris. I had hopes that her stated plan – to come to the capital for the sake of a little pleasure – was a sign of her recovery. I suspect now from your letter that my hope was false: she went to Paris in order to search for Gravot and his wife, and it is evident that she found them. She was missing for three weeks. I fear to imagine how she must have spent those days. I brought her body back from the city the week before Christmas and she rests now next to my father.

I close with a word of advice which I hope you will heed, even if it comes from a stranger. If you have not yet handed money to M. Gravot, do not, under any circumstances do so. If you have, consider it lost. I also request that if you have repeated to anyone the slanders of M. Gravot regarding my family, you will correct that error.

Begging you to accept the assurances of my best regard,

Jean Prideux

The women read the letter in turn.

'The poor woman,' Tanya said at last, handing the letter back to Maud.

Maud nodded and wondered about her own behaviour when Mme Prideux had arrived on her doorstep. If only the old lady hadn't been so frightening. She had shut the door on someone who might have saved her – all to protect the peace of the monsters within. The thought made her afternoon black and kept her from sleeping half the long, dreary night.

CHAPTER 8

15 January 1910

*T*HE DAY AFTER THEY RECEIVED THE LETTER FROM Jean Prideux, Maud woke late. She was still weak, and the pain of her continual headache increased once she had hastily dressed and gone outside on the street. The bells of the trams rang and jangled, the horses struck their hooves on the cobbles and the motor-taxis darted among the omnibuses, their iron wheels tearing the road. She crossed Boulevard de Clichy and hugged the west side of Place Pigalle. A huge clock hung above the *épicerie*; it was already a little after twelve, much later than she had thought. She glanced across at the fountain. Only a few women were there, lounging and smoking cigarettes. Other women in their long winter coats and furs shepherded children in sailor hats along the pavements, making for home or the park in hopes the showers would keep off. The two groups were from different worlds and blind to each other.

Maud stumbled against one of the tables set outside *Le Rat Mort*. A waiter, his hair and moustache so slick and oiled they looked freshly painted, started towards her, his look something between concern and suspicion as he tried to decide what world she belonged to. When she straightened up and gave him a slight nod, his face flickered with recognition, and with a cautious bow he let her pass by.

Maud tried to step a little more firmly after that, down the hill along Avenue Frochot, but had to pause and lean against a wall as soon as the bend in the road provided her with a moment of privacy. The people passing might think her drunk, she knew. Her clothes were respectable but she had no hat, no gloves, and in Paris everyone stared. A policeman might pass at any moment. She forced herself to walk on till she found herself in Place St Georges and at the Countess's front door – then before her courage could fail her, she rang the bell.

The butler showed her into the library and took her name. He was English and recognised her accent as that of an educated woman. The library seemed to serve the same purpose in France as it did in England, a place to receive that doubtful class of person one could not introduce immediately into the salon, but whom it might be dangerous to leave waiting in the hall to be gossiped over or noticed by other guests. Maud did not sit down, unsure if she would be able to stand up again if she did. Instead she rested against the window that opened out onto a pretty little garden at the back of the house. It was all in greys and purples at this time of year, sage greens and soil. Earth tones. There was a fountain in the centre of the lawn, silent now; the mermaid pouring nothing into the little pond under the rock on which she sat. A gardener was pulling dead leaves out of her granite hair.

The door was thrown open and Maud turned round to face the Countess. The American cried out and looked behind her as if unsure whether she needed to summon help. Maud felt the familiar nausea and weakness in her limbs. Her head swam and her legs, tired and unwilling, started to give way. I will wake in a prison cell, she thought, and it will be my own fault. The Countess crossed the room and caught her as she fell, lowering her down onto a sofa with an arm around her waist. She was stronger than Maud had expected. Maud didn't quite faint, just breathed steadily till the sensation of falling and spinning began to fade, and opened her eyes.

'You are not a ghost, I think,' the Countess said and released her. Her voice had become calm but her tone was fierce, the words sharply enunciated. 'Has someone been playing a trick on me, Miss Heighton? Is someone laughing at me?'

Maud could only shake her head.

The Countess leaned forward and rang a little bell on the table. Maud stiffened, but when the butler bowed his way in at the door, she only asked him to bring brandy and water. Maud began to speak, but the Countess lifted her hand – no. The brandy arrived on a silver tray with tumblers cut from crystal rather than the great balloons at Hôtel Chopin. They looked as if they'd been blasted from ice. When the Countess filled one and put it into her hand, Maud was surprised the glass was not cold. The Countess then poured herself a generous slug and knocked it back like a worker in a cheap bar. She stared into the empty glass as she spoke.

'That man Morel came to me on New Year's Eve and handed me my tiara. He said you stole it then threw yourself in the river out of guilt, so now I have to ask myself, Miss Heighton, was there some mistake? Or did you steal it, but just not feel that guilty, after all?'

Maud felt the brandy burning her throat and coughed. 'I did not steal it.'

'So you just picked it up and forgot to put it down?'

Maud felt herself being watched now. The Countess was sitting on the edge of the sofa, her empty brandy glass held by its rim with the fingers of her right hand. Her left hand supported her sharp chin. She looked wary now the first shock of seeing the dead girl walking had passed, caught somewhere between suspicious and angry and not sure which way to jump. Her eyes travelled over Maud's face, back and forth.

'I took nothing, and I did not throw myself in the river.'

There was a tap at the door and the butler reappeared. He addressed the air somewhere above their heads.

'Madame, there is a Miss Koltsova demanding to see you. She says she is a friend of Miss Heighton's.'

'I wonder how they found me?' Maud said, amazed.

'Slipped your leash, did you, Miss Heighton? Do you wish to speak to me alone? I can have Arthur stand outside the door with a truncheon to safeguard our privacy.'

Maud swallowed. 'Tanya would not want me to come. But I have nothing to say to you I cannot say in front of her.'

'Then let her come, Arthur!' The Countess's American accent had become a great deal more pronounced since she had entered the room. The butler cleared his throat. 'What is it, Arthur?'

'There is another . . . person with her.'

The Countess looked at Maud, one eyebrow raised.

'Yvette, probably. She is a model.'

'Well, Arthur, bring them all in. And a couple more glasses, I guess.' He bowed and the Countess poured herself another drink. 'Funny thing is, I thought today was going to be a really dull day.'

Yvette and Tanya were both ushered in and Arthur placed glasses for them on the table. He seemed to move with exaggerated slowness. Yvette was flushed and glaring at Maud. Tanya was all but bouncing out of her chair. The moment Arthur withdrew, stately as a swan in a tailcoat, Tanya began speaking in rapid French.

'She is innocent. You cannot arrest her. She did nothing wrong.'

The Countess held up her hand again and the look she directed at Tanya was so fierce that even Yvette shrank away from her a little.

'I wish to hell,' the Countess said very distinctly and in English, 'that people would stop telling me what didn't happen and tell me what *did*. You two shut up and drink the brandy if you have a taste for it. Miss Heighton, explain yourself.'

She did. The words came uneasily at first, but the brandy smoothed her throat, and after the first few sentences, when she began to describe Sylvie taking opium and sending her out for supplies, they came fluently. She told the Countess of Mme Prideux and her accusations. To Maud it seemed that someone else was speaking. She heard her own words, calm, apparently well-chosen, but all she felt was that great black rage that washed over her every night as she slept. Her words floated above the sea of pain in her head. She told the Countess of the night she had been thrown in the river, her illness on waking and the help she had received from her friends, then she explained about writing her own letter to the Prideux family. She then passed the reply from Jean Prideux to the Countess and watched her read it in silence. Madame de Civray then handed the letter back to Maud and set her brandy glass on the table with a click. She proceeded to ask Yvette a question or two about events after Maud was dragged from the water. Tanya, very respectfully, told her of her own meeting with Morel in Passage des Panoramas.

'Interesting. Yet, ladies, I have my tiara.'

'But Madame,' Yvette said – and it was strange to hear her speak English so carefully, her usual profanities and freedom buttoned up by the unfamiliar language – 'are you sure that the *tiare*, it is the same as the one you lost?'

The Countess got up and went to her desk. 'Miss, get this straight. I did not *lose* anything. That is one thing I am sure of.' She picked up pen and paper and wrote something, then rang the bell for Arthur. The butler appeared at once. She met him in the doorway and there was a short conversation of which the girls heard nothing.

'Why are you here, Maud?' Tanya said in a whisper. 'Sasha saw you from the motor as we passed Place Pigalle! Yvette said you'd be here, but I couldn't believe you'd be that stupid.'

The Countess turned back into the room. 'I'm afraid I must ask you to wait a few minutes,' she told them, then closed the door behind her.

'Shit! She's going for the police!' Yvette said, knocking back the last of her brandy like a sailor. 'I say we run.'

'Where?' Tanya hissed back. 'She knows me. And look at the colour of Maud's face. She couldn't escape a tortoise if it really wanted to catch her.'

'What's your idea then, princess?'

'I'm not running,' Maud said simply before Tanya could reply. 'I know I shouldn't have come, but I couldn't do anything else.'

'Yes, you could have done,' Yvette said brutally. 'Look at you! You could have stayed in bed and waited until . . .' She waved her hand in the air.

'Until what, Yvette?'

'Oh, I don't know! Until we'd persuaded you to go home to England.'

Some thirty minutes passed. Maud was not sure if she was calm or simply exhausted. Tanya and Yvette were nervous. Yvette could not stay still and wandered around the room picking up one object then another until Tanya snapped at her. She did not stop, however, just handled the objects she picked up a little more carelessly when she knew Tanya was watching.

When the door finally opened again, the Countess was carrying a dark blue travelling case. Beside her was a thin, elderly man in a high starched collar with a thick white moustache and a slightly apprehensive air. He did not look like a policeman. He stared at the three women, obviously curious. Maud guessed what was in the case and looked away from it.

'Monsieur Beauclerc, these ladies are friends of mine. You may speak frankly in front of them,' the Countess said. M. Beauclerc looked startled at the prospect of speaking frankly in front of anyone. 'Ladies, this is Monsieur Beauclerc from Maison Lacloche in Rue de la Paix.' Her voice was still dry and controlled. She nodded Beauclerc onto the sofa and sat beside him, then placed the travel case in front of him on the veined marble table-top. 'Tell me about this piece, sir.'

Beauclerc looked as if he thought some trick might be played on him, and he glanced hopefully at the Countess in case she might offer some more information, a little guidance. None seemed to be forthcoming, so he gave a tiny sigh, drew the case towards him and opened it. Then, having glanced at it briefly, turned to the Countess. Maud heard Tanya and Yvette inhale sharply. Of course, they had never seen the thing before. The sight of it seemed to pull Maud back into Rue de Seine and she felt thoroughly ill. Beauclerc's voice when he spoke was pitched quite high, and oddly neat and precise for a Frenchman. Each word came out cut and brilliant.

'This is the diamond tiara of Empress Eugénie, Countess. I know it, of course. We cleaned it for your father before he gave it to you as a wedding gift. The piece was designed and created by Bapst Frères in 1819 for Marie-Thérèse. It was made with jewels from the State Treasury so was returned to the State in 1848, then later became a favourite of Empress Eugénie, hence the name.' He blinked owlishly.

Maud heard Yvette whimper. Another day, the sound might have amused her. The diamonds covered the tiara like frost on a winter hedgerow. The larger stones were like light captured and frozen – clarity held.

M. Beauclerc smiled slightly and turned the case towards Tanya and Yvette.

'Is it heavy?' Tanya asked.

He shook his head then looked, questioningly, at the Countess. She nodded and he pushed the case forward so Tanya could pick it up. Yvette crouched by her chair and with one nervous finger touched the glittering stones. M. Beauclerc continued to speak to the Countess.

'After the founding of the Third Republic, many of the French crown jewels were sold at auction.' He was relaxing into his role as narrator now and crossed his ankles. 'The tiara was bought by Asprey in London, I believe, then passed into the hands of Tiffany, from where it was purchased by your father, as I understand it, Countess. The case I made myself, the old one having become really very shabby.' He sounded so distressed at the idea that Tanya looked up briefly and smiled. 'The grand stone is a golconda of the first water, some twenty-two carats in weight. Not the size of the fabled Royal Blue, of course, but some might think it superior, given the clarity and quality . . . of . . . its . . . cut.'

He had glanced towards the tiara that Tanya and Yvette were holding between them as he spoke, and his words slowed down. His face became white, then angry red patches appeared on his cheeks. He clicked his fingers and held out his hand, and Tanya passed the tiara over to him. As the Countess sat back and watched, he began to turn it in his hands, confusion and disgust making his movements brittle; and his shoulders twitched as if he was receiving a series of electric shocks.

'This . . . this was worn by the Queen of France,' he hissed. 'What foul outrage . . .'

The Countess raised her eyebrows, but he was too engaged in staring at the tiara to notice it. 'Explain yourself, sir.'

'These are fakes! The central stone and her larger sisters! The foliage scrolls still hold the original stones, perhaps . . .' He covered his eyes with his hands as if the sight distressed him too much.

'Try and contain your emotion, Monsieur Beauclerc,' the Countess said. Her voice was so tight it sounded like a crack in the air.

'My apologies, Madame. But the shock . . .' He cleared his throat and Maud thought his eyes looked a little damp. 'I would need more time to tell you exactly what has been taken and what remains. Madame, I would be grateful if you could explain—'

'You will have to forgive me, Monsieur,' the Countess interrupted. She stood and walked over to the window, and looked out into the garden at the rear of the house. 'I'm a little short on information at the moment. Let me just say this. Someone took the tiara and a few days later returned it to me in its current condition.'

'Then you have been robbed. We must summon the authorities.'

'I *have* been robbed, sir – but the circumstances are complex. I ask you to keep this visit confidential.'

He looked as if he was about to protest, but after meeting the Countess's eye he dropped his chin.

Yvette had curled up onto the floor where she could keep her eyes level with the shifting lights of the tiara. 'This is good work, isn't it?'

He looked at her with a frown. 'Evrard and Frédéric Bapst were craftsmen of the first rank, miss. It is a classic piece, the symmetry of the foliage—'

'No, not that. The faking, I mean. I know you saw it as soon as you looked *properly*, but you did have to look, didn't you? And you said you're not sure about the smaller stones. To fool a man like you, with all your cleverness, even for a second,' she snapped her fingers and they all jumped, 'that has to be a good fake.'

Beauclerc rubbed the bridge of his nose again. 'If there is such a thing, then yes, they are good imitations. But there are many people in Paris making fake jewels, expert ones. You'll see the signs saying "imitation" hung over half the displays in the boutiques of the Palais Royal.'

'And the settings?' Yvette pressed on. 'I mean, to get the real diamond out and stick in a glass one without it looking wrong? You'd have to know what you were doing, yes?'

Beauclerc looked once more towards the Countess for guidance, but she seemed absorbed in the view of her garden. 'Yes, certainly. But this is Paris – centre of the world for fashion and jewellery. The best craftsmen from all Europe find their way here. I could name a hundred men who could make these fakes, and a hundred others who could set them.'

Now Tanya leaned forward in her chair, her eyes bright. 'But you all know, don't you? All of you jewellers and designers, you all know this tiara and who owns it. It's famous.'

He stroked his chin. 'Yes, of course. I admit that the list of people who, without an express command from the Countess herself, would be willing to do this work and had the capacity *is* rather shorter . . .'

'Well then,' Tanya said, drawing a tiny notebook from her bag and pulling out a pencil thin as a spider's leg from its spine. 'Give us *that* list.'

CHAPTER 9

Caveau des Innocents oil on canvas 64.8 × 76.3 cm

One of the most notorious bars in Paris near Les Halles and known until the First World War as a haunt for the destitute and desperate. Though the patrons are huddled in the rough clothing of the working poor and seen by the light of smoking oil lamps, there is a sense of life and community in the painting. The focus of attention is the singer seated at the back table with her bright red shawl and the violinist who accompanies her, the handkerchief around his neck echoing the same red. The performance seems to transport her listeners, who lean in towards her just as the viewer is drawn towards her – and away from the surrounding shadows.

Extract from the catalogue notes to the exhibition 'The Paris Winter: Anonymous Treasures from the de Civray Collection', Southwark Picture Gallery, London, 2010

When Beauclerc had been hurried, sniffing and unhappy, from the house, Yvette assured the Countess that she could find which of the men on the list had done the work on the tiara if she were given a few days to look for them in the lower haunts of Paris. One of them would have more money than he should, she said, or would have been busy while everyone else was drinking over Christmas and New Year.

Maud lay back on the Countess's settee while they discussed it and let the talk flow over her. She had expected some relief from coming here. She remembered the middle-class living rooms of her mother's friends where she had been petted and praised – the glow of self-worth she had felt. She had felt it again when the Countess gave her the portfolio of photographs during those perfect days before Christmas when she was loved and useful. Now, lying back empty and hollow while the others were so full of purpose, she realised she had been hoping to feel that again, had imagined the Countess tearful and grateful, praising and pitying her back into the world. It had not happened.

'Fine!' the Countess said at last, holding up her hand to stop the talk of the two other women. 'Find who did the work and come and tell me. We shall see about the police after that.'

'You mustn't do anything that puts Maud in danger,' Tanya protested. 'If you do, I shall . . . I shall . . .'

'What? Faint?' Madame de Civray replied sharply. 'Do not fret, Miss Koltsova. I'm sure we can persuade whoever did the work to turn in Morel, or Gravot if that is his real name. Such people do not normally keep their mouths shut for their friends.' She took a breath. 'I'm sorry, girls. Seeing the dead walk and then finding out about that damned tiara has rattled me.'

Yvette looked up at her, eyes slightly narrowed. 'It was brave of Maud to come here, Madame.'

The older woman pursed her lips. 'Yes, it was. I thank her for it and I shan't forget it.' But she did not look at Maud. 'Do you mind if Arthur shows you out of the back door?'

⤫

Tanya let them off at Place Pigalle before being carried off to the Louvre to play the part of the devoted student and Yvette supported Maud on her arm back to Valadon's.

'Let me come with you tonight,' Maud said as she sat down on the bed and began to unbutton her boots.

'No. No bloody way,' Yvette said, shocked. 'It is not the place for you and besides, you are not well enough. I can't ask the questions I need to with you hanging over my shoulder. You don't know the language – this is not drawing-room French – and you don't know how to be.'

'And where *is* my place?' Maud's disappointment at the Countess's house was thickening, curdling into something bleak and wretched. 'I will come if I have to follow you through the streets until I fall in the gutter. I want to see. And I cannot sit here quietly while other people plan and do around me. No more.'

Yvette sat down heavily on the bed beside her, making the springs complain. 'Where is your place? Who knows? No one does, Maud.' She pulled her knife from her pocket and flicked it open, then began to pare her short nails. 'Your place is just where you end up, I suppose.'

'Tell everyone I am a new model just turned up with a few francs, and you're using me to buy you drinks.'

Yvette looked at her sideways and spoke softly. 'Why? Why do you want to come? There's nothing to see but misery and stink. A month ago, you would have swooned at the very idea of going

221

somewhere like that. Anyone seeing you go into these places will assume you are a whore or a thief, possibly both.'

'But now I am a ghost, Yvette, I can go anywhere. And I shall. I want to see, and why should I care what strangers think?'

Yvette squeezed the blade shut, slipped the knife back into her pocket then hugged herself. 'Christ, Maud, I hate it when you talk like that. You've always cared what other people think, and you're *not* a ghost.'

'I feel like one. An angry one. I can't carry on thinking the world can be made into what I want it to be, Yvette. That got me killed. I want to see it *as it is*.'

Yvette waited for a while then nodded. 'All right – but say as little as you can. If they think you are not one of them in the Caveau des Innocents, they will kill you. Rest now. I'll come back for you at midnight.'

An arched doorway, an entrance into the cellars of what was once a great house in a dim street a stone's throw from Les Halles. There was a man, hunched against the cold, leaning on the wall outside. His eyes drifted over them and he nodded. Maud wore clothes she'd borrowed from Valadon. A simple skirt and threadbare cotton blouse under a short black coat worn shiny at the elbows. She felt more comfortable than she had in the rose evening gown.

Yvette pushed open the door and led Maud down a narrow stone staircase. The only light was from smoking candles stuck into the tops of bottles on the steps or occasional oil lamps swinging from large metal hooks, and the air was thick with the stench of sweat, sour alcohol and cheap black tobacco. The grey plaster walls were scrawled with names in household paint, a dark vermilion:

Panther, Ugly Henry, Fat Emily. Not decoration, but some sort of declaration of existence.

At the bottom of the stairs, the two women reached the first of a series of low, vaulted rooms. There was a bar of sorts, with smeared glasses and unlabelled bottles. Yvette pointed at one then waited, leaning her folded arms on the bar, for Maud to pay. Against the walls were wooden benches and tables. Yvette picked up the bottle and a pair of glasses and took Maud to a spot in the corner of a second vault that led off from the first, poured the drinks and emptied the first glass immediately down her throat. Maud did the same. The wine scorched her throat, but after the first sting she felt it warm her, drive some of the noxious stink out of her blood.

She began to pick out the details of the room. A man at the far end of the room was playing a violin, and seated at the table next to him, another was singing. The patrons nearest to them swayed with the music and joined in with the chorus. Maud could only make out a few of the words. He was lamenting his girl, shut away in Saint-Lazare, complaining that he had no comfort in life while she was gone. It seemed the song was addressed to the girl's little sister. He was asking her to take up her elder's duties. Each verse seemed to end with a joke or a pun that sent the crowd into fits of laughter before they sang out the chorus.

The bar was beginning to fill and the reek of unwashed bodies, warmed by their closeness, soured the thin air. Yvette held her tumbler close to her face, observing the distorted crowd through the dirty glass. The song ended and another began, a woman singing this time in a low growl. Maud looked at the faces, mournful or intent, the way the men and women watched each other as much with their bodies as their eyes. Yvette slid out of her place and went to lean on the bar again; after a few minutes Maud realised she was talking to the man next to her. Yvette was nodding at him now, her eyes flickering to right and left while he spoke, making sure she was not overheard.

While Maud watched, another man, his hair greased back from his forehead, took Yvette's place beside her and said something to her she didn't understand. She shrugged then felt his arm slide around her waist. His skin smelled of stale bread and onion and she could feel the warmth of his body through her clothes. He was whispering into her ear a mixture of compliments and obscenities, his fingers pressing into the flesh of her hip, his breath on her neck. Suddenly she was yanked to her feet. Yvette had pulled her up and was now leaning into her face in a rage, shaking her arm, talking fast and loud. The man who had been embracing her laughed, said something and grabbed his crotch. The others near to him hooted and applauded. Looking as submissive as she could, Maud took hold of Yvette's hand and kissed her knuckles. She saw the slight flicker of surprise and amusement cross Yvette's face before the girl remembered to be angry again. She delivered one last insult to the man, then wrapped her arm around Maud's waist and carried her off.

Her act of furious indignation lasted until they turned the corner into Rue Berger when she dropped her grip on Maud, leaned against the wall and began to laugh so hard the tears ran down her face. The street was quiet, the shop-fronts and pitches around Les Halles closed away for the night and the doors to the warehouses locked. A dog barked from behind one of the gates and Yvette pulled herself straight.

'Oh Lord, oh I thought I would die when you kissed my hand! Did you understand what I was saying to you?'

Maud put her head on one side. 'Something about being a faithless bitch, I think. What did you find out about the names on the list?'

Yvette waited to see some spark of amusement in Maud's face, some acknowledgement of the adventure, but none came. She wiped her eyes on her cuff.

'According to Freddy, one is dead. Another left Paris last year to try his luck in the provinces. Two of the others have been seen out and drinking most nights since Christmas. But there are two that no one has seen around for a while. The man I spoke to said the bloke who was the pick of Beauclerc's list was Henri Bouchard, and he's one of the ones not seen since before the holidays. Apparently he'd been trying to go straight, working out of a shop in the Palais Royal – but he's not turned up there since then either.'

Maud nodded shortly and Yvette felt a chill in her bones that had nothing to do with the coldness of the evening or damp in the air. 'How did you get him to tell you these things?'

Yvette pulled her shawl over her shoulders and turned north back towards Montmartre, walking briskly. 'I told him I had a fellow interested in getting into the game of swapping real stones for fakes in the shops. Freddy used to do that too – before he got his face cut. Everyone could spot him after that so now he sweats in Les Halles butchering meat.' She could hear Maud following her.

'Are you angry with me, Yvette?' Her voice was calm.

'No,' Yvette took her arm. 'Just a little frightened for you. What would your lawyer brother say if he knew that you had been in that bar? With that man?'

Maud considered it a while and as they passed through the pool of light from a gas-lamp, Yvette saw the suggestion of a smile cross her friend's gaunt face. 'He would have me committed, I think, and what's more, if I had heard the story told about another woman from our town, of our class, I might have agreed with him. Isn't it strange? A place you can go every day if you wish to, yet my brother would probably lock me away forever if he knew I'd let that man put his arm around my waist. Let us go and see the Countess.'

Despite the lateness of the hour, it was still a little while before Madame de Civray returned from her evening engagements. The two women were summoned to her dressing room. The Countess sat in front of the three-part mirror taking the powder from her face with cold cream and brushing out her hair while Yvette told her what she had learned. After consulting her diary, she gave them a date.

CHAPTER 10

19 January 1910

*H*ENRI BOUCHARD WAS DRUNK. HENRI BOUCHARD made a habit of being drunk whenever he had the money and he had money now. It was not half of what he deserved though, not for a job like that. He let out a curse and some tart on the next table looked at him over her shoulder then turned back to her friends. He was a craftsman. They had treated him unfairly. Rushed him through his work and then paid him badly for it. Still, he had enough to get drunk in one of his favourite bars – one with a proper band and lots of girls dancing. Not like in Les Innocents where you had to face nose to nose what a failure you'd become. Only the desperate got drunk in that stink-hole. Here you still got a lively crowd ready to fight and flirt till dawn, but your drinks came in a clean glass.

'What's up, Uncle?'

A young woman slid along the bench towards him. He growled and turned away. 'Oh come on, Uncle, don't be like that! My friends haven't arrived and you look like you could use cheering up. Buy us a drink and I'll sing you a song.'

He half-turned towards her, his eyes narrow. She was pretty

enough. Prettier than the women who normally offered to keep him company these days. Perhaps she could smell the money on him, little enough though it was. Still, what harm could a song do? He nodded to the waiter and the girl put her arm through his. He felt the ease of her warm his flank. A good feeling that, when it was cold in Paris – to feel the heat of a girl next to you, the smoky animal comfort of it. It made it almost a pleasure to remember the hell of the work camps on the shores of Guiana, where you were slick with your own sweat, and hunger clawed every breath, just to feel more sweetly the comfort of this now.

If they'd paid him what the work was worth, he could have lived like this for good, but that Gravot was a swine. He knew too much about the old days – quoted him his own words back from the camp when Henri had liked to boast about the society ladies locking away paste worth five francs in their strong-boxes. And he remembered things – oh, Gravot had a memory on him. That was what had cost Henri his proper fee on this job: Gravot's memory and Henri's boasting. Henri recalled him arriving in the camp. Scrap of a lad; thought he was as like to die in his first week as live, but he held on, the little devil, learning from the old lags around him – sucking it all in with the burning air. And the men liked to talk. There was nothing else to do when they'd done fighting each other for scraps. Then there were his funny turns. They'd caught a wild pig once, and the guards were willing to look the other way for the best cuts of it. Killing it had turned into a bit of a festival and Gravot had seemed as blood-happy as any of them till Vogel had stuck a knife in its belly – and then he'd gone white as paper under his prison tan and started beating him up. Knocked Vogel flying and would have killed him too if they hadn't dragged him off. Such strength he had in his wiry little bones . . .

The band started up with one of the songs he remembered from his youth, and Henri's foot tapped along to it before he even knew he was listening. Gravot was quite the gentleman these days. A fake gentleman, a gentleman of glass and gilt, but a good copy. Henri had been pleased to see him at first. Could hardly hear his 'Good morning' on the street outside the back yard lean-to where he worked for the blare of tropical birdsong Gravot seemed to bring with him. Then when it came to agreeing the price for the job, he showed what sort of 'friend' he was. No wonder he'd got rich while Henri was rotting in the back room of one of the cheapest jewellers in Paris, never allowed to handle anything worth more than a franc and with the steward's eye always on him.

'Uncle, I swear you haven't heard a word I've said.' The girl was filling up his glass and he half-smiled at her. She had pretty hair the colour of sand. Not one of the whores, nicer than that.

'Something about a hat?'

'Oh Uncle, you are funny. No, a skirt I made, and pricked my fingers open to do it and the madame comes in and it's "no, no, not like that" – and I'm to do it all over, and it had taken me hours. Such fine work, and do they understand the quality? Not a chance. If I'd known the price they'd pay me I'd have stitched it so the seams would split on first wearing.' She sighed and put her chin in her hands.

'Now then, flower, I know how that feels.' Poor lass, he thought. 'Same thing happened to me and I thought he was a friend too. But enough of our worries, let's have that song, eh?' She smiled and nodded like a little girl.

Three hours later he was as happy as he had ever been, wandering down the hill past Place Pigalle with this pretty girl chirruping and whistling on his arm. If she wanted his company on the way home it was worth a walk into Rue Laferrière. She actually seemed to like him. He thought so right up to the moment two men stepped

out of a doorway and threw a sack over his head. Something struck
him and he fell into their waiting arms.

∾∽∾

Tanya was seated at dinner between the owner of one of the daily
newspapers and Perov, but neither got a great deal of her attention.
She tried to talk pleasantly to each of them, but realised she missed
their questions and her answers were often vague to the point of
rudeness. Perov would probably interpret her distraction as modesty
and embarrassment, and draw his own egotistical conclusions. The
newspaper-owner probably thought her an imbecile. There was
nothing to be done about it, Tanya could not draw herself away
from the sight of the Morels seated opposite her. Sylvie was clear-
eyed and smiling, and making a conquest of the men who sat either
side of her. Tanya occasionally heard her light laugh or her
questions. The men were bankers apparently, and both falling over
themselves to answer her naive enquiries about their business.
They glowed and swelled as Tanya watched.

Further up the table, Morel was talking to the American opposite him, who seemed to have some interests in construction, about
his plan to leave France for America, telling him how impressed he
was by the buildings of New York he'd seen in photographs. The
man, handsome, clean-shaven, in his fifties, was much more taken
with Tanya's aunts, who sat either side of him. Their view of
America as a land of savages and cowboys obviously amused him.
They asked if there were theatres in America and whether they had
managed to educate their peasants as yet. Tanya could almost
admire the way Morel stuck to it until the man in construction said
yes, he would be happy to receive Morel in New York when he
happened to be there. Morel smiled around the table as if expecting

general applause and, belatedly, tried to charm the very bored woman to his left.

Tanya could not eat. The food was all too rich, and wondering if Yvette had found the man she was looking for and led him to the Countess's house had twisted her stomach into a knot. She wished Allardyce were here. Even if he knew nothing about Maud or the horrors of what had been done to her, she knew that seeing him smile at her across the silverware would have helped her to get through the evening. Being next to Perov was making her skin crawl. His cuff links were diamonds.

She looked again at Sylvie. What had that girl done to surround herself with luxury? Lied and stolen and play-acted, killed and tried to kill, all for money, ordinary boring money. Tanya pushed at a piece of fat white flesh on her plate. The lobsters had come up alive on a special train from Normandy that morning. If she married Perov, perhaps everything would taste this stale – even his proposal seemed to have drained the joy out of Paris – but her father was adamant that this would be a good match.

The newspaper-owner asked her what she was thinking, and before she could stop herself she answered truthfully. 'I was wondering what it might be like to be poor, or at least have very little money compared with what I have now. I'm wondering if I would miss lobster.' She looked round guiltily but Perov was explaining wheat imports to the woman next to him and had not heard her.

The newspaper-man smiled and nodded into his wine. 'My father was a carpenter. A good one, but there were times when he couldn't get enough work to feed us all. I'm one of seven, you know. The little brother!' She looked at his wide belly and the length of his white moustaches and he laughed at her. 'A long time ago, dear child, even old men like me were once boys.'

'Forgive me, I did not mean . . .'

'I can hardly believe it myself. Now I am as rich as any man at this table, I think, and have seen every stage of wealth in between.'

'Being rich is much better, isn't it?' Tanya said sadly, jabbing at her plate again.

'It's a great deal better than being very poor, but I think I was happiest in those early days, when as a young man I set out to do something all fire and fluster! Working next to my wife, wondering if we were going to have enough money to print the next issue, then gradually, gradually watching the circulation rise. Those were the best days.'

'Your wife worked with you?' Tanya said.

'Indeed. She was one of my best writers and still does the odd piece for Marguerite at *La Fronde* – though I can't get her to write for me any more. She says she has too much fun playing with the grandchildren to bleed ink for me.' He raised his glass and Tanya realised he was toasting the woman next to Morel. He was explaining something to her a little loudly; she still looked bored, but when she caught her husband's glance she rolled her eyes and grinned at him. Tanya looked back in time to see the man beside her wink. They were like children, signalling in church. He leaned towards Tanya and said in an undertone, 'You are aware, I am sure, dear child, how many men complain that their wives do not understand them. I always complain that my wife understands me only too well.'

The butler entered and approached the Countess's chair, then bowed low to whisper in her ear. She stood up with a quiet apology to the men next to her and a nod towards her husband. Tanya felt anxiety twist in her chest and fought the impulse to stare at the Morels again, so comfortable and pleased with themselves. She looked instead at the Count at the far end of the table. He was a blandly handsome man who seemed charmed by everything around him and delighted in his ability to pay for it. He had already told those close to him the story of the journey of the lobster, and now he was describing how his wife had bought the plates and bullied the manufacturer for a better price. He noticed he was being observed and raised his glass to Tanya with a smile. She nodded back to him and returned to the glitter of her cutlery, the frosted whiteness of the tablecloth and tried to imagine what was happening elsewhere in the house.

'Happy as a king, isn't he? Happier.' The newspaperman was addressing her again. 'Every time I argue with my wife I tell her I should have married a rich American, but there weren't so many around in my day. She says that none of them would have had me anyway.'

Perov, it seemed, thought it was time to pay a little attention to them. 'An American like that comes at a cost,' he said in his thin pale voice. The newspaperman shrugged. 'I'm deadly serious, sir,' Perov went on. 'Her father made his fortune in oil in the wildest hinterlands of that vast continent, and she, rather than receiving a proper education, used to travel with him. They say she saw three men killed, one by her own father, before she was ten years old. I tell you, *she* runs this house now. Iron hand in a velvet glove, you know. All very comfortable for the Count if he behaves himself, but what civilised man could want a wife such as that?' Tanya felt his gaze slide over her and did not look at him, afraid if she did she would hiss like a cat. 'No, some accomplishments are desirable, certainly, and the taste to create a fashionable and elegant home for her husband, but nothing of the new woman about her, please.'

'Have you ever had your portrait painted, sir?' Tanya asked the newspaperman.

'Indeed, I have, last year. We have hung it in the entrance hall of our building to scare the staff and intimidate the creditors.'

'And how much did you pay for it?'

He laughed. 'A thousand francs, dear.'

'That is very interesting,' Tanya said, and tried to do better justice to her lobster. Perov said nothing, then returned his attentions to the woman on his other side.

Some twenty minutes later, the Countess came back into the room and retook her seat. Tanya looked at her and she gave a quick nod.

CHAPTER 11

*W*HEN HE WOKE, THE WORLD WAS THE INSIDE OF a flour bag; he could taste the dust on his lips. There was a rag in his mouth; it tasted dry. He was sitting on a chair and with his hands tied behind him. The air was cold and as he shifted his feet he felt his boots drag against stone. Someone must have seen him move. The flour sack was pulled off him and he blinked hard. A cellar. He looked side to side. Wine bottles all round the walls in heavy, expensive ranks. His view forward was blocked by the bodies of two wide gentlemen in long dark coats. They wore round hats. One looked smooth and well-fed. The other had long sloping shoulders, the broken nose and evil eyes of a prize-fighter. The sort that gouges. Henri steadied himself; he knew the signs of a beating coming but he was confused too. He owed no one money. Not today! And if it was just the francs in his boots they were after, why had they bothered to tie him up and bring him down here? The little *grisette* in the bar was cheese on a trap then. He sighed.

The smooth man turned away once he had seen that Henri was awake, and said something in English. A woman's voice replied, and straining in his chair Henri saw between the two men a woman standing further back in the shadows. She was wearing an evening

gown and her throat sparkled with sapphires and diamonds. They
seemed to gather the light from the oil-lamps and turn it into
fireworks. Whatever she had said meant no good for him, for as
the woman turned to go, the big man dropped into a fighting
stance and drew back his arm. Henri closed his eyes and braced
himself. Then another voice, female and rapid. The girl from the
bar, but speaking English. Why was she still here? He opened one
eye very cautiously. Her words had made the big fella hesitate. It
seemed the jewelled lady was in charge, they were all looking at her
now. She sighed and nodded to the girl, who then came trotting
up to him. She bent down low and spoke in French.

'Henri, I'm going to take that rag out of your mouth. Would
you like that?' He nodded. 'But if you say anything foul, I'll shove
it right back in your gob. Understand?' He nodded again.

She yanked out the rag and he spat on the ground at her feet,
but held his tongue. She waited, but when it became clear he was
going to keep quiet she dropped into a crouch next to him, holding
on to the back of his chair for balance. He leaned away from her
slightly.

'Look, Henri, I'm sorry. These men are Americans. They work
for the lady and they think you'll be more likely to talk to us if they
beat you up first.' That was probably true. He looked at the prize-
fighter again. The man was rolling his shoulders. 'I say you're not
that bad a fella. Just made a few mistakes long ago, didn't you?'
This whole thing was odd, but by the sound of her voice it was best
to agree so he nodded hard. It made the pain in his head wake up
and beat on the inside of his skull. 'So will you answer this lady's
questions? Then we'll let you go.'

'Without the beating?' She nodded and flashed a grin at him.
'They ain't police?'

'They are Pinkertons.' She breathed the word into his ear and he shivered. 'American thugs for rich people. Clean-shaved, both of them! The gendarmes wouldn't have them even if they could speak French worth a damn.' He shot a quick look at the men. They looked wary, but obviously had not understood her.

'You staying here?'

She put her hand on his shoulder as if he was a schoolboy being presented to the headmaster by his mother, and said, 'He's happy to talk.'

The woman in sapphires stepped towards them. 'Yvette, remember I *can* speak French and I'm not so old I can't hear what you're whispering.'

His champion lost some of her bravery and looked down at the floor. 'Yes, Madame.'

Sparkles looked him up and down for a moment or two. 'You are sure this is the man?'

'Yes, Madame. Henri Bouchard. He's been talking tonight about not getting paid what he's owed, and people taking advantage of his bad luck. I'm sure it's him.'

Had he said that? Probably. Red wine and a big smile like that and he would run on. The tunes the band had been playing had made him mournful too, for his youth when the world seemed like a good place. Then the world took to teaching him the same lesson time and time again. People took advantage. And he'd never found the trick of making a woman like him without making her sorry for him, and he *had* been unlucky! He'd been caught swapping real stones for fakes when cleaning a necklace in 1893 and done five years for it. Now here he was, an artist really stuck making pennies in the back room of a dump that catered to shop girls. And he'd tried to keep his nose clean – at least till that shit Gravot turned up.

Sparkles was staring at him. He found he couldn't look her in the eye so concentrated on the hem of her long dress. It shimmered with all sorts of fancy stuff.

'The tiara, Henri? Who brought it to you?'

That fucking tiara. Of course it was the tiara. He got half – no, half of half – what his work was worth, and now he was in a cellar. 'I'm saying nothing.' Sparkles said something in English to the two men; they started moving towards him. Yvette went pale. Not a good sign.

'They are going to break your fingers, Henri!'

Shit. 'Gravot! Christian Gravot!' Sparkles held up her hand and the prize-fighter looked disappointed. Henri tried to catch his breath. 'He found me. He . . . he knows about a couple of little jobs I did that the cops never caught on to: enough to send me away a good few more years. He said I had to do the job or "the information would get to them". Bastard.'

Sparkles nodded. 'How did you do it so fast, Henri?'

'There are lots of drawings of that tiara. It's famous, isn't it? And they had a good photo of some American chit wearing it, so I had a few weeks to get ready.' He couldn't resist a little smirk. 'Four days was plenty to polish them up nice and swap out the real ones.' Sparkles raised her eyebrows and suddenly she looked sickeningly familiar. Shit again. The smirk disappeared and his shoulders slumped.

'How many stones did you replace?'

'Twenty plus the main stone,' he mumbled miserably to his boots. 'All the big ones. And the great fat cushion I recut. Been working on it since before Christmas.' Sparkles flinched when she heard that. 'Make it easier to sell. Just got the polishing done last night. Been doing nothing else since he brought it to me, but I did it fast even with Gravot breathing down my neck. Had to quit my job to do it. He made me. I just hope they'll take me back. He said he'd give me the rest of the week, but all of a sudden it's hurry hurry, can't stand another stinking evening with me, won't leave me alone for as much as a piss while I'm working.'

'Why hasn't he run, Henri?' Yvette asked. 'Why is he still in Paris?'

Henri looked up at her and shook his head. It made his jowls wobble like a bulldog's. So they knew Gravot. Good. Let *him* sit in a cellar with the big fella then.

'Why should he?' he said. The thought of the prize-fighter catching up with Christian on a dark night and messing up his fancy suit gave him a twinge of pleasure. He could feel it under the pain in his head, his hands. 'He thinks he's in the clear. Good conman never runs. Just ambles off when he feels like it. He's going to sell a few of the little 'uns here, then head off to America. Use the rest to found his business empire.

Henry spat on the ground again, thinking of Gravot sitting behind him while he worked, reading the business pages of the American newspapers, talking about opportunities. How America was the *real* place for a man with ambitions, not France. The country was full of peasants, he'd said while Henri sweated over that great rock for him, hardly losing any of its weight, but disguising it, keeping it just as beautiful, but anonymous. Like dyeing a girl's hair and dressing her in a new frock.

The girl patted him. 'Now Henri, you didn't keep any for yourself, did you? I know you didn't like the price he gave you, so weren't you tempted just to keep one for your trouble?'

Of course he'd been tempted, feeling all that real ice at his fingertips. Such high-grade stones – the clarity, the neatness of the cut. 'That arsehole knows his diamonds and he wouldn't leave me alone with 'em for a second.'

Sparkles was taking the news pretty well, Henri thought. She hadn't set the thugs on him or started crying or yelling yet. Just looked at the wine racks and frowned like she'd seen the Bordeaux sniggering.

'Thank you, Mr Bouchard. Christian Gravot will be arrested and you shall testify that he brought you the tiara and what you did with it.'

Henri jerked up so hard the chair juddered and he almost fell. 'No! No chance! I'm not going back to that hellhole.' They were all looking at him like this was a surprise. 'You don't know what it's like over there.' No one did. The heat and disease, the men dying round you, the ones that lived beating you for rations or for sport even when they knew you had nothing to steal. He blinked hard. 'You can kill me here, but take me to a cop and I'll deny it all. I'll say you lied and I never saw that dog . . . I'm not going back.' He realised it was true as the words were going out of his mouth. 'You can't prove nothing. Only told you to be civil.' He was not a brave man, he knew that, but letting those men kill him here and now with that girl Yvette fresh in his mind and a belly full of red wine would be a fine death compared with what waited in Guiana.

The American men might not understand French, but they knew a refusal when they saw it. The prize-fighter stepped in and swung hard into Henri's kidney. The pain ran through his body like wine spilled on a white cloth and pushed the air out of his lungs. He heard Yvette cry out, and he squeezed his eyes shut, steeling himself for the next strike. Sparkles said a word and no blow came. He opened one eye cautiously.

'You mean that,' Sparkles said. It was a statement not a question, but he nodded anyway. For a long time there was silence then she said, 'How do we know you won't warn Gravot?'

He'd bitten his tongue under the surprise of that last blow. He spat out the blood. 'Because that shit got me here, and I'd love to see him here instead.'

Yvette put her hand on his shoulder again. 'What's he planning, Henri? Tell us something else.' She leaned in very close to him. 'Tell us, and I won't tell them you keep your money in your stocking.' Her breath tickled the inner shell of his ear like the sound of distant water on sand.

'He hasn't sold any yet. Rheims. He had tickets for Rheims in his hand. He's been planning a little jaunt in that direction to sell a few stones and congratulate himself for driving me crazy. He leaves on Friday – back on the Sunday-evening train. He was going to give me till then to finish the polishing, but these last three days he's been at my back every minute chivvying me along.'

'Any more, Henri?'

Ah, fuck him. 'Five of the smaller stones I put in a bracelet for him. Bit of a rush job, but they're easier to smuggle about that way than loose. He wanted the others set too, but I told him he'd had all the work from me I could stomach. Thought he was going to blow, but in the end he just smiled and wandered off like a little king. The sod.'

Sparkles nodded. 'Very well. I must go back to dinner. Boys, clean him up and get him out of here. Don't leave town, Monsieur Bouchard, will you?'

He shrugged as well as his bonds would let him. 'Where would I go?'

She looked into the shadows behind her. 'Come on, my dear.' A figure stood up from the darkness. Another woman, tall and shapely but dressed a little plain and pale in the face. Sparkles took her arm. They began to walk towards the cellar stairs. Sparkles looked over her shoulder. 'Yvette?'

The girl bent down to kiss his forehead. 'Sorry, Henri. You're not a bad old devil.' He looked at his boots and managed another shrug. The place where she'd kissed him glowed in the darkness she left behind.

* * *

'Well done, Yvette,' the Countess said. Yvette almost thanked her but bit her tongue. 'So, Miss Heighton, you are vindicated. I believe you, but the law will take us no further. Still, again I thank you for bringing this matter to our attention and I promise it will not be forgotten. You look a little tired still. Go home and rest, honey. I must be getting back to dinner. Arthur will see you out.'

'But what next, Countess?' Yvette said.

'Steps will be taken, dear.'

'What steps?'

'Oh, you'll be informed. Now take that girl home before she falls over.'

'Are *they* here?' Maud said. Her voice sounded heavy and thick. Yvette tightened her grip on Maud's arm and the Countess glanced behind her as if checking that Arthur was still standing at her shoulder.

'They are here,' she said.

Maud took half a step forward and Yvette saw such a look of animal rage on her face that she was afraid. The Countess did not move but the butler stepped closer to her. Yvette kept Maud pinned to her side.

'Maud, you cannot,' she whispered frantically into her ear. 'Please, they will deny everything and accuse you, and nothing will be done but you will go to prison and die there.' Maud was still staring up the hallway towards the receiving rooms of the Countess's home. 'For God's sake, Maud, *come away.*'

'I should not have let you in the house tonight, Miss Heighton. I hoped you would be sensible.' Madame de Civray turned on her heel and crossed the hallway, the train of her gown perfectly pooling and slippering behind her on the polished parquet.

'Maud – please, sweetie – come away,' Yvette said, her voice sounding almost tearful. It was not that Maud was pulling against her, only she could sense the power of her anger ready to burst forward and felt, if it did, she would not be able to restrain her and Maud would be lost.

'His business opportunities,' Maud hissed. 'His trip to America. How lucky that I was there to teach his "sister" better English. Yvette, take me away before I start to scream.' Maud turned back towards the kitchen, and without any more ado let herself be led out of the house, the butler staying two steps behind the women until they were safe in the night and the door was locked and bolted behind them.

When dinner was over and the guests were being ushered back into the drawing room, the Countess claimed Tanya's arm. 'Sweetness, I have a new acquisition to show you, do let me steal you away.' She ushered her into the morning room where they had met M. Beauclerc. There was a man in a grey suit sitting on the sofa, a round hat in his hands. As the ladies entered he got to his feet, but the Countess waved him back.

'Honey, this is Mr Carter of the Pinkerton Agency. We had a very interesting chat with a new friend of Yvette's this evening and the law is a no-go, I'm afraid.'

'She found him? Oh, she is a wonder! But you know Maud is innocent?'

'Oh, as the day is long, dear. But this fellow Henri refuses to say anything to the police.'

'And did you send people to Rue de Seine? Did you find the stones?'

The Countess smiled. 'It was worth a try, but no, they were not there.' She turned towards Carter. 'Your people left no sign the place had been searched?'

'None, ma'am.'

Tanya was confused. They had not found the diamonds and this Henri would not talk to the police – and yet the Countess looked perfectly content.

'We have a chance to play the long game,' the Countess continued. 'It seems Morel is going to deliver himself into our hands.'

'I don't understand.'

'Well then, shush kitten, and we shall explain. Mr Carter? You OK if he goes in English?' Tanya nodded.

'There are limits to what we can do in Europe, ma'am,' Carter said. 'Taking a known criminal like Henri off the street and getting him to talk – well, that's one thing, but it wouldn't do for us to give the same treatment to a fellow like Morel. He hasn't pulled any scams we can pin on him in Paris and he's spent freely enough around town to make some friends. Even this Miss Priddy woman . . .'

'Prideux,' Tanya said.

'Prideux,' he gave a respectful nod. 'From what I hear, her son the solicitor said there was no use chasing the money, and we've asked around about the accident. No one saw anything suspicious, and we can't find anyone who saw her with Morel that night. No surprise there – he's not dumb, but I'm just saying he can't be touched on that.' He cleared his throat and Tanya waited without speaking. 'Now he plans to get a boat over to New York at the end of the month. There our life will be a lot easier. We can reverse-scam him. We've the people for it, the contacts, and we can take him for every penny he's got. Perhaps if we're lucky we'll even get the big stone back. Take it as security on some deal.' Tanya noticed he had a light baritone, the same camel colour as his overcoat. 'There's no way to stop him selling a few stones in Rheims, but we'll get back what's owed to the Countess in the end.'

'That is all?' Tanya said.

The Countess laughed. 'Honey, it's perfect! The fooler fixed. We'll make him good and uncomfortable, and I'll get my money back. Shame about the grand stone, but if Henri is as good as they say he is, and we con Morel out of it in New York, then perhaps I can make something pretty out of it.'

Tanya shook her head. 'And that is all?'

Mr Carter frowned as if she was making a joke he couldn't quite understand. 'The money will be recovered and he'll be sorry he took the stones. That's what we want. Sure, if we took him to the law he might get his neck stretched, but that's not going to happen, like the lady says, and I can't go round assassinating people, Miss Koltsova. Not in Europe at any rate!' The Countess made a little cooing noise between amusement and sympathy.

Tanya spoke quietly, though there was a shimmer of distress in her voice. 'They threw Maud in the river. They told her friends she was a thief then a suicide. I ask you again: *is that all?*'

Mr Carter stroked his smooth chin. 'I suppose, given Miss Heighton's honesty in coming to you, ma'am, and at some risk to herself . . . a reward of some sort perhaps?'

'Of course. I shall arrange something nice,' Madame de Civray said in her usual bright voice. Tanya was disgusted, but the Countess was not even looking at her. 'Oh, and while we are tidying things up . . .' She rang the bell and her butler appeared in the doorway. 'Tell her to come in now, Arthur.'

A maid, certainly less than twenty with thick ankles and apple cheeks, was ushered into the room. She looked very frightened. 'You wished to see me, Madame?'

'I did, dear. I'm afraid you'll have to leave my service at once. You will go tonight, and I will not be giving you a recommendation to future employers.' From her tone of voice you'd have guessed she was sharing plans for some surprise party for her children.

The girl went white and her eyes became watery. 'But, Madame . . . ? If I have not pleased you I will work harder. Please, Madame. My mother, my little brother all rely on my wages here. If you send me away without a reference, what shall I do?'

'You should have thought of that before you entertained gentlemen callers here, shouldn't you?' The girl covered her mouth with her hand and the tears began to run down her face. 'You have my sympathy, honey, but what would it look like if I were to just let you go with a thank you and a recommendation? I would be inviting riot into my home. Mr Carter, would you be so kind as to watch her pack and check her luggage in case she takes any souvenirs?'

Mr Carter stood up and placed his hand on the girl's shoulder. She looked up at him, astonished and afraid.

'Come on, dear,' he said, and steered her out of the room. The girl herself seemed too stunned at the sudden collapse of her world to speak.

The Countess stood and gave herself a little shake. 'There, that is done. Oh, I shall enjoy hearing all about Morel's plans for New York.'

'*She* let Morel into your house?' Tanya said.

The Countess smoothed her gloves up her arm. 'Yes, honey. I

was wondering, you see, taking Maud in like that . . . all the preparation. They knew exactly what they wanted and where it was. The cook wormed the truth out of Odette. That she had been walking out with a gentleman and had brought him here. Not that any of them know about the tiara being plucked, of course.' She took Tanya's arm. 'If they ask you, honey, you can say I was showing you that little Morisot in the corner.'

Tanya pulled away. 'Perhaps you can tell them I am still lost in admiration for a few moments more.'

The Countess shrugged. 'If you wish, dear.' She left the room and the butler slipped in through the door to wait with Tanya. His eyes were fixed straight ahead and his hands clasped behind his back.

'Arthur, are there writing materials I may use in this desk?'

'Yes, miss.'

She opened the drawer and found a plain sheet and envelope and a slim fountain pen. Hoping she would ruin the nib forever, she wrote, *To whomsoever it may concern, I give this gift to* . . . 'What is that girl's name, Arthur?'

'Odette, miss. Odette Suchet.'

. . . *Odette Suchet, to do with as she will.* She unfastened a bracelet at her wrist, fumbling a little with her evening gloves and her indignation, then added to the page, *It is a bracelet of diamonds and sapphires.* She signed the note and added her Paris address below, then put note and bracelet into an envelope and handed it to Arthur.

'See that this reaches her, please, Arthur, and that Mr Carter does not take it back. Have I made myself clear?'

He tucked it into the inside pocket of his coat and bowed to her. 'Perfectly, Miss Koltsova.'

∽∽

Maud hardly heard Yvette wishing her good night. Every word that Henri had said about Morel burned in her, made her drunk. How pleased he must have been with himself, ready to wander out of town whenever they liked and start their new life in America, stepping over her corpse to do it without a thought. If they thought of her now it was as a nothing, carried away by the river with the rest of the rubbish. They were there now, untouchable in the lamplight, scraping their knives on the Countess's plates and drinking her wine while Maud remained here, neither dead nor alive.

She undressed and slid shivering under the sheets and again dreamed of her drowning. She must have cried out in her sleep because when she woke suddenly, she found one of Suzanne's waifs standing in her doorway. He was a good-looking young man in his twenties, though the flesh on his face looked rather loose and pale, his eyes yellowish. She started.

'Don't be afraid! I heard you shout and I wanted to see you were not needing help. I am Amedeo.' He put out his hand and smiled. His Italian accent was heavy, curling his words and throwing them at odd angles into the air.

'I recognise your voice. You're the Dante scholar?' She sat up in bed and took his hand. It did not seem shocking now, this man wandering into her bedroom in the middle of the night and she found she was not frightened.

'I am!' He stared at her thoughtfully. 'You look ill.'

'So do you.'

'Ha! Perhaps! But I am not really drunk yet. I came looking for Suzanne. When I find her she will give me money to get drunk and I will be well again. You need nothing?'

Maud shook her head and he shrugged and began to saunter back towards the door.

'Amedeo?'

'Yes, young lady?'

'What does Dante say of revenge?'

He turned back. 'That it is a sin. A sin of anger, and those who commit it are surrounded by a rank fog, forever tearing each other apart or gnawing at their own limbs. They are trapped in the marsh.' He sighed. 'I shall not waste the poetry on you if you do not speak Italian. I shall tell you instead what my mother told me when I came home from school covered in bruises from the bullies there.'

'What did she say?'

'To forget a wrong is the best revenge. But she was not right. Some wrong you must get a hot blade into it, take out the poison matter even if it costs you a little flesh. She said I must trust in God – but why should I trust Him to punish my enemies? He let them hurt me in the first place. Good night, young lady.'

CHAPTER 12

20 January 1910

*M*AUD WAS WOKEN BY TANYA, STILL UPSET AND carrying a basket of pastries. The young women ate them sitting on the bed while Sasha made coffee on the stove, Tanya biting down angrily on each one and refusing to talk until Maud said she could eat nothing else. Only then did they exchange their stories of the previous evening. When Maud had heard Tanya spit out the scheme the Countess and the Pinkerton man had dreamed up, she rested her chin on her knees.

'Yvette thought I was going to strike Madame de Civray last night,' she said.

'I wish you had,' Tanya replied. 'It would make me happy. A reward, she says! Like a bone for a dog.'

'The butler would have broken my arm.' Maud put her hand out in front of her and it did not shake. 'You have to go to Lafond's, Tanya. I shall take a trip to Printemps this morning. I need to buy something with a veil.' She saw the question in the tilt of Tanya's chin. 'I don't want anyone from the Académie to see me and ask questions.'

Tanya wiped the flakes of pastry slowly from her dress. 'You are not going home then, Maud? The Countess is a selfish monster, but if there is nothing to be done here . . . I would happily pay your fare if that would be of help.'

'Are you going to tell me to go home and forget it ever happened as well, Tanya?'

'What else can be done?' Maud said nothing. 'It makes me afraid for you, Maud.'

'Why?'

'You are too calm. Too quiet. I feel as if you have made some decision and you are not telling me what it is. Oh Maud, it was such a brief flowering you had. Those few weeks when you were with the Morels, you bloomed. You were easy to be with, less serious, and now there is this . . . I wish to God I had never taken you to Miss Harris.'

'Don't you think in a way it is funny, Tanya? I spent the happiest weeks of my life with people who intended to murder me from the start. I think that's funny.'

'No, it's not,' Tanya whispered fiercely. 'It's tragic. And don't tell me those are different sides of the same coin. I shall shriek here and now if you do.'

Maud shrugged. 'I thought that talking to the Countess, letting her know I was innocent would make me feel easier, but it hasn't. *They* are still out there in the world, and the Countess's answer, the plan of her little men in long coats – it's not enough for me. Morel has to suffer and he has to know why.'

Tanya took her hands between her own. 'You have a life. You have talent. Of course it is wrong, it is unjust, but you know life is not fair. Leave them to God.'

'No. I told you – it's not enough. You know that. And I *don't* have a life, Tanya. I'm still drowned in the river somehow and I need to get out.' She spoke softly and simply as if she were reciting her plans for the day – a walk in the park, a little sketching, revenge.

'And will this . . . punishment – will it help you?'

'I don't know. It cannot make me worse.'

Tanya stood up quickly and a small leather notebook fell from her pocket onto the bed. Maud picked it up ready to hand it to her, but something in Tanya's expression made her curious and she opened the pages. Tanya protested, but seeing it was already too late turned away to pick up her hat from the armchair. Maud looked through the pages and saw neat lists of figures of groceries and rents, the prices of meals in the cheaper restaurants. 'Tanya?'

'Do you remember what Valadon said, that I will never be an artist because I like things to be pretty?'

Maud handed the notebook back to her. 'I do.'

'Well, it's true. But I think wanting things to be pretty might make me some money. Portraits. Ones of wives and children in comfortable homes that might pay five hundred francs a time. I have been about it half the night and it seems to me that five hundred francs can buy a great deal.' She looked both proud and a little ashamed, and frightened too that Maud would laugh at her. 'I know that it is a lot for a portrait, but I think men would rather have me in their home, painting their families, than most other artists.' She looked at the neat lists of figures again, then touched the jewelled pin at her throat. 'Am I being stupid?'

'Five hundred francs does buy a great deal, Tanya. And many husbands might think of hiring you where they would not hire anyone else.' Maud got out of the bed and the world did not spin or lurch. She felt as if she had new black blood in her veins. 'I am going to see Miss Harris later this morning.'

Tanya put the notebook back into her pocket. 'Do you wish me to come with you?'

'No, this I had better do by myself. And in your lists, Tanya, put something aside for sickness or accident.'

◌◌◌

Charlotte was with Miss Harris going through the accounts when Maud called, and though she had thought she would speak to Miss Harris alone, she remembered what Charlotte had said about Morel smiling too much and invited her to stay. They had heard nothing from the Morels about her supposed disgrace and so greeted her with pleasure. Miss Harris seemed a little disappointed when Maud lifted her veil and Miss Harris noticed she still looked rather drawn. Then Maud began her story. It felt as if she were relating someone else's history. Once or twice Miss Harris put her hands together, palm to palm, and lifted the fingertips to her lips. It was something between a prayer and an attempt to stifle an exclamation.

When Maud had finished speaking, Miss Harris was silent for some time. Then she reached out to take Maud's hand across the table.

'Oh Miss Heighton! I am so sorry.'

Maud wondered whether, if the Countess had offered that generous sympathy, she might be back in England by now.

'I want justice, Miss Harris,' she said. 'And I would like you to help me.'

Miss Harris still held her hand. 'He is leaving Paris, you say? The Countess intends to reclaim her money from him there before he can do more harm? Well, my dear. Certainly it seems that justice has been denied you in this world, but you shall have it in the next.' Maud tried to pull her hand away, but Miss Harris kept hold of her. 'No, my dear. You shall hear me. There is nothing – *nothing*

263

– you can do to this man that will compare with the agony he will feel when he finds himself judged before his Creator. His sufferings will be terrible. He will see what he has done in God's Holy Light and you will pity him. Yes, you shall. Pray for him, Miss Heighton. That is my advice. Go home, lead a good and useful life and pray for them both. They have damned themselves. God has saved you for some purpose, I am sure, but I am just as sure it was not to take revenge on the Morels. This is my advice to you, dear Miss Heighton. I shall not help you in any other way.'

Maud's hand was released. She stood and curtsied to Miss Harris with the greatest respect, but left without saying another word.

☙❧

She walked across Paris. The rain had been steady all day but rather than return to her grey room in Montmartre she walked the length of the Champs Élysées, passing the twin domes of the Grand and Petit Palais and crossing Place de la Concorde. She did not look at the place where Sylvie had shown her the stolen brooch or search for any sign of where Mme Prideux had died. The cars raced by her and the high omnibuses teetered past. When she crossed the river on the Solferino Bridge the embankments became quieter. The rain persisted but the cafés were still full, men and women going about their sanctioned public lives under the striped awnings and behind low, burning braziers. Some of the men stared, tried to speak to her, but she simply looked over the tops of their heads and they melted back into the crowds. She reached the Quai Conti, but only when she was at the bottom of Rue de Seine did she hesitate. Her chest ached again, a dark flowering. She could walk past the door, the windows, and glance up. If, at that moment someone – Miss Harris, Tanya or Yvette – had happened on her and offered her again their comfort and friendship, perhaps she would have left Paris that evening and she would have been saved. But no one came.

She walked down the street looking straight ahead of her, crossed the Boulevard Saint-Germain, then just as she came opposite the house, she looked up and froze. Sylvie was standing in the window with her back to it, facing into the room. She still *is*, Maud thought. She still is when I am not there. How can that be? Knowing that Sylvie was in the Countess's house had been pain enough, but to see her – her white neck with the blond hair gathered on top of her head – it was pain beyond all imagining. Then *he* appeared at her side. Morel. He took her in his arms and held her. Sylvie was laughing, her head thrown back. They are happy because I am dead, Maud thought. The idea seemed to take the air from her. Morel. The man who had thrown her into the water without a qualm, now wrapped around Sylvie and murmuring into her neck, telling her the places they would go with the money they had stolen, the wonderful, delightful life they would have together now Maud was rotting in the Seine and he had his fist full of diamonds.

Morel seemed to feel something – he lifted his head and glanced out of the window, but Maud was already gone, dragging her bitter heart with her. As she walked away, the sellers of the afternoon newspapers began to call out for custom. 'The waters are rising! The river mounts!'

When she returned to the room she was soaked to the skin. At first she didn't see Charlotte sitting by the stove with her legs crossed. She was smoking a cigarette, and on her knee was propped a book; it had the tell-tale thin paper and gilded edges of a Bible. She looked up at Maud's bedraggled form.

'I've lit the stove – I hope that's not a problem. The room was freezing and I wasn't sure how long I'd have to wait.'

'Of course,' Maud said, taking off the veiled hat and putting it on the bed. 'What can I do for you, Miss . . .'

'Just call me Charlotte,' the woman said, waving the cigarette and looking back down to her reading. 'It will wait. Put something dry on before you get sick again.'

Maud did so, glancing at her visitor out of the corner of her eye as she changed out of her wet clothes. Charlotte was dressed, as ever, in black and wore thick-soled shoes. Her forehead was a little lined and Maud wondered if she could be as much as forty. When she had dressed, Maud dragged one of the wicker chairs over so she could sit opposite Charlotte by the fire. Charlotte closed her Bible and reached behind her chair, hauling onto her knee a basket complete with red gingham cover and took out a flask and bread and butter wrapped in greaseproof paper. Without saying anything she poured out milky tea into one of the china cups she had brought with her and handed it to Maud, along with one of the parcels of bread and butter. Then, when she had served herself, she said, 'Miss Heighton, I wish you to know first of all that Miss Harris has done more good in this world than any other individual I have ever met.'

'I understand,' Maud said. She sipped the tea and a wave of nostalgia broke over her so sudden and complete it seemed an outside force. She thought of the tea room in Reeth where her mother had taken her once when she was a child, the charabanc ride up the North Yorkshire Dales and the shifting banks of green on the moor. It lasted only a moment and then she was back in her grey Paris room and listening to Charlotte.

'She has brought more lost souls to God than you can imagine.

Creatures that no one else would think worth a moment of their time have become good and useful members of their community. She has, through nothing but patience and kindness, turned drunks into true believers, whores into nurses. Even those who are still too lost in their own misery to conceive of a God who loves them will follow *her* into church because she believes – and they believe in her. She does not preach. She prays for them and offers them her love, no matter how miserable their condition. I am blessed indeed to see what wonders God can work through her.'

Maud had nothing to say in reply, but continued to drink her tea and watch her. Charlotte leaned forward, lifting her index finger: 'And she is right, absolutely right that you should leave the Morels to God and pray for them, *but . . .*'

Maud looked at her over the edge of her teacup. 'But you are not Miss Harris?'

Charlotte sat back again, her plain face twisted with a half-smile. 'Indeed, I am not.' She put her tea onto the floor and from the basket produced a notebook. 'Explain to me what you have in mind.'

Maud reached for the bread and butter. 'I mean to haunt him.'

When Yvette swung into the room an hour later, Charlotte had finished taking her notes. She smiled with real affection at the model and when Yvette crossed the room to kiss her, lifted up her cheek to receive the salutation with a slight blush.

'There is still a good English community at Rheims,' she said to Maud. 'We have sent a number of girls there who needed to leave Paris and its associations behind them and they will have made friends. Every community relies on shared intelligence.'

'And they will have the necessary authority?'

'Naturally,' Charlotte said, packing her basket again. 'They are trusted. And we shall tell them to make it clear that if anyone buys those diamonds, their names will become mud amongst all of our rich American and English donors. And our Russian ones,' she added with a vague smile. 'It is easy to do the same in Paris. We shall shut all the doors to him and leave him loose on the streets for you to hunt.'

Maud stood to shake her hand and see her to the door. It was strange how these habits of politeness re-emerged in the company of another middle-class Englishwoman.

'Thank you.'

The woman shook her head. 'Do not. I suspect it is weak of me to assist you, but I cannot help myself, and as I have the nature God gave me, I suppose He must have some plan of which I know nothing. Or perhaps He means to test us and we are failing.'

Yvette had thrown herself down on the bed and waved as Charlotte left them. She had snatched up one of the packets of bread and butter and now ate it lying on her back and staring up at the ceiling while Maud told her what Madame de Civray had said to Tanya, and then began to explain her own plans.

'Morel goes to Rheims tomorrow. He returns on the twenty-third. If Charlotte is as successful as she hopes, he won't be able to sell the diamonds. And while the Pinkertons may not be able to do anything illegal in France, I can. I am a ghost, after all.' Perhaps she expected Yvette to protest in some way at this point, but she did not, just waited for Maud to continue. 'I want to hire a pick-pocket to steal them back from him and frighten him at the same time. I want him to wonder if he is being pursued.' She sat down on the bed. 'I saw him this afternoon in the window at Rue de Seine.' And when Yvette turned to stare at her: 'I know I shouldn't have gone. Don't say it. He looked so happy, so pleased with himself.'

'He won't stay like that if the Pinkertons have their way. He'll end up ruined,' Yvette said evenly.

'It's not enough. I want him to be frightened. Scared. And for as long as I can keep him that way.'

Yvette took her hand, wound her fingers around Maud's and unravelled them again as if playing with a toy. 'We want him punished too, Maud. Tanya and I. But we don't want you to put yourself in danger again. You don't care about that though, do you?'

'I'd drag him down to hell myself if I could, even if I had to stay there with him.'

'So you want to find a pick-pocket?'

'Yes.' There was a long pause.

'But you don't ask me for an introduction.'

'I didn't like to assume.'

Yvette groaned and threw herself backwards onto the bed. 'Oh Maud! You've become an avenging angel but kept the manners of an English miss and a proper sense of decorum to your inferiors.'

'You're not my inferior, Yvette. I know that,' Maud said.

'You thought I was when you first saw me. You proper English girls always do. More meat to be put up on the dais and stared at. Don't be sorry. If we worried about the soul of every person we saw on the street, we'd go mad.' Yvette clambered out of the bed and went to the cracked mirror to peer at herself. She saw lines beginning at the corners of her eyes. 'I can help you. I would tell you to stay quiet and let me do the talking, but that's never a problem with you. Are you strong enough for Rue Lepic after all your wanderings?'

'Now?'

'Now. Before I change my mind.'

CHAPTER 13

*R*UE LEPIC WAS THE STEEP NARROW ROAD THAT LED
to the summit of Montmartre, kinking and twisting up
the hill. It seemed to get poorer and dirtier with every step climbed
until suddenly they turned a corner and everything changed. They
were surrounded by neat gardens in their winter rest, fruit trees
and comfortable freshly painted villas. The street-lamps were being
lit, and new patches of light and shadow lifted and glowed along
the damp road. A man with long hair and velvet trousers sauntered
past and nodded at Yvette. Maud recognised him, his grubby silk
scarf. He was one of the men she had seen on the Boulevard Saint-
Michel selling his sketches for two francs a time. He looked too
old to be a student. Perhaps he was another of these men who had
come to Paris in their youth and never escaped it. Maud shivered.
To be trapped in Paris seemed no better to her than being trapped
in her father's home. As they passed the *Lapin Agile* on Rue Saint-
Vincent they heard a great shout of laughter from inside. Someone
was singing.

Yvette didn't look round and Maud followed, watching her.
The model's usual animation seemed to be draining away. She
didn't look at the people passing her and her shoulders were
hunched. There had been something of this in her that evening in

the bar behind Les Halles, but this was different. She was not playing at anything now; the strain showed on her thin face and made her look older. She turned into Rue des Saules and the respectable country village disappeared like fog. Here the apartment buildings were crushed and dirty, windows broken and boarded up with ragged-edged planks. In the thickening darkness, small groups of men and women watched them from the doorways and steps. The women wore clogs and skirts that showed their ankles, their hair short and framing their faces in straight black lines. The men were young in flat caps and striped shirts, coloured handkerchiefs tied around their throats. The uniform of the *apaches*.

In the first boarding-house Maud had lived in, before she learned the brutal truths of Paris economy and moved somewhere colder and cheaper, there had been a rather silly middle-aged English couple who had invited her on a spree one evening. She had been lonely enough to accept and watched her money disappear in a couple of second-rate hostelries. The couple were determined to see the *real* Paris, and they had taken her to a restaurant where they claimed all the great writers of the city came to dine. Maud thought the clientèle were mostly tourists and the *escargots* were likely made of cat. Their pièce-de-résistance was to take her to an *apache* club. It was an over-priced and soulless little dance hall with rude waiters and a dispirited band, but it delighted them – and when a couple of young men fought on the dance floor for the attentions of a girl, they looked as if they would burst with excitement. The fight appeared unconvincing to Maud, and the gendarmes who arrived to break it up and throw the gawking English out onto the street did not make her think it was any more genuine. Their uniforms didn't fit. Maud had seen a drunk hit a woman; the hissing violence of it, the suddenness of the action, the silence of the blow. These people made too much noise to be in any genuine pain or fear. Her hosts asked if she wished to come out with them again for another evening, and she refused as politely as she could, knowing that they would take it as a sign of her fear and fragility at the wild and debauched life they had shown her, and be rather thrilled at frightening her.

These men here, talking and smoking in the muddy alleyways behind the Rue des Saules were not imitations of outlaws. What Maud had seen in that club was a blurred reproduction and here were the originals in vivid colour. The men and women she had seen at the Caveau des Innocents were older, worn with work and anxious only to distract themselves with drink and song and human warmth. Here the air crackled with calculation and suspicion and suppressed violence. One man stepped forward, his hands in his pockets. His face had a long pink scar that ran from just over his eye down to his jaw. 'Yvette. Haven't seen you in months, little sister.' He looked at Maud, and she felt him weighing her up. She was wearing her veil and gloves. 'Have you brought us a chicken for the pot?'

Yvette took the knife from her pocket and opened it with a click that sounded like a gunshot in the quiet street. She spoke softly. 'I'm here to see Mother, Louis. Touch my friend here and I'll gut you like the pig you are.'

He grinned. 'Oh, Yvette with her little knife! Always ready to defend someone.' He scratched the side of his nose. 'Keep her then. We're off to the Bois to find something fatter anyway. Come with us if you like. You can watch while I throttle some gentleman walking his poodle a little late. Even give you first go of his pockets.'

A young woman appeared beside him and wound her arm through his. Her face looked like an angel's, soft and clear with Prussian-blue eyes. The whites showed round the edge of them, making her face seem oddly bright, attentive. She could not have been more than fifteen. She pressed herself up close to Louis's side. When she spoke, her voice was sharp-edged and her pretty face became older and harder.

'Your real mummy hasn't come to find you yet, Yvette? What was she – a princess? A lady? No sign of her after all these years? Remember the stories you used to tell us – how she was going to take us all away in a white carriage. Poor old Yvette. They never came to look for you, did they?' She gazed up at Louis and whined, 'She was always crazy, Louis. Don't let her come.'

Yvette lifted her chin. 'Don't fret yourself, Nina. I wouldn't go anywhere with *him*.'

He put his arm around the girl's waist and she chirruped with pleasure like a cat grateful for its feed. 'Too right. Leave her to her pipes and books till she has to earn her smoke money on her back. Maybe I'll let you be one of my girls if you're good.'

'Get out of my way, Louis.'

He stood back slowly to let them pass into the yard. 'See you soon, sister. You're starting to look old, you know. Another five years and you'll be selling it for a franc a time with my other pets.' He laughed and returned to the group he'd been standing with at the kerb, taking the girl along with him.

Maud looked sideways at Yvette. Her eyes were bright and her face a little flushed. 'Come on.'

She took her through a dirty yard into a kitchen that opened straight off the cobbles. The table was scrubbed and the floor was being swept by a child about seven years of age dressed in a wool shift but bare-footed despite the season. At the head of the table sat a thin middle-aged female with black buttoned boots and a plum silk dress. It was of an old-fashioned style and for a second Maud was struck by her resemblance to Tanya's aunt Vera. This woman seemed like the dark face of the same coin. She was drinking tea from a delicate service decorated with birds of paradise. She looked up when she heard them approach and smiled. Her lips were dark red, and she spread them to show her yellow teeth.

'Yvette! How nice. And you've brought a friend.'

Yvette clicked the knife shut and slipped it back into her pocket. '*Maman*. I hope you are well.'

❧❧

Maud did as she was told and took no part in the negotiations other than nod her assent to the price agreed and offer the necessary advance. There was a bitumen delight in offering up her stock of money so easily, without noting each small amount paid and making impossible calculations for her keep in the future. This had to be done and this was the cost. The future would take care of itself.

Much of the discussion between Yvette and the woman in purple she did not understand. They spoke in a French Maud did not recognise – some sort of slang that was slippery and bewildering. The money was folded and placed in an embossed silver purse. The woman nodded to them and returned to sipping her tea with her little finger crooked away from the cup. The streets outside were quiet – the *apaches*, it seemed, had left for the hunt.

Yvette did not speak to her again until they had reached Place du Tertre. She hesitated there, looking at the cafés, the noise and light biting away at the wintry edges of the square, but when Maud asked if she wished to visit one of them, she shook her head. 'I need to breathe.' She took Maud instead to the terrace below the Sacré Coeur, and there they took possession of one of the benches that faced away from the new cathedral, its shocking white and squeezed domes ghostly behind them. Maud opened her umbrella, not a rich silk and tortoiseshell beauty like Tanya's but something more modest from Printemps, and held it over both of them. Their bodies touched shoulder to thigh and warmed each other. Yvette lit a cigarette and folded her arm across her chest. 'Go on then. Ask.'

'Is that your mother?'

She turned away, looking towards the west of the city. 'I don't know. She always said she was, but she takes in babies from time to time for a fee. The little ones always work as pick-pockets for her. I did until I was thirteen.'

'Like Fagin.' Yvette said nothing and Maud glanced at her. 'He's a character in a book, *Oliver Twist*, by Dickens.'

'I know who Fagin is, Maud. The nuns taught us to read. That's where all that . . . what Nina was saying came from. The stories I used to tell of the rich men and women coming to save us from life on the Butte.'

Maud thought of Yvette as a child telling stories about the heroes who were going to rescue her and her playmates, thought how often she had woken in her sickness to see her at the end of her bed with a book in her hands, thought of her attention and mimicry in the studio, of her retreats into the peace and warmth of opium. Maud had hidden from her misery in drawing, in paint; Yvette obviously had her methods of escape too.

'I never thought of you as having family, Yvette.'

'Thought I just sprang up with the weeds from between the cobblestones, did you?'

'I suppose I did in a way.'

Yvette grunted. 'It's not much of a family. *Maman* rules a little shit-heap and sells souls to do it. I thought I was better than that, but who knows. Maybe I will end up back there.' Maud said nothing. 'Thanks for not telling me I'm wrong.'

'I hope you are, but sometimes it takes chance or accident to cut our moorings.'

Yvette glowered out over the city like an angry angel. 'I'm not sure I believe it is ever possible. We are all set on a course the first day we open our eyes. Tanya with her money, you so proper and good. I shall earn what I can and spend it on dope, remembering books and dreaming myself into them. I am only putting off what has to happen by keeping away from the dens now.'

Maud followed her gaze. The city was coming alive with light, its unnatural brilliance affronting the darkness, but the wind and rain still blew across it in waves. 'I have been to the Caveau des Innocents.'

'And within a day you are shaking hands with Charlotte and seeing her out. You can't escape what you are.'

Maud watched her profile, the cigarette smoke tugged away from her lips in the wind and thought of Sylvie in the graveyard, her glamour, her genteelly faked craving for opium that had so convinced Maud. She breathed in deeply as she watched the rain falling through the lamplight, then spoke. 'After my father died and my step-mother left town, I set the fire that burned down the warehouse and our old house.' Yvette turned away from the city and stared at her. Maud blinked rapidly but continued. 'Everyone was telling me to stop putting off the inevitable and join my brother's household. I could not paint well enough to earn my own living and I had no other talents. I should become a wife and mother. But I just couldn't – I couldn't believe that was the only choice. It seemed so wrong. And I hated that house. Then I thought about the fire and it seemed like the only thing to do.'

Yvette put out her cigarette, grinding the butt into the damp ground. It was some time before she spoke and when she did it was almost in a whisper. 'Were you frightened?'

It came back to Maud at once, the smell of burning wood, the sound of her own footsteps hurrying through the empty house once the fire had caught. 'Yes. I had to go back up the stairs after I had set it going and wait for the smoke to reach me. I thought that would make it look more real. And they did believe me, no one thought for a second I could have started it. Poor Maud, running into the street in her dressing-gown and bare feet to escape the flames.'

'But you were free?' Maud nodded. 'I don't think I have anything to burn down.' Yvette turned back towards the city and Maud said nothing. She had always told herself that she set the fire for the insurance, now she wondered if that were true. Someone would have bought the property at some point. She had burned it because she loathed it, because under her mild ways and respectable speech Maud was thwarted, indignant and shimmering with rage. The fire had burned so hot the air seemed to ripple. She remembered what Valadon had said, how her fists were clenched and sore when she woke up in the mornings. Maud thought of herself as a good woman, but now she was beginning to wonder. She wished she still believed in God, believed in Him with all that passionate conviction of Miss Harris or Charlotte. Then she could pray for Yvette and herself and think it would do some good.

'You still want this, Maud? I can call it off if you want.'

She stared out over the soaking city. 'It is what I want. I will not go meekly back to England with him free and happy.'

'Then I had better explain what we agreed.'

CHAPTER 14

CHRISTIAN MOREL LEFT FOR RHEIMS A HAPPY MAN. HE made himself comfortable in the first-class compartment and gazed smugly at his reflection in the polished glass as the train pulled away. He had planned this as a jaunt; a little pleasure trip to ease his mind now the task of keeping a close watch on Henri was done. Still, putting constant pressure on the old codger had done some good. He had done the recutting and polishing faster than Morel could have hoped, and done it well in spite of his indignation. What's more, stealing from the Countess had brought extra benefits. Her gratitude to him for returning the tiara discreetly and with due deference meant he had now made some very valuable contacts with rich Americans. America was the thing. A new, ambitious nation not dead and dried up like France, crisped, its juices all run out and lapped up before Christian had had more than a taste of it. Then he frowned, and still watching himself in the glass, raised one eyebrow. The brilliant man of business considers. Perhaps he should abandon the name Morel in Paris and disappear into that vast new continent as Gravot again. He had heard a couple of men in the club talking about Los Angeles as a place that looked likely to boom. And did he really want to swap Paris for the constrictions of Boston? He and Sylvie would travel quietly to New York, then head out west, sell the great stone in Chicago and arrive on the Pacific Coast like heroes. Yes, let Morel live and die in Paris. He stroked his chin. He was clean-shaven, a modern man. All the ambitious young men in America would recognise him as one of their own.

He went to the best jeweller in Rheims straight from the station with his story ready and waiting on the tip of his smooth tongue. He planned to say he was selling the bracelet on behalf of his sister, a woman of fashion in Paris who had accepted it from an admirer. Now the admirer was replaced by a respectable husband and it would be better if his sister became a wife with an equally respectable bundle of banknotes rather than another man's jewels. They would take it from him with a vague smile, but then seeing the quality and clarity of the stones their hands would twitch to close round it. He would see the gulp of desire in their throats, the sheen in their eyes as they imagined the potential profit.

He took the tram to Place Royale rehearsing these pleasant conversations in his mind. He would seem a little uncertain when the first price was offered. He would say perhaps he should try another of the jewellers in the city, these happy few who supplied the champagne merchants with their diamonds and rubies. The jeweller would begin to sweat and gradually increase his price until he got to a reasonable amount – fifty thousand francs or so. Morel would then agree and everyone would be delighted with their bargain.

He hopped down from the tram and tipped his hat to the statue of the old King watching the square and providing a perch for the pigeons to watch it too, and chose his first target – an elegant little shop tucked into the corner of the square with a discreet window display of luxury and taste. The doorbell rang out and the girl behind the counter smiled at him sweetly as he pushed the door open, wished him good morning and asked if she could show him anything. She had the trace of a foreign accent which reminded him suddenly of Maud, her precise and mannered French. It almost made him stumble, but as soon as he began his story of the sister and the admirer his tongue gained its usual fluency. Her expression did not change, but there was somehow a slight chill in the air. He produced the bracelet, uncoiling it from a velvet pouch he kept in his breast-pocket. She nodded at it, but did not reach out to take it. Instead she rang a tiny brass bell on the counter and an old gentleman with powdery skin and wearing a black suit emerged from a door behind the counter. He had a slight stoop and the flesh hung from his thin face in loose pouches.

The young girl moved away, only very lightly touching his old liver-spotted hand as she passed. The old man glanced at the bracelet and at once came that tell-tale swallow. It was as obvious as licking his lips. He put his hand out and took it, then for fully five minutes examined the stones. Christian began to feel impatient. There could be no doubt about the quality of the stones, and he knew he looked like a respectable man, a man of means – the sort of man who would inspire trust in a well-brought-up Englishwoman, in fact. That he had proved in the last few weeks. The old goat should have named a price already, or at least be making himself friendly.

Christian never thought about his father when he could avoid it, or about his father's death, but sometimes when he was tired or under some sudden strain the images would roll back over him. For a moment, the bracelet in the old man's hands changed, became those half-remembered gleams smeared in his father's blood. He was there again. The crack of gunfire in the distance and the caustic smell of smoke from burning buildings. Petrol thrown onto the barricades and ignited – the stink of it clung to him. He wondered if the old man examining the diamonds could smell it. He felt his mother's hand – he had struggled to hang onto her when she screamed and started running across the square. He would have run the other way, away from the man kneeling over his father's corpse but he had to follow her so he did. He looked away from the man in the shop, tried to concentrate on the mosaic borders in blue and gold that ran around the top of the walls. Instead he saw the woman holding back his mother. She had the build of a peasant and his mother, so thin and uncomfortable to lean against, had not half her strength. He threw himself at the man on the ground. He saw his father's blank and empty face, the bullet-wound in his forehead and the man pawing at his innards. The man struck at him with his elbow and he fell back slightly stunned. Perhaps he could have got up again but he did not, only watched as the man held up one of the stones. He cleared his throat. He was sweating.

The elderly jeweller looked up finally and shook his head. 'I'm sorry, sir. We are not buying today.' *But you want them,* Christian wanted to say. *I know you want them.* And without even making an offer? How could a man have got so old and still be such a fool?

'Very well. Do you recommend any other jeweller in town?'

Did he imagine it, or did the old goat's eyes flicker towards the girl? 'I respect all my colleagues in the city, but I suspect you will not find many willing to buy at this time.' He handed the bracelet back to Christian, and he seemed in the moment the diamonds left his grip, to age a little further. He had the obvious hunger of the connoisseur, but he did not want them?

Christian controlled himself enough to give them a curt nod of farewell and went back out into the square. He had the feeling that the statue of the King was looking at him with a slight sneer. It reminded him a little of Jean Prideux, that self-righteous prig. Well, he had beaten him in the end. He crossed the square and swore violently at the driver of a tiny, ridiculous little motor-car who almost knocked him from his feet, coming out of nowhere and with no regard for the safety of others. Just when he was thinking of Prideux too – it was too much. Morel had to pause for a moment, smooth down his hair and adjust his high collar to reassure himself.

The rival jewellery shop on the square was rather more brash in its display than the first place, and there were two women on the premises already gossiping as the assistant wrapped up their packages. The man behind the counter was younger. He looked prosperous, modern. Christian noticed with approval that the fittings and furnishing of the place made the one opposite look drab and stately. True, this man did not look the type to become emotional about diamonds, and would probably be a greater challenge to bargain with, but surely he could be relied on not to turn down such an excellent offer. And anyway, a little hard bargaining got Christian's blood flowing. However, the jeweller did not even look at the bracelet. As Christian fetched it from his pocket the man was already telling him he had no intention of buying today and with shocking rudeness turned away from his customer. Had a new mine been discovered? Had Rheims suddenly found a river of huge diamonds flowing through their cellars? Had they all become too simple-minded to see the bargain of a lifetime laid out in front of them?

Christian took a room at the Lion d'Or and retreated to it shivering. He had thought his business would be done by now and that he would have the whole of the next day to stretch his legs and buy foolish gifts for his wife. Instead, he ate a poor dinner that cramped his stomach all night and woke to a grey morning with the work still to do. He consulted the directory in the hotel and chose another three places of business that should, by rights, snatch the stones from him in gratitude and delight. All three turned him down.

On the second night in the hotel he tried half-heartedly to seduce a young woman who had travelled from London to see the cathedral, but something in the way she ate her food and mispronounced her French reminded him again of Maud and he lost his appetite for the game. He wondered if he were ill. The lean-to he had rented off Cours du Commerce to house Henri and his equipment had been damp with this continual rain, and he had been bored there, watching, always watching for any tricks from the resentful old devil. Locking him in at night with a bottle of red so he didn't go off on his wanderings, hiding the diamonds in their place. Then that invitation from the Countess and badgering Henri to finish the job, so that the dinner would be a celebration of their cleverness.

He had worked hard for this, Christian thought. The continual restraint, the constant watch he had to keep on his behaviour while the English miss was in their hands. There was that one night after dealing with Prideux when he had drunk whisky late into the night. Sylvie had been angry with him, afraid that drunkenness would scare off their little English bird, but Miss Heighton had slept through his stumblings and he had needed a drink. It was a strain on the nerves to arrange an accident like that, even among the chaos of Paris.

After his story-telling to Maud he had gone in search of Madame Prideux at the raggedy guest-house where she was staying and greeted her like an old friend. He embraced her and insisted on taking her out to dinner, his second that evening, and all the time sympathised, apologised. All a misunderstanding. Letters gone astray. He showed her the stubs in his chequebook to demonstrate the amounts that he had tried to send to her. They had been cashed, he said. So he had assumed all was well. He'd been a little hurt not to receive any letter from her, of course but . . . By saying very little he all but convinced her that her own son was stealing from her. Funny. It seemed she's rather believe that than believe she'd been fooled by him and Sylvie. He praised her brilliance at finding him against all the odds and learned she had seen him crossing Boulevard Saint-Germain but lost him in the crowd again and had spent the next four days asking after him until at last her questions had led her to his house on Rue de Seine.

How glad he was that she had persisted, he said, at which she blushed like a virgin. To explain his use of a new name had been trickier. He told her he associated the name of Gravot with his terrible past so had decided to take his wife's maiden name as his own. He upset himself talking to her about his struggle with those awful memories; real tears trembled on his eyelashes. It was their time in his home town that had done it, he said. He had finally visited his mother's grave and the emotion had been too much. That was why the couple had left so quickly. But he had never, never intended to desert his dear friend Mme Prideux. How could she think it? She could not have lost faith in him? Surely?

The woman was overjoyed to love him again and swallowed his charm like champagne. By the time he led her across the Champs with the promise of one more glass of wine at one of the really good restaurants to celebrate their reunion, she was happy as a child . . . then it was only a matter of waiting till the right moment when the crowd was thick and the traffic was charging by.

Christian took another drink and loosened his tie. He had not wished her to die, though he supposed in the long run, that was easier. A broken leg, the clanging of ambulances, her off her feet and out of the way for a few weeks was all that was necessary, but the car caught her and threw her in the air and into the path of another. He had walked away from the crowd gathering round the accident a little unsteadily. Killing was not easy. Maud too, the way she had tried to cling onto him. Disgusting, but necessary. It would make them rich, but still. Bloody diamonds.

He and Sylvie had arrived in Paris planning another 'investment scheme', called there by all that beautiful American money flowing through the city like the river. One only had to dip in one's hand . . . He had only seduced the maid to gather a little more information about the rich circle Madame de Civray had around her. Then he'd seen the tiara and thirsted for the stones – and the way she just left the tiara in its case in the dressing room! She didn't wear it more than once a year, the girl had said. It was more temptation than he could bear. He came home and told Sylvie. Explained his hunger. She understood and worked out how he could have the diamonds. Dear girl. All her cleverness. The opium had been his suggestion. They both enjoyed a smoke from time to time, and it added just the right thickening to the story of Maud's downfall. It had all gone beautifully. Even Lafond, who seemed sceptical at first, hadn't been able to resist the testimony of the shop girl and clerk at the pawn office. The body hadn't turned up at the morgue, but no doubt it would some day. The Countess had been an angel. Yet after two days of refusals, of seeing the diamonds turned away as if he were trying to sell paste, they began to feel like a curse.

'Hey, fella, you look like I feel.' A man in a brown suit was addressing him. Another American. Why did they always want to talk to everyone? It was as if they were constantly astonished to find other human beings on this side of the Atlantic.

'Can I buy you a drink?' the man went on. 'I've been in this town three days and it's been three days too long. There's no sense of business in this place. No vision. No sense of opportunity. And my Gawd, the food! Still, the champagne is good. I buy for the best hotels in New York, but the way these people are, you'd think they were doing *me* the favour.'

This chimed so neatly with what Morel himself thought about the place that he sat up and began to look more fondly on the man in brown. A drink or two later and he was positively cheerful. Feeling more secure now the drink was in him, he took out the little pouch with the bracelet in and showed it to his new friend.

'What were you asking for them?' Christian told him and the man laughed. 'What, that's about five thousand dollars, yeah? Hell, I know a bargain when I see one. Sure, I'll take them off you for that. We'll go to my bank first thing in the morning.'

The clouds lifted from Christian and in the little bar, the sun began to shine. They ordered another bottle to seal their deal and their new friendship when the maid approached and told the gentleman there was a phone call for him at the booth by the reception desk. He shrugged. 'Only be a minute, friend.'

Time passed. The champagne in the American's glass lost its sparkle. Who spends so long on the telephone? Christian put the bracelet back into his breast-pocket and went out into the lobby where the reception desk stood; the telephone booth behind it was empty. The clerk looked up with a polite smile and a slight gesture of the head that seemed to convey she was at her guest's disposal, of course.

'That American man – came out to take a phone call. We were having a drink together. Where is he?'

The clerk smiled, though something in her eyes was blank and unwelcoming. 'Our only American guest checked out a few minutes ago, sir.'

Morel controlled his temper and went to pay the bar bill. Each note seemed to burn as he passed it over. He hated this town.

CHAPTER 15

23 January 1910

THE TRAIN ROLLED INTO PARIS VERY LATE. MOREL had enjoyed a carriage to himself for most of the journey, but for the last slow part of the trip his privacy had been invaded by a businessman from Éperney who sighed and shook his head over the newspaper. Christian tried to ignore him, staring fixedly out into the darkness and seeing his own handsome face ghostly in the glass. Why had that damned American run off? The diamonds burned next to his heart. Five thousand dollars for the bracelet was a bargain: he would take no less than seventy thousand for the grand jewel when they reached America, yet if he had no buyers they were worth no more than cobblestones. Of all the luck! No doubt the call was from one of the American's contacts in the city and the deals he had thought dead had risen into life again. It was just a coincidence. That and the strange resistance of the diamond dealers in the city to grab a bargain. It meant nothing, it could mean nothing. He and Sylvie had been clever and this strange little trip aside there was nothing to indicate there was any sort of trouble brewing. Miss Koltsova had swallowed the story, so had the Countess and Lafond. He could smell the gunsmoke on the streets of Paris again, see the man, his hands all bloody. He wished Sylvie was with him. If this carried on, he might have one of those moments when he lost himself and came to, not knowing how much time had passed or where he was.

'The waters are rising.'

Christian turned away from his own reflection. 'I'm sorry?'

'The waters, sir. Rising. Such losses in the provinces and now it seems Paris herself is threatened. The river is already higher than it has been for ten years and the waters keep coming.'

'Indeed.'

The man was so determined to talk that even this was taken as an invitation to conversation. 'Our sins will find us out. Be assured, sir.'

'What did you say?'

'Our sins. Look at us with our electric lights and our underground railways. Motor-cars everywhere. The moving walkways at the exhibition in 1900. We rebel against Nature and she will punish us. It is the cutting down of the trees, it makes the wood spirits angry . . .'

The man's first words had sent a tremor of shock through Christian, but as he began to chatter about such nonsense, he relaxed a little. Still, high water in Paris. The river had been full when he left, but floods? Would it affect him, his hiding-place? No, not in a hundred years would the waters reach it. He felt a deep urgency to leave Paris as soon as they could. He would risk selling the bracelet there, after all. The chances of the Countess happening to hear that he had been selling diamonds was infinitesimal, and even if she did, what connection could it have to her with her tiara back in its case and the woman who had stolen it at the bottom of the river?

Finally the train drew into the station in great clouds of hissing steam and Morel descended into the usual maelstrom of porters and guards, stepping round hatboxes and breathing in the cold heavy air of a damp Parisian evening. He walked out into the square in front of the station. After hours penned up in the train his instinct was to walk, but the rain fell steadily, and spiteful gusts of wind threw handfuls of it into his face, where it stung like gravel. He unstrapped his umbrella from the travelling bag and as he stood there he heard a shout in the centre of the square.

'I've been robbed! My wallet!' A tall man in a suit the same cut as his own was turning in circles like a dog chasing its tail. He spotted a gendarme and trotted off towards him, his umbrella raised. Like most of the other gentlemen in the crowd, Christian checked his valuables were still with him, slipping his hand into the breast-pocket of his coat and feeling the diamond bracelet in its little bag.

'Madame Prideux!' A voice shouted the name almost next to his ear. He took a step back and collided with a young man in working clothes. The young man steadied him.

'Careful there, Dad!' Then he disappeared into the crowd. Morel strained to see who had shouted the name and saw another man, older, approaching a young woman on the other side of the crowd and taking her arm. Christian could not see her face, since she was veiled and had her back to him, but there was something familiar about the shape of her. Before the impression could fully form, the man and woman were lost in the crowd.

How common a name was Prideux? He had not met many, but the woman he had killed had two married sons. Had she had brothers? There were probably cousins scattered all over the country. Coincidence. The trip to Rheims, the disappointment was making him nervous and now he was seeing ghosts. The man probably didn't say Prideux at all.

Christian opened his umbrella and bent down to pick up his travelling case. He would walk, rain or no. The exercise would calm his nerves and he would take a glass in Café Procope before returning to the apartment. He did not like Sylvie to see him in this state, it made him feel weak in her eyes and he would wonder why she stayed with him; she with all her cleverness and beauty, she could pick whatever life she wished but she had come along with him, loved him when she said she had loved nothing in her life before. But she had not felt the fabric of those women's clothes, felt their last breath on her cheek.

Enough.

'Disaster approaches!' the newspaper-seller yelled as he crossed the square, pushing through the crowds. 'The water is rising!'

Christian took his time over his walk through the city and across the river. It was high, certainly. The steamers had stopped and the water seemed to be full of wreckage. Wine barrels and timber swirled along, tumbling under the Pont Neuf. It was an impressive sight in the darkness. The lamps shone down on the turbulent black waters, the noise of them had increased to a dark rush, punctuated by occasional muffled blasts as the flotsam and jetsam smashed against the stone piers. He glanced up at the pneumatic clock on the bridge and frowned; seven minutes to eleven. He was sure that he had seen the same time on the clock when he left the station. One of the other gentlemen crossing the bridge noticed his confusion.

'There's water in the works, sir. The clocks have frozen and we are out of time. Still, was there ever a better excuse for coming home a little late?'

Christian managed to smile and nod, and felt for his pocket-watch. The movement shifted his coat against him and he sensed something different about the way the cloth lay against his waistcoat. He reached into his breast-pocket, then with the sweat starting out on his forehead in spite of the chill in the air, he turned out the rest. The diamond bracelet was gone.

He looked up and saw the shape of a woman standing under one of the lamps one hundred yards behind him on the bridge. The waters must have started to disturb the gas supply, as he was sure the shadows were deeper than usual, but something about her, her figure, the way she held herself so straight was familiar – and she was staring at him. He felt a coldness wash over him, a fear that began in his body rather than his brain. Another barrel slammed against the support of the bridge and he turned instinctively towards the sound. When he looked back, the woman was gone but his fear seemed to rise in his throat. He began to walk quickly back the way he had come, examining the pavement and concentrating hard, trying to recall every face in the crowds he had passed through and refusing, refusing to think of that familiar silhouette on the bridge. Just a girl, an ordinary girl. Then he remembered the station, the shouted name, the young man with whom he had collided. His heart seemed to stutter and pound till he could not hear his own thoughts. He felt as if the smooth pavement under his feet was cracking open, showing the corpses and rot below.

When Maud arrived back at Impasse Guelma, Yvette sprang across the room and grabbed her by the shoulders. Maud just had time to notice Charlotte sitting by the stove with her cigarette and her Bible on her knee.

'Maud! You should have been here hours ago. What happened to you? We got the diamonds. Where did you go?'

Maud took off her hat and set it down on the bed and started to pull off her gloves. Her hands were stiff with the cold and the damp. It seemed strange that they were so chilled, given the warmth she had felt spreading through her ever since the moment she had seen Morel's panic.

'Look,' Yvette said, her face flushed. She pulled open the velvet pouch and Maud glanced at the string of fat square diamonds. They were a strange collection of lights. Pure reds, greens and purples flickered along their facets, made little bursts in their hearts.

'They are very pretty. I can see why he was so upset at losing them.'

Yvette looked at her, her mouth slightly open. 'You followed him? That was where you were. You followed him.' She sat down heavily on the bed then reached across and before Maud could resist, grabbed her wrist, squeezing the delicate bones until Maud winced. 'You did not die, Maud. Do not make this your only reason for living.'

She pulled her hand away. '*I* did not make this my only reason for living. *He* did.' The room was very still and the words seemed to hang in the air between them.

'Did it please you to see it? Did you think of us worrying about you at all?' Yvette's voice sounded dull and empty.

'I did not worry,' Charlotte said in English. 'I thought you would want to see him suffer rather than come here and gloat over the diamonds with Yvette.'

'What is "gloat"? I am sure I do not do it. But I wanted you to come back, Maud.'

Maud sat down and tried to put her arm around Yvette's shoulder, but the young woman shook her off and stood again. 'I am not your pet,' she said.

Maud began to undo her hair. 'No. I think more often we are yours, Tanya and I. We're the innocents and you are wise Yvette who knows everything about poverty and opium and sex and crime and laughs at us. Well, I am learning. And Yvette, you do not know what it is like to be alone. You can surround yourself with people who admire you every day. You do not know what it is to be useless and alone and thrown away like rubbish. That man made me worthless. I want to see his mind crack and I want him to think of me as it happens – and I cannot care about anything else until I do see it.' Her voice rose as she spoke until it was almost a shout.

Yvette hesitated, then threw the diamond bracelet on the bed and left the room, slamming the door behind her. Charlotte stood up with a sigh and picked the bracelet up. Maud did not move. 'What shall we do with this then?'

Maud shrugged. 'Keep it.'

Charlotte turned it between her fingers. 'It is the property of the Countess, but I suppose you do not necessarily want her to know what you are doing. Is that so?'

'I suppose not. Her Pinkertons might wish to stop me so that Morel can take his money to America and they can steal it back there. I am like Henri. They would have no scruples about tying me up in a cellar, would they? I am dead already, after all.'

Charlotte nodded, then rolled up her sleeve and fastened the bracelet around her wrist, and smoothed the material back down again to cover it. 'I shall keep it for the time being and we shall see what happens. It is in God's hands.' She reached for her cloak and wrapped it around herself, looking more like a monk than ever.

'Miss Heighton,' she said, 'I understand you feel guilty. Yvette went to a great deal of trouble to save your life, and risking it so blatantly in front of her must stir your conscience, but do not be cruel. I suspect that Yvette would much rather have been brought up in England as a respectable young woman than raised by wolves in the back streets of Paris, don't you? That she manages to make friends with anyone who is willing to speak to her is a sign of her good and generous soul, and you throw it back at her as if it is a sign of *her* lack of worth. She has saved people, Miss Heighton. She has helped Miss Harris take children out of the hands of criminals and she has helped women like you survive where many have starved, sickened and died, or gone mad and destroyed themselves with no one to care. I have to ask, what have *you* done?' She then smiled and picked up her Bible. 'Good night, Miss Heighton.'

CHAPTER 16

Flood oil on canvas 61 × 46 cm

The picture seems to show the famous floods of January 1910 which brought Paris to a standstill for some weeks. It is unusual in that, rather than show us a grand vista of the floods with recognisable landmarks in the distance, the artist concentrates on the waters themselves, looking down into them. At the centre of the frame, the base of a lamp-post stands out at an angle, and though its lamp is beyond the frame, we can see the effect of its light on the water. Here an Impressionist technique is used for a painting of concentrated intensity. The waters are made of thick strokes of pure colour in a dizzying array of tints, circling round the pure black of the base of the street-lamp and almost completely filling the frame.

Extract from the catalogue notes to the exhibition 'The Paris Winter: Anonymous Treasures from the de Civray Collection', Southwark Picture Gallery, London, 2010

24 January 1910

When Tanya arrived at the Académie on Monday morning she found Yvette sitting at the top of the narrow staircase smoking and shifting her weight from hip to hip as if dancing to some tune in her head. As soon as Tanya rounded the curve in the stairs, she jumped to her feet. 'Ah, you're here!'

'Where else should I be? Tanya said. 'Why is the studio shut?'

Yvette reached behind herself to tap at a piece of paper pinned to the door. 'No school today! Monsieur Lafond encourages all his little students out onto the streets to see Paris face to face with disaster.'

Tanya looked behind her doubtfully. 'But it is raining.'

'Tanya, show a little spirit! Anyway, we can drive around in your car, can't we? They are talking of blowing up the Pont de l'Alma. I was worrying that your aunts wouldn't let you out today. Five minutes more and I'd have been off without you. Aren't they afraid you'll be swept away?'

'Perov has been invited to lunch to tell us all the news, but is it really so bad? I thought there were just a few streets flooded near Rue Felicien David. Lila and Vera went yesterday afternoon to see the people going up and down the streets in boats and came back with postcards. And what of Maud? She was going to meet Miss Harris on Thursday and I haven't seen her since.'

Yvette put out her cigarette and wrapped her arms around her stomach. 'She has had a victory over Morel, but I think she has gone mad. I cannot be with her today.'

Tanya was still on the step below, her eyes wide. 'Oh, you have to tell me everything!'

Yvette raised her arms. 'Oh, I shall, I shall. Only not here. Can we drive out in your little car or not?'

Tanya looked angry, then relented. 'Very well. Come along.'

Yvette ran past her and down the stairs.

Maud had found her in one of the back rooms of the Bâteau-Lavoir almost two hours after she had stormed out of Valadon's place. It was one of the better places to smoke a pipe in Montmartre, and Yvette had gone there to enjoy the utter peace and happiness of the drug, the feeling of floating through one's favourite dreams, recalling them so vividly it was like living them again, but better. No fear, only a sense of wonder and awe at the beauty dancing behind one's half-shut eyes.

She had brought with her the basket of oysters and three bottles of red wine the strange woman who ran the place always charged for entrance, and had intended on indulging herself entirely. Let Maud go mad. It was no business of hers. A day, two days. The hours would have no meaning. She knew she was supposed to model at Passage des Panoramas the next day, and that if she did not go they might not let her work there again, but at that moment she did not care.

She was welcomed in and made her way into the back room where the floor was covered with rush mats and the walls were hung with silks. Men and women reclined on the floor or on benches round the walls, their clothing loosened and their drowsy faces content or thoughtful. She was shown a space at the back wall on one of the raised hard wooden beds and settled herself. The silks were frayed at the edges. She knew that after a few pipes she would think that beautiful.

A few boys and women made their way slowly and carefully among the smokers, preparing the pipes and offering them to the customers. The men and women in the centre of the room – the wealthiest, judging by their clothes – looked quietly ecstatic. They spoke to each other, telling stories in low voices, but Yvette noticed others in the darker shadows of the room, their faces appearing from time to time in the light of the lamps. They were deeper in their affair with the drug and no longer wished to talk. One ran his fingernails through his hair, scratching at his scalp with an expression of complete bliss. Yvette felt a stab of envy and pity. The women who tended the pipes were thin. They did the skilled work of rolling pills in return for the occasional pipe from the customers. The usual rate was one for every five they prepared.

A boy approached her, the tray in his hand, and lit the lamp then picked up the pipe with a smile, offering to ready it for her. It had been a month since she last smoked. She shook her head and sat up, pressing her back to the wall and drawing up her knees, and the boy moved away to look after someone else. When Maud arrived she had still not taken one from him. The English girl took a place beside her and for a long while stared at the other smokers from the shadows just as Yvette was doing.

'I am sorry, Yvette.'

'You should be in bed. You'll get ill again.'

'I'll rest tomorrow.'

Yvette watched for a moment longer. One of the women serving in the centre of the room wasn't much older than her. Thirty, perhaps. She watched her inhale the smoke through the ivory mouthpiece of the pipe while the opium pill vaporised with the smallest hiss. Yvette wondered how long it would be before she herself surrendered and made pipes for strangers. Perhaps a little longer. 'Let's go, Maud.'

They departed with the smell of the smoke on their clothes and the curious stares of the proprietor at their back. Maud left her at the corner of the street where Yvette shared a room with two other girls who used it as a refuge between men, and Yvette watched her start the descent of Rue Lepic, that straight slim back, the falling snow pale yellow in the lamplight.

Tanya directed her patient chauffeur up and down the quayside in increasing excitement. The snow, which had been falling all night and into this morning, added to the sense of a Paris lost in some sort of strange apocalyptic dream. It clung to the bare trees along the river; the pavements had disappeared under the water. Workers were building raised walkways out of narrow planks so the people could get to and fro without a soaking. Here and there, parts of the road were closed off; the water had eaten away the ground beneath, leaving sudden pits and trenches that reached the sewers.

On the Pont de la Tournelle they clambered out of the car and were for a moment silenced by the sight of the river grown so vast and threatening. Notre Dame seemed to have shrunk, cowering from the waters. The Seine surged forward. The public bathhouses moored along the banks were already floating near the level of the embankment. They tugged at their moorings, fighting the speed and strength of the current. Standing in the open, Tanya could see the wreckage in the water – great planks of timber hurtling past them on the river's broad back, heading straight for the six great arches of the bridge. The sightseeing boats passed under this bridge every day, but now there was hardly twenty feet of room between the water and the road where they stood. Another barrel crashed against the stone and the whole structure seemed to shake.

Tanya turned her back on Notre Dame and crossed the bridge to join the crowd on the other side. Yvette took her arm and together they elbowed their way to the front of the throng of whispering sightseers to see what the river was hurling into the city. Furniture, shutters and doors that must have been torn from houses further upstream careered towards them and struck against the stonework. A parade of barrels carried away from the Quai des Vins swam with the current like swans, apparently stately in the distance, till as they approached they seemed to speed up and spin, colliding with the arches or sucked through the diminishing space below them.

For the first time, Tanya found the floods something more than a diverting break from the usual patterns of life: she saw them as a threat. One of the barrels cracked below her and she started. The ground under her feet was being knocked away. Yvette tugged on her arm. 'Look!' There was a group of men hanging over the edge of the Pont de Sully further upstream, trying to catch the barrels out of the water with long poles as they swept by. As they watched, one man, leaning far out over the water, managed to fix his hook into one. For a moment it seemed as if the barrel was going to drag him with it, but one of his companions managed to reach it too and share the strain. They walked it out of the heavy flow of the water to the sound of distant cheers.

The crowd around Yvette and Tanya was mostly quiet; there was only the occasional murmured remark of fear and awe as the waters clambered over all obstructions, tearing at the walls that confined them. 'The river will eat Paris,' a voice behind them said. 'She already has,' another replied. 'The pavements are giving way, the cellars are all flooded. Thousands of homes gone already.' 'When will it end?' 'Not before it gets worse, that's certain.'

There was a loud shout of laughter behind them and Tanya

turned round. At the back of the crowd, someone still wearing evening clothes was climbing up on top of a car. Once established, he helped drag up a friend to sit beside him. 'Ten louis on the dresser beating the table to the bridge,' the man said. He was fat, young, and spoke French with a strong English accent. The friend he was helping scrambled to a sitting position and peered into the river.

'Which table?' he said, his voice high and nasal. Tanya groaned – it was Perov.

'Too late! The dresser has it. You owe me ten. Double or quits if that tree gets to us before I can count to twenty-five.'

'Done! Did we bring anything to drink?'

The Englishman reached down to instruct his chauffeur, realised he had stopped counting and hurried to catch up.

Tanya pushed back into the crowd and was standing directly below them when the tree struck just as the first gentleman reached twenty-three. Perov cheered, then seeming to sense the angry stares from beneath him, looked down.

'Miss Koltsova!'

'Mr Perov,' she said firmly, 'this wreckage did not come from nowhere. You are making asinine bets over the terrible misfortunes of others.'

He went quite red. Tanya was speaking French, and loudly too. There were murmurs of agreement in the crowd. 'The city is under threat and this is all you can do?' she continued, her sense of outrage in no way diminished by her own sightseeing. 'Factories have been destroyed, homes inundated and still it rains. Can you not find useful employment even now?'

He slid back down from his perch on the roof. 'Miss Koltsova, you are too harsh.'

Behind them came another crash against the stonework. The

impact seemed to run through Tanya like an electric shock. She said more softly and in Russian, 'I will not marry you, Mikhail Pavlovich. I do not need any more time to decide. Thank you for your offer and your patience. I shall explain to my aunts why we cannot have the pleasure of your company at lunch today and write to my father myself.'

His mouth hung open. 'Because you see me making bets on the wreckage of some peasant dwelling?' he managed to say at last, his cheeks still red.

'No.' She reached out and patted his arm. 'It is because we are not friends – and no amount of money or family interest can make up for that.' He opened and closed his mouth a couple of times.

His friend also slid down from the roof, nearly tripped then cleared his throat. 'Natives . . . restless. Better view from further upstream.'

Perov took control of himself. 'As you wish it, Tatiana Sergeyevna. Perhaps it would have been more fitting to choose another moment to tell me of your decision.'

Tanya nodded. 'Probably, but I see no reason to keep you in suspense a moment longer than necessary.'

His friend pulled on his sleeve. 'Stop jabbering in that barbaric tongue and come on, will you, Micky?'

Perov said no more, but now rather pale, he made a smart bow and climbed back into the car. The crowd cheered their departure.

Yvette struggled to Tanya's side in time to stare after it. 'Was that . . . ? Did you just . . . ?'

Tanya took a deep breath. 'Yes, it was, and yes, I did. And I am very glad.' Her eyes dropped to the sable muff that had been warming her hands. 'At least I think I am glad. Still, now I will marry Paul so that is good.' She looked up at Yvette, her eyes huge and black and her skin rather pink. 'You don't think Paul will *mind* marrying me, do you?'

Yvette laughed.

Before Tanya returned to her aunts to break the news, she had the story of the weekend from Yvette. She leaned back in the car and blinked rapidly. 'Poor Maud! Do you think she *is* mad?'

Yvette shook her head. 'No – at least not yet. It is this way she has of talking about herself as if she were already dead, yet she is still there somehow. She came looking for me last night, after all.'

Tanya smiled sadly out of the window. 'It gives her licence. Like Akaky in *The Overcoat*, I think. When she is a ghost she can take revenge. She can't as a living breathing English girl. Why are you looking at me like that?'

'I never thought of you as a great reader, Tanya.'

She rolled her eyes. 'All Russians have to read Gogol. It's a rule we have.' Still watching the streets through the window, Tanya rested her delicate pointed chin on her thumb and forefinger. 'I have to tell my aunts about Perov now. Oh, I hope I've done the right thing.' She turned round as she said it, all appeal.

'Of course you have. I saw the man for ten seconds and would rather marry Valadon's dog. Much rather.' Tanya smiled again. 'Do you have time to drop me in Place Pigalle?'

The letter was waiting for her on Maud's bed. Yvette sat down and opened the envelope. It was cold in the room; the stove was unlit and the snow and rain fell in turn outside. She clambered under the blankets and pulled them up around her as she read.

> *Yvette,*
>
> *I know I have not repaid you very well for saving my life. I thought that making the Countess believe I was innocent would make me easy, then that taking something from Morel would do the same. It made me glad to see the fear on his face tonight, but it was a dark, hungry sort of gladness. After we left that place I came home thinking I should rest as I promised you, that just as you could resist that drug, perhaps I could resist haunting Morel any further and leave Paris, but I find I cannot. He will try and convince himself it was all accident. Even if Charlotte's conspiracy of shop girls prevent him from selling any of the other diamonds he has stolen in Paris, I'm sure he and Sylvie will have money enough to get to America by some means – and what if the Countess misses him there? I would disappear from his conscience and he would be happy forever. The idea of that stops me from sleeping.*
>
> *I must be his shadow.*
>
> *Maud*

'Oh, Maud,' Yvette said and curled the thin blankets more closely around her, letting the note hang from her fingers. Outside the window she could see the snow falling from the clotted skies. Like feathers, that was what they always said of snow in books, wasn't it? That it was like feathers.

When she was a child she used to dance and sing for the gentry as they drank their coffee outside the cafés on the Champs. One of her *maman*'s other little charges would go among the crowd with his cap out collecting coppers and anything that they might have taken their eye off, wallets and trinkets from inside the ladies' handbags, watches and rings.

Once, one of the women had called her over to pet her and stroke her hair and tell her what a pretty child she was. Yvette had submitted happily enough. There was a pigeon feather caught on her blouse. She thought it was dirty and made to brush it away but the woman stopped her and told her it was good luck, a sign that her guardian angel was looking after her. She thought maybe the woman was going to take her home but then the kind lady had released her and turned back to her coffee and her friends. Yvette's companion gave her the signal his work was done and she ran away, disappointed again, but the idea of the guardian angel stayed in her mind. She had thought of it the first time an artist on Montmartre had asked her to model and then paid her, the time she turned down a man as a lover who later turned out to be violent and cruel to his girl. She had thought of it too the second or third time she had smoked opium, the first time the drug had let her fully appreciate its beauty, and thought that in that moment she was finally settling back into her angel's embrace and feeling his wings close over her. That was then. She had not believed in him for a long time. Then in the last year or two, since she could not find him she had tried to become a guardian angel to others, or not an angel, but something hopeful in the world. Imperfect and muddy from the streets, but still . . .

She rested her head on her knee. The whole point of a guardian angel was that they were with you whether you deserved it or not, that they stayed with you, that even if they could not save you, they were there. She threw off the blankets and went in search of Maud.

CHAPTER 17

*S*COLDING, THREATS, LONG LECTURES ON HER LACK
of character, her ingratitude, her gross stupidity – all of
this Tanya had been expecting, but when her Aunt Vera said
nothing at all to the news, only burst into tears and ran out of the
room, the girl was shocked. Aunt Lila stayed where she was, her
hands folded in her lap and she too said nothing for several minutes.
Tanya's bravery began to shiver and retreat.

'Aunty Lila, please say something. I have thought very carefully.
I cannot marry someone I do not respect, and Mr Allardyce is a
good man.'

Eventually Lila looked up, her features sharp and angry.
'I'm glad you think so, Tanya.' She stood up and smoothed the
heavy silk of her dress. 'Do you realise why Vera ran away like
that?'

'She wishes me to marry Perov,' Tanya answered a little sulkily.
'I know that.'

Lila shook her head. 'You are a deeply selfish child, Tanya. You
always have been, fainting and sighing into getting your way. I
never thought you were as delicate as you pretended, but it has
suited you, hasn't it, to make your father think you are a weakling
in need of constant care? Now you announce to us that you are a

modern woman able to make her own way, that you care and think nothing of us and throw all that care back in our faces.'

'Aunt, I do not mean—'

'Do be quiet and listen. You have humiliated Vera. Your father needed someone to look after you and she volunteered. She asked for your father's trust and now he will think that she has failed. You know that neither of us would have a penny if he didn't give it to us. It is easier for me, I have played the shrinking violet for fifty years so no one will blame me, but Vera has actually tried to do something in this world. She tried to help her husband in business but he threw it away at the gambling tables, she has had to beg and flatter to get her son a decent position in the Ministry and hears hardly a word from him. She tried to guide and protect you in a foreign city and you have done nothing but sneer at her and defy her since the moment we arrived. She only wanted to love you, Tanya. She is a busy old woman but she only wanted your love and your father's respect. You never offered her the first and have robbed her of the second. It is very badly done, my girl. Very badly indeed.'

She left Tanya sitting pale and alone. Her first impulse was to cry; first at the injustice and then because she suspected that sweet compliant Lila might be right.

Sylvie wanted to see the floods. Christian had told her about the unsuccessful trip to Rheims and the theft, when he arrived home in the early hours of the morning. After a few moments of stunned silence, she had burst into laughter and kissed him. She would never stop surprising him. It was the gods taking their cut of their good fortune, she said, and now that was done they had nothing left to fear. Now she was in a festive mood and wished to be in the open air. He had been worried that in the days he had spent watching Henri work she would have grown bored and begun smoking the drug more than before, but she had not. Her will was iron when it suited her. She showed no sign of missing it and spent her days reading English novels and working on her sketches. Her English and her drawing had improved greatly under Maud's tuition.

Today, Morel's first thought was to collect more of the stones from their hiding-place and sell them in Paris. She dissuaded him. Paris was not herself at the moment, she said. There would be no fun buying or selling while the waters were boiling up through the streets. Much better to have a holiday here until the waters drained away and then they could make the sale and leave the country quickly and quietly as planned.

Morel allowed himself to be convinced. The couple left Rue de Seine after lunch well rested and wrapped in furs and overcoats to see the sight of Paris slowly drowning.

It happened first when they climbed the towers of Notre Dame. It was Sylvie's idea and she was right – it was something to see, with the river swelling and racing under the bridges. The snow had settled on the gargoyles, who stared down on the city with horrified pleasure. It made Sylvie laugh. Occasionally the sky would suddenly, miraculously, clear – and a stream of sunlight would dance over the snow on the roofs, warm the sand-coloured stone and turn the yellow river green and gold. It was at such a moment that he looked down and saw the figure in the middle of the square. You could not pick anyone out at such a distance and name them, of course. The streets were full of people – workers whose factories had been shut down by the water, had brought their wives and children out to see it fighting through the city, but Morel was sure it was *her*, and that her attention was fixed on him.

He called Sylvie, putting out his hand to her and pulling her near to him as soon as her fingers brushed his. He looked down, ready to point her out, confess what he thought he had seen on the bridge the previous night . . . but she was gone. The crowd was one mass again, flowing through the square in waves like the river itself.

'What is it, Christian?'

'Nothing. Nothing, my darling.'

By the time they had reached the Quai de Passy and marvelled at the people punting themselves through the streets in little boats and rafts, he had almost forgotten. Sylvie bought photographs from a street-hawker and clung onto Morel's arm watching the water and the men putting up the wooden walkways along the side of the street.

'I *can* get through there!' Morel turned around. An elderly man, made almost spherical in his greatcoat, was arguing in a good-natured way with one of the policemen on the road just where the waters were lapping up towards them. 'Look, officer, you can see by the tree the water's not more than three foot deep and the cart has a clearance of four – four and a half feet probably! My aunt's just pulled everything she owns out of the basement on Rue des Eaux and I can't leave it sitting on the street for the *apaches* to rifle through.'

'But my friend, the ground is like porridge!' the policeman protested. 'Look, the lamp halfway along is already sinking.'

Morel looked where he was pointing. The street-lamps were still lit and glowing in the afternoon light. No one could get to them to shut off the gas. It did seem to be tilting. The cart-driver waved his hand. 'Pah! I'll trust my horse to know not to step in a sewer.'

A woman stepped out of the crowd, her cheeks pink with the

cold and the same look of glee on her face that Sylvie had. 'Give me a ride, Dad! I want to go through and my husband will help you with the stuff at the other end if you do.' She pulled on the arm of a young man beside her and he touched his cap. If it was to the driver or the policeman wasn't quite clear.

The policeman shrugged. 'Be careful, that's all I'm saying – and don't blame me if you get a soaking.' The mood seemed to have caught him too. He was smiling as he said it.

'All right then,' the carter said, and put his hand down to help the girl up beside him.

Sylvie stepped forward. 'Oh, us too please, my friend!' Morel let himself be led to the cart's side. The older man was looking down at her in the fine furs a little doubtfully. She pulled the butterfly brooch from her lapel. 'I'll give you this.' Morel frowned briefly. It was the brooch she'd given Maud for Christmas and then reclaimed from her little store of possessions after she had gone into the river. Morel felt a creeping sense of cold on the back of his neck, but Sylvie was already scrambling onto the cart and making herself comfortable with the girl and her husband. Before Morel had even managed to take his seat beside her, she had found out he worked in one of the flooded factories in Bercy. She was bright and joking with the young couple. Sylvie always knew how to be with whomever she came across. Never needed a hint. It made him proud.

'All secure?' the carter called out, then urged his horse forward into the water. It was as if they were part of the river. The women linked arms and laughed, half-lifting themselves off the wooden bench-seats to see over the parapet and into the river. The Eiffel Tower stood high and lonely on the other bank. 'It moved,' the girl shrieked suddenly. 'Did you not see it move! Ahh, it will fall at last and crush all the rich in Suffren.' Her eyes were shining. The horse was moving slowly but steadily, and the water was deepening. It was up almost to its chest. The water splashed up and the women squealed. Morel looked back to see if the Tower *was* moving, monstrous thing. He couldn't see any sign of a shift.

Their progress was being watched by the crowd they had left behind. They waved and whistled at each other. Then he saw her. Not ten yards away yet and veiled, the familiar thin shape standing on the very edge of the water. She put up her hands and lifted the black netting that hung in front of her eyes. *Hell and all its devils!*

Morel gave a shout and pushed past Sylvie and the girl, the motion of the cart making him stumble onto his knees. The young man tried to hold onto his arm, but Morel shook him off. He heard Sylvie call to him but looked instead into the crowd. She was still there. The dead woman staring at him. He clambered awkwardly off the back of the cart and fell into the water. The cold seized him as if it had claws and forced the air out of his lungs. The horse whinnied, protesting at the movement, and then surged forward away from him a few paces. The ground felt weak and soft under his feet and some current caught him before he had regained his balance. He fell forward on his hands and was choked by the filthy water. The confusion and sound of it, cold air and freezing water spluttering in his throat. He tried to push himself up but stumbled again. Above the noise of the water he could hear Sylvie shouting his name. An arm suddenly caught him and lifted him clear. Two men, one the policeman who had warned them to be careful and another, a labourer who had been working on the thin wooden walkways, half-dragged him up towards the crowd again. His coat was sodden and pulled him down. The dead woman in the crowd was gone, leaving only these amazed faces – disgusted, frightened or angry. 'Are you mad? Are you mad?' the policeman kept saying.

Morel slid out of their arms onto the cold cobbles. He looked up at them, not understanding what they wanted from him; there was a circle of sky showing between their faces, and the air filled with another of those sudden flurries of snow. Someone was pushing through the crowd. Sylvie. In those few moments she had run all the way back along the walkway. She helped him stand and guided him away from the curious stares. He shivered, and feeling his teeth rattle he clenched his jaw. 'She's coming for me, Sylvie,' he said. 'She hates me and I was kind to her.' It seemed unjust suddenly. He had paid her, fed her and now her ghost felt only rage. He shivered again. The taste of the river was in his mouth, in his hair. If he had been able to use his skinned and stiffened hands properly he would have torn his clothes off right there on the street. He wanted to explain to Sylvie, make her understand – but when he tried to speak again, his throat closed and he retched.

Sylvie waved down a taxicab and after a fierce debate the driver agreed to take them all the way back to Rue de Seine – if he got the fare in advance, plus extra for the wet.

⌒⌒

When the Morels arrived back at Rue de Seine, him with his head down and her not letting go of his arm and hurrying him in, Yvette was not sure if she should be proud of Maud or frightened for her. Something had happened – Morel's dishevelled state and wretched stoop told as much – but where was Maud? Taken up by the gendarmes? Murdered? But the couple looked as if their problems were falling over them like the flood, rather than done with, so Yvette let herself hope. She paced back and forth on the Boulevard Saint-Germain, keeping a close eye on the crowds around her. It was not the sort of day when people noticed a girl such as her. The whole city felt strangely tense. She heard snatches of news from the people passing by; of pavements collapsing, more ragged holes appearing in the streets far away from the river. The water was climbing up through the sewers and underground tunnels: all those clever modern tricks of control of which the city was so proud were being turned against her by the river. The level of the water was still rising fast; so much debris collecting against the Pont de l'Alma that engineers were talking of blowing it up before it became a dam. The factories were shutting, the waste-works were closed.

She had been looking for Maud in the crowd for so long, that when she finally saw her, it came as a shock. Maud walked straight past without seeing her, her face a mask. Yvette ran a few paces to catch her up and touched her arm. In the first moment she glanced round, Maud looked irritated, ready to knock away a beggar or a man, then surprised.

'Yvette.' She looked up Rue de Seine towards the Palais du Luxembourg. 'They are at home?'

Yvette was not sure what greeting she had expected, but one with a little more warmth than this. 'Yup,' she replied. 'They rolled up an hour ago and nothing moving since. He looks as sick as a dog. What did you do?'

Maud smiled, cat-like, discreet – but there was such an animal pleasure in it Yvette was shocked. 'I frightened him.'

Again Yvette wondered if Maud was still quite sane. She kept her own voice slow and even. 'You will keep watching him?'

'I shall, as long as I can.'

Yvette had used her time well. 'If you must. There is a woman living in the house opposite with a room on the second floor. We may rent it by the hour if you wish it, though it will be expensive. I shall watch while you rest, if you can.'

Maud looked around her as if noticing for the first time that the sky was growing thick with darkness. 'Good. Why is it darker than normal?'

'Floodwater. In the electricity works, the basements. The lights have failed in places all over the city,' Yvette said. Another scrap of information gathered from the crowds around her. 'Take my arm.'

'I was ready to do this alone,' Maud said. 'Why are you helping me?'

'I don't know – because something tells me I should? For God's sake, the ground is going under our feet. Who knows what is right today?'

CHAPTER 18

*A*UNT VERA WAS IN THE DRAWING ROOM BUT THE lights had not been turned on and the afternoon gloom had silted the room with purple shadows. She did not move when Tanya let herself into the room and settled down beside her. Tanya did not try to touch her.

'Aunty, I think the world is changing and I wish to change too. I love Paul and I think we can be happy together, but I shall have to manage on a great deal less money.' She had her notebook with her. 'I know you only want me to be happy, but I think there are more ways to be happy now for women like us, with an education and some talent, than there were. Don't you think?'

Her aunt still did not move, but Tanya thought she was listening. 'Mr Allardyce once told me he thought you were a remarkable woman. I think so too, and I need your help. With Papa, of course, but also with the other things. Life has been easy for me and I shall have to learn how to manage my money.' Vera was certainly listening now. 'We shall need to entertain, but only in a modest fashion, and I shall need an apartment with three bedchambers at least. Sasha will need one, and I wish to always have a room for you and Aunty Lila, always there when you wish it. Can you help me a little to work it all out?'

Vera sniffed and put out her hand. Tanya meekly handed over the book and heard her aunt beginning to turn the pages. After a few minutes she said, 'You've forgotten you'll need to pay to keep the place warm, Tanya. In these Paris winters . . . Do you wish to have an apartment with an American bath? He will want it, I suppose. Turn that light on so I can see what I am about.' Tanya leaped up to do so, and her aunt stood and carried the notebook over to her writing-table. She carried on studying Tanya's notes then looked round, a spark of interest in her faded blue eyes. 'You think it is likely you will get five hundred for a portrait?'

'I think so. I have asked a few of your friends and they seem to agree it is a reasonable amount. I think I could complete one like that in a week's painting. One needs the commissions, of course.'

Her aunt drew a fresh sheet of writing paper from the desk and put it down in front of her. 'It seems to me you should work to get a portrait in the Salon next year. Something of the style you wish to make a living from.'

Tanya joined her at the writing-table and for a little while as the evening thickened around them they spoke about costs and careers, who they knew who might become a patron, whether Sasha would be willing to learn enough French to become a housekeeper to the young couple.

Vera was writing something down on her growing numbered list when she lifted her head and said: 'Your father must modernise, Tanya. He is too stuck in the old ways of managing a family, his women. Your mother was a good person, but she never thought of anything other than looking pretty and reading novels. He must realise that we new women have our place too.'

'Yes, Aunty.'

'And tell your young man to call on us.'

'He will be reporting on the flood, Aunty. He might not know when he can come, or have the chance to dress.'

'We are not some stuffy household that insists on such things. Tell him to come when he can and covered in mud if need be.'

'Yes, Aunty.'

Tanya excused herself for a few moments and sent a note to Paul's lodgings, then spent another hour with Vera and the figures. It was a little after six when the footman came in to tell them a young girl named Odette wished to speak to Miss Koltsova.

Sylvie would not hear of him leaving the apartment. 'You are still shivering, Christian. I will not let you.' She did not seem to understand the importance of it – that *she* was coming and would creep up with the water into the cellar and snake her way around the diamonds and take them back into the river with her. He could not explain it to Sylvie. She would not believe him. She brought him foul-tasting teas and tried to get him to rest, telling him everything was well and that soon they would be sailing away to America, and that dirty lying Paris, which always looked so fine but was full of holes, torn-up pavements and gunfire, would be behind them. They would be in a country where there were no graves and tunnels.

Again he tried to get up, and again she pushed him down onto the pillows. 'I will go and fetch them, Christian,' she said at last. 'In the morning I will go, but only if you promise to stay still and rest now.' That gave him some measure of peace but when he slept he dreamed he was drowning.

Paul Allardyce arrived at Tanya's house just before nine o'clock that evening and was shown at once into the drawing room where Miss Koltsova was waiting for him alone. He was exhausted, having spent the whole day tracking the floods through the streets, gathering figures and trying to talk to officials whose faces were pale with worry. He had crossed the city half-a-dozen times, guessing the size of the sink-holes and attempting to find words for the strange softness of the ground. He tried to remember what he had heard of the catacombs and quarries, the sewers and underground tunnels, then wrote furiously for an hour before going to the telegraph office and sending his full report, at great expense, to New York. Tanya's message found him at his lodgings where he had gone simply to change his shirt before travelling out once more to watch the river crawling higher and higher.

She was such a beautiful woman, and after the dirt and worry of the day, the poor who had lost everything, the widow of the man who had killed himself rather than leave his home, just looking at her was some sort of relief. She began by saying how glad she was her message had reached him now the *petit bleu* system had failed and half the telephones were not working, that she had been trying to contact her friends with no success . . . He lost track for a minute – she was speaking English but rather fast and low. It took him a few moments to realise the topic of conversation had changed. She was telling him that she had rejected the Russian millionaire and was proposing to marry him; that she was sure she would be able to make money painting, and if her estimate of his income was not wildly inaccurate they should be able to live in Paris quite comfortably and even save against future emergency. He must have been looking at her with a slightly foolish expression because after a minute or two her words trailed away. She stared at the ground in front of her and as ever Paul found himself fascinated by the furious darkness of her thick hair. He took a step forward and tried to find his voice.

'Tanya, I have been awake since dawn. I can hardly think, but are you saying you wish to marry me? Is that what I am to understand?'

She gave a very small nod. 'If you think, that is . . . if you would like me as a wife.' She bent down and picked up a sheaf of papers from the low table in front of her. 'Aunt Vera has been helping me with the sums and says she will teach me to keep an account book.' She thrust the papers out towards him, her black eyes very wide as if she wanted him to examine them. He pushed them out of the way and took her in his arms, kissing her hard. For a moment she was still and frightened in his embrace, then she began to return the kiss with a heat that burned him. He had to pull himself away, breathing hard. She looked at him, her face flushed.

'So you think, Paul, you might love me a little without all the flim-flam?'

He took her hand and thought for a second; his feelings almost choked him. 'Tanya, your smile is one of the great sights of the world to me. The feeling I have when I see it, it's like . . . like seeing a great clipper ship under full sail, or walking through the Alps on a clear day. It stops my heart. I love you very, very much.' He cleared his throat. 'Now let me do this properly. I am only ever going to do it once in my life.' He lowered himself to the ground, supporting himself on the table with his palm until he was on one knee, crumpling some of the sheets of figures in the process, then he reached up for her hand again and with it between both of his own, he began: 'Tatiana Sergeyevna Koltsova, would you do me the honour . . .'

CHAPTER 19

The Reader oil on canvas 56.1 × 33.1 cm

A subject that was a favourite of Edwardian genre painters, this image of a young woman reading by a window is given extra interest by the late-night setting, the treatment of the light falling across the figure, the burning end of her cigarette and the psychological realism of the model's absorption in her book. What can be saccharine in some renderings here becomes an intimate portrait of a state of mind.

Extract from the catalogue notes to the exhibition 'The Paris Winter: Anonymous Treasures from the de Civray Collection', Southwark Picture Gallery, London, 2010

25 January 1910

Maud jerked awake. Yvette was sitting in the chair by the window as she had promised she would. The faint glow of the street-lamps softened the sharp angles of her face and made her look younger

again, and gave her enough light to read by. She had borrowed
some historical romance from the owner of the house and sat with
it now on her knee, a cigarette burning in her other hand and an
ashtray improvised from a soapdish sitting on the floor at her feet.
The filigree ironwork outside cast vague curling shadows over the
folds of her skirt. She heard Maud move but did not look up.

'The rooms are still dark,' she said and turned a page. 'Go back
to sleep.'

For a few minutes Maud thought she would, then a sudden
explosion shook the room, a great throb of thunder. 'God!' Yvette
said, getting to her feet and opening the window as Maud sat
upright in the bed, her heart beating wildly. 'They must have blown
the Pont de l'Alma after all. Heaven help us.'

Maud slid out of the bed and went to stand next to her. Yvette
pointed across the street. A light had come on in the Morels'
apartment and one of the shutters was being pulled back. Maud
shifted back into the shadows, looking down and sideways as Sylvie
appeared in the frame, leaning her small white hand on the ironwork
and looking towards the river. The light spilled over her shoulders,
the sapphire-blue of her silk dressing-gown, her blond hair loose
and long over her shoulders. Other figures appeared on the street,
all looking in the same direction. Only Maud was not looking
north and west where the sound had come from; she focused
instead on the lines of Sylvie's face and her hand on the rail,
remembering that head resting on her shoulder, that hand in hers.

∽∾

Some hours later, Yvette brought coffee, bread and news from the
woman on the ground floor. 'The bridge is still there,' she said,
handing Maud a sliced and buttered roll. 'It was some factory in

Ivry blew up, but the fire didn't spread. The water is still rising though. Anything from over the way?' Maud shook her head. The shutters to the Morels' drawing room were half-opened but there was no other sign of life. 'Eat something, Maud.' It was the sadness in Yvette's voice that made her try the food, but even so she did not stop looking out of the window. 'I want to get some message to Tanya if I can, to tell her we are well . . .'

The concierge of the Morels' apartment came out into the street pulling her shawl over her head. The snow was falling again and melting onto the soaked pavements as if the ground were drinking it up. Maud sat up in the chair and peered after her. She remained there, her pose one of fixed attention until the woman returned. There was a man with her in a long pearl-grey overcoat and a large leather bag at his side.

'She has been for a doctor,' Maud said and licked her lips. Yvette looked up from the novel she was reading again then set it down and brushed the crumbs of her breakfast from her dress.

'I shall go and see if I can find out what's happening,' she said, and went to the door. Maud did not look round to see her leave.

The concierge was happy to talk. Her older sister had nearly been killed by typhoid and now with her best tenant ill it was all she could think about. 'He came back shivering and soaked last night – fell in the waters, she said – and I don't like the sound of him today. Groaning! There is groaning! And what if the floods come up this far? What are we supposed to do? Leave him to drown or carry him off with us, nasty diseases and all?' Everything she said was in a fierce whisper and spoken out of the corner of her mouth, as if they were at the theatre and speaking at all was bad manners.

'But the water won't come this far. We're safe, surely?' Yvette said, huddling away from the sudden cold wind that ran up the street. She felt it like Maud's impatience, pulling her back to the room to tell her about the fever, the groaning.

'Don't you bet on it, sweetheart! You don't have to walk half so far to see the river today, I tell you. Go and have a look. My Georges has been down there already. He took one look and back he came, emptied out our bit of storage in the cellar and moved it all up to the attic. Now he's a strong man, but a lazy one. There's no way he would have carried my mother's second-best mattress up to the roof if he didn't think it had a good chance of a soaking. That I can tell you for free.'

Yvette ignored the wind tugging at her back and went to look for herself. The shock was sudden and absolute: water everywhere. It rippled along the quays and ate away at the islands; the naked trees, shivering with wet snow, hung at strange angles along the Quai de Conti. The streets were sinking. She turned back up Rue Bonaparte and saw the same fear on each face. The nervous excitement of the previous day had become something darker. Paris was being throttled slowly by her own river, and what had looked like another spectacle laid on by the city for the entertainment of her citizens was twisting into a slow act of violence.

❧❧

Tanya was certain that Maud or Yvette would call for her early in the morning. The only possible reason why she had not heard from them already was that they had received her messages too late last night to respond – but nothing came. She stared at the clock until she thought it must be broken, and when Sasha came into her room with tea just after ten, she was shaking it vigorously. The old maid took it from her with a frown and set it back on the mantelpiece, then she pulled a telegram form from her apron and handed it to Tanya. She snatched it from her, then a second later crumpled it in her fist and threw it in the general direction of the fire.

'All well? *All well?* That's what they have to say to me?'

Sasha bent down to pick up the note, smoothed it out again then tucked it into her pocket. She thought all such things had value and should be preserved against emergency like short threads and off-cuts of wax paper. 'They think I can have *nothing* important to tell them. That is it. They think all I'm doing is worrying about them and of course I am, but I *do* have something important to tell them.' She turned and pointed an angry finger at Sasha who only stared at it with her eyebrows raised. '*And* I am engaged.'

'I think you mentioned that a time or two last night as I put you to bed, pumpkin,' Sasha said.

'But they don't know that! Yvette only knows I refused Perov . . .'

Sasha yawned and sat on the bed. 'Maybe they can't tell you where they are. Fact they sent this,' she patted her stomach where the pocket of her apron sat, 'means that they *are* thinking of you, so stop wailing. Now I mean to get you out and useful before you tear the house apart. The Red Cross are collecting, and what they are collecting needs sorting.' Tanya started to protest but the look in Sasha's eyes made her stop. 'We shall send a heap of your messages around so they know where to find you and leave word here too. We might as well enjoy having footmen to spare before you make beggars of us, I suppose. Now put something on a sensible woman might wear and let's hurry along, shall we?' She got to her feet again with a grunt and pulled out one of Tanya's more conservative walking dresses from the armoire.

'Sasha, when I marry will you come with me?'

Sasha helped her lift the morning gown she was wearing over her head. 'I'm not sure that's how they manage things here, dear.

Normally you'll just have a girl in to clean and fetch for you by the hour.'

When Tanya's face re-emerged from the white chiffon it was pale and slightly tearful. 'If you wish to go back to Saint Petersburg, of course I shall understand.'

Sasha picked up the walking dress and bent down, fanning out the skirt so that Tanya could step into it. She felt the girl's hand on her shoulder as she steadied herself. 'Don't fret, chicken. I'll help you settle in – you've got some learning to do. Vera and I will teach you.' She stood, pulling the dress up with her and held it so Tanya could slide her long slim arms through the tight sleeves. 'Then I shall open a little restaurant, I think.' Tanya's eyes sprang open and Sasha sniffed. 'There're lots of Russians in Paris might like a taste of proper food from their homeland, and none of these Frenchies can cook a damn. All sauce, sauce, sauce till you don't know what you're eating.'

Tanya turned to let her fasten the dress, thinking the world was a more surprising place than she could have ever imagined.

☙❧

He kept asking her if she had been to fetch them, though at times he wasn't sure if he had said the words out loud or just dreamed them. She always said, 'In a little while, Christian my love, in a little while. I cannot leave you just now.' He was afraid he had mentioned the ghost of the woman and might have made her angry, but whenever he managed to open his eyes she was smiling at him kindly enough. She knew where they were, she'd take care of it. He sank into a sort of half-dream where he could see nothing, but the air was tainted with corruption and there was a constant sound of trickling water.

∞∞∞

Maud watched by the window, eating whatever Yvette handed to her and watching the shutters of the house opposite. The day passed slow as ice. That night she slept a while and let Yvette watch, and for the first time her dreams were not of drowning. She seemed to be again on the terrace outside Sacré Coeur; the rain was falling but it felt warm as a blessing against her skin. She knew Yvette and Tanya were there watching with her as the floodwaters consumed Paris, and below them the lights went out one by one till the city of lights was dark and cold and victory blossomed in her.

CHAPTER 20

26 January 1910

*Y*VETTE BROUGHT HER COFFEE AGAIN IN THE morning and declared her intention to go back to Valadon's place and her own. 'My clothes are stinking,' she said. 'If you insist on staying here until we have not got a franc between us, well and good, but I shall do so in clean clothes.'

Maud only nodded and Yvette began her weary slog across a shattering Paris. The Cours de Rome was becoming a lake fed by the Metro tunnels, and they said part of Place de l'Opéra was collapsing. Back at her room she found four messages from Tanya pinned to her bundle and then another crop at Valadon's. She fished out a length of cord to tie up Maud's clean clothes and cut it to length with her knife. A present from *Maman* the day she had finished her schooling with the nuns. She would rather have had a book as the nuns only handed out Bibles, and Yvette had already decided there was nothing much in those pages for her. She had used the knife to scare other children away from her things and twice used it to protect herself. Once from Louis. After the other men on the hill saw his scar they kept away when she told them to. It was the only gift she remembered being given and she had carved her name into the bone handle and gone out into the world with it. Not gone very far into the world though. She put it back into her pocket and headed to Saint-Sulpice where the latest appeals from Tanya had directed her.

∽∽

Most of the refugees flooded out of their homes round Paris, Bercy and Javel had been directed here, and Saint-Sulpice had been transformed to receive them. There were cots and mattresses every-where you looked, and people huddled into little groups round portable heaters. At the back of the church a procession of men and women collected bowls of soup from a trestle table. It was strangely quiet given the number of people there. Even the children were silent. The air smelled slightly rotten. A woman in a Red Cross uniform at the door looked relieved when she realised that Yvette was looking for someone rather than a place to sleep. 'We are nearly full and the waters still rise,' she said. 'On the first night we had only five, now there are five hundred. Oh, it breaks my heart to see them praying. They can only be praying for other people, since they have already lost everything. Miss Koltsova is in the back with a few of the children while their mothers sleep. Take her out for a little while if you can. She was here half the night and from early this morning too.'

When Yvette approached, Tanya saw her through the crowd and put a blonde girl off her knee, kissing her dirty head as she did. Then she flung her arms around Yvette's neck and held her for a moment. 'Oh, you are here! Thank the Lord!' Before Yvette could do anything more than grin at her, Tanya took her by the hand and led her into a quieter corner. 'What I have to tell you seems less important after what I have seen here,' she whispered. 'Oh, it is dreadful. Have you been near the river today?'

Yvette nodded. 'It is higher than the road near Concorde. Only the wall holds it back. And there are crowds everywhere . . . But what is your news, Tanya? Are you engaged to Paul?'

She blushed. 'I am. He is here, talking with the refugees. His paper had already set up an appeal and the American Ambassador has already pledged *such* a sum.' Yvette thought she looked rather proud of this, as if every generous American action reflected rather well on her now. 'But Maud? What news?'

'All my congratulations, sweetheart. There, now you are resolved to work for a living I shall stop calling you Princess.'

Tanya looked pleased. 'Sasha says she will believe I can earn money when I learn to dress myself.' Yvette snorted with laughter and Tanya's eyes danced. 'Yes, I know, but some of these very expensive dresses are terribly complicated. I'm sure it will be much easier with cheaper clothes.' She tried to say it stoutly but Yvette was not convinced. 'But Maud . . . ?'

Yvette told her what she could, murmuring low so that the passing men and women would not hear her, but each seemed so sunk in their own distress and shock she could have sung it. 'Now she watches and waits, for what I do not know. Perhaps if she sees him sick, sees that he believes she is haunting him it will be enough, but she seems . . . not herself. She frightens me.'

Tanya nodded. 'Sasha said she found something dark in the river and brought it back into the air with her.'

'She found the strength to live, that's something. But I must go back to her. Kiss your fiancé for me and tell him he is a lucky man, even if his wife-to-be can't dress herself.'

Tanya put out her hand to stop her. 'Yvette, it wasn't just to tell you I was engaged. That girl, the maid the Countess threw out, came to see me.' Yvette waited, frowning a little. 'She wanted to thank me. She is going to take a stenographer's course, but the thing is, she followed Morel. Yvette, I know where the diamonds are.'

CO&CO

They found Maud still in her place at the window but looking more animated than she had been the previous day. She told them she had seen Morel himself at the window twice since Yvette had left, looking anxiously towards the river then shivering and looking up and down the street, searching the faces of the people coming and going on the pavements, their steps hurried or cautious as if afraid the road was going to give way beneath them. She greeted Tanya with warmth and congratulated her, though even as she did so her eyes flitted towards the window again. When Tanya began to tell them of Odette's visit, however, she became more attentive.

'Morel had taken her to Café Procope in Cour du Commerce once or twice,' Tanya explained. 'Poor thing, she was rather in love with him, I think, and she went back there a few times after he gave her up.' Tanya looked tired; her work at Saint-Sulpice seemed to have drained her, but her eyes were bright. Yvette found it strange to see her in such a plain dress, but she seemed more substantial sitting there than in her usual silks and chiffon. 'She was hoping to see him, and see him she did, going into Cour de Rohan. She followed him whenever she could. Apparently he spent hours a day there, and she said she saw him go into the cellars in the yard a couple of times. The second time she tried to speak to him and he was cruel.' Yvette could imagine. 'Then that very evening the Countess cast her off.' Yvette remembered what Valadon had said about women being fools and wondered if she were right.

320

'So you think he's keeping the diamonds there?' Maud said. 'In the cellars below Cour de Rohan?'

'What else could it be?' Tanya said, looking up at them with her round dark eyes. 'Close, but not too close. Secluded but somewhere a man like him might easily be dining in the cafés.'

'And you think we should go and search for them?' Maud said, looking back again over her shoulder.

'Of course we should!' Tanya said. 'They can be returned to the Countess and he will have lost what he has worked for so hard. Then Maud, you can be free again. You will have beaten him.'

Yvette watched the Englishwoman's face. There was a moment of light there, like a shifting of the clouds against a stormy sky, as if she had perhaps caught some scent of a future free of this, but then she shook her head. 'I don't care about the diamonds. What is their theft, taking jewels from a woman who has too many already, compared to what he did to me?'

Yvette put out her hand and rested it on Maud's knee. 'It is not what is important that counts, but what is important to *him*, isn't it, Maud?' For herself she thought collecting the diamonds would be by far the best idea. Tanya was right, and for the first time since they had left Henri in the cellar she thought there might be a chance of an ending which Maud might survive. Maud hesitated, then nodded.

'We should go at once,' Tanya said, standing up. 'The waters are reaching higher and higher through the cellars and sewers. If we don't go now it might be weeks before we get another chance, and he might be well enough by then to stop us.'

They hurried Maud up and into her long coat and into the street, but she could not resist looking back towards the apartment. He was there again, looking out of the window towards them, his face grey and his mouth a gape of despair. She turned away and let her friends sweep her along the street.

∽∞

Still Sylvie would not go. He begged her to but she would not. She tried to dose him with laudanum but he tasted it in the wine and spat it out. He could stand today, and in those moments she left him to himself, he went to the window and strained to see how near the waters were approaching. What if *she* came in the night? If the waters reached to the road under the window, would she be able to leap up to the first floor and throttle him? Would he wake up to find her squatting on his chest, dripping with the foul waters of the Seine? He thought of her face, livid with rot like those of the drowning victims he had seen at the morgue. She would bare her yellow teeth and wring out her sodden clothes so the poisonous damp would trickle into his throat.

His heart thudding, he leaned out again. And he saw her looking up at him from the street below, her eyes a-glimmer with hatred. She was going to take the diamonds, his beautiful diamonds, the emerald-cut great stone five times the size of all the rest that would make him a king in America. She would take it and then force it down his throat with the riverwater and cut it out of his belly again. He saw it in her eyes. He whimpered. Sylvie could come back any moment and she would tell him he was ill, that his imagination was disturbed and his fever high, but she had not seen it, had not felt the hatred of the ghost as he had.

Morel dressed as quickly as he could. The buttons were difficult to fasten with his shaking hands and the sweat on his forehead stung his eyes. He took his coat and waited behind his door for a moment till he was sure the corridor outside was empty then made a dash for the front door, scooping up the large key to the apartment door as he passed the hall-table. His hand caught the flower vase and it went crashing to the floor but he didn't pause until he was outside and had turned the key in the lock. He heard Sylvie call his name and hesitated on the landing; her footsteps came close and then the door handle rattled. He could hear her breathing and put his fingers lightly onto the wood, knowing she was just the other side.

'Christian?' she said softly. 'Christian, my love, I know you are there. Come back and come to bed. Let me look after you, my darling, you know you are not well.'

He felt tears in his eyes; her voice was so soft but she could not protect him from the dead. 'She is coming for the diamonds, Sylvie,' he whispered, pressing his cheek to the wood. 'For *our* diamonds – and we shall not be tricked. No, I will fetch them and then I will come home and you will care for me.' His mind would not work as he wanted it to, his forehead was damp. 'I know I am not well.'

'Christian, unlock the door. We shall go together.'

He smiled, a wave of love for his pretty clever wife lifting his heart as it had lifted the first time he laid eyes on her. 'No, Sylvie. You will stop me. Be patient. I will fetch them and then we will be happy for all times, best beloved.' He let his cheek rest against the wood one moment more then turned and stumbled down the stairs. He could hear her calling his name and the rattle of the door handle as he went.

CHAPTER 21

'*W*AIT HERE FOR ME,' MAUD SAID AS THEY TURNED into Cour de Rohan.

Yvette frowned. 'No, we go together. I don't think he will have put them in a big barrel marked *Diamonds*. You'll need help to look, Maud.'

'And if someone comes?'

'Everyone is helping their neighbours nearer to the waters,' Yvette said, then looked at Tanya. 'But you stay here anyway, Tanya. Just in case.'

Tanya was busy preparing the lanterns they had brought from the ironmongers. 'Why?' she said indignantly.

'Because! And anyway, Maud and I have spare clothes at Rue de Seine and you do not. It might already be flooding down there, and even if it isn't it will smell and there will be rats.'

'Rats?' Tanya said, taking a slight step backwards.

'Yes,' Yvette said with a certain glee creeping into her voice. 'They panic as the water rises and come swarming out through the tunnels. They will probably try and climb up your dress to escape the flood.'

'Oh, all right! I'll wait.' She sat down on the edge of the water-trough and put her chin in her hand.

The entrance to the cellar was in the corner of the courtyard: a wooden cover set in a stone surround with two large iron rings to lift it, sunk into the wood. Yvette and Maud lifted it off together, the rust flaking off on Maud's pale brown leather gloves like dried blood. Yvette swung herself nimbly down onto the ladder in front of her and when she had reached the bottom, she lit her lantern. From where she watched above, Maud could see nothing but shadows – ghosts of barrels and wooden struts in the ashy Indian Yellow glow.

'Come on down.'

The ground at the bottom of the ladder was dry, but the tunnels smelled of riverwater, and it was clear even in the half-light that the cellar tunnel led quite steeply downwards. The floor was earth, the walls brick. After three or four yards the tunnel ended in a T-junction. In front of them were half-a-dozen arched doorways.

'You start there,' Yvette said, pointing to her left, and with a determined step went right. None of the doors were locked and it seemed that whatever was usually stored in them had already been cleared away. There were wine racks on the walls of the first two rooms that Maud went into, simple shelving in the third.

Yvette suddenly appeared beside her in a blur of diffused light that made her look ghostly, her voice breathy with excitement. 'I've found something.'

'Can you hear water?' Maud said. It was a whispering sound like rain in the trees.

'The sewers will run just underneath here. The ground is still dry. But come on – there's another room leading off this one.'

Maud followed her out through to the T-junction and back into the next store room. At first it looked just like the others, but at the back there was a space of deeper darkness. Yvette lifted her lamp, to reveal a low opening leading back into some older, deeper vault.

Yvette was pushing aside a barrel that blocked the path. Whatever dread Maud felt settling on her shoulders, it seemed as if Yvette felt none of it. Without speaking to Maud she ducked through the opening, and a moment or two later reappeared, grinning. 'It opens out again, Maud. Come through.'

She did. The sound of running water had faded here, but the air seemed heavier; even the flames in their lamps seemed to shrink from it. She straightened up and looked around her. She was in a vault perhaps seven foot at its highest point and all lined with thin and crumbling bricks. It was divided in two by a wall of larger stone blocks that looked as if they could have been pulled from the medieval walls of the city. They did not quite reach the roof. Around the walls, strange shapes gathered – broken furniture and split barrels. It was a dead space, a forgotten dumping ground.

'You go left of the wall,' Yvette said cheerfully. 'Look for something that has been disturbed.'

Morel remembered his gun only when he was out on the street. He could not go back now but the thought of seizing the diamonds back from Maud's ghost frightened him. He felt in the pockets of his coat and found a five-franc piece then half-stumbled across the threshold of the ironmonger's shop on the corner of Saint-Germain and Rue Grégoire de Tours. The old man behind the counter looked up at him in some alarm.

'Are the waters coming?' he said. 'We've emptied the cellars and my son is searching for sandbags. Is it coming up the street yet?'

Christian ignored him, trying to focus on the display of knives hanging on the wall opposite the counter. The reflections of the oil lamps lit about the place confused him and the air was smoky. He made a grab at one almost at random – a hunting knife, its blade four-inches long and curved. Then he put the coin down on the counter and went to leave.

'Sir, are you well, sir?'

He waved his hand as if the man was merely some insect and stumbled out again, shoving the knife into his belt. The crowd seemed to work against him. The street furniture set out to trip him, the men buffeted at him with their shoulders. The crowd became a mass of hostile glances. He leaned against the flaking bark of a plane tree and drew his breath in and out until the world steadied a little and his vision cleared. He thought of her again, the ghost searching for his diamonds. He pushed on and turned onto the cobblestones of Cour du Commerce. It was narrow and ancient here, the old walls of the city cramping towards each other, then the open air of Cour de Rohan. There was the lean-to where he had watched old Henri sweating day after day. He spat on the ground. Then, feeling a hand on his sleeve, he recoiled. A dark young woman was speaking to him. The Russian girl! What was *she* doing here? Could a ghost have human companions? Her voice buzzed into his brain; she was chattering about the floods, asking him for some assistance. He tried to form some reply and free himself from her, but she continued pulling at his arm. His rage, his desperation suddenly broke free and he struck her across the face with all his force. She fell to the ground and did not move. The cover to the cellar steps had been lifted away and he clambered down into the darkness, his hands and feet clumsy on the ladder. There was his candle on the barrel. He took it, lit it and lurched onwards.

The rear cellar extended back a long way. The texture of the ground changed. It felt slippery under Maud's feet. The dividing medieval-looking blocks didn't sit flush with this back wall either. The end wall was made of thin, old-looking bricks; the mortar was crumbling. Lowering her lantern, she saw the earth floor was black and muddy. She heard a dry whisper in the walls and lifted her light again; the mortar between the bricks was trickling out in a thin stream as she watched. She put her hand on the stone and it felt cold. She pressed herself against the wall, listening. It was not the rush of water, but something else. A sense of mass and weight, of pressure. She felt, horribly, the stones shift under her palms and took a step backwards. Her heel caught on the curl of an old piece of railing and she tripped and dropped her lamp. The flame died. Above the wall that almost divided the chamber in two she could see the glimmer of Yvette's light. She pulled herself upright, fighting free of the railings as if she had fallen in a briar patch.

'Yvette, I've lost my light!'

'One moment, I'll come for you. Maud, I think I've found them.' There was the sound of something shifting then a rattle. 'Oh my God. They are beautiful.' Her voice was soft, reverential. 'I am coming now.'

The light shifted and Maud felt her way cautiously along the central wall. In the darkness the pressure of the caged water nearby was palpable in the air. The trickling of mortar seemed louder and there was another noise, a slow scraping of brick. She reached the edge of the dividing wall and saw Yvette stepping towards her over the wreckage, the light in her left hand and a box in her right. Maud recognised it, the phoenix rising on its edge, and she felt her rage lift into her throat.

On Yvette's face was an expression of bliss. She showed Maud the open box. The grand stone cushioned by its smaller fellows. 'We have him now, don't we?' Without waiting for Maud to answer she set it down for a moment to relight Maud's lamp then picked it up again. She was about to speak but before she could, there was a sound in the darkness in the outer cellar and a curse. Someone had missed their footing and knocked into the barrel Yvette had moved.

'Get back, and cover your light,' Yvette said in a harsh whisper and Maud crept back again along the wall, sheltering the reluctant glow of her lantern under her coat. She could hear a heavy laboured breathing. Maud's fingers brushed one of the tangle of short railings again and her hand closed round the free end.

'Mademoiselle?' It was Morel's voice, a little slurred but him, without a doubt. He was on the other side of the partition with Yvette. Maud set down her lamp and pulled the railing free. It was very heavy.

Yvette gave a little shriek. 'Oh! Monsieur, you startled me.'

'What? Why are you here?'

Maud shifted her grip on the iron bar. The water was so close. Even if Morel was ill he might still be strong enough to kill them both, but he was not as strong as the water was, whispering to her on the other side of the thin bricks. It had eaten Paris, it should eat him too. It became her ally. He would not think to harm them if he felt it coming for him – he would run. She moved her palm along the bricks looking for the place where the cold pressure was greatest.

∞∞

'What are you holding?'

Yvette stood frozen in front of him, the box half-concealed in

329

her right hand, in her left the lantern held high. She put her weight onto one hip and made her eyes wide.

'My aunty swears she left a picture here among the rubbish. A landscape, I think, though she can't like it much, otherwise why would she have left it to rot here for years? But today she must save it from the flood. Will you help me, sir? You've a kind face! Let's have a look around, eh?'

His face was grey and sweating; his eyes darted around the room. He saw the empty place where the little round box had been sitting, its cover clearly lit by her lamp. He dropped the candle into the mud and pulled the knife from his belt. 'Give it to me.' He shuffled forward a step.

Maud closed her eyes and with all her strength swung at the wall. The bricks crumbled under the blow and the water leaped out of its confinement in a joyous blast, taking more of the rotten masonry with it.

The noise made him step back, and at once water gushed in behind Yvette; she could feel its frozen force pushing against her legs. She screamed, and while he was still looking at the sudden rush in horror and confusion, she threw the box towards him. The diamonds cascaded out, striking him in the face, and the great stone fell over his shoulder. He half-turned and dropped to his knees, scrabbling in the rushing filth. Yvette ran past him, but his left arm shot out and caught her round her thigh, tripping her into the roaring waters. The lantern flew from her hands, landing and bouncing against the broken barrels. She fell hard on her hands then twisted round to pull her face from the deepening water. 'Bitch!' he screamed and as the lantern began to splutter and fail she watched, fascinated, as he raised his right arm, the knife hovering in the darkness above her.

'Morel,' Maud said, her voice clear above the sound of the water. She uncovered the lantern so he could see her face. He went absolutely still.

Yvette pulled her own knife from her pocket, struggling to get it free under the water. It rushed up her body, splashing into her mouth and eyes, gushing around Morel's thighs as if he were a stone in a stream. She scrabbled the knife free of her soaked skirts and opened the blade under the flow of dirty water.

'Maud,' Morel said in a whisper. Then Yvette thrust up, her thumb on the blade. She felt a terrible resistance then a release as the knife went deep into his chest. He gasped and toppled forwards. She dropped the knife and scrabbled away from him. Maud pulled her upright. He was floating face down in the water.

'My God!' Yvette screamed and reached towards him as if she thought she might be allowed to change her mind. Maud moved her aside and went to him, pushing his floating body into the wreckage and turning him by his shoulder until she could see his face. The eyes were open and sightless.

'He's dead,' Maud said. The water was nearly at their waist. 'We have to go.'

'Oh Jesus, my knife!' Yvette said, dropping into a crouch, feeling around on the floor and spitting the water out of her mouth as it reached her lips and eyes.

'*Now*, Yvette. Now or we're dead too.' Maud grabbed her and began to drag her towards the opening into the main cellar. Yvette reached out one more time and felt something in the water; she managed to get her fingers around it. Maud pulled harder at her shoulder, helping her to her feet against the force of the river racing ever faster to fill its new space. Together they struggled through towards the storage room, and both had to duck under the slapping water to get through the low opening. Maud let the waters tear the lamp from her hand. There followed moments of death, thunder and darkness with their heads underwater and all the lights gone. *Air.* They stumbled onwards – and ahead of them they heard their names being called – then screamed.

Yvette got her arm under Maud's and they moved forward, their hands pushed against the walls to keep their footing. Rats were swimming alongside them, scrabbling up the walls and along the roof over their heads, falling over themselves in their panic. The track of the cellar began to rise.

'Here!' Maud managed to shout. Tanya came splashing to meet them, her lantern held high, the rats swimming past her and up to her knees in water. She reached for her friends, and pulled them over to the ladder.

'Yvette first,' Maud gasped. Tanya nodded and guided Yvette's shivering hands onto the ladder and went up behind her, pushing her onwards and out, shoving her lantern after her. Then she turned back.

'Now you, Maud.'

Maud hesitated. Around her the waters were still lifting and the rats were screaming and scattering into what escape routes they could find; above her was her friend, framed by the patch of wan Parisian sky. She put out her hand and let Tanya drag her out of the darkness.

CHAPTER 22

*I*T WAS SOME TIME BEFORE TANYA COULD PERSUADE
Yvette to move or speak. Like a mother with a child, she
managed at last to persuade her to come over to the water trough
in the courtyard and clean some of the contaminated waters of the
flood from her with the slightly cleaner water still coming from the
old pump. She put her own coat round Yvette's shoulders then
went to Café Procope to beg towels and a messenger to send to
Paul.

With Maud and Yvette as well protected from the cold as she
could manage, she led them the short distance to Paul's rooms on
Rue Racine. The concierge was a friend of Mr Allardyce's so knew
Tanya's name, and on hearing it, and seeing her and her friends,
she put her usual moral scruples aside and took them in. She
brought hot water, blankets from her own store, and soup. Maud
and Yvette let Tanya attend to them. Maud watched her remove
Yvette's filthy clothes and sponge her pale skin with soap and hot
water, dry her and wrap her in blankets then wash the foul waters
from her hair. Then she settled Yvette on the sofa near the fire and
turned her attention to Maud.

It was when she put her head back to let Tanya pour warm
water from an enamel jug over her hair that Maud saw for the first

time the livid bruise on the Russian girl's cheek. She put up her hand to touch it with her fingertips.

'Tanya?'

The girl smiled and shook her head. 'Don't worry, darling. It left me dizzy for a while, but it was nothing to the sickness I felt when I came to and realised that monster had got past me. Don't fret. Sasha and Paul will be here in a little while, and they will make a great deal more of a fuss over me than I have made over you.' She poured another jug of hot water over Maud's hair, lifting the strands apart with her fingers. 'Can you tell me what happened?'

Maud looked over to the couch where Yvette appeared to have drifted off into an uneasy sleep, wrapped in a mound of blankets. 'He found her with the diamonds. He would have killed her if she hadn't been so quick with her knife.'

Tanya nodded, then took one of her towels from the pile and began to rub Maud's hair dry between her palms.

'What is she holding onto so tight? All the time I have been washing her she's kept her hand clenched over something.'

'Her knife, I think,' Maud said. 'She was searching for it in the water. Tanya, when Paul comes, do you think he might collect our things from the room in Rue de Seine and pay the woman? I have silver enough in my purse, I think.'

'Of course, darling.'

∞∞

Paul did what he was asked, though it took some time before he was reassured that Tanya was not severely injured. Tanya asked him for his trust and he gave it as easily as he had given his love. Sasha had come with him from the church and now mounted a furious watch over them all, seated on a stool by the stove and working her needles, getting up from time to time to examine them all for signs of fever.

As soon as Paul had delivered their bundles, he left again to continue reporting the water's rise. Maud watched his expression as he exchanged hurried goodbyes with Tanya in the open doorway, and thought her friend had as good a chance as anyone of happiness in marriage.

Maud went behind the screen to dress. She slipped her feet into the cold damp leather of her boots and was catching the last of the buttons together when she heard the sound of something dropping to the floor and a low gasp from the main room. She emerged and saw Tanya kneeling by Yvette. She imagined that the knife had fallen from her hand finally as she slept, and that Tanya's sigh was a sign she had found it with Morel's blood on it . . . but when Tanya turned towards her and opened her palm, she was not holding the knife, but the golconda diamond.

'Maud,' Tanya said, her voice tight, 'the knife is still there. When the waters go down, they will find him and it. She carved her name into it. She must get away.'

Maud stared at the stone. Seeing it in Tanya's palm, the way it shifted the light around it, it seemed ridiculous that even for a moment she could have been fooled by the fake she had seen. The diamond had a power and presence to it that could not be described or captured.

She knelt down and closed Tanya's fingers over it. She never wanted to see it again. 'Do you think Yvette might like to come to England with me? We will need papers perhaps, but there will be some time before the waters go down.'

Tanya touched Yvette's forehead and she murmured something in her sleep. 'Yes, yes I do. Oh Lord, yes, I think that would be best.'

There was a light tap at the door and Sasha went to answer it. Charlotte was there looking weary but otherwise just the same. 'I met Mr Allardyce at Saint-Sulpice,' she said before they had even asked the question. 'And he told me where you were. I thought I'd come along and be warm for an hour before going back to the refugees. It seems everyone knows you are here, by the way. There was a woman waiting in the street and she asked me to give you this, Miss Heighton.' She passed her a piece of notepaper. Maud felt her body shiver as she took it. There was no other woman who might be waiting for them there.

It read: *Pont des Arts, an hour.*

Maud passed it to Tanya. 'From Sylvie.'

Tanya glanced at it then looked back at her. 'Maud, you can't go.'

'Of course I am going, Tanya. You know that.'

Tanya clenched her fists in frustration. 'Then I shall come too. Charlotte, will you watch Yvette with Sasha until we get back?'

Charlotte settled herself into one of the armchairs and glanced at the sleeping girl. 'Of course I shall.'

Maud was shaking her head. 'Tanya, please, you have to take care of Yvette. You are getting married . . .'

Tanya had already put on her long coat and was doing up the buttons angrily. 'No, Maud. Don't worry, I shall not interfere. But whatever happens . . . there should be a witness. You will not disappear into that horrible greedy river again with no one knowing of it. You don't know what it was like, just to be told, to be told something like that by a stranger.'

CHAPTER 23

Pont des Arts oil on panel 29.3 × 23.6 cm

Though this also seems to show the Seine in flood, the focus is on the effect of the lamplight on the snow that has gathered along the railings, and the landmarks of Paris have disappeared into the darkness behind it. The mood of the painting is simultaneously one of calm and threat. We are drawn towards an absence in the centre of the frame.

Extract from the catalogue notes to the exhibition 'The Paris Winter: Anonymous Treasures from the de Civray Collection', Southwark Picture Gallery, London, 2010

'Mademoiselle! By all that's holy!' Maud felt a hand on her shoulder. A policeman in gaiters and a short cape was holding her back. She could see Sylvie on the bridge ahead of her, lit by a gas-light on the centre of the bridge. The river roared around her.

'Let me by, I don't mind getting wet.'

'That's your choice, mademoiselle, but the road is unsafe. It falls away under you, look!' He pointed along the quay, to the men

building up the embankment in the sullen yellow glow of oil-
lamps. The trees fell sideways like drunks, and the lamp-posts had
sunk and tilted to their knees, though some were still lit, struggling
to do their duty, to lift their lights above the water.

'That woman on the bridge – I know her.'

He turned round, and seeing Sylvie sitting on the railings of the
bridge, he swore and blew his whistle till another policeman some
twenty yards along the way signalled that he'd heard and pointed
towards the bridge.

'Let me go to her,' Maud said.

'We'll go across together,' the policeman replied. 'If one of us
falls in a sink-hole, the other one has to try and drag 'em out.
You'll be soaked, you know.'

'I don't care.'

Tanya took Maud in her arms and held her a moment. 'You
must come back to us, Maud. All will be well if you come back to
us.'

The tenderness in her voice made Maud's throat tighten and
she found she couldn't reply.

The officer took her arm and together they battled through the
dark waters which showed parchment yellow where the light
reached them till they reached the steps up onto the bridge. Maud
was soaked to her waist and felt as if she was dragging the river up
with her as her heavy wool skirt pulled and coiled around her legs.
She looked up. There was someone else on the bridge now with
Sylvie. Another policeman was standing some yards from her, to
the north. He held his hands wide and low like a man trying to
urge a dangerous animal back into its cage. Maud and her guardian
approached from the south.

'Good evening, Maud,' Sylvie said lightly, though she was still
looking at the other man.

'Sylvie.'

'She has a gun,' the officer to the north said, his voice calm but loud enough for them all to hear.

Sylvie nodded. 'Yes, I do. That is true. I do have a gun.' She held it up into the lamplight to show them, clasping it between her two hands, a finger around the trigger, but somehow relaxed. 'Gentlemen, I wish to have some private conversation with this lady. Would you be so kind as to retreat a little way?'

'I shan't leave you with a gun pointing at you, miss,' the man on Maud's side said. She looked at him. He had a kind face, and was probably not much older than herself. There was no sign of fear on him. Only determination. She had a sudden vision of him walking down the Champs Elysées with his girl on his arm.

'Please do as she says,' she told him, and when he hesitated, 'I promise she can't hurt me. Let me talk to her.'

'I don't like it.'

'I know you don't.'

He looked into her face and she met his gaze steadily, evenly.

'If she aims,' he said, 'don't think, just run.' He nodded to his colleague to the north and they both stepped backwards slowly a yard or two, while Maud advanced until she was in the middle of the bridge and facing Sylvie. Morel's wife looked lovely in the lamplight. She was wearing a dark blue dress, close-fitting, with her fur-lined coat open over it. The snow fell silently onto her hair and shoulders, and along the railings either side of her while the river lunged and roared beneath them.

'Aren't you afraid I'll shoot you?'

Maud realised she had never thought of this moment. She had wanted Morel to suffer, imagined him suffering. When she thought of Sylvie it was only in the past. Sylvie walking in Père Lachaise, Sylvie stretched out reading in the drawing room, Sylvie lighting a cigarette and laughing. Sylvie stepping over her body. She looked just as beautiful as ever, just as graceful, as kind. Maud thought of how it had felt when she had rested her head on Maud's shoulder, rested her light weight on her arm.

'How many times can you kill one person, Sylvie? I think if you are holding the gun, the bullets would pass straight through me.'

'Careful, Maud. You'll make me curious to try. Strange. You were such a slight breath of a girl, tiptoeing about. You seem different.'

'What can I possibly fear now?' Maud asked.

The slightly mocking smile fell from Sylvie's lips and she looked sideways and down into the waters surging just below the bridge, their suck and groan as they pushed through the arches, carrying their loot of debris, planks and barrels with them. 'He's dead, isn't he?'

'Yes.'

She nodded and continued to watch the waters while she spoke. 'He shut me in at Rue de Seine – it took forever for the concierge to hear me. I ran out after him, and all I saw was you and your friends being led away from Cour de Rohen. I followed you to those rooms. I hoped perhaps he'd been arrested, but there were no police. I went back to the cellars and saw they were flooded.' She paused as if trying to work out some impossible puzzle and her voice was wondering when she said, 'I couldn't calm him. I could always calm him – but not today. He thought he had seen your ghost, that you were in league with the river and coming to take him. He didn't say "The river is flooding the cellars"; he said, "*She* is doing it – *She* is coming to take them. To take *us*". Oh, I told him he was wrong, that he was imagining it. But he grew nervous when we couldn't sell the diamonds and you began to appear to him. You never showed yourself to me, did you?'

'No. Only him. It was he who threw me in the river like rubbish.'

'Yes, but the plan was mine.'

The words struck Maud in the centre of her being. It seemed to smash some dam inside her – and her feeling was one of release. Grief flowed from her and the river carried it away.

'Have you ever loved anyone, Maud? Other than me? Someone who might love you back?'

Maud shook her head.

'You cannot know then, what it is like to love someone and not be able to save them. The pain of that! It leaves you breathless.'

'I think I do know what that feels like, Sylvie.'

She looked up at her under her long lashes and smiled suddenly, sadly. 'I understand. Yes, perhaps you do.' She lifted her chin and looked along the river behind Maud. 'Paris is beautiful tonight. All this water, the way the light swims in it. Notre Dame behind you, covered in snow. It looks like a palace. Oh Maud! I loved him so very much, my handsome man. It's strange. I knew he was dead before you told me. The moment I lost sight of him as he ran up the street this afternoon I felt my heart stop, my soul just snap out of existence, like turning off an electric light. I knew I'd never see him again.'

The water from Maud's dress was pooling beneath her like an extra, deeper shadow in the lamplight. Sylvie made a noise halfway between a sob and a laugh. 'Such a little thing. A tiny movement of the wrist. A drop more laudanum and you'd have drowned, just disappeared, and he would be alive and we would be happy. Damn it.' She tilted her head back and blinked rapidly, not letting her tears fall. 'I was such a fool! I was afraid you would taste it in the wine. I should have known I could have added the whole bottle and you'd have drunk it all down like a good girl and thanked me.

Always so grateful! So helpful! It made it so easy. I couldn't believe we had found such a sweet fool. And now here you are to judge me. Perhaps you do look like a ghost, after all. Perhaps you are dead. Surely my dear Maud would be leading me to safety by now? But you just stand there and judge. Not like nice helpful Maud at all. Are you real? I'd like to know.'

Maud looked straight into her blue-grey eyes: they were calm, curious. She took in the curve of her waist, the tight cut of her dress across her shoulders, the lace on her chest, the curls of blond hair over her small ears, the single pearl earrings, caught like globes of smoke. 'I am Maud Heighton. You and your lover tried to kill me, but I lived. I told the Countess what you had done, and we stopped you selling the diamonds. I let Morel see me, hoping it would make him mad. And yes, I do judge you.'

Sylvie swallowed, then licked her lips and took a great shuddering breath. 'What a beautiful night this is.' She looked up into the sky. 'Oh, the glory of it! Very well, Maud. You have that right. Judge away.'

She lifted the gun and placed it between her teeth and pulled the trigger. A mist of red appeared in the air behind her. Maud lurched forward, but while the sound of the shot was still cracking in the air, Sylvie's body crumpled and fell backwards into the black waters. The policemen ran forward from either side of the bridge and Maud collapsed onto her knees. The officer who had helped her across, crouched at her side. 'Are you injured?'

She shook her head and he left her. She couldn't breathe. It was as if the air stuck in her mouth. She put her hands on the ground in front of her and tried desperately to make her lungs open and find air. The world swam and quivered around her; whistles blew and somewhere she could hear Tanya screaming. With an enormous effort, she struggled to her feet and ran from the bridge, lurching through the vile waters, until she felt her friends' arms around her again, gathering her up and pulling her free for the second time.

When Paul Allardyce returned to his rooms that night he found they were filled with sleeping women. They had made nests for themselves on his sofa and chairs. His fiancée was asleep on his second-best greatcoat by the stove and her maid snored next to her on an armchair, using his steamer trunk as a foot stool. He crept through them and collapsed on his bed, where he slept dreamlessly in his dirty clothes.

CHAPTER 24

27 January 1910

THE RIVER HAD ALMOST REACHED BOULEVARD Saint-Germain and the cellars were filling on both sides of the street. It was easy for Sasha to deliver some note of pretended appeal to the concierge which sent her a safe distance into Rue Mazarine. Dawn was still an hour away when Maud walked briskly through the hall and up to the first floor. The door was unlocked, as she had thought it would be. One key was still in the cellar in Morel's coat, the other belonged to the concierge and would never leave the ring on her belt. The image of the moment Sylvie pulled the trigger kept appearing in her mind like the pulse under her skin, the explosion of red under the lamplight.

She let herself into the flat and flicked on the electric light. The smashed vase on the floor reminded her of Mrs Prideux. She walked through the drawing room to Christian's room. It was the part of the apartment she hadn't entered before. The bed was unmade, an angry twist of blankets and sheets. His sickbed. His desk was up against the right-hand wall, cherrywood and roll-topped. She pushed it open and began to make her way carefully through the papers. She looked in herself for grief or doubt, for guilt, but could not find anything so simple. She was bruised, hollowed-out, and her heart seemed to beat slowly – an exhausted animal finally allowed sight of home, but not there yet. Whatever she had to feel about the Morels would come later – slowly, she hoped. Home. Not Alnwick, but Richmond or Darlington perhaps. Somewhere honest with wide landscapes. Countryside you could walk through for days on end where the light changed because of the moods of the sky, not the electric glare of Paris. Peace. There she would be strong enough to feel, let these bruises heal. The Quaker families in Darlington had built libraries large enough to keep Yvette happy for months, and James had mentioned there was a lady doctor in town. He seemed to approve of her. If the town could accept a lady doctor they would probably accept a female painter and a Frenchwoman.

She sighed and went back to her task. There was some correspondence – bills for the most part, but there were also the papers she needed: a birth certificate in the name of Sylvie Morel, born 1 January 1888, in Toulouse. She had lied about her age, just a little. Just as she couldn't stop herself thieving just a little under Maud's nose from the jewellery shop. Maud took it and put it in her handbag, along with any other piece of paper with the name Sylvie Morel on it, and then she made a fire in the grate and burned the rest.

After that she went into Sylvie's room, took a pair of suitcases from under the bed and packed them with the dead woman's clothes – the delicate lace underthings, a pale chemise and long white skirts. A dark blue tea-gown, collars and cuffs. She filled the lacquered jewel-box with the loose trinkets scattered on the table-top, fitted in brushes and combs, stockings and shoes. Everything a respectable Frenchwoman might take with her on a trip to England. She would not ask Yvette to wear them, but they gave the proper impression as they travelled, and selling them in London would give them some money. Might they travel a little around England before deciding where to settle?

She thought of the plans Sylvie had been making with Morel: the vision of her pulling the trigger returned and she felt the soreness in her heart. Regret and hope folded their arms around her like twin angels. She took the two suitcases into the hall and checked that the papers in the grate were fully consumed and the embers dark. Suddenly the lights fizzled and went out. She closed her eyes and waited, a ghost among ghosts, to see who might come for her, but there was no sound apart from the gentle fall of the rain against the glass. The power had finally gone in this building as the water wound its way in, that was all. The ghosts were gone. She went back into the hall, picked up the suitcases and left.

Portrait of Madame de Civray oil on canvas 31.7 × 26.7 cm

The warm earth tones of this portrait give it an unusual intimacy, as does the casual posture of the sitter. Note the reflections of light on her evening clothes and jewels. Uniquely among the anonymous paintings in the de Civray collection, this picture has at some point been clumsily re-touched: you can see with the naked eye the uneven patch of colour on the table in front of the Countess. X-rays suggest that this patching was done to cover an egg-shaped white object that lay there in the original. Some have suggested this was the golconda diamond that Madame de Civray had removed from the Empress Eugénie tiara and converted into a pendant at some time before World War I. Her removal of many of the original stones from the tiara was discovered only after her death, and was greeted with horror in France where the tiara had once formed part of the crown jewels. She left no explanation for what some regarded as an act of vandalism, other than a note in the case itself which said only, *It was a fair trade*. The pendant was eventually bequeathed to the Smithsonian Institute in New York, in spite of protests from some French newspapers.

Extract from the catalogue notes to the exhibition 'The Paris Winter: Anonymous Treasures from the de Civray Collection', Southwark Picture Gallery, London, 2010

'So, Tanya, I have come. What do you want of me? Talk quickly, honey, I'm already late.'

The Countess looked around the drawing room in Rue Chalgrin and seemed to approve. The room was lit only by fire and candles, giving it the feel of an eighteenth-century salon. She dropped the furs from her shoulders and took a seat on the sofa, her arm stretched out along the back. Tanya stood to one side of the fireplace, her hands clasped in front of her as if about to recite or sing to the company.

'I want you to leave Maud Heighton alone, and Yvette. I want you to never mention either of them again. Or the Morels. Please do not employ any of your Pinkertons in France or anywhere else to look for them or enquire after them – and if you ever hear of them again, please do not give any sign you know anything of them.'

The Countess's face had grown serious while Tanya spoke. She raised her eyebrows. 'That is a great deal to ask, Miss Koltsova. In light of what has been taken from me, a very great deal. Why should I do this?'

Tanya stepped away from the fireplace and put the stone she had been holding on top of the table in front of the Countess. The woman looked at it, but did not pick it up. 'That is my diamond, I assume.'

Tanya went back to the fire. 'It is, though I do not think you could ever prove it. Not if Henri has done his work well.'

The Countess looked up again. 'And the rest, Miss Koltsova? The other twenty stones Henri chiselled out and gave to Morel? Where are they?'

Tanya could not meet her eyes; instead she stared into the fire. 'No one will profit by them and the guilty couple are dead.'

'I guess you don't want to tell me any of the particulars?' Tanya shook her head. 'That's a lot of diamonds to lose, Miss Koltsova.' There was a decanter of whisky on the table next to the diamond and a glass. The Countess poured herself a drink and continued to stare past Tanya into the flames as she sipped it. She still did not touch the huge diamond next to her. 'Is she here? Miss Heighton, I mean.' She stabbed a finger suddenly onto the table. 'In this building?'

Tanya hesitated and then nodded. 'Yes, she is.'

'So why am I having this conversation with you, honey?' She was looking at Tanya with fierce concentration.

Tanya remembered the maid, the dismissal, how charming the Countess of Civray could be until she stopped trying. 'Because she doesn't like you much any more, Madame, and thought there was a danger she might spit in your eye if she saw you. So I said *I'd* return your stupid diamond.'

For a moment the Countess was completely still and then she burst into laughter. 'Oh, you girls! God, you kill me.' She wiped her eyes. 'It won't be the first time I've negotiated with people who want to spit in my eye. Tell her – no, please *ask* her – to come in and bring any work of her own she happens to have with her.'

'This is not a negotiation,' Tanya said stiffly.

'Like hell it isn't,' the Countess said and poured herself another drink. Tanya still hadn't moved. 'Please, Tanya, I'd be very grateful if you could ask Miss Heighton to step in.'

Tanya could not refuse her when she asked that way; all her breeding demanded it. The Countess studied the diamond in front of her, watching its colours dance in the firelight until Tanya returned with Maud beside her. Maud came in and stood in front of her, looking, the Countess thought, very much like the polite, thoughtful young English girl she had welcomed into her house before Christmas. She examined her for a while in silence. She liked it when people came to her house and admired her paintings, admired her – and she realised with a slow smile that she was not so sure she liked it when they did anything else. Well, that was one new thing she had learned – and her father always told her that the best lessons were the ones you paid for. Those you remembered.

Maud put a painting on the table beside the diamond and her whisky glass. It was a portrait of Sylvie Morel with her opium pipe. The Countess considered it for a while, thinking hard, and then looked up at the artist.

'Miss Heighton, I'm going to guess a couple of things and you're going to tell me if I'm right or wrong. You are leaving Paris?'

'I am.'

'And I think that model Yvette I am not allowed to ask about in future is going too?'

'She is.'

The Countess sighed and leaned back again, cradling her whisky. 'My father taught me never to come out of a bargain with what you are first offered, and I take his advice very seriously. Now this diamond is here and I'm told this lady,' she tapped the portrait, 'and her brother or husband or whatever he was are dead, so I think I have an idea of what happened. The guilty will not profit, you say, and I don't think you'd be able to look me in the eye if you were taking the rest of the haul back to England.' She saw Tanya glance at Maud, but the Englishwoman made no sign.

The Countess was impressed. 'No – scratch that. *You* might be able to, Miss Heighton, but Miss Koltsova could not.' She drummed her fingers on the table-top. 'Twenty, five-carat diamonds.' She tapped at the portrait again. 'They are worth a fortune. Not as much as this big one, of course, but still a fortune. I tell you what – I'll sell them to you, Miss Heighton. I'll take this picture, and every year for the next twenty years – if both of us live that long – I want you to send me the best thing you've painted. For that you can have my silence. I'll also pass on any rumours I hear that might disturb your peace, and,' she nodded to Tanya, 'I'll give this girl a commission to paint me, and to paint my children. Then I'll tell everyone in Paris what a clever artist she is. How's that?'

Tanya had blushed a little and was looking at Maud hopefully now, but the Englishwoman's voice was even. 'I'll paint something for you, specifically for you, whenever I wish to. I promise I will never do any less than the best I can for you, and you shall have twenty paintings within twenty years if not before.' She paused. 'But for our safety, in case anyone makes the connection between the pictures, the diamonds and what has happened here, I shall not sign them.'

The Countess considered for a second then knocked back the last of her whisky and stood up.

'Deal. You'll go far, Miss Heighton, and I'm glad you're not dead. The world is more interesting with you in it.' She slung her furs around her shoulders again then picked up the diamond and put it in her pocket as casually as if it had been a cigarette-case.

'Miss Koltsova, have that picture mounted on canvas, framed and sent to me, please. So just nineteen to go now, Miss Heighton. Now if you'll excuse me, the Comédie Française are having a candlelit benefit for the flood victims, and absolutely *everyone* is going to be there. Good night.'

She walked out of the room and left them in the glow of the firelight. As soon as the door shut, Tanya flung herself onto the sofa, filled the whisky glass to the brim and drank.

'Oouf! That woman terrifies me!' She looked at Maud and frowned. 'How is Yvette?'

Maud came and sat down beside her, took the whisky glass from her hand and drank her own share. 'She's nervous, but she is willing to come to England and live under the name of Sylvie Morel. I've told her she could give French lessons to the schoolchildren of Darlington if she promises not to teach them to swear. She says it sounds a better future than the one she thought was waiting for her here.' She handed Tanya the glass back.

Tanya looked a little doubtful. 'Darlington is where your brother lives, is it not? Will he approve? I thought you might go to London or the West Country.'

Maud sighed. 'Oh Tanya, if I know one thing I know I can cope with James now, and I want to see Albert, my little half-brother, grow up. I shall remain Maud Heighton so he can always disown me, and London is too like Paris. No air.' She saw Tanya's confusion and put her arm through hers. 'And I absolutely guarantee there are no opium dens in Darlington. Just a great many Quakers. Yvette is giving your Aunt Vera lessons at the moment on the rates models should be paid, which are the best colour shops, and how to get the best prices.' Tanya laughed. 'Will you come to see us in England? When you are married? You will like the North, and however modestly you dress, the whole county will be amazed at your wonderful sense of style and flock round you like moths.'

Tanya took her hand. 'Then yes, I shall. I will bring my husband and my two – no, my three – children and Sasha, and we will leave all the ghosts behind us.'

Maud laid her head on her shoulder and they were still there when Yvette came to find them a few minutes later. She claimed the whisky glass and sat on the floor between them as they told her of the conversation with the Countess.

'You really won't sign them, Maud? The risk is very small, isn't it?'

'Yes, it is,' Maud replied, taking back the glass. 'But I still don't like her.'

Yvette snorted. 'You're buying those diamonds from her in a way, aren't you? A picture for each one.'

'In a way, yes, I suppose I am,' Maud replied.

Yvette twisted round so she was looking up at them both. 'That must make you one of the most expensive artists in the world.' Maud almost dropped her glass and Tanya put her head back and laughed. 'Oh and Maud, I sold that picture of Tanya you did in class to her Aunt Lila. It should be enough for travelling clothes, if you still have enough for tickets.'

CHAPTER 25

28 January 1910

*T*HE WATERS HAD FINALLY STARTED TO RECEDE. IN Saint-Sulpice the refugees continued to warm themselves under the Delacroix frescos, huddled on mattresses, the women trying to quiet the children and the men staring at their hands as if asking where and how they would find the strength to rebuild. Charlotte was folding blankets and organising into neat baskets the different items of clothing that had been donated. In Paris, for a few days at least, it had become fashionable to be generous. The rich cleaned their closets out and congratulated themselves, knowing that the waters were losing their power and would soon slink back, like the poor, into their proper course and continue to serve them.

Charlotte felt their approach and looked up to see two smart young women dressed for travel with handbags in the crook of their arms and folded umbrellas in their gloved hands. It took her a moment to recognise them. She left her station and embraced Yvette, then shook Maud's hand.

'You know what happened?' Yvette said quietly and the older woman nodded.

'You talked enough in your sleep for me to guess, and there have been rumours about a woman killing herself on Pont des Arts.' Her voice sounded deeply tired. 'I do not know what God means by it all. Perhaps He will forgive them at the last, and you, and me for helping you.' She rolled her sleeve up a little to show the flash of the bracelet with the five fat stones. 'What of this?'

Yvette took Charlotte's arm and pulled the sleeve back over it again. 'The Countess is not looking for them. Make sure you get a good deal from one of your shop girls on Rue Royale and build another home for waifs.'

She nodded. 'An anonymous donation? Well, Miss Harris has been concerned about some of the English dancers who perform in Paris. They get paid late and the accommodation the company provides is wholly unsuitable.'

'Well then,' Yvette said, 'it will do more good sheltering them than decorating the Countess, don't you think?'

Charlotte nodded, her round face thoughtful. She reminded Maud of the Spaniard's portrait of Miss Stein. She had the same uncompromised beauty of intelligence and belief, handsome where so many fashionable women were merely decorative. She realised with a smile that recognising Charlotte's spirit in the painting had made her appreciate it a great deal more. Maud shook hands with her again. 'Give Miss Harris our best love and thanks.'

'She will pray for you.'

'I do not doubt it,' Maud replied, and turned to leave. Tanya was waiting for them.

∽◦∽

Yvette did not want to say a formal farewell to Montmartre or anyone on it, but she consented to come close enough to say goodbye to Valadon at Impasse de Guelma. Suzanne's farewell was gruff but heartfelt, and she promised to spread the story on the hill that Yvette had found a rich protector and been swept off to Monte Carlo.

'Good luck out there,' she said, shaking Maud's hand then kissing Yvette's pale cheek. 'I know there is a world beyond Paris, but I can't really understand it myself.' Then she whistled into the cold air for her dog and set off up the hill under a white sun and the cobalt wash of the sky.

Vladimir waited by the car, the engine idling, ready to drive them out of Paris and on to solid ground so they could make their way to the coast. 'You could still call me Yvette, couldn't you, Maud? Even if we say my legal name is Sylvie.' Her voice was soft and cold as the snow.

'I will.'

'Are you ready then?' Yvette's voice was firmer now, more like herself than she had been since that moment in the cellar. 'Show me this England of yours.'

Maud turned and looked down the Boulevard Clichy; the flâneurs and thieves, street-hawkers and shop girls, the philan-thropists, chancers and visionaries, the blandishments of Paris wrapped round its dirty, defiant soul. She put her arm through Yvette's and nodded to the chauffeur. He opened the rear door for them and bowed. 'Yes, I am ready.'

EPILOGUE

'The Paris Winter: Anonymous Treasures from the de Civray Collection', Southwark Picture Gallery, London, 2010

Press Release

Since the opening of the exhibition, the Gallery and the de Civray Foundation have been shown sketchbooks belonging to the family of the artist Maud Heighton which suggest that she is the artist behind this remarkable collection of works. Maud Heighton studied in Paris between 1908 and 1910, and afterwards enjoyed a long career as a portraitist in Darlington and throughout the surrounding area. Her reputation as one of the UK's forgotten female Post-Impressionists has been on the rise for some time, and with the addition of these works to her oeuvre it is set to soar. Heighton was successful in her own lifetime, though it is thought that she and her lifetime companion Sylvie Morel supported their comfortable manner of living largely due to the popularity of the novels written by the latter. These were melodramas of the Parisian underworld, written under the pen name 'Yvette of Montmartre'. Her famous book, *The Death of Cristophe Grimaud*, was filmed in 1932 and starred Claude Rains and Janet Gaynor. The two women owned a large house in Darlington, a cottage in Reeth, a villa in the South of France and toured regularly on the continent. Their work is likely now to reach a much wider audience, and the trustees of the de Civray Foundation are delighted to have contributed to the enhancement of their reputations. By arrangement with their heirs, the works of both women, including Heighton's sketchbooks and the manuscripts of Sylvie Morel, are available to all interested scholars who wish to consult them by appointment and subject to suitable references.

Historical Notes

Académie Lafond and all those who teach or study there are fictional but the school is based on Académie Julian which did have premises in Passage des Panoramas and Rue Vivienne and offered expert training to male and female artists, many of whom are household names today. On the work in the Women's Ateliers I recommend *Overcoming All Obstacles: The Women of the Académie Julian*, ed. Gabriel P. Weisberg and Jane R. Becker.

Suzanne Valadon (1865–1938) was a model and painter, friend and muse to both Toulouse Lautrec and Erik Satie and mother to Maurice Utrillo as well as being a great artist in her own right. For an account of her life I recommend *Mistress of Montmartre: A life of Suzanne Valadon* by June Rose. She was living in Impasse de Guelma at the time *The Paris Winter* is set, but her accommodation was cramped so she probably didn't sub-let. Amedeo Modigliani (1884–1920) was in the habit of reciting Dante to her.

For the description of Gertrude Stein's salon in Rue de Fleurus I've relied on her book, *The Autobiography of Alice B. Toklas*. The paintings that Maud and Tanya notice in particular on the walls are, of course, Picasso's.

Miss Harris is also a fictional character, but inspired by Ada Leigh (1840–1931), a remarkable woman who ran a house for penniless English and American women in Paris during this period in

Avenue de Wagram. I have made great use of her short book *Homeless in Paris: The Founding of the 'Ada Leigh' Homes* published privately under her married name, Mrs Travers Lewis. It gives a rare account of destitute women in Paris during the Belle Époque and many of 'Miss Harris's' anecdotes and victories are in fact Ada Leigh's. Her maid did at times lock her out on the balcony so she could get some fresh air.

For all things opium related I am deeply indebted to *Opium Fiend: A 21st Century Slave to a 19th Century Addiction* by Steven Martin, a gripping historical and personal account of opium smoking and addiction.

The best account in English I have come across about the Siege of Paris and the Commune is *The Fall of Paris* by Alistair Horne.

For a non-fiction English account of the flooding of Paris in 1910 I recommend *Paris Under Water* by Jeffrey H. Jackson. I've also drawn heavily on the reporting of the floods in *The Times* and *Le Matin*, and in *La Vie à Paris 1910* by Jules Arsene Arnaud Claretie, though I've occasionally distorted what was flooded when to suit my own purposes.

I think any twenty-first-century woman might fear for her blood pressure reading *The Modern Parisienne* by Octave Uzanne, but it shed a great deal of light on both the economics of women's lives in the period and the unthinking misogyny dressed up as an 'appreciation of the feminine' current during the period. For other views on women during the Belle Époque I recommend *Feminisms of the Belle Époque* edited by Jennifer Waelti-Walters and Steven C. Hause and *Career Stories: Belle Époque Novels of Professional Development* by Juliette M. Rogers.

Many other books of travel and discovery have been consulted during the writing of this novel, but I'd like to mention two in particular: the charming *Paris Vistas* by Helen Davenport Gibbons which includes a great description of the floods and *Magnetic Paris* by Adelaide Mack which includes an account of the New Year celebrations at Bal Tabarin and some wonderful scenes of life on the Paris streets. I also thoroughly enjoyed *Paris à la carte* by Julian Street and made use of his accounts of the different grades of Parisian bars and cafés. All these are out of print at the moment, but you can read them online at the Internet Archive at www.archive.org. You can read *The Modern Parisienne* there too if you are feeling up to it.

As always all mistakes, misunderstandings and anachronisms are my fault and mine alone.